KNIFE'S EDGE

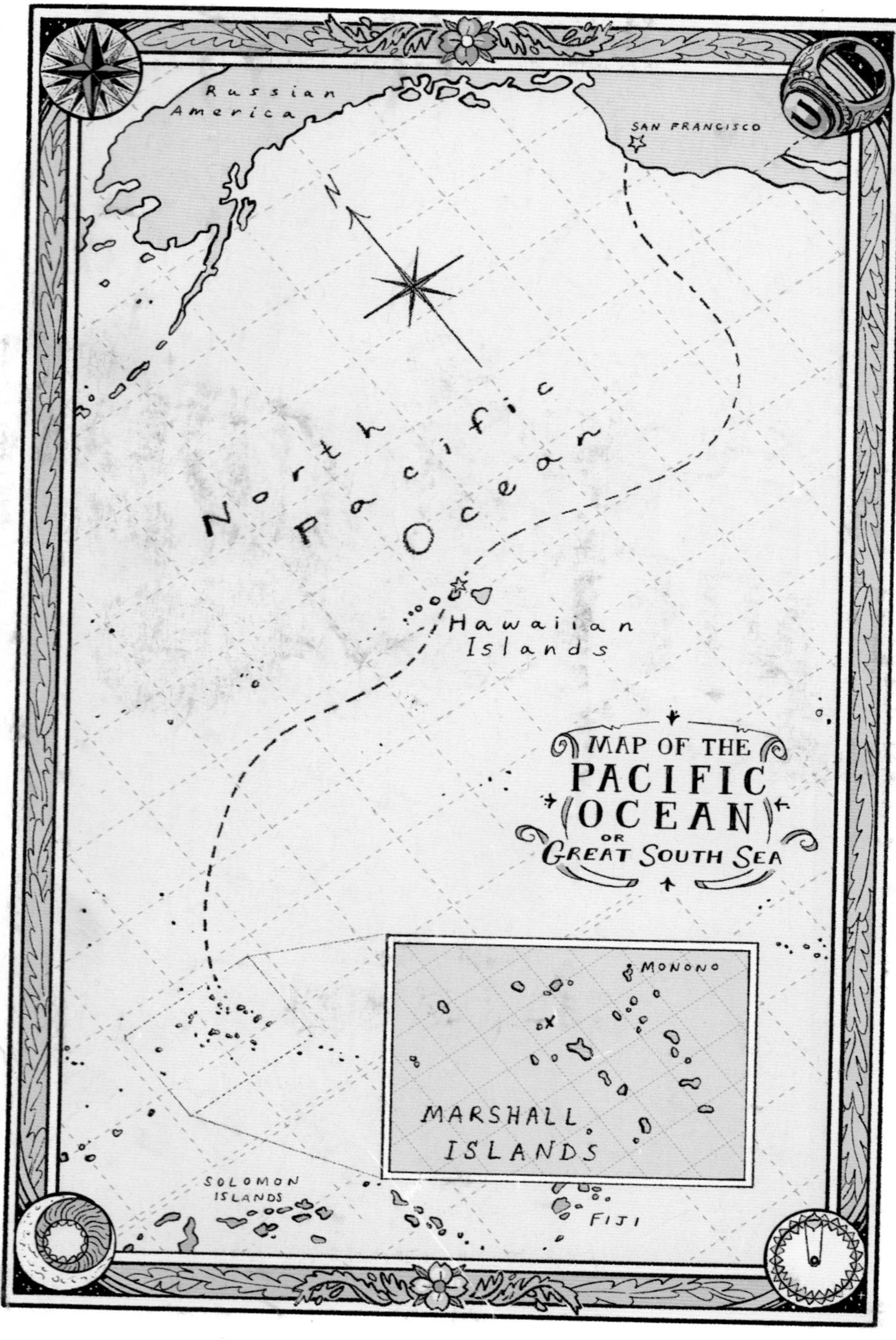
Russian America
SAN FRANCISCO
N
North Pacific Ocean
Hawaiian Islands
MAP OF THE PACIFIC OCEAN OR GREAT SOUTH SEA
MONONO
MARSHALL ISLANDS
SOLOMON ISLANDS
FIJI

HOPE LARSON

KNIFE'S EDGE
FOUR POINTS
BOOK 2

Illustrations by
REBECCA MOCK

SQUARE
FISH

MARGARET FERGUSON BOOKS
FARRAR STRAUS GIROUX
New York

To Sydney, Megan, and Emily
—H.L.

To my mother, Kathy, and my father, David
—R.M.

SQUARE
FISH

An imprint of Macmillan Publishing Group, LLC
175 Fifth Avenue, New York, NY 10010
mackids.com

Our books may be purchased in bulk for promotional, educational, or
business use. Please contact your local bookseller or the Macmillan Corporate
and Premium Sales Department at (800) 221-7945 ext. 5442
or by e-mail at MacmillanSpecialMarkets@macmillan.com.

Library of Congress Control Number: 2016951407
ISBN 978-1-250-15846-8 (paperback)

Originally published in the United States by Farrar Straus Giroux
First Square Fish edition, 2018
Book designed by Andrew Arnold
Square Fish logo designed by Filomena Tuosto

1 3 5 7 9 10 8 6 4 2

AR: 2.6 / LEXILE: GN290L

TABLE OF CONTENTS

1 No Safer Place 7

2 Mercy 39

3 B Is for Brandel 55

4 A Marked Man 73

5 The Ship and Her Master 91

6 Reconstruction 107

7 Monono 125

8 Truce 143

9 A Taste of Sunshine 161

10 Eternity 181

11 Echoes 215

CHAPTER ONE
NO SAFER PLACE

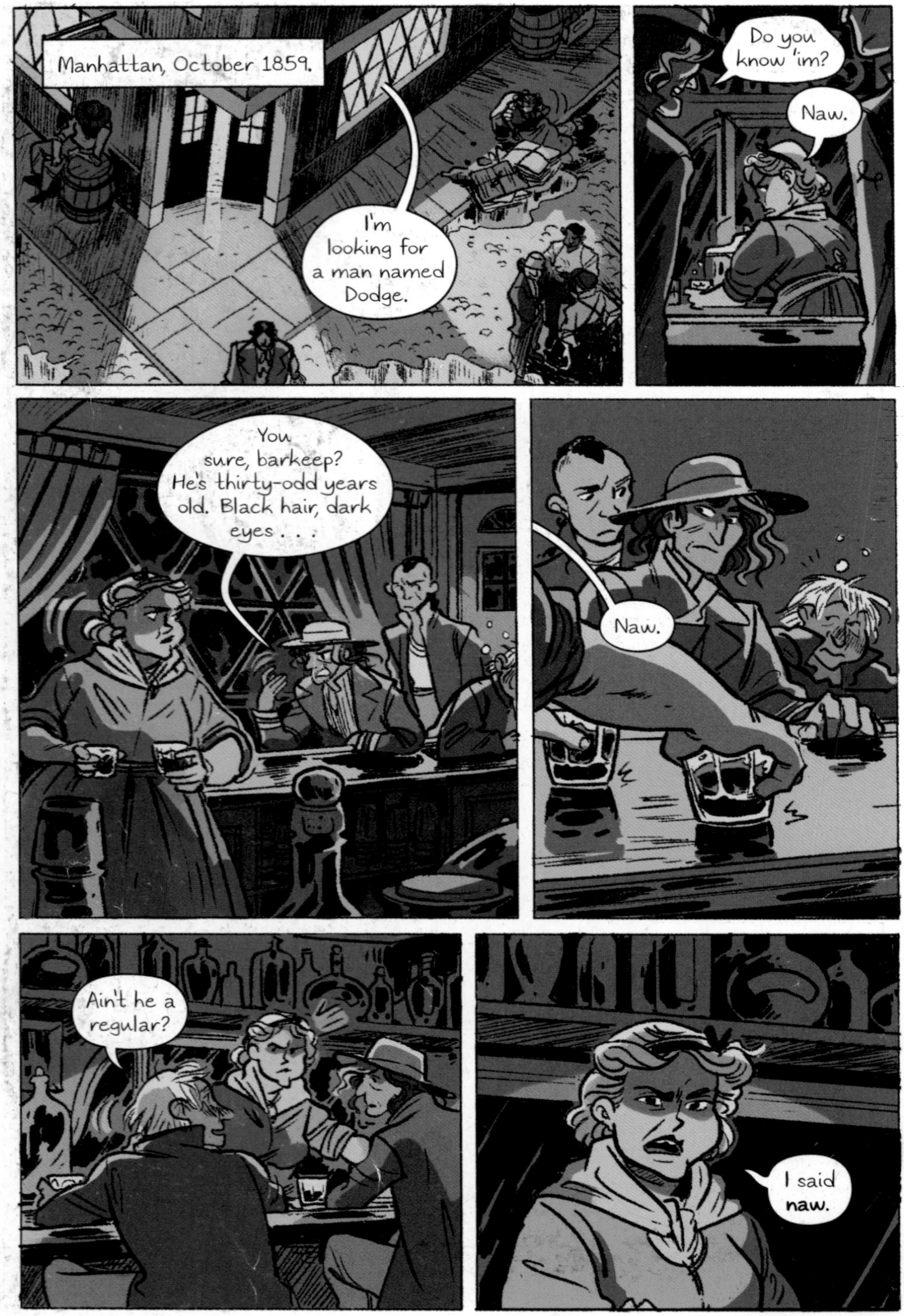
Manhattan, October 1859.
I'm looking for a man named Dodge.
Do you know 'im?
Naw.
You sure, barkeep? He's thirty-odd years old. Black hair, dark eyes . . .
Naw.
Ain't he a regular?
I said **naw.**

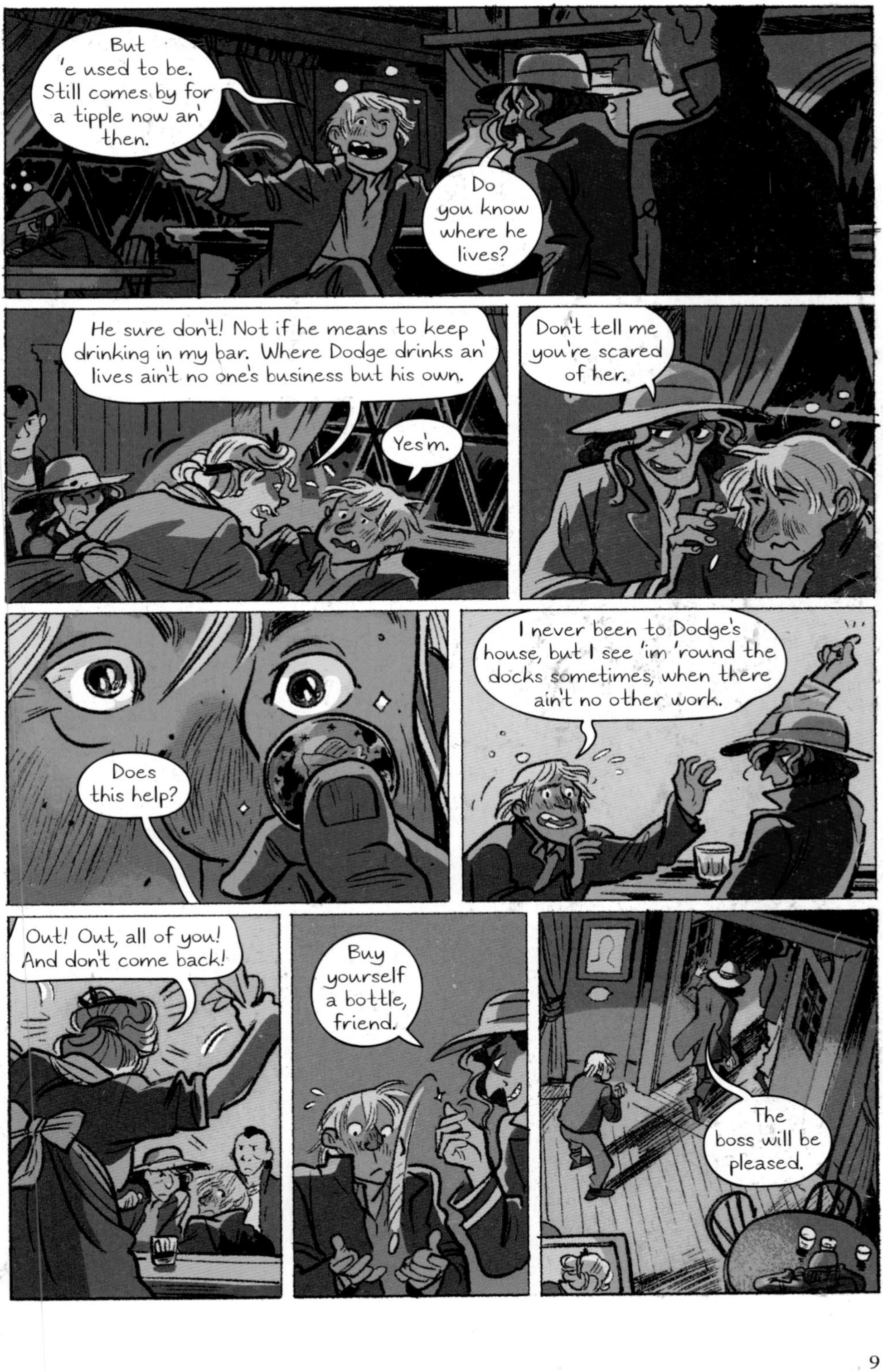
But 'e used to be. Still comes by for a tipple now an' then.
Do you know where he lives?
He sure don't! Not if he means to keep drinking in my bar. Where Dodge drinks an' lives ain't no one's business but his own.
Yes'm.
Don't tell me you're scared of her.
Does this help?
I never been to Dodge's house, but I see 'im 'round the docks sometimes, when there ain't no other work.
Out! Out, all of you! And don't come back!
Buy yourself a bottle, friend.
The boss will be pleased.

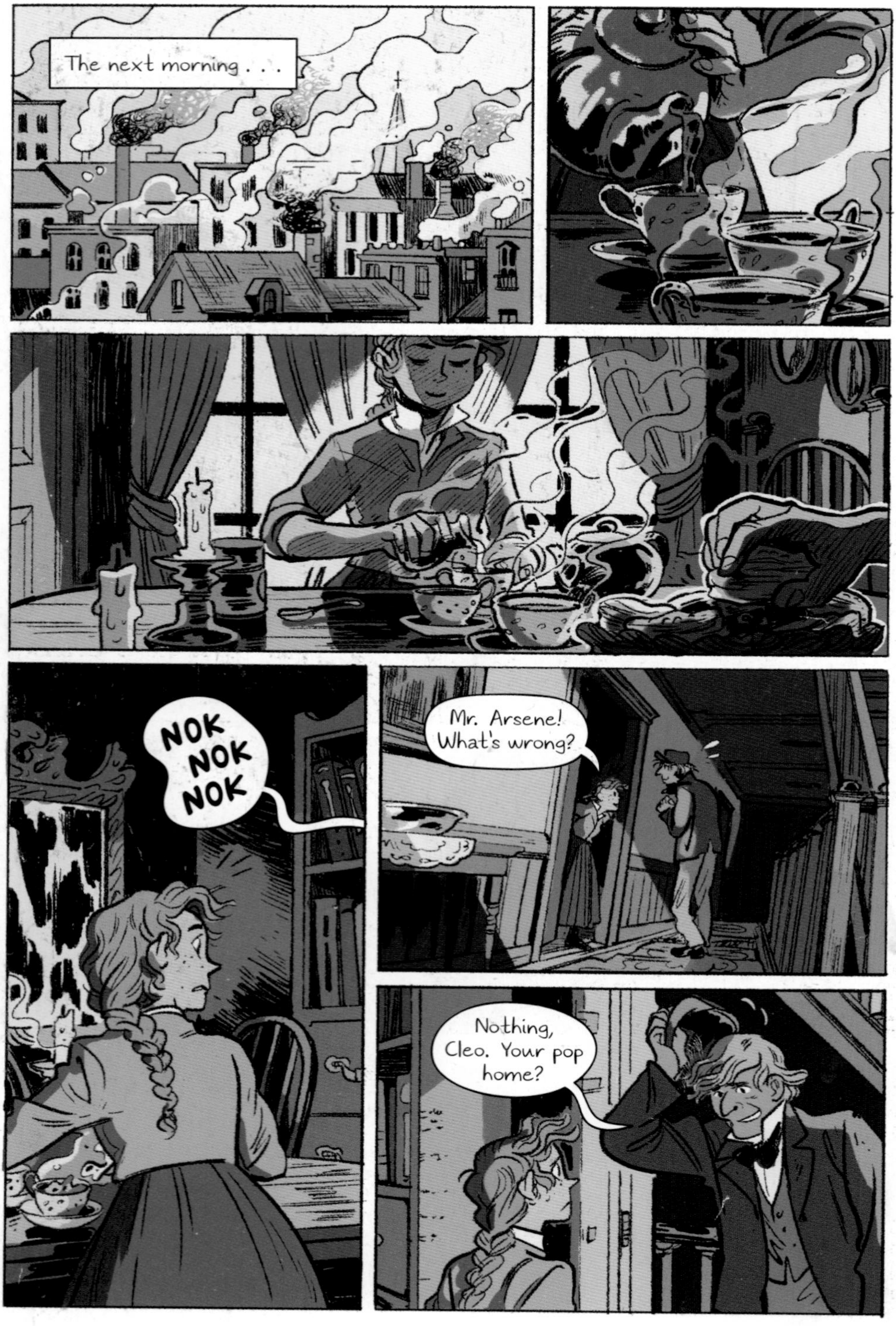
The next morning . . .
NOK NOK NOK
Mr. Arsene! What's wrong?
Nothing, Cleo. Your pop home?

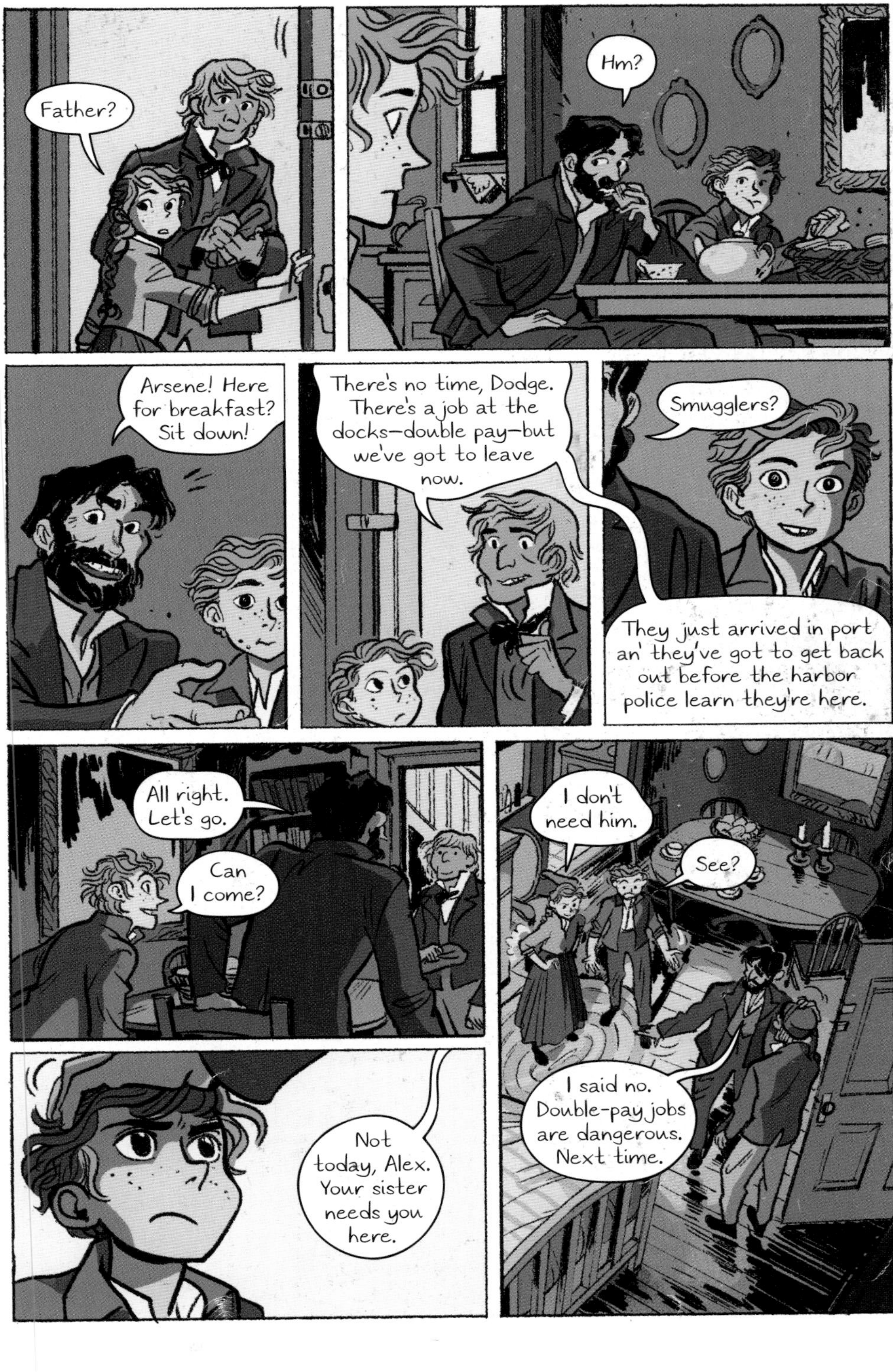
Father?
Hm?
Arsene! Here for breakfast? Sit down!
There's no time, Dodge. There's a job at the docks—double pay—but we've got to leave now.
Smugglers?
They just arrived in port an' they've got to get back out before the harbor police learn they're here.
All right. Let's go.
Can I come?
Not today, Alex. Your sister needs you here.
I don't need him.
See?
I said no. Double-pay jobs are dangerous. Next time.

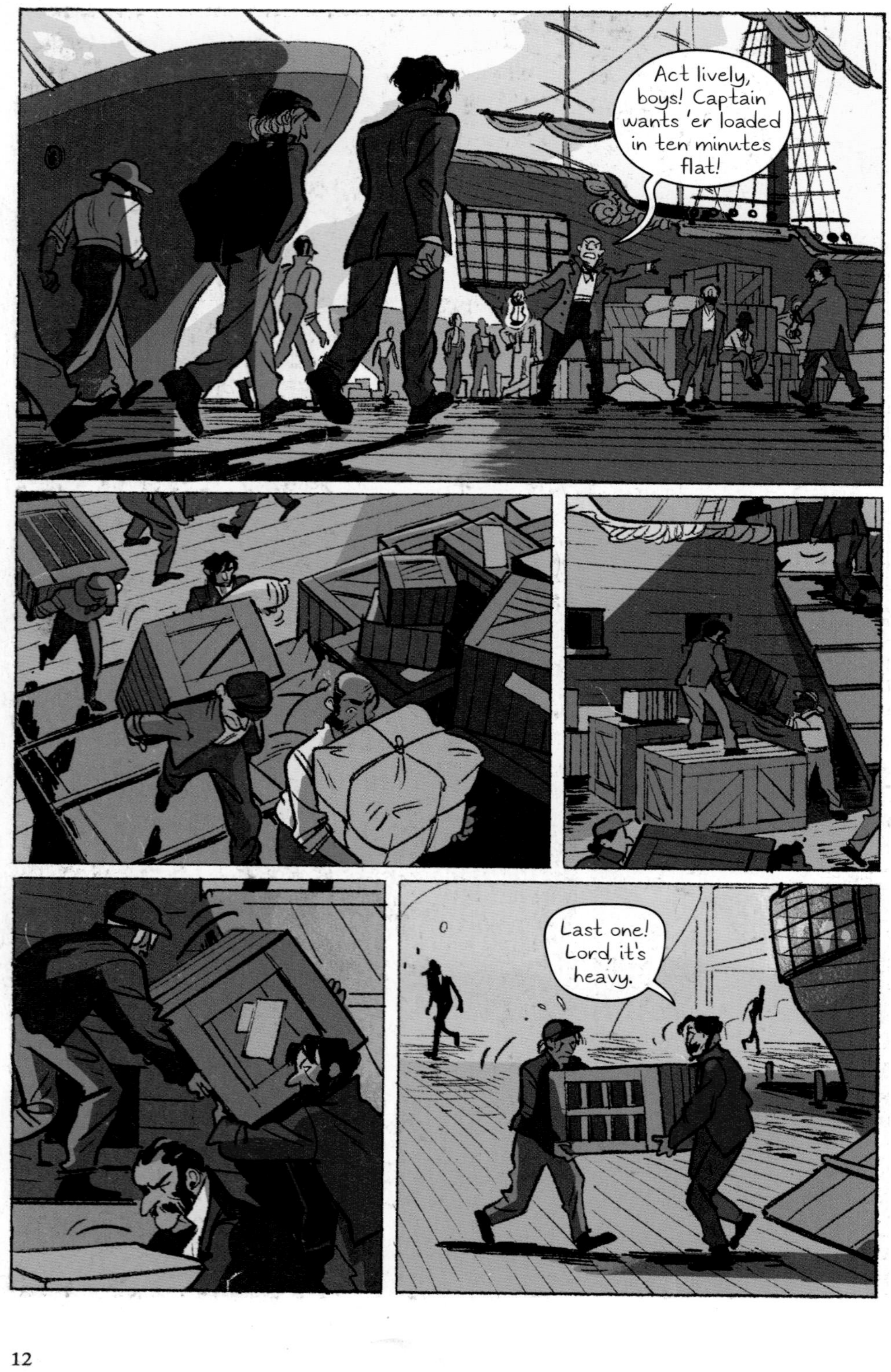
Act lively, boys! Captain wants 'er loaded in ten minutes flat!
Last one! Lord, it's heavy.

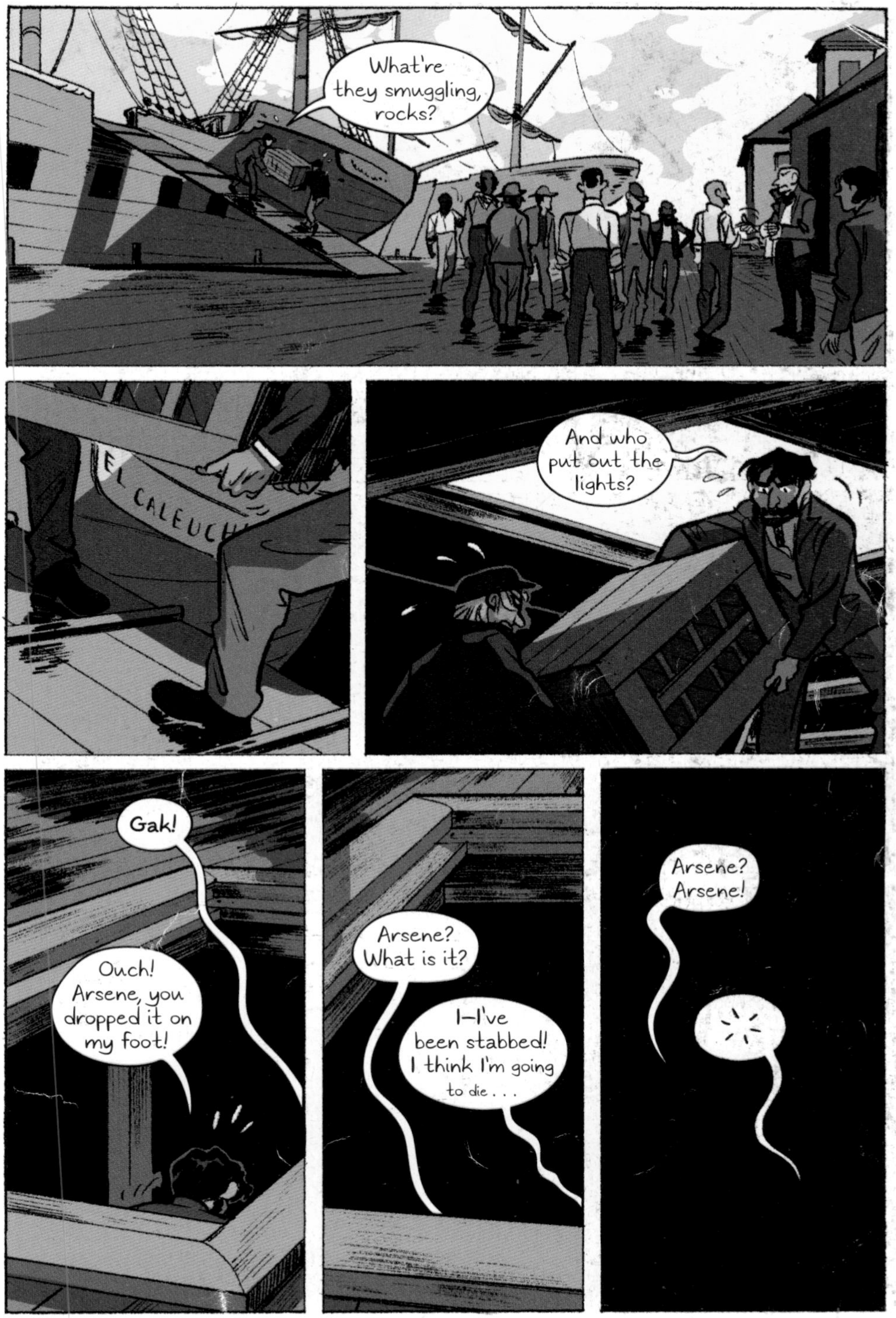
What're they smuggling, rocks?
EL CALEUCH
And who put out the lights?
Gak!
Ouch! Arsene, you dropped it on my foot!
Arsene? What is it?
I—I've been stabbed! I think I'm going to die . . .
Arsene? Arsene!

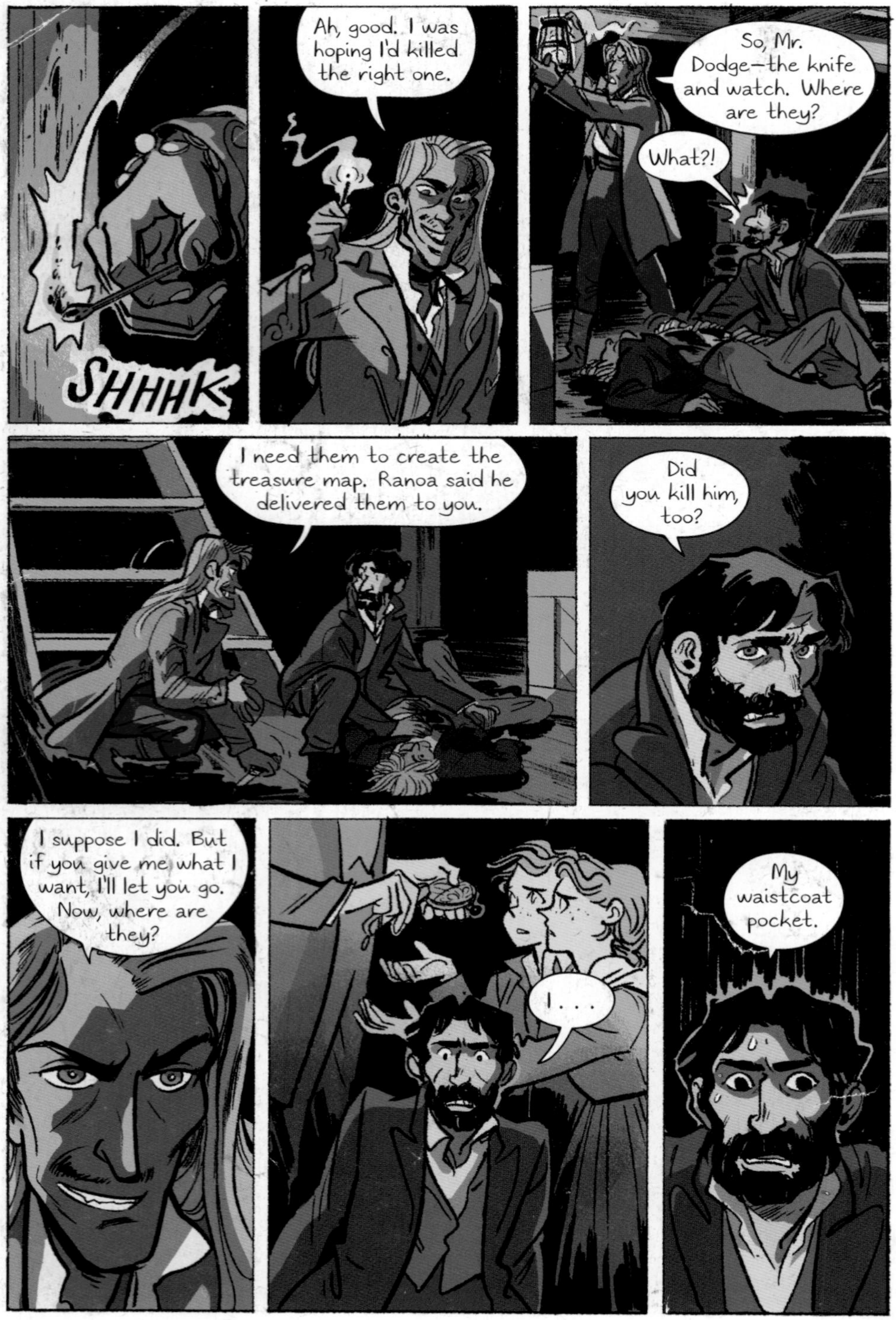
SHHHK
Ah, good. I was hoping I'd killed the right one.
So, Mr. Dodge—the knife and watch. Where are they?
What?!
I need them to create the treasure map. Ranoa said he delivered them to you.
Did you kill him, too?
I suppose I did. But if you give me what I want, I'll let you go. Now, where are they?
I . . .
My waistcoat pocket.

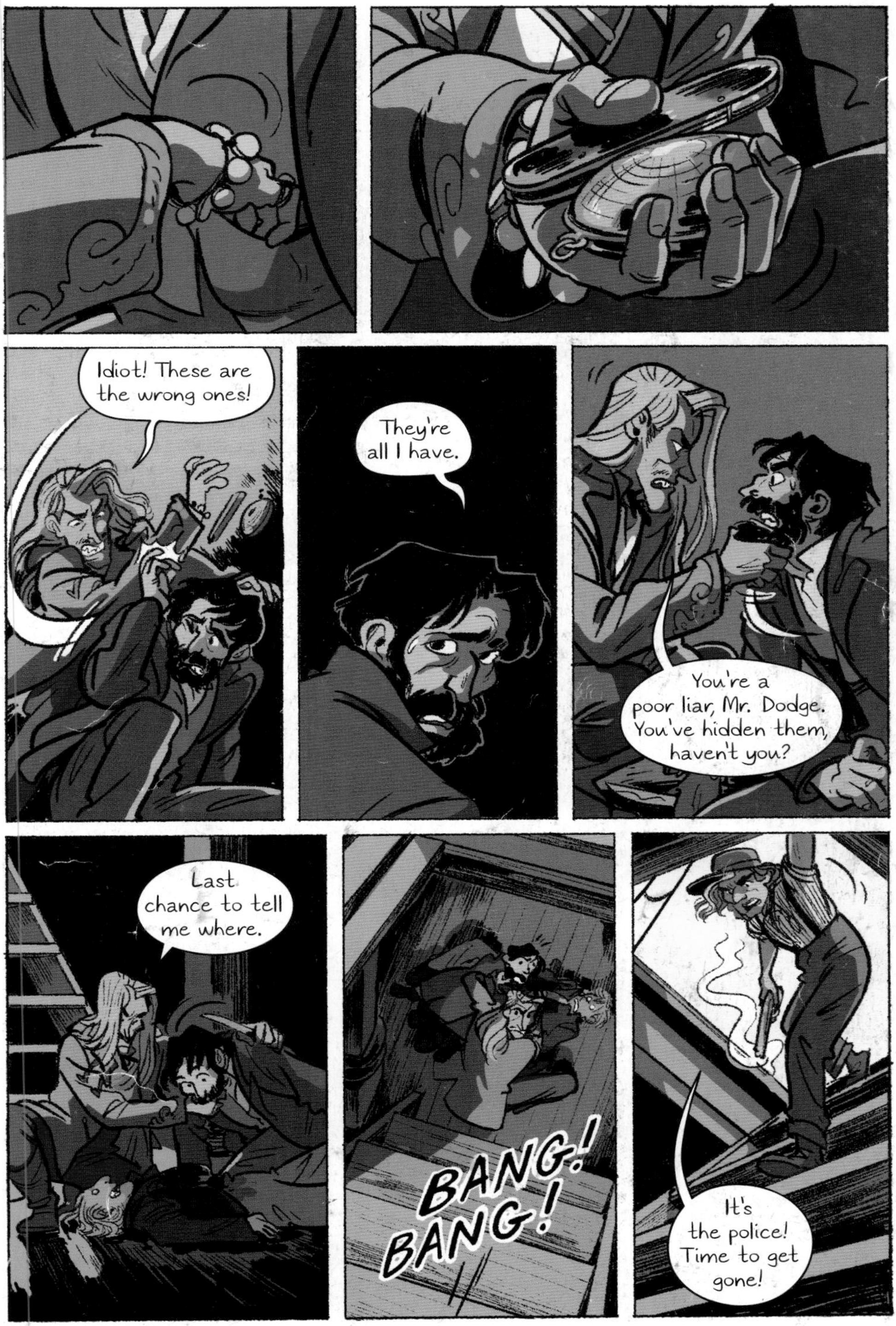
Idiot! These are the wrong ones!
They're all I have.
You're a poor liar, Mr. Dodge. You've hidden them, haven't you?
Last chance to tell me where.
BANG! BANG!
It's the police! Time to get gone!

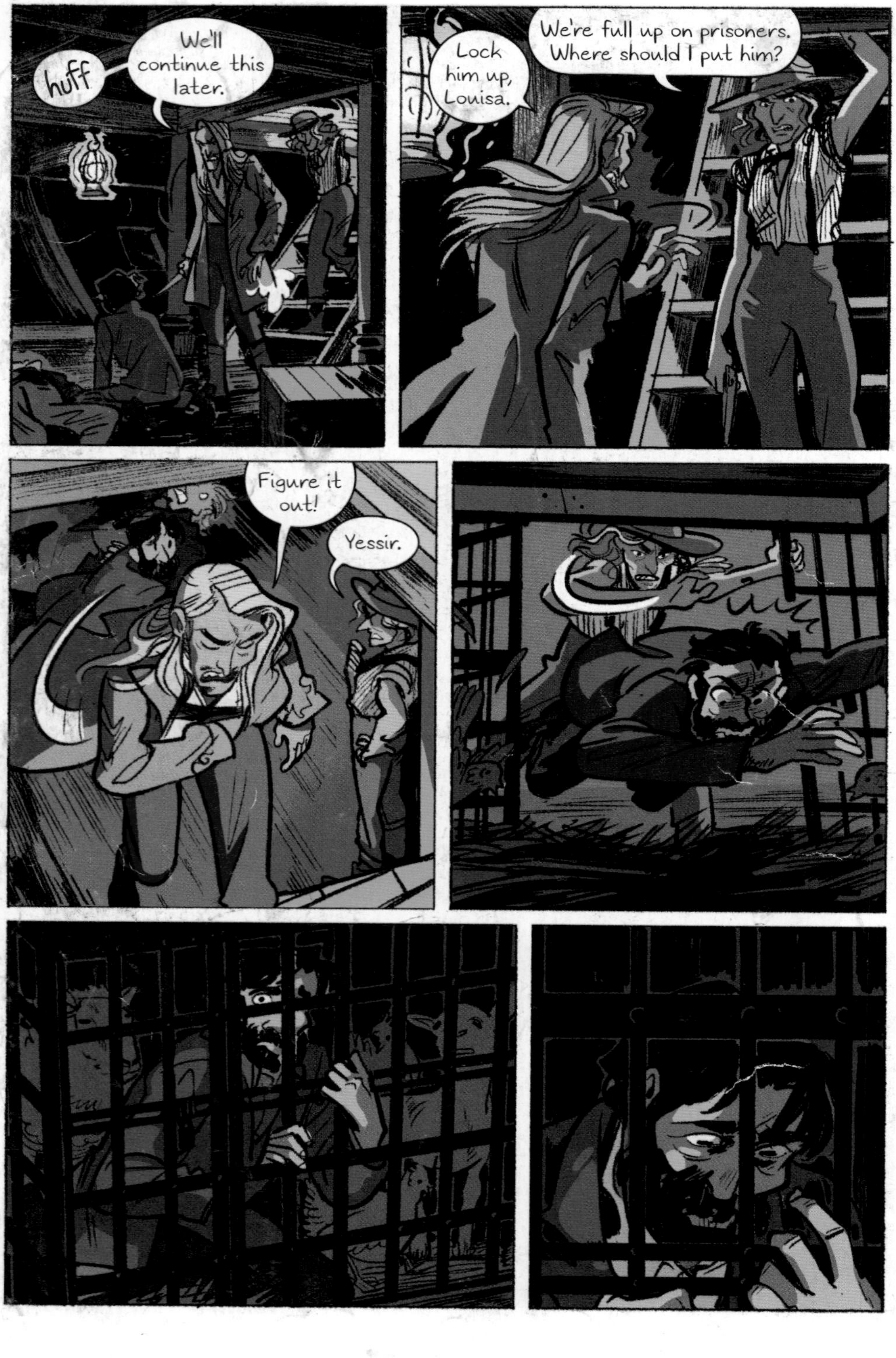
huff
We'll continue this later.
Lock him up, Louisa.
We're full up on prisoners. Where should I put him?
Figure it out!
Yessir.

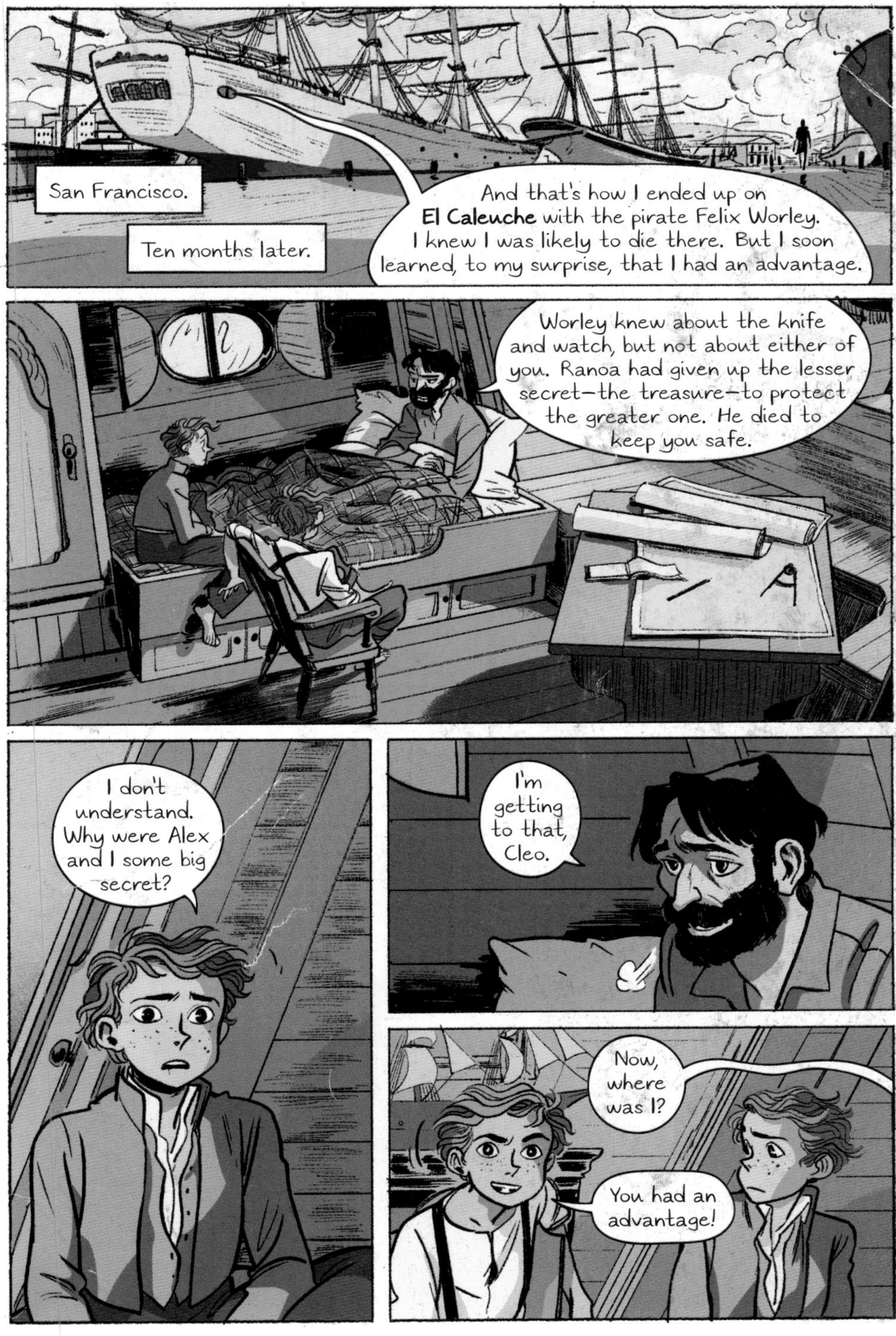
San Francisco.
Ten months later.
And that's how I ended up on **El Caleuche** with the pirate Felix Worley. I knew I was likely to die there. But I soon learned, to my surprise, that I had an advantage.
Worley knew about the knife and watch, but not about either of you. Ranoa had given up the lesser secret—the treasure—to protect the greater one. He died to keep you safe.
I don't understand. Why were Alex and I some big secret?
I'm getting to that, Cleo.
Now, where was I?
You had an advantage!

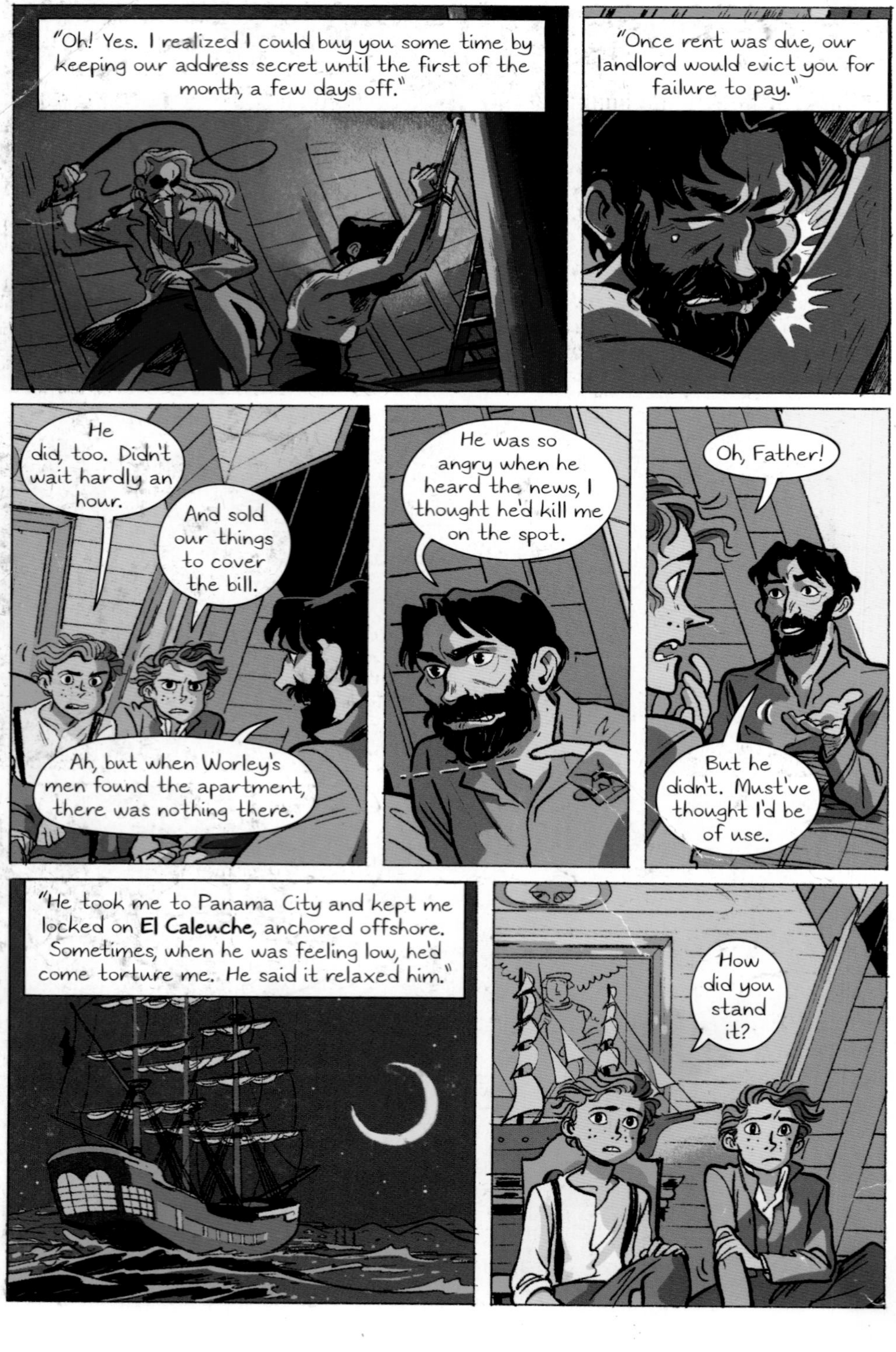
"Oh! Yes. I realized I could buy you some time by keeping our address secret until the first of the month, a few days off."
"Once rent was due, our landlord would evict you for failure to pay."
He did, too. Didn't wait hardly an hour.
And sold our things to cover the bill.
Ah, but when Worley's men found the apartment, there was nothing there.
He was so angry when he heard the news, I thought he'd kill me on the spot.
Oh, Father!
But he didn't. Must've thought I'd be of use.
"He took me to Panama City and kept me locked on **El Caleuche**, anchored offshore. Sometimes, when he was feeling low, he'd come torture me. He said it relaxed him."
How did you stand it?

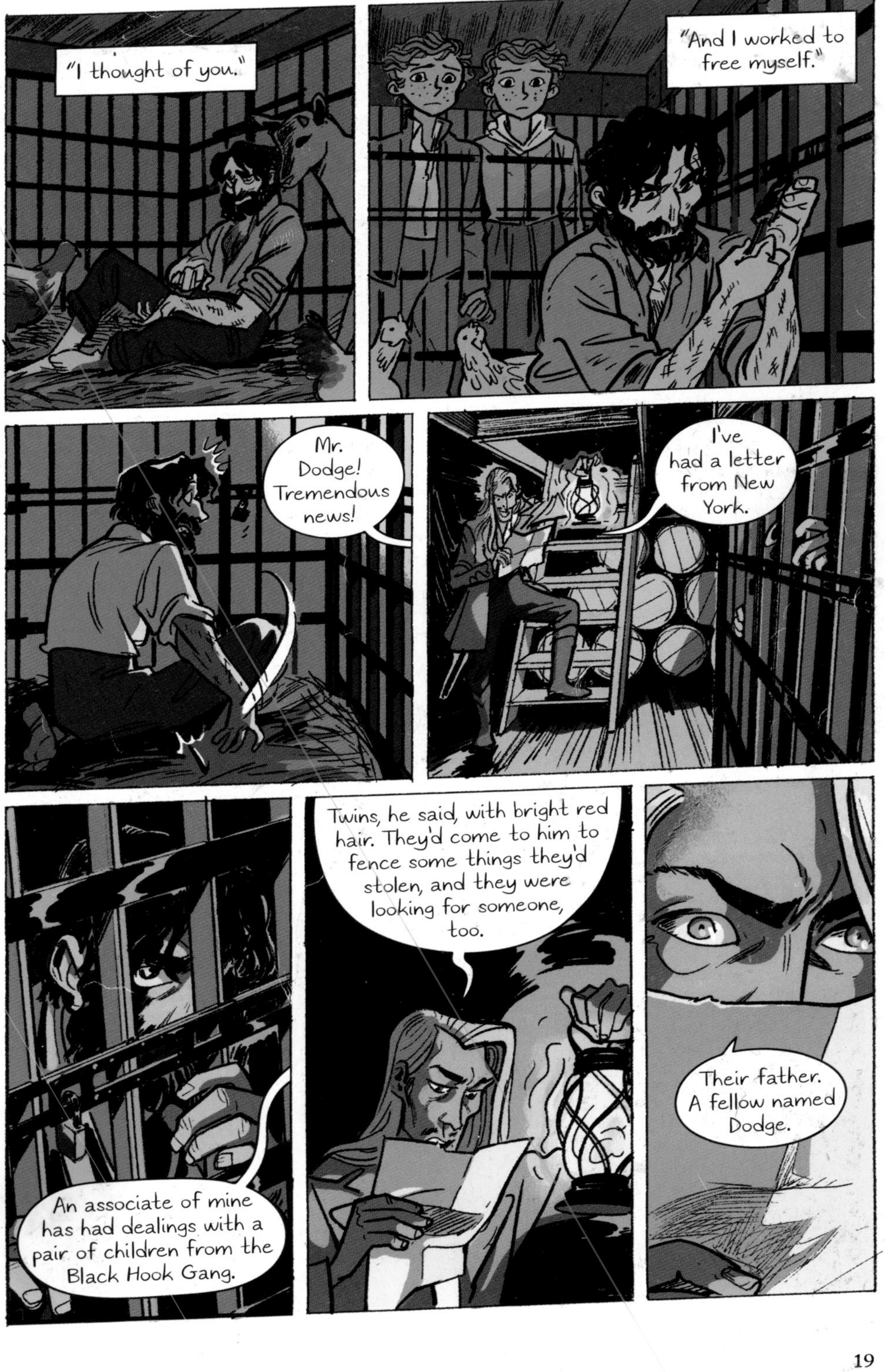
"I thought of you."
"And I worked to free myself."
Mr. Dodge! Tremendous news!
I've had a letter from New York.
An associate of mine has had dealings with a pair of children from the Black Hook Gang.
Twins, he said, with bright red hair. They'd come to him to fence some things they'd stolen, and they were looking for someone, too.
Their father. A fellow named Dodge.

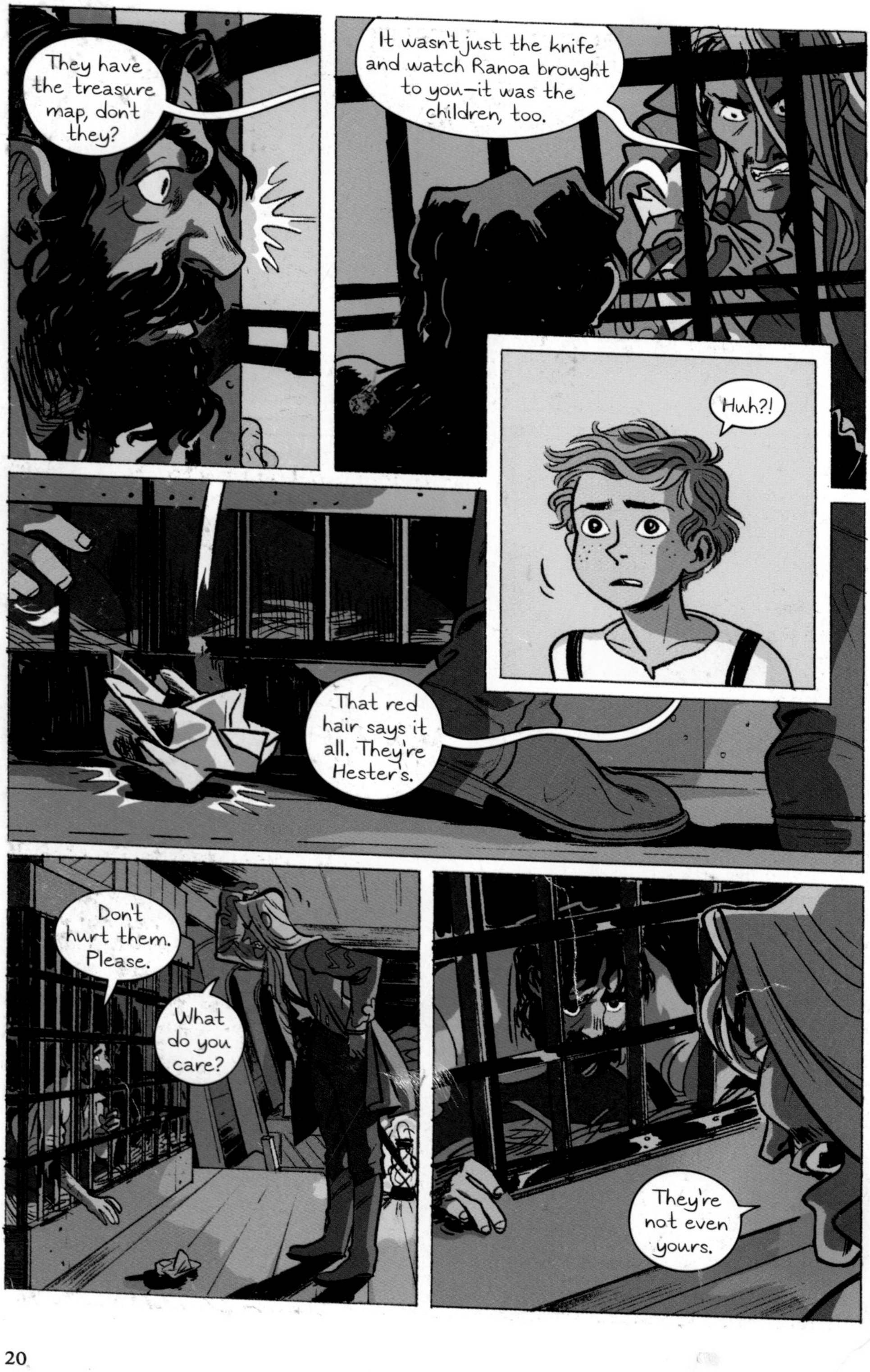
They have the treasure map, don't they?
It wasn't just the knife and watch Ranoa brought to you—it was the children, too.
Huh?!
That red hair says it all. They're Hester's.
Don't hurt them. Please.
What do you care?
They're not even yours.

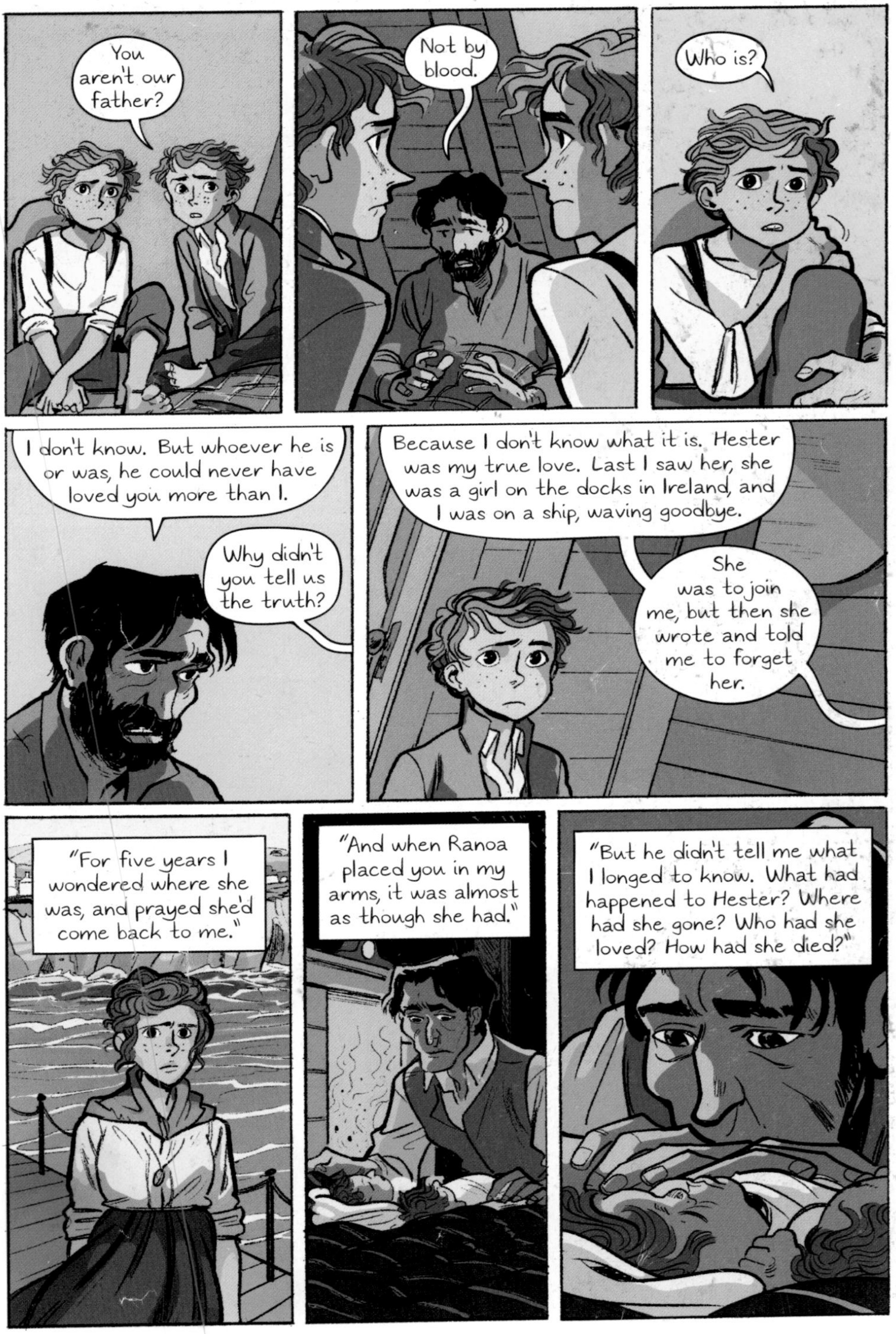
You aren't our father?
Not by blood.
Who is?
I don't know. But whoever he is or was, he could never have loved you more than I.
Why didn't you tell us the truth?
Because I don't know what it is. Hester was my true love. Last I saw her, she was a girl on the docks in Ireland, and I was on a ship, waving goodbye.
She was to join me, but then she wrote and told me to forget her.
"For five years I wondered where she was, and prayed she'd come back to me."
"And when Ranoa placed you in my arms, it was almost as though she had."
"But he didn't tell me what I longed to know. What had happened to Hester? Where had she gone? Who had she loved? How had she died?"

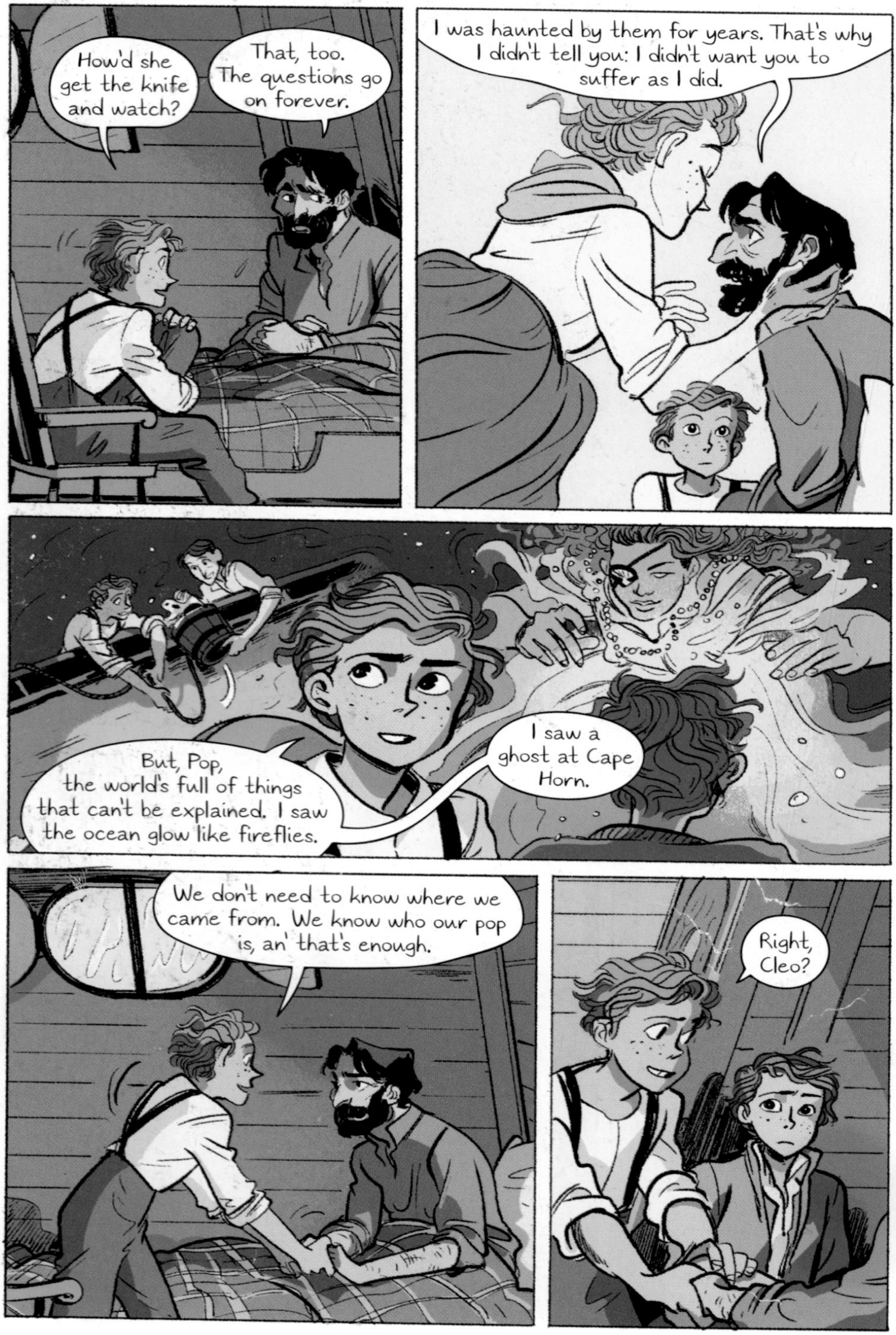
How'd she get the knife and watch?
That, too. The questions go on forever.
I was haunted by them for years. That's why I didn't tell you: I didn't want you to suffer as I did.
But, Pop, the world's full of things that can't be explained. I saw the ocean glow like fireflies.
I saw a ghost at Cape Horn.
We don't need to know where we came from. We know who our pop is, an' that's enough.
Right, Cleo?

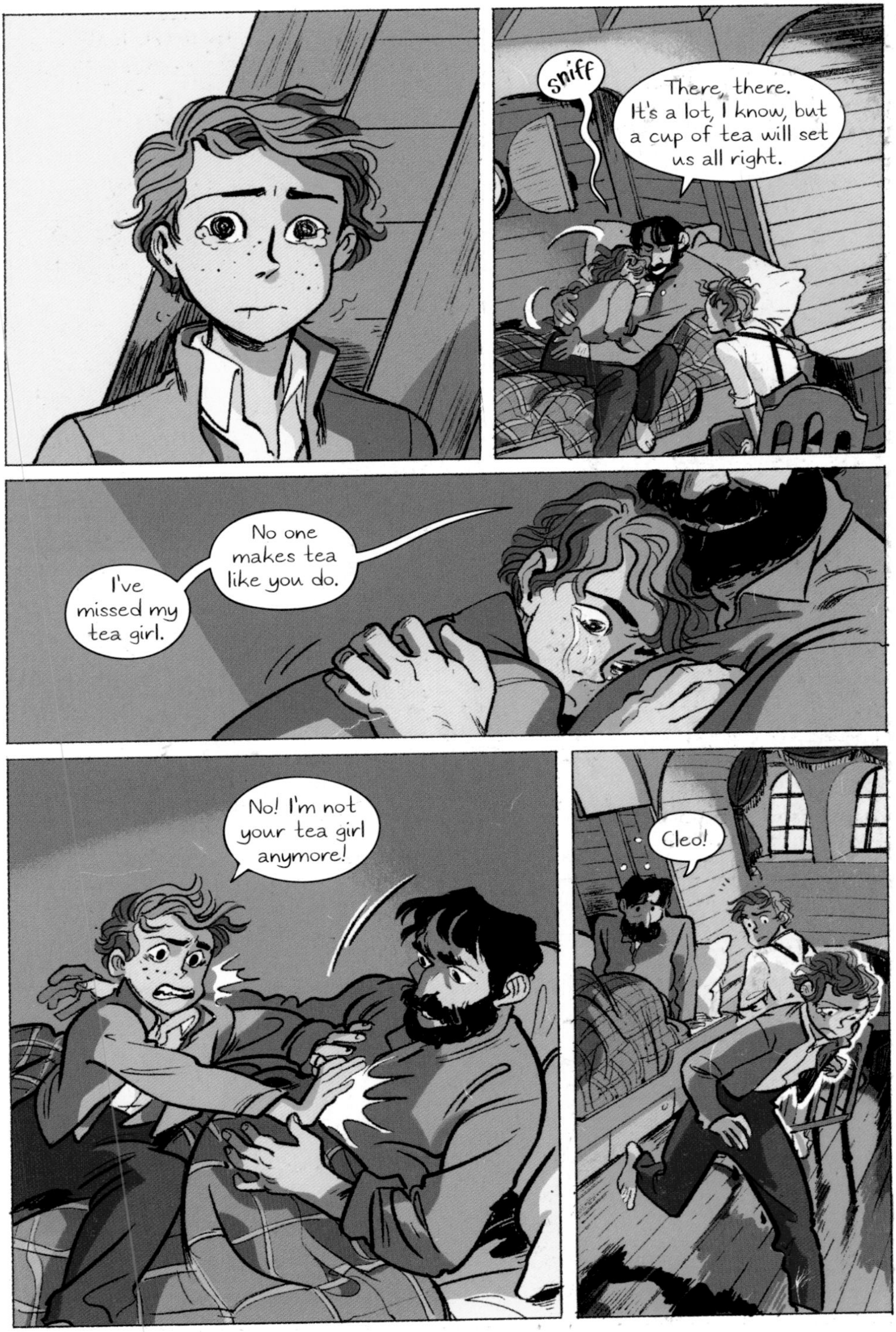
sniff
There, there. It's a lot, I know, but a cup of tea will set us all right.
I've missed my tea girl.
No one makes tea like you do.
No! I'm not your tea girl anymore!
Cleo!

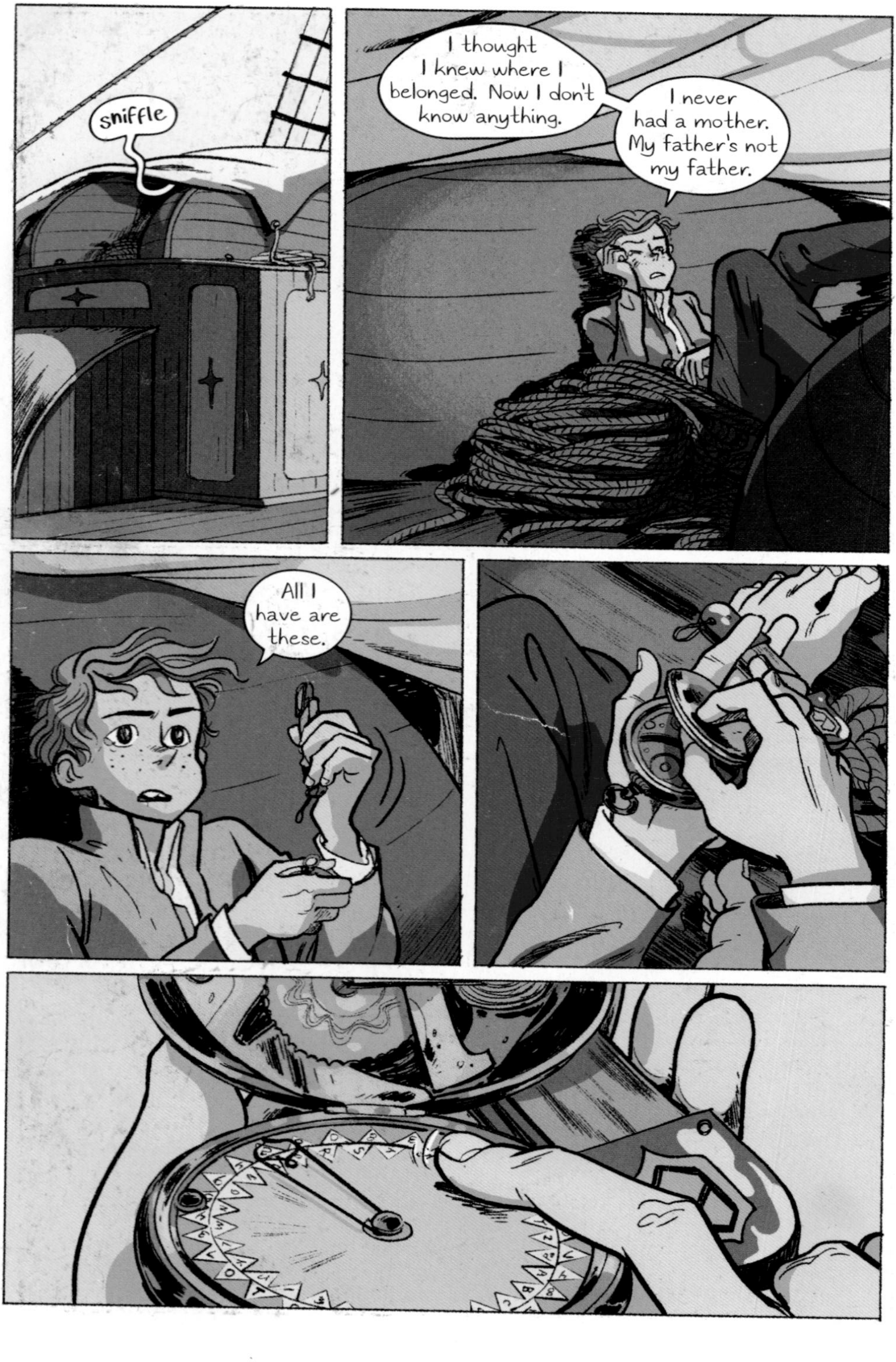
sniffle
I thought I knew where I belonged. Now I don't know anything.
I never had a mother. My father's not my father.
All I have are these.

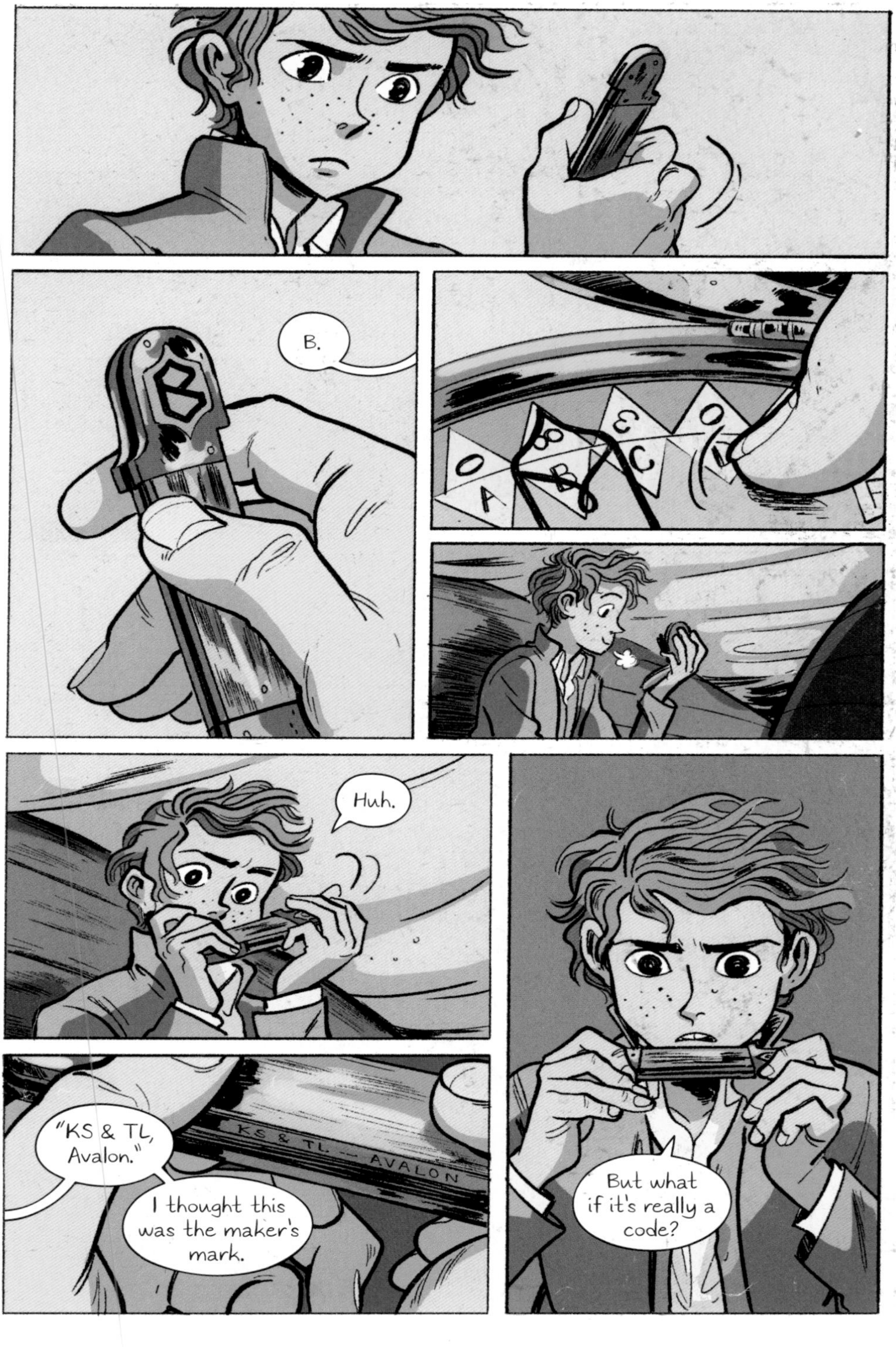
B.
Huh.
"KS & TL, Avalon."
I thought this was the maker's mark.
KS & TL — AVALON
But what if it's really a code?

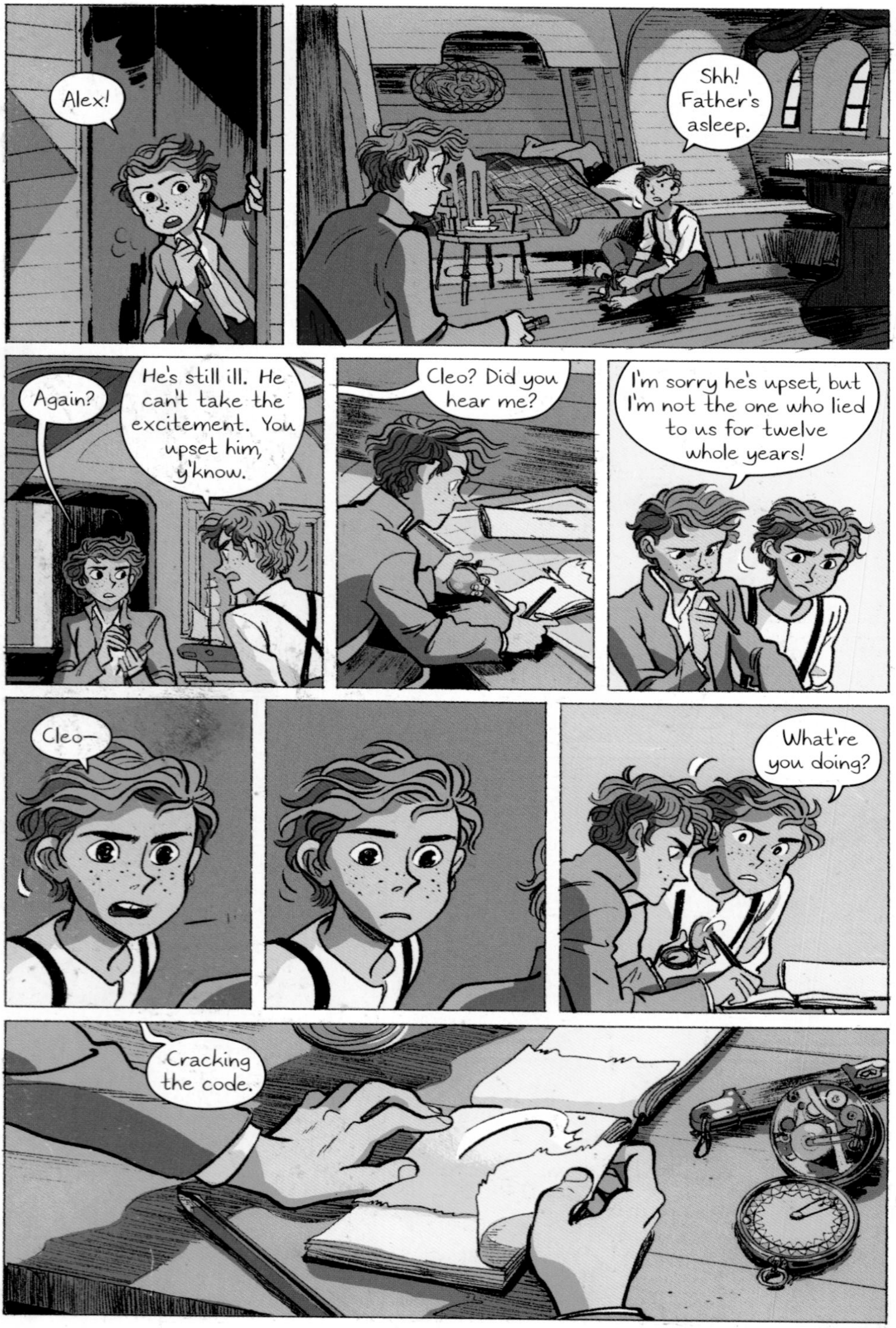

Alex!
Shh! Father's asleep.
Again?
He's still ill. He can't take the excitement. You upset him, y'know.
Cleo? Did you hear me?
I'm sorry he's upset, but I'm not the one who lied to us for twelve whole years!
Cleo—
What're you doing?
Cracking the code.

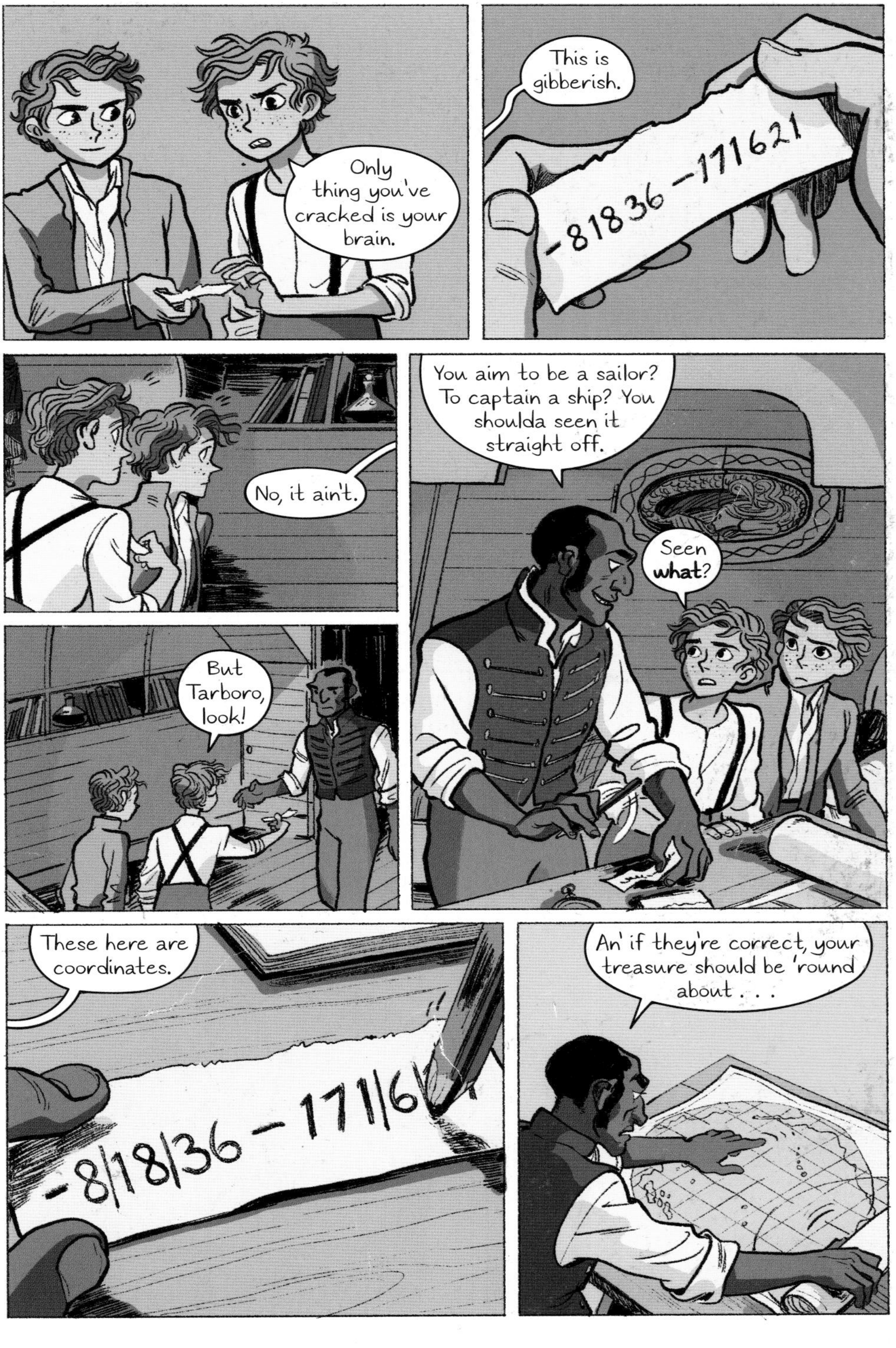
Only thing you've cracked is your brain.
This is gibberish.
-81836-171621
No, it ain't.
But Tarboro, look!
You aim to be a sailor? To captain a ship? You shoulda seen it straight off.
Seen **what**?
These here are coordinates.
-8|18|36 - 17|1|6
An' if they're correct, your treasure should be 'round about . . .

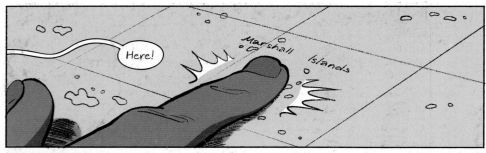

Here!

Marshall Islands

The Marshall Islands. Largely uncharted an' swarming with sharks and hostile natives.

There's no safer place to hide a treasure—which is to say, there's nowhere more dangerous.

But you'll take us there, won't you?

I passed through the Marshalls once, some years ago, aboard the **Gleam** . . .

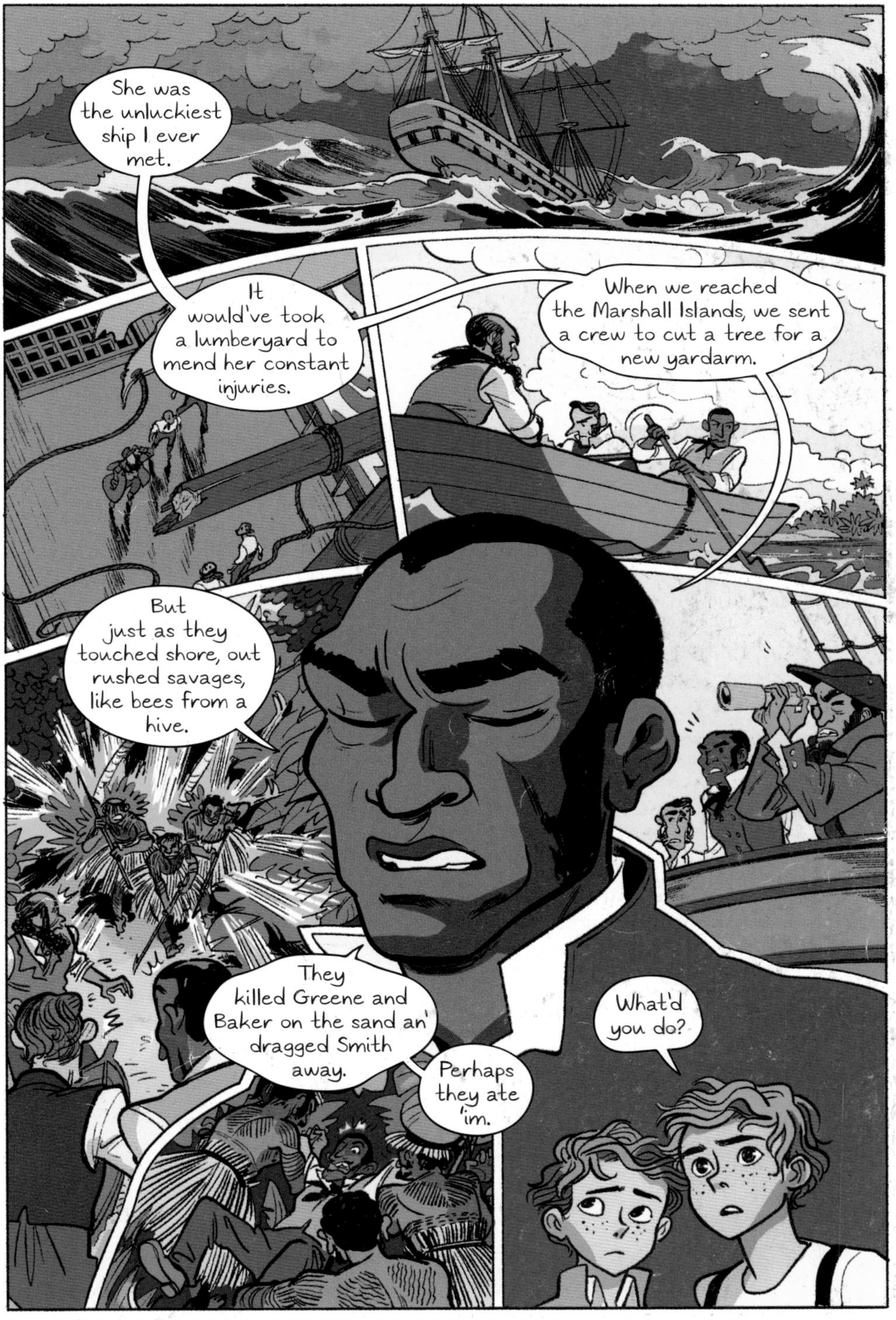
She was the unluckiest ship I ever met.
It would've took a lumberyard to mend her constant injuries.
When we reached the Marshall Islands, we sent a crew to cut a tree for a new yardarm.
But just as they touched shore, out rushed savages, like bees from a hive.
They killed Greene and Baker on the sand an' dragged Smith away.
Perhaps they ate 'im.
What'd you do?

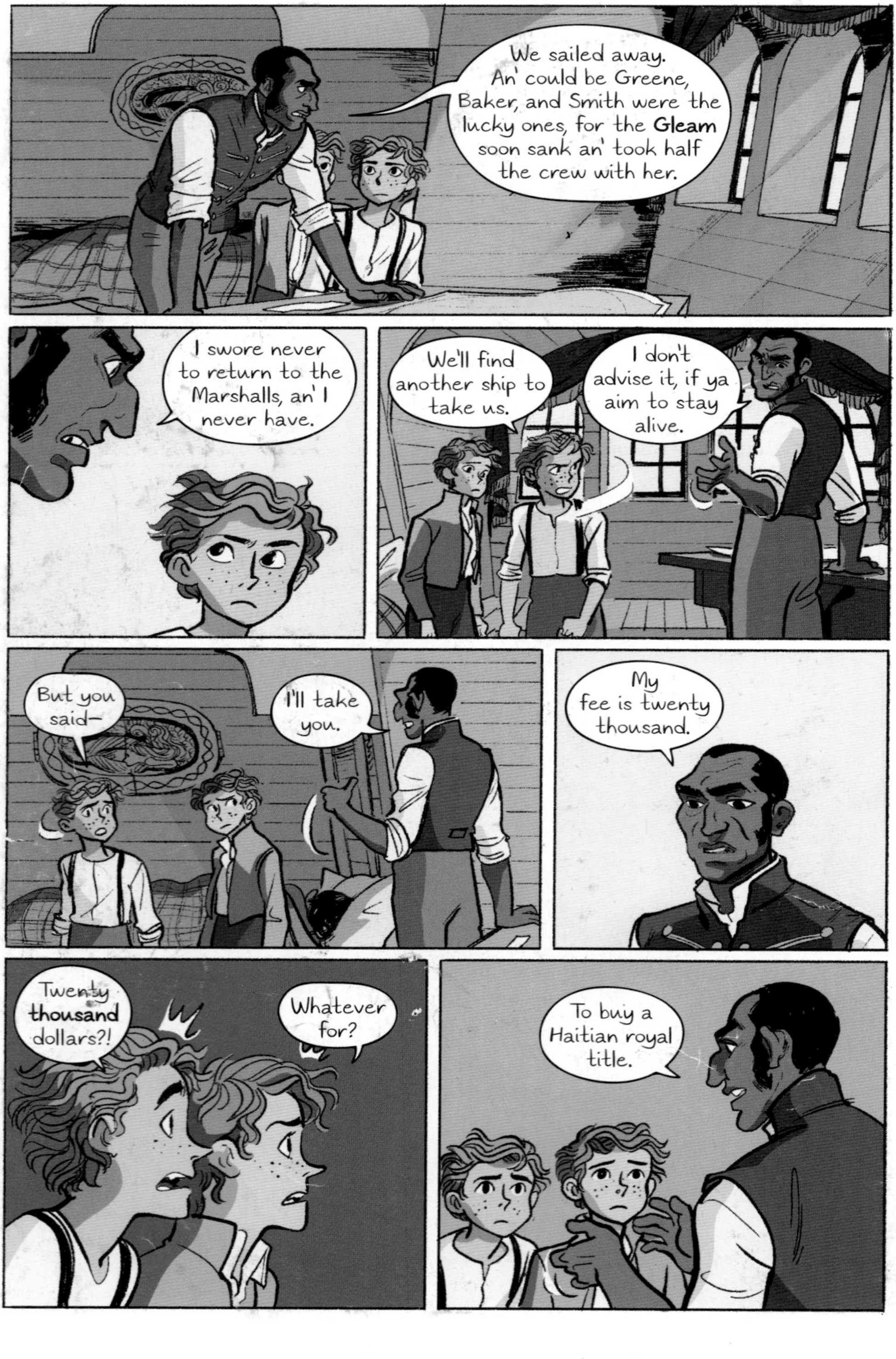
We sailed away. An' could be Greene, Baker, and Smith were the lucky ones, for the **Gleam** soon sank an' took half the crew with her.
I swore never to return to the Marshalls, an' I never have.
We'll find another ship to take us.
I don't advise it, if ya aim to stay alive.
But you said—
I'll take you.
My fee is twenty thousand.
Twenty **thousand** dollars?!
Whatever for?
To buy a Haitian royal title.

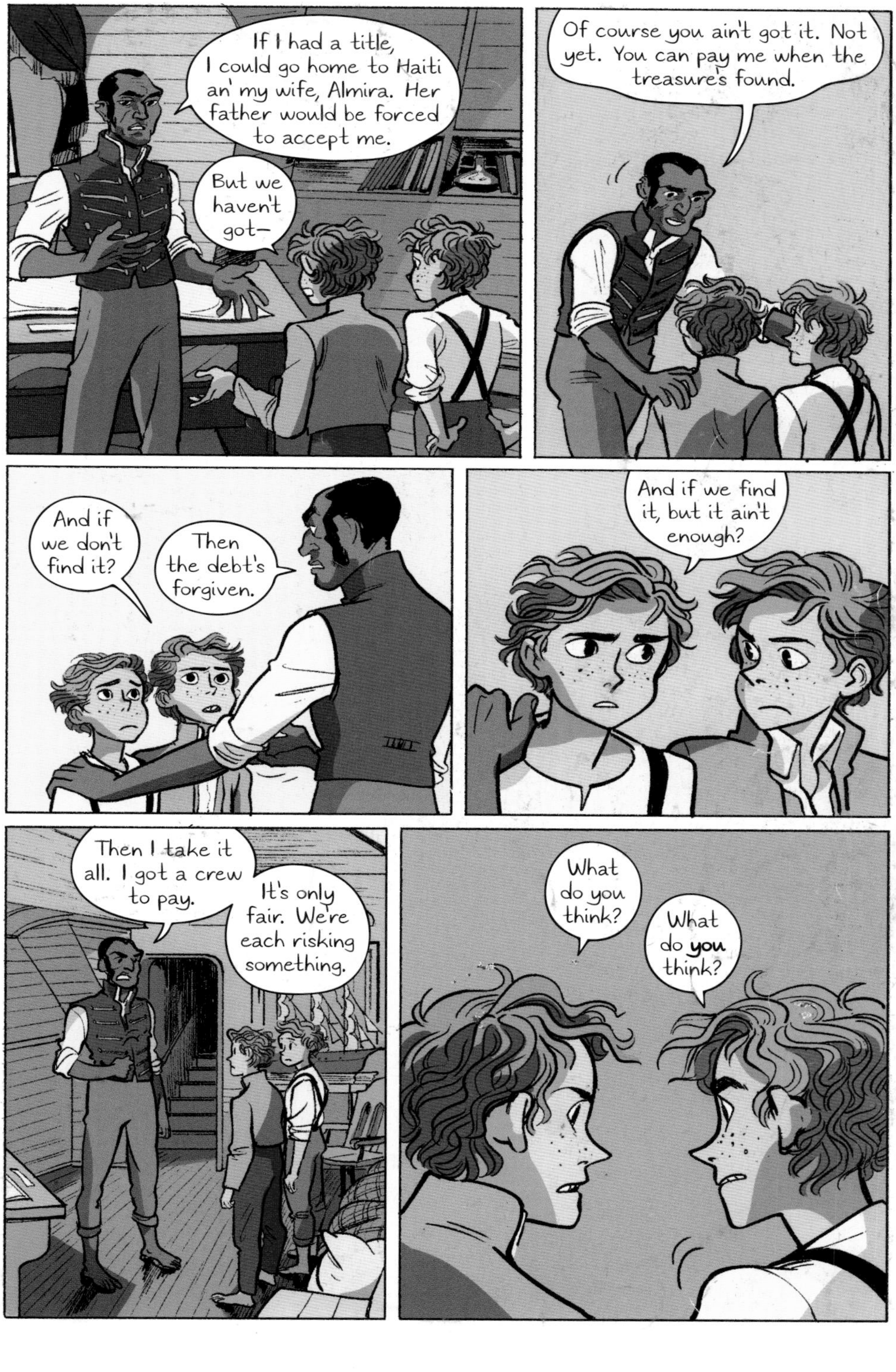
If I had a title, I could go home to Haiti an' my wife, Almira. Her father would be forced to accept me.
But we haven't got—
Of course you ain't got it. Not yet. You can pay me when the treasure's found.
And if we don't find it?
Then the debt's forgiven.
And if we find it, but it ain't enough?
Then I take it all. I got a crew to pay.
It's only fair. We're each risking something.
What do you think?
What do **you** think?

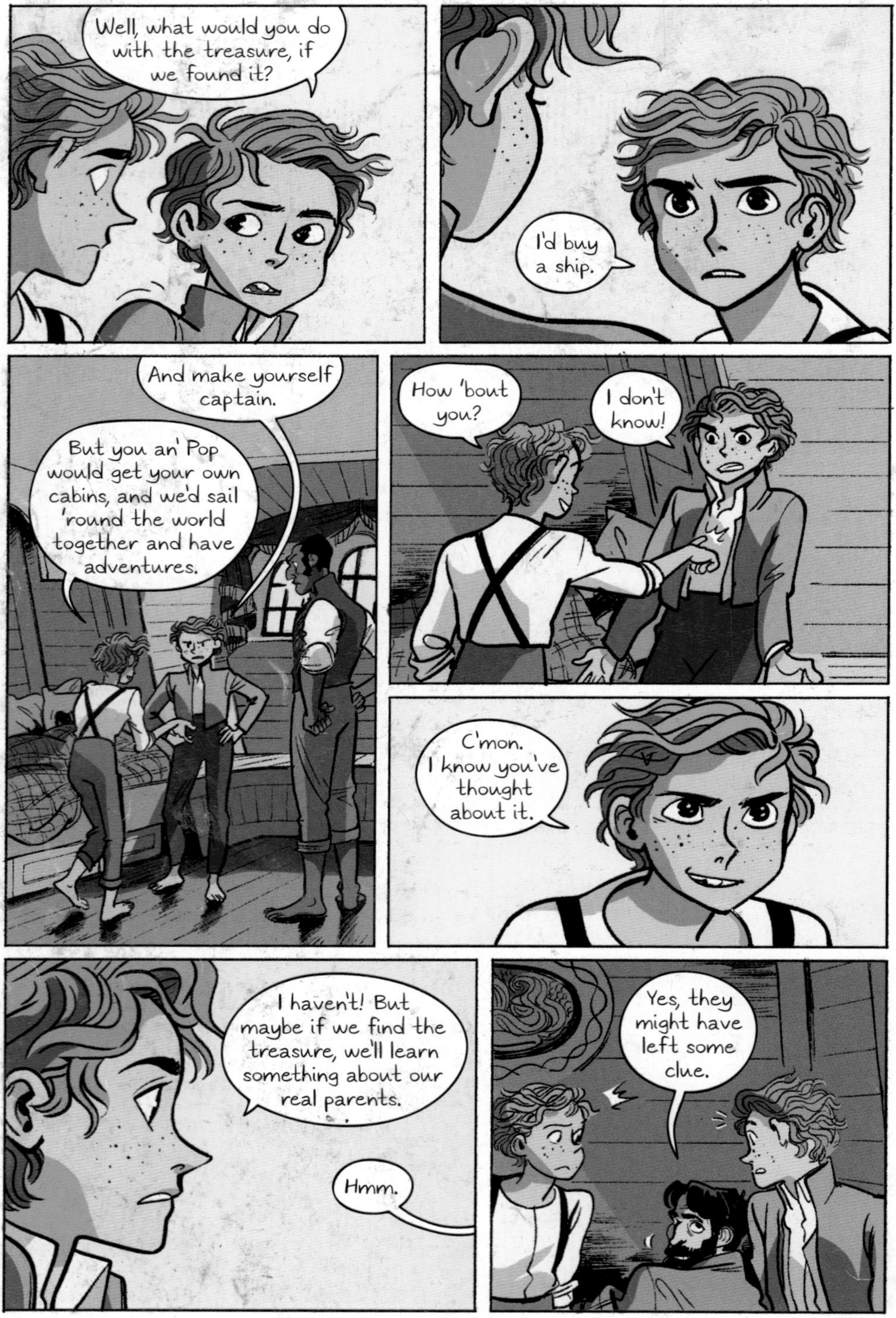
Well, what would you do with the treasure, if we found it?
I'd buy a ship.
And make yourself captain.
But you an' Pop would get your own cabins, and we'd sail 'round the world together and have adventures.
How 'bout you?
I don't know!
C'mon. I know you've thought about it.
I haven't! But maybe if we find the treasure, we'll learn something about our real parents.
Hmm.
Yes, they might have left some clue.

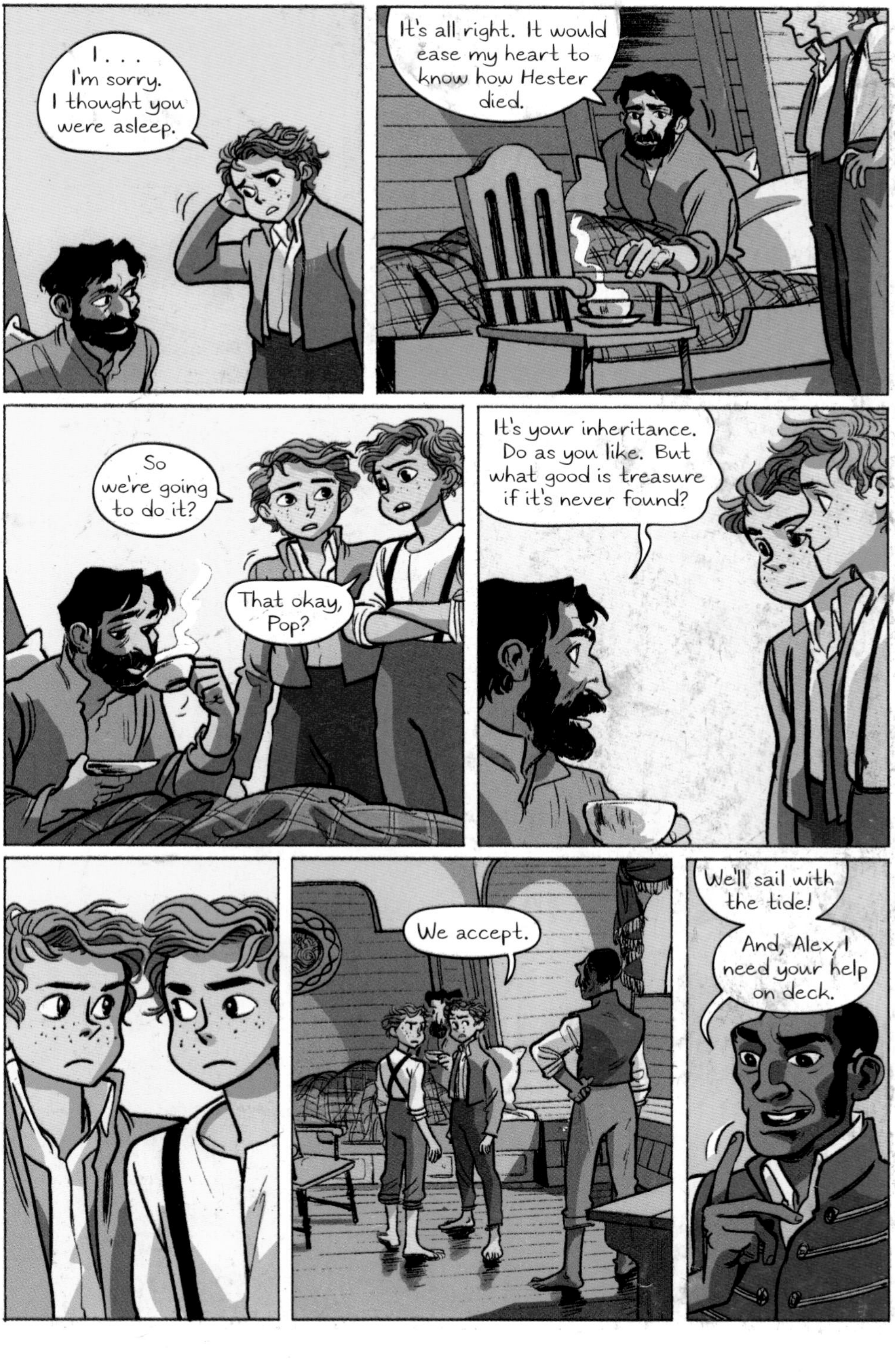
I . . .
I'm sorry. I thought you were asleep.
It's all right. It would ease my heart to know how Hester died.
So we're going to do it?
That okay, Pop?
It's your inheritance. Do as you like. But what good is treasure if it's never found?
We accept.
We'll sail with the tide!
And, Alex, I need your help on deck.

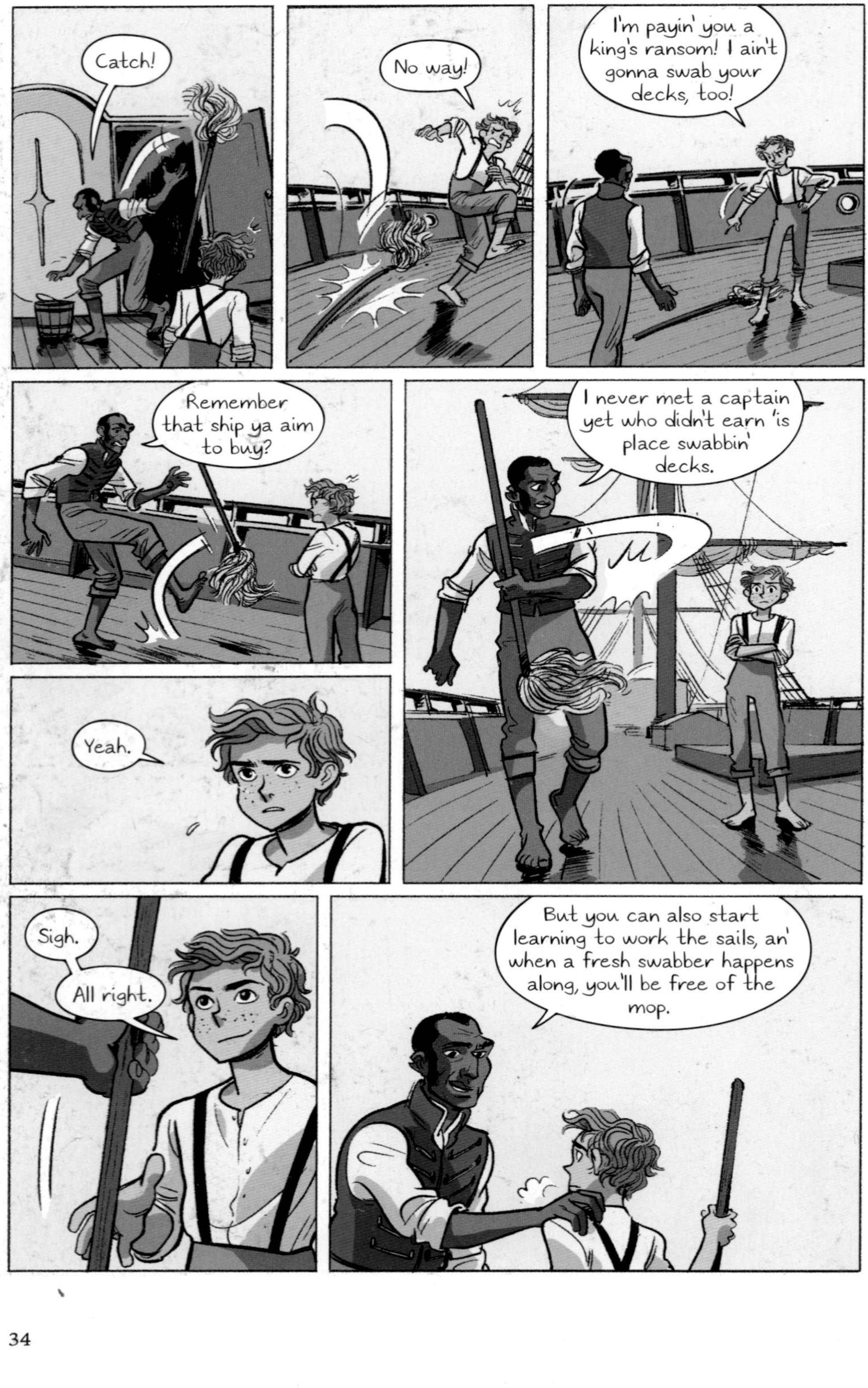
Catch!
No way!
I'm payin' you a king's ransom! I ain't gonna swab your decks, too!
Remember that ship ya aim to buy?
I never met a captain yet who didn't earn 'is place swabbin' decks.
Yeah.
Sigh.
All right.
But you can also start learning to work the sails, an' when a fresh swabber happens along, you'll be free of the mop.

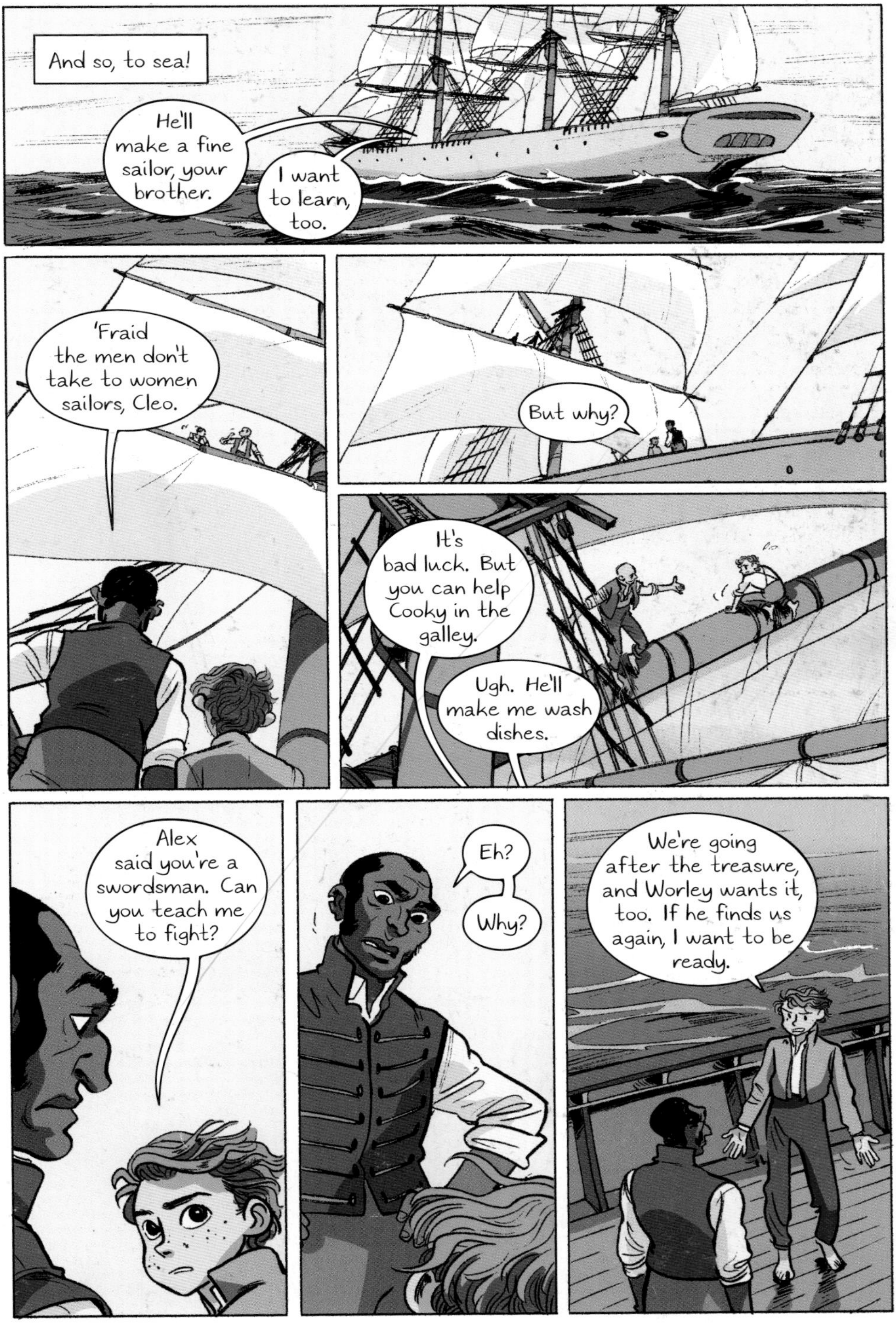
And so, to sea!
He'll make a fine sailor, your brother.
I want to learn, too.
'Fraid the men don't take to women sailors, Cleo.
But why?
It's bad luck. But you can help Cooky in the galley.
Ugh. He'll make me wash dishes.
Alex said you're a swordsman. Can you teach me to fight?
Eh?
Why?
We're going after the treasure, and Worley wants it, too. If he finds us again, I want to be ready.

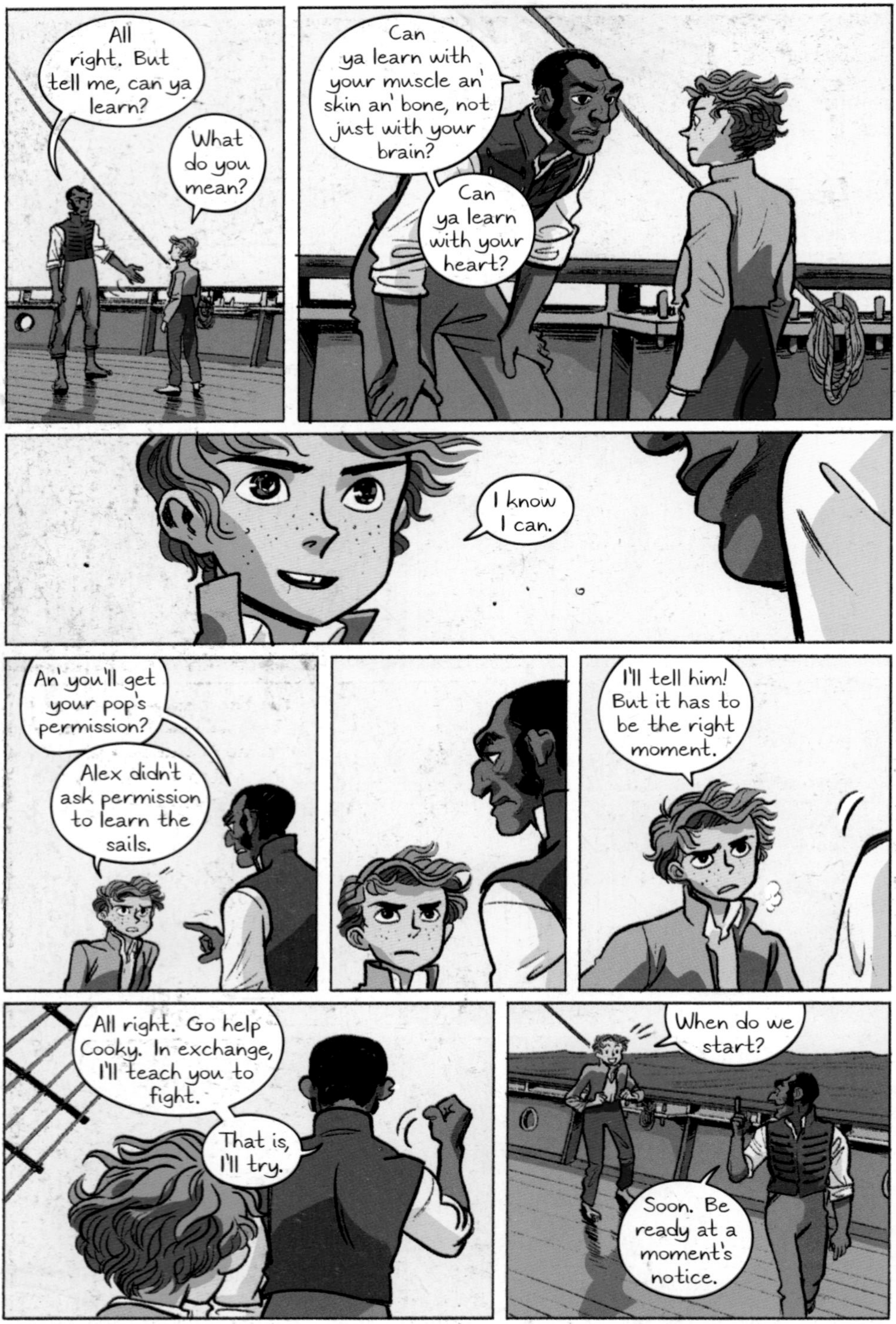
All right. But tell me, can ya learn?
What do you mean?
Can ya learn with your muscle an' skin an' bone, not just with your brain?
Can ya learn with your heart?
I know I can.
An' you'll get your pop's permission?
Alex didn't ask permission to learn the sails.
I'll tell him! But it has to be the right moment.
All right. Go help Cooky. In exchange, I'll teach you to fight.
That is, I'll try.
When do we start?
Soon. Be ready at a moment's notice.

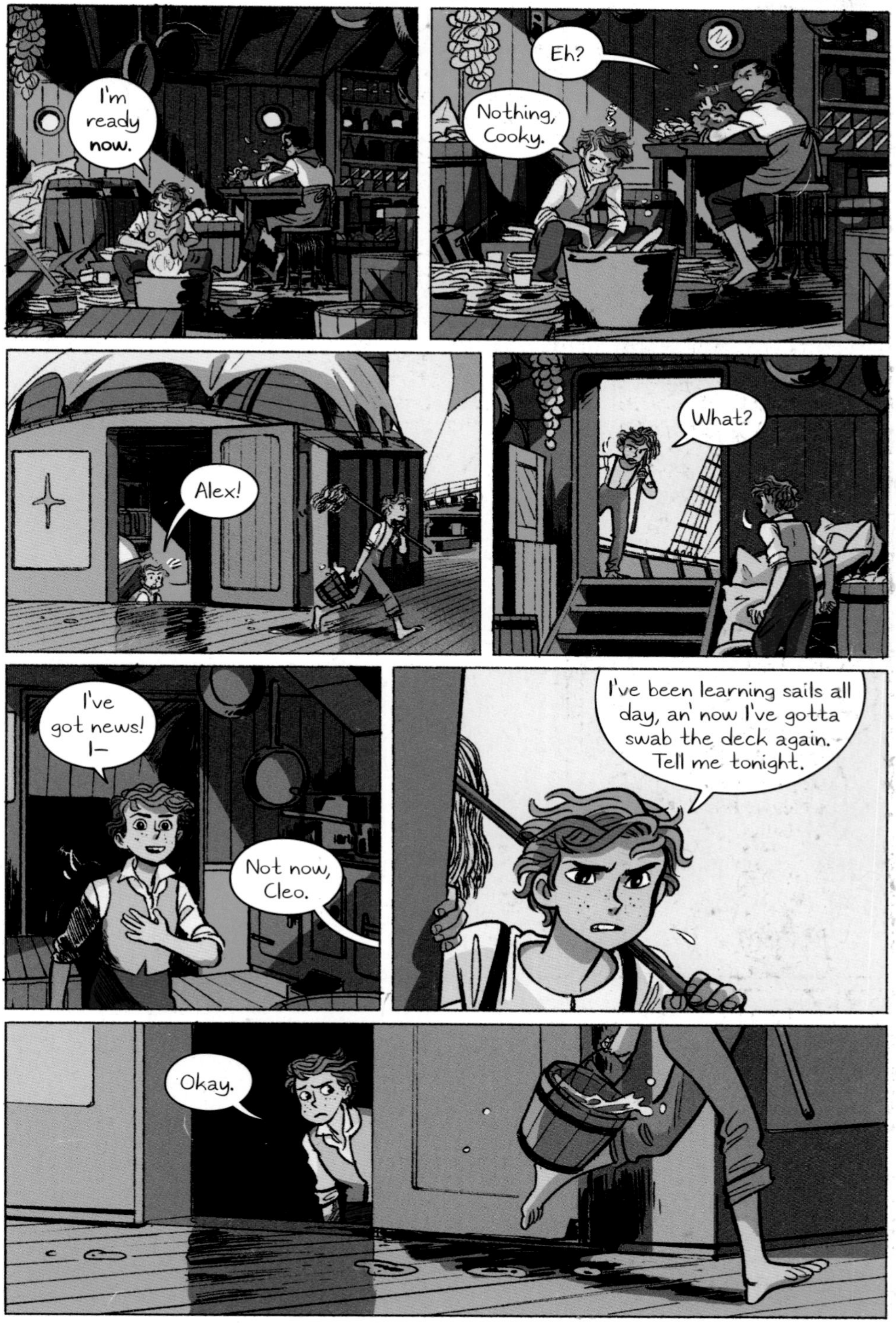
I'm ready now.
Eh?
Nothing, Cooky.
Alex!
What?
I've got news! I—
Not now, Cleo.
I've been learning sails all day, an' now I've gotta swab the deck again. Tell me tonight.
Okay.

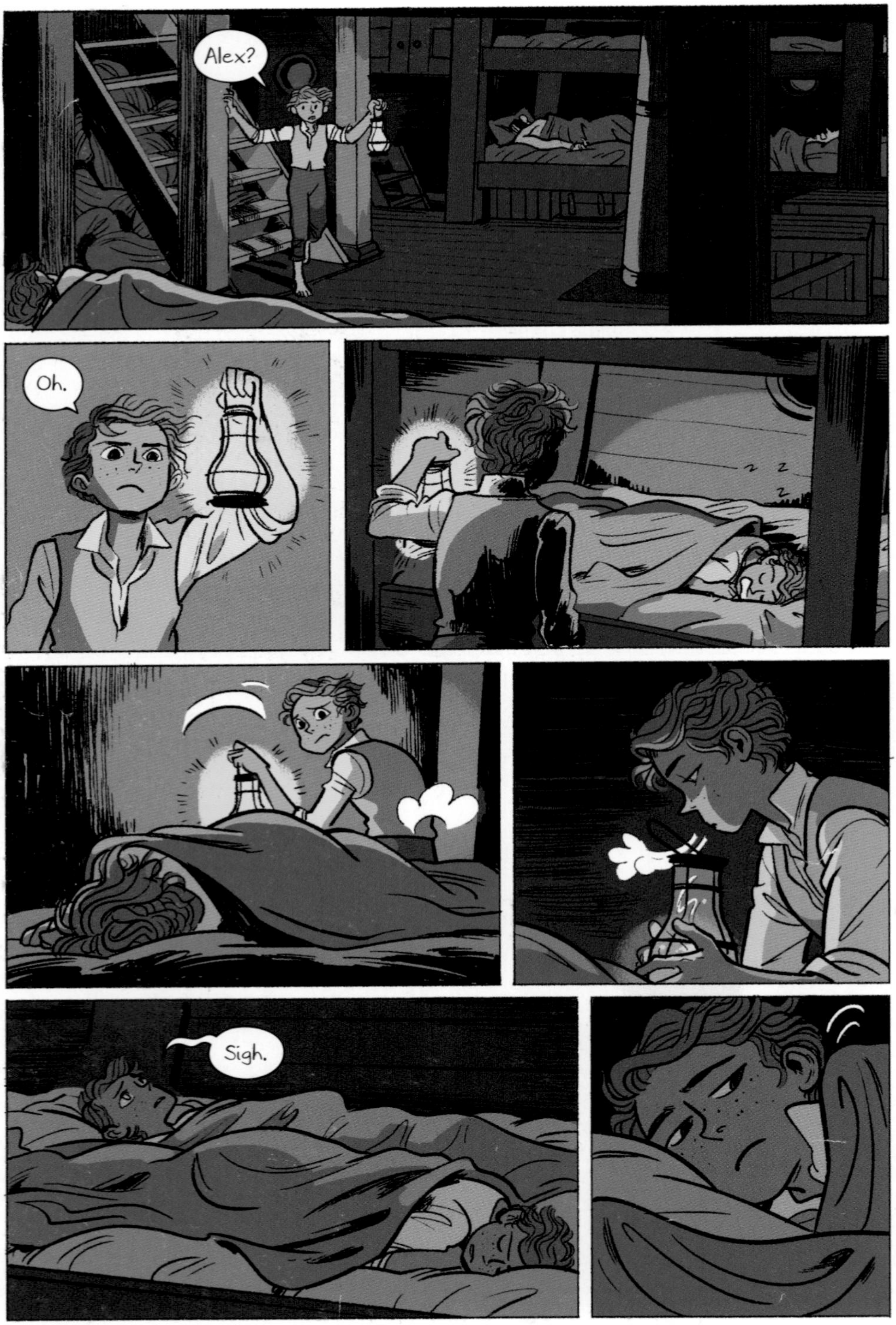
Alex?
Oh.
Sigh.

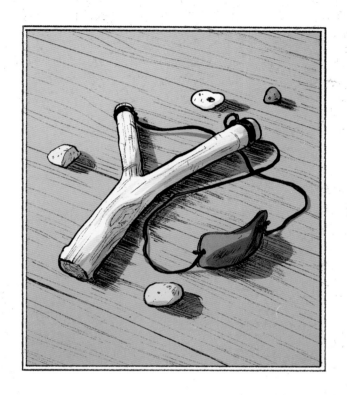

CHAPTER TWO
MERCY

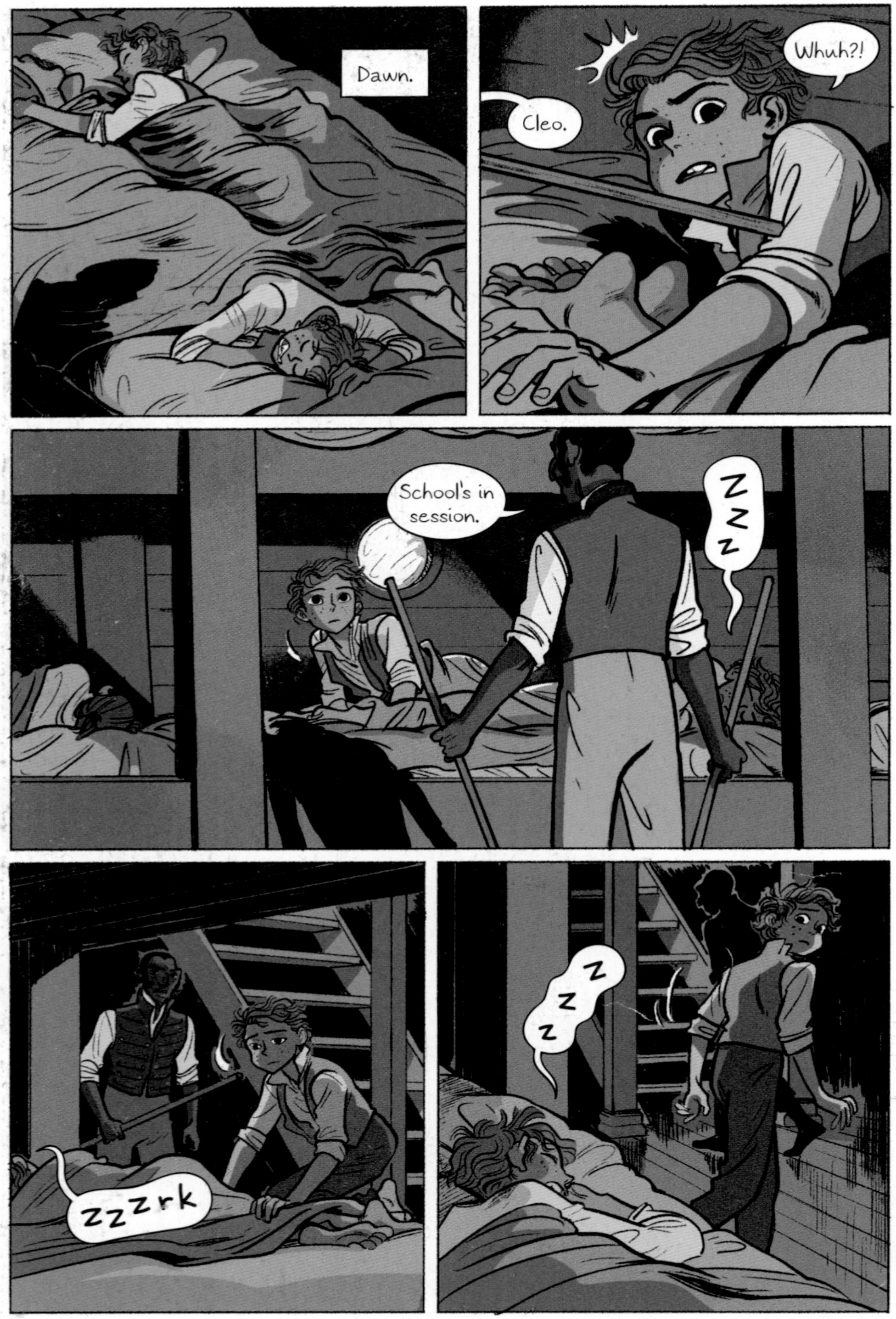
Dawn.
Cleo.
Whuh?!
School's in session.
ZZZ
zzzrk
ZZZ

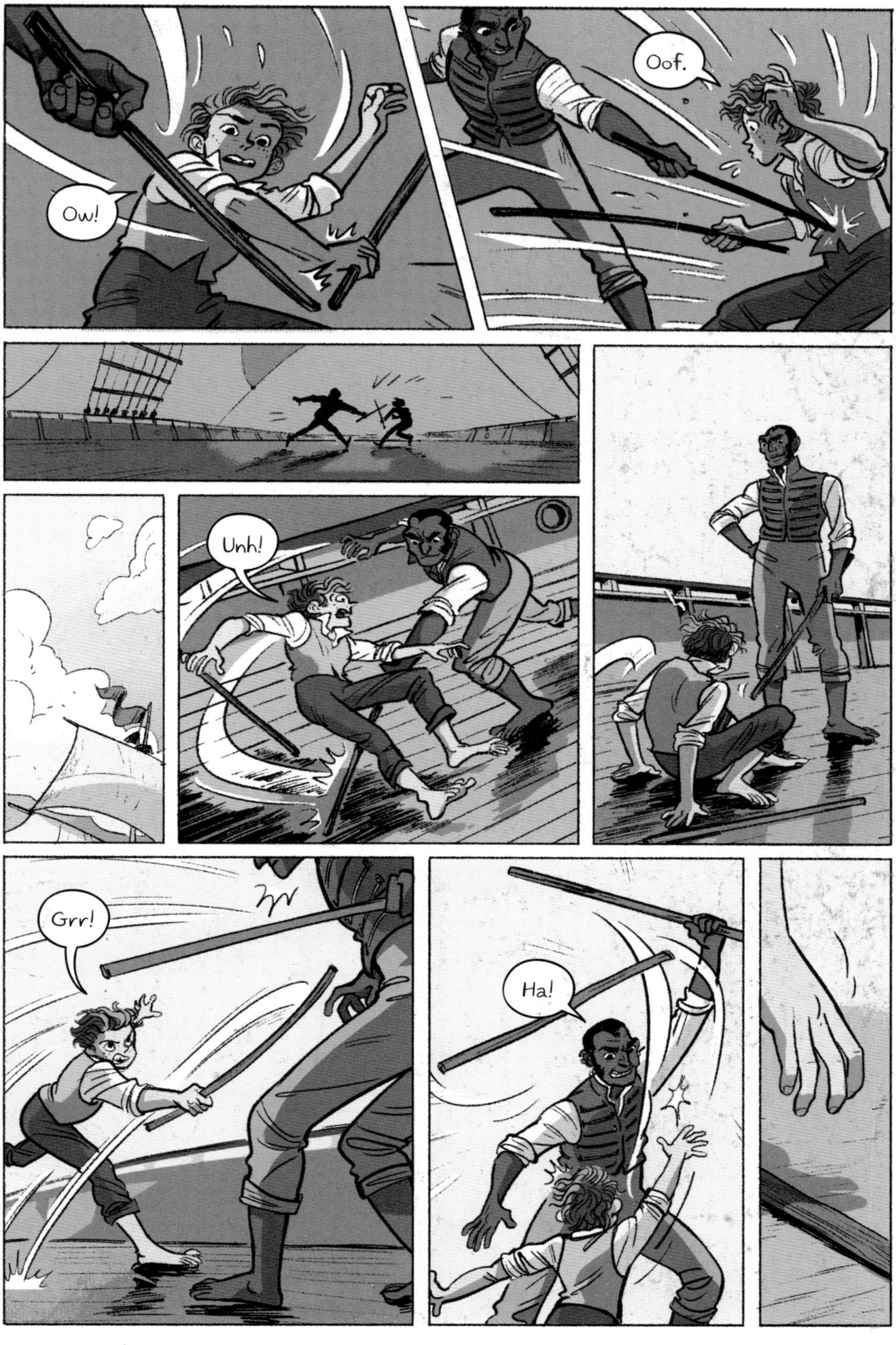
Ow!
Oof.
Unh!
Grr!
Ha!

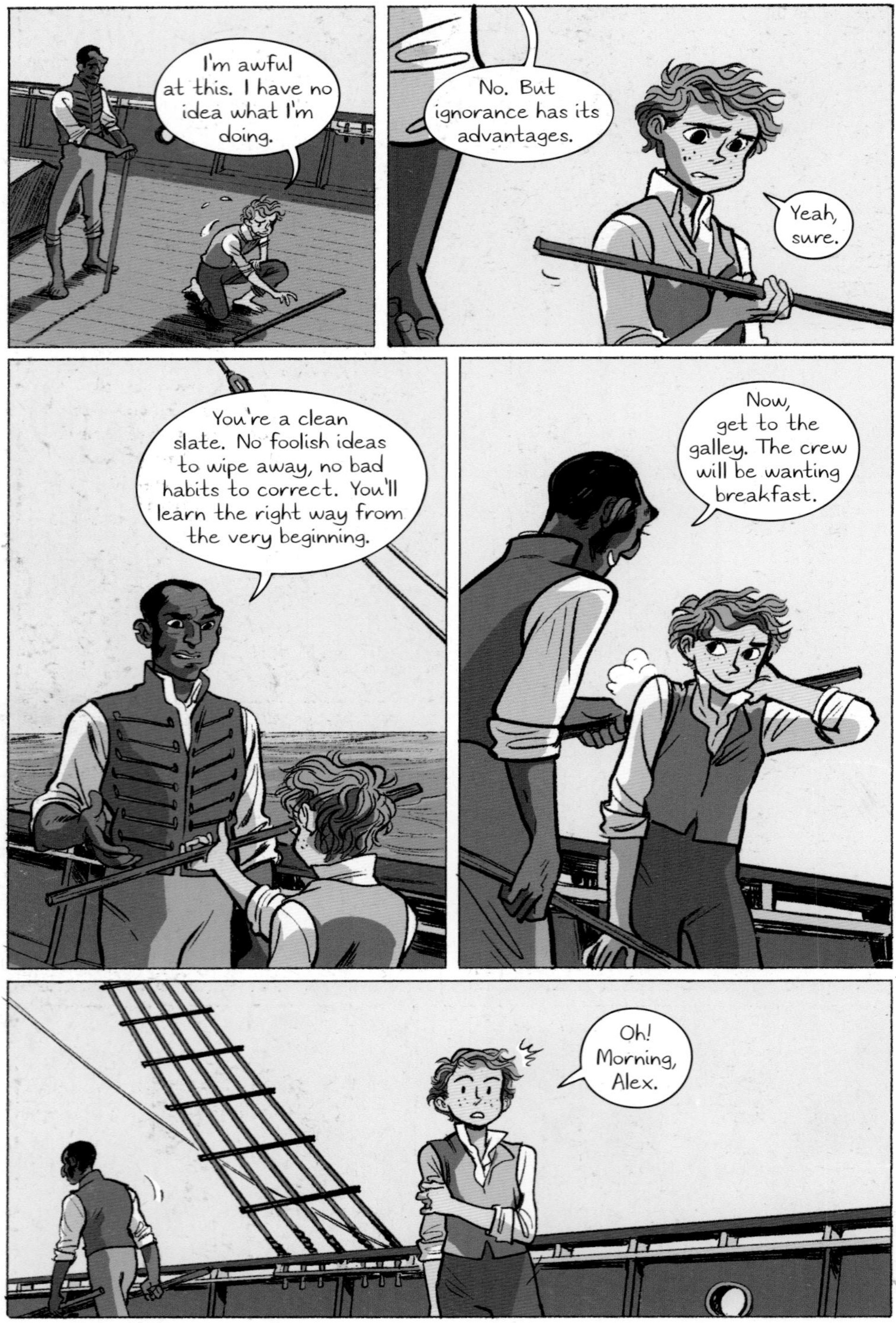
I'm awful at this. I have no idea what I'm doing.
No. But ignorance has its advantages.
Yeah, sure.
You're a clean slate. No foolish ideas to wipe away, no bad habits to correct. You'll learn the right way from the very beginning.
Now, get to the galley. The crew will be wanting breakfast.
Oh! Morning, Alex.

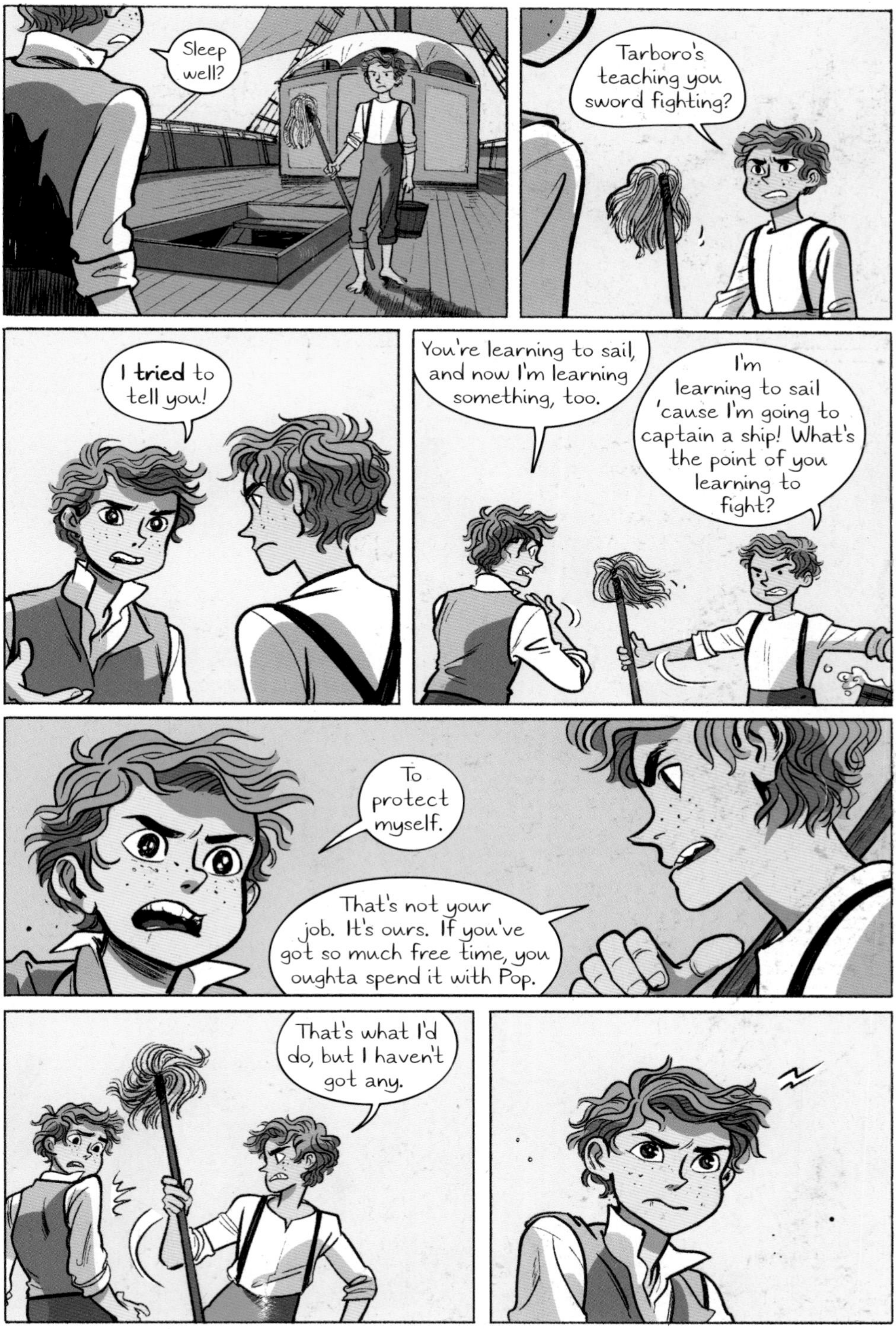
Sleep well?
Tarboro's teaching you sword fighting?
I **tried** to tell you!
You're learning to sail, and now I'm learning something, too.
I'm learning to sail 'cause I'm going to captain a ship! What's the point of you learning to fight?
To protect myself.
That's not your job. It's ours. If you've got so much free time, you oughta spend it with Pop.
That's what I'd do, but I haven't got any.

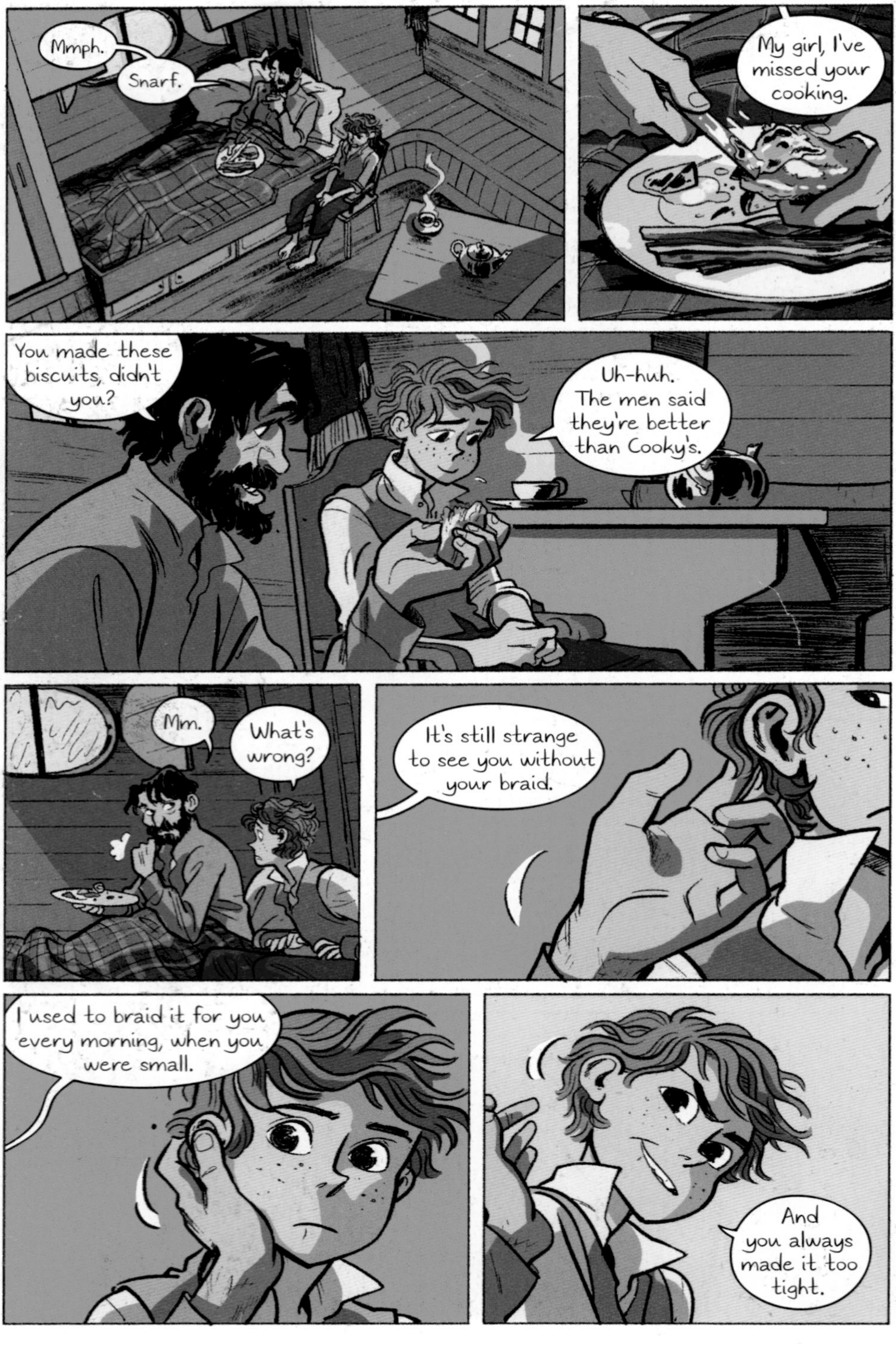
Mmph.
Snarf.
My girl, I've missed your cooking.
You made these biscuits, didn't you?
Uh-huh. The men said they're better than Cooky's.
Mm.
What's wrong?
It's still strange to see you without your braid.
I used to braid it for you every morning, when you were small.
And you always made it too tight.

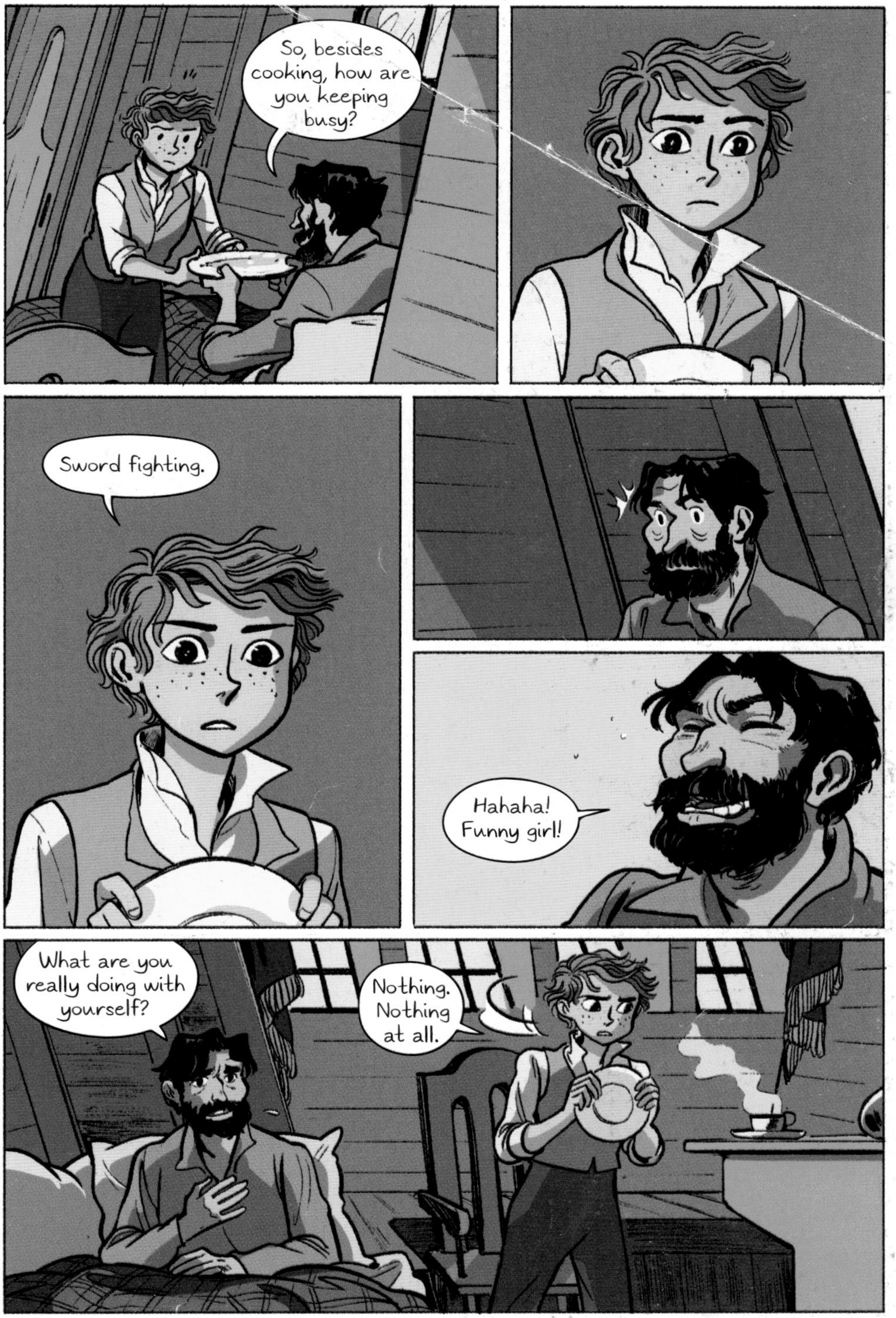
So, besides cooking, how are you keeping busy?
Sword fighting.
Hahaha! Funny girl!
What are you really doing with yourself?
Nothing. Nothing at all.

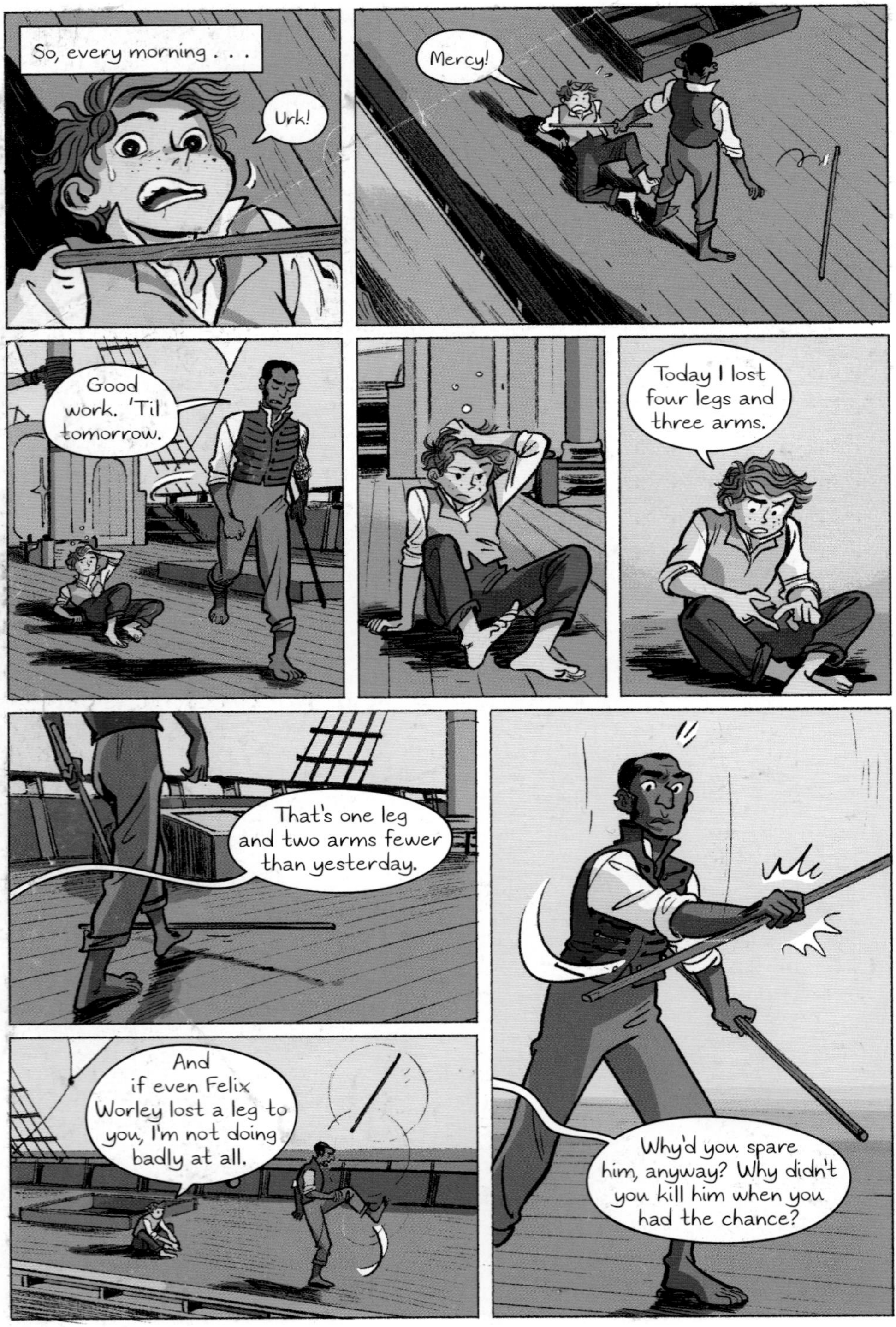
So, every morning . . .
Urk!
Mercy!
Good work. 'Til tomorrow.
Today I lost four legs and three arms.
That's one leg and two arms fewer than yesterday.
And if even Felix Worley lost a leg to you, I'm not doing badly at all.
Why'd you spare him, anyway? Why didn't you kill him when you had the chance?

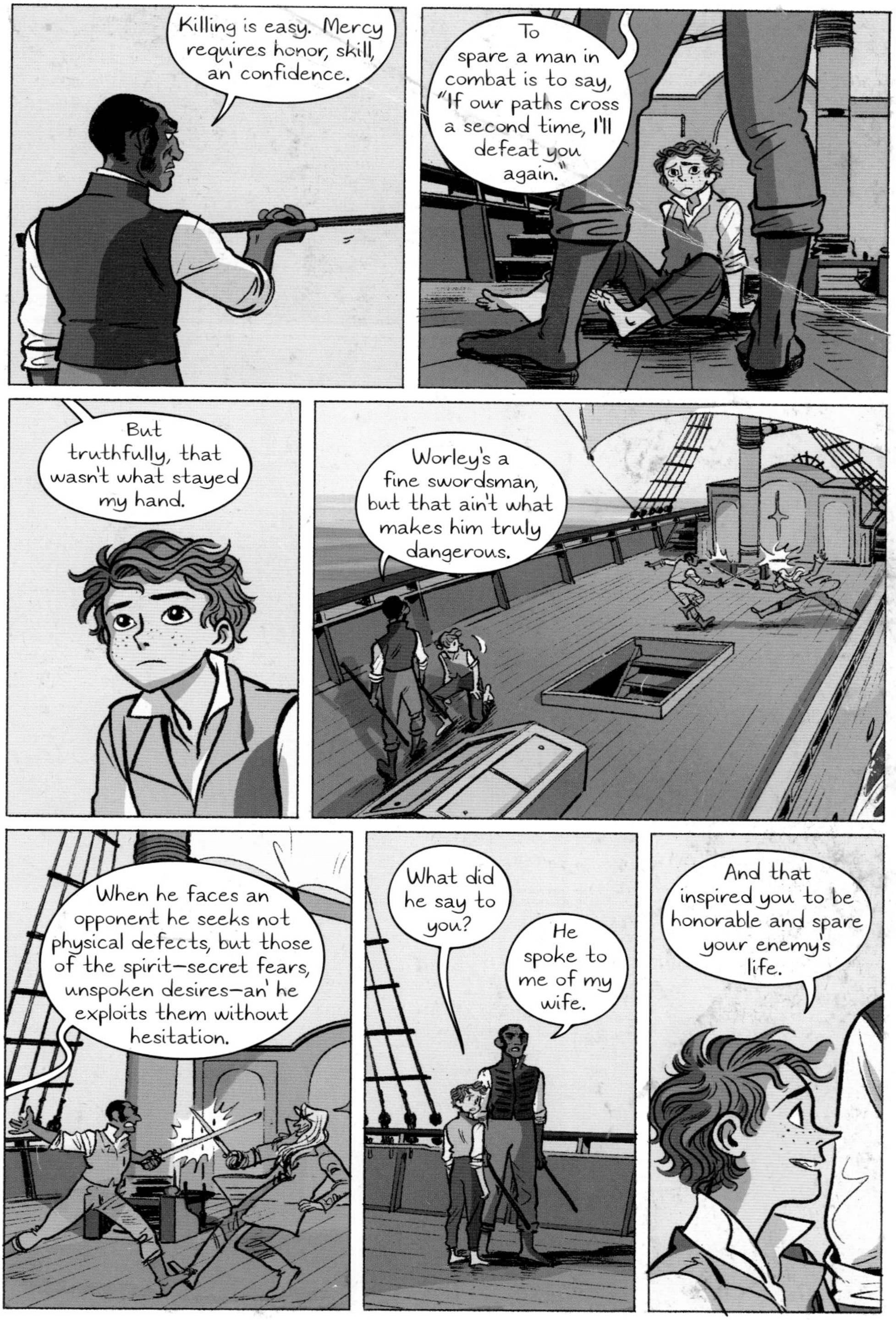
Killing is easy. Mercy requires honor, skill, an' confidence.
To spare a man in combat is to say, "If our paths cross a second time, I'll defeat you again."
But truthfully, that wasn't what stayed my hand.
Worley's a fine swordsman, but that ain't what makes him truly dangerous.
When he faces an opponent he seeks not physical defects, but those of the spirit—secret fears, unspoken desires—an' he exploits them without hesitation.
What did he say to you?
He spoke to me of my wife.
And that inspired you to be honorable and spare your enemy's life.

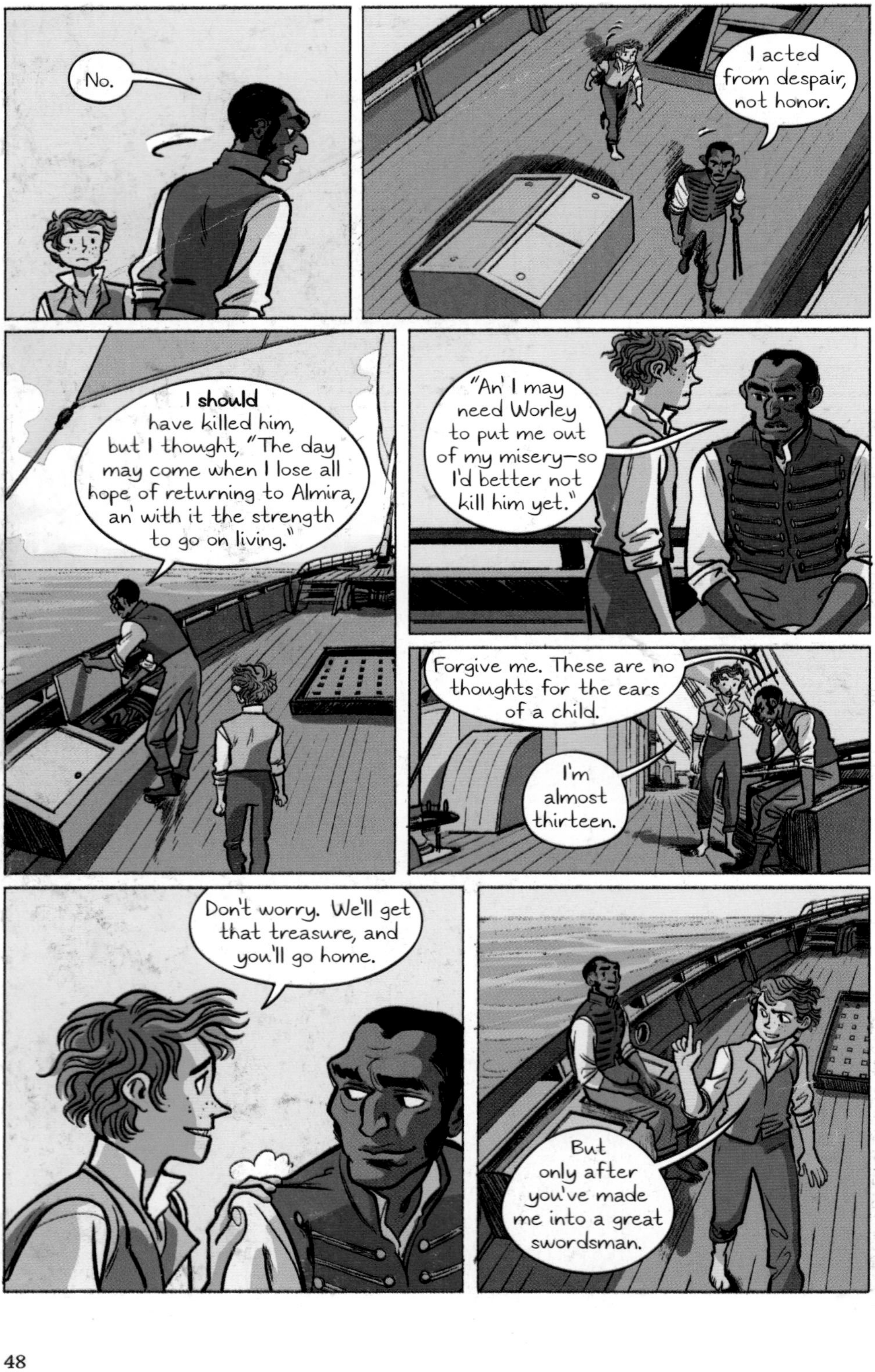
No.
I acted from despair, not honor.
I should have killed him, but I thought, "The day may come when I lose all hope of returning to Almira, an' with it the strength to go on living."
"An' I may need Worley to put me out of my misery—so I'd better not kill him yet."
Forgive me. These are no thoughts for the ears of a child.
I'm almost thirteen.
Don't worry. We'll get that treasure, and you'll go home.
But only after you've made me into a great swordsman.

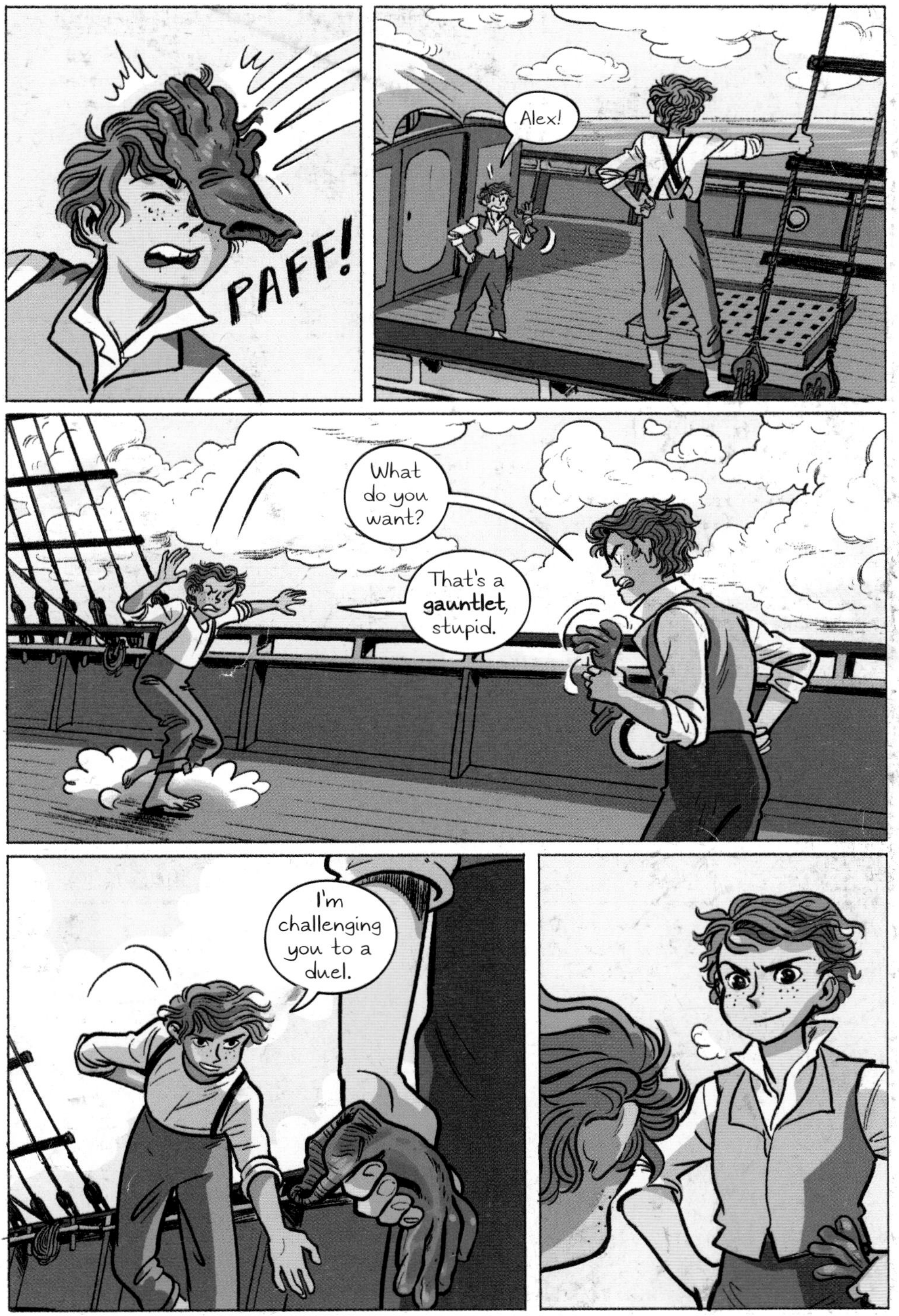

PAFF!
Alex!
What do you want?
That's a **gauntlet**, stupid.
I'm challenging you to a duel.

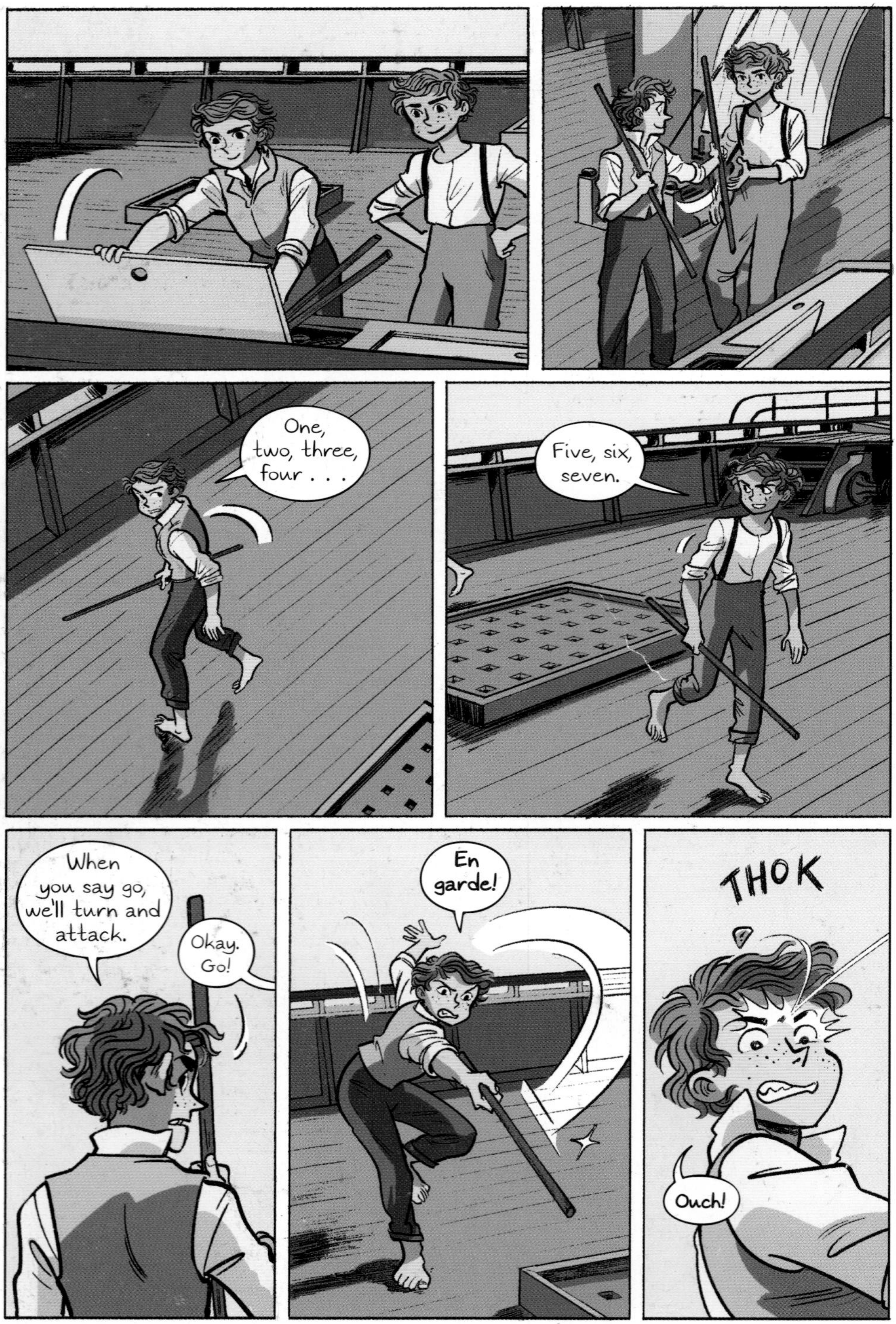
One, two, three, four . . .
Five, six, seven.
When you say go, we'll turn and attack.
Okay. Go!
En garde!
THOK
Ouch!

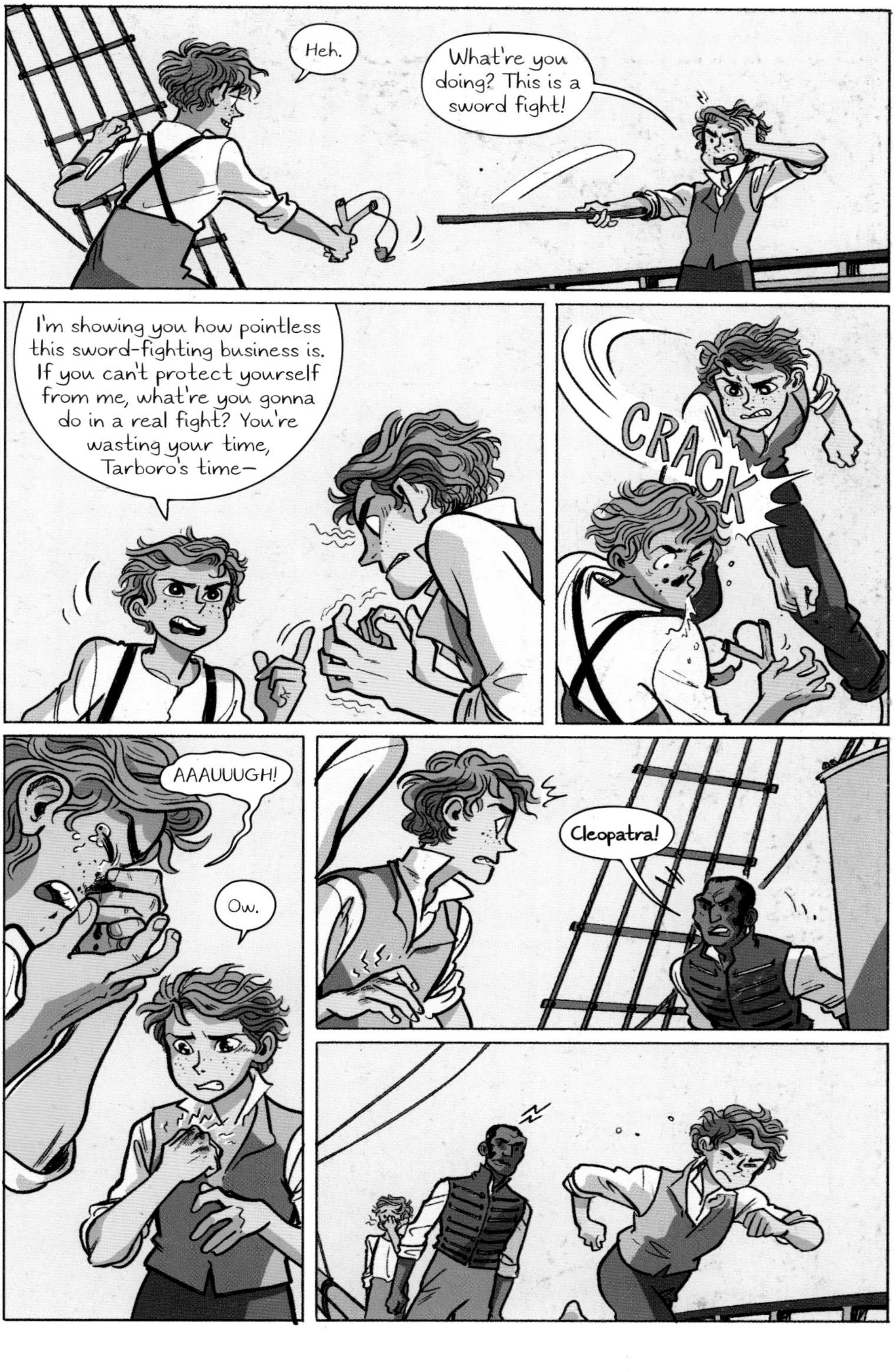
Heh.
What're you doing? This is a sword fight!
I'm showing you how pointless this sword-fighting business is. If you can't protect yourself from me, what're you gonna do in a real fight? You're wasting your time, Tarboro's time—
CRACK
AAAUUUGH!
Ow.
Cleopatra!

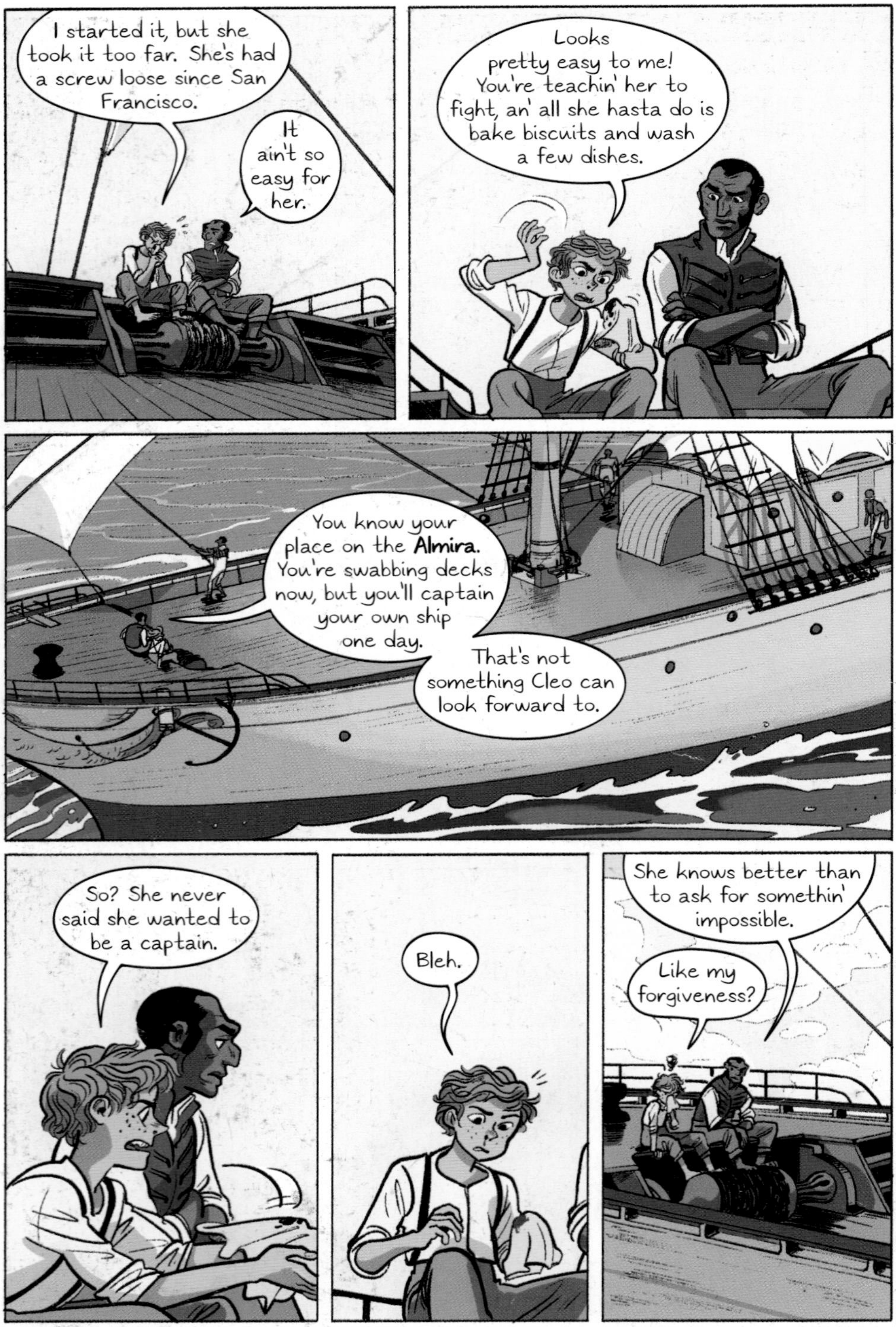
I started it, but she took it too far. She's had a screw loose since San Francisco.
It ain't so easy for her.
Looks pretty easy to me! You're teachin' her to fight, an' all she hasta do is bake biscuits and wash a few dishes.
You know your place on the **Almira**. You're swabbing decks now, but you'll captain your own ship one day.
That's not something Cleo can look forward to.
So? She never said she wanted to be a captain.
Bleh.
She knows better than to ask for somethin' impossible.
Like my forgiveness?

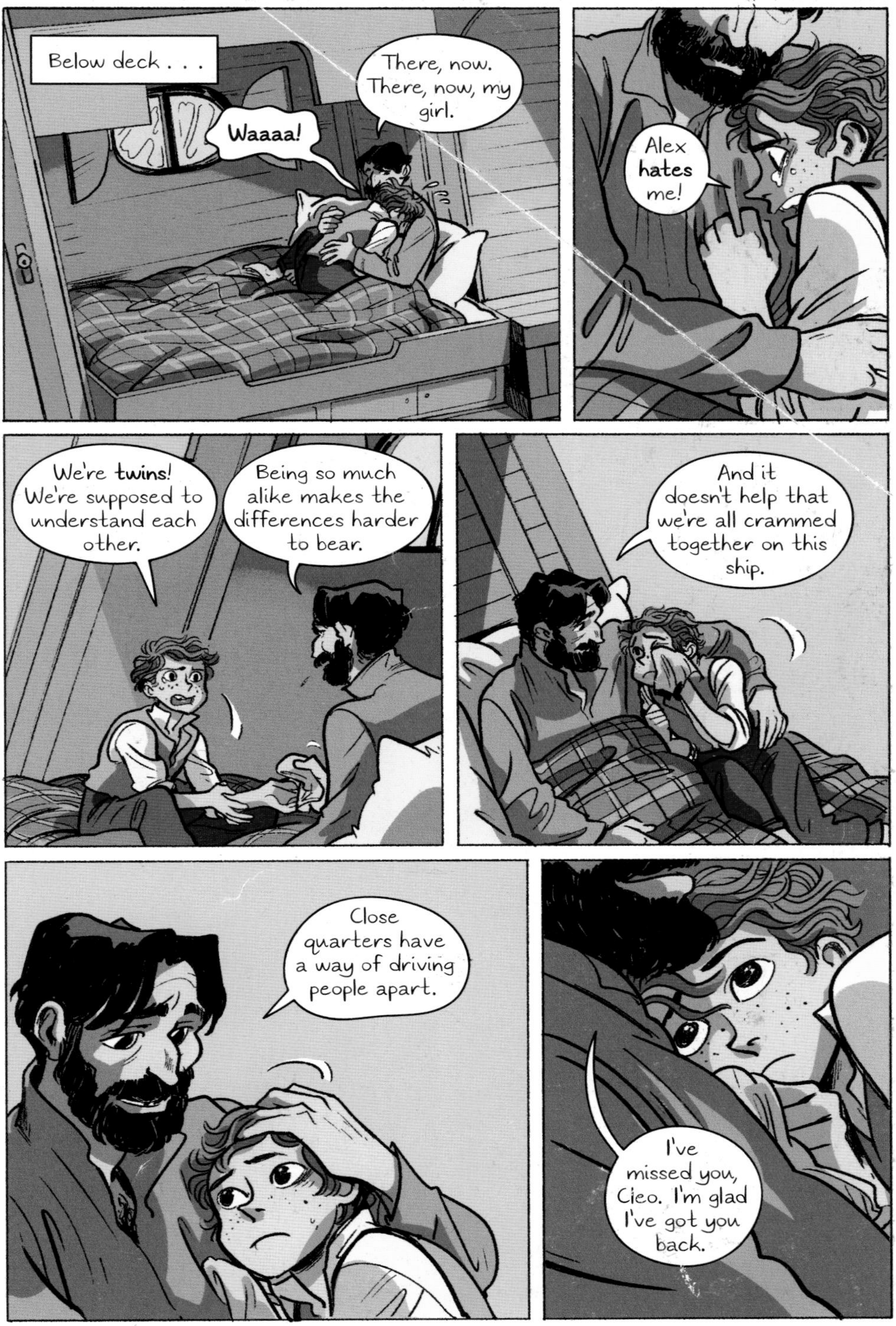
Below deck . . .
Waaaa!
There, now. There, now, my girl.
Alex **hates** me!
We're **twins**! We're supposed to understand each other.
Being so much alike makes the differences harder to bear.
And it doesn't help that we're all crammed together on this ship.
Close quarters have a way of driving people apart.
I've missed you, Cleo. I'm glad I've got you back.

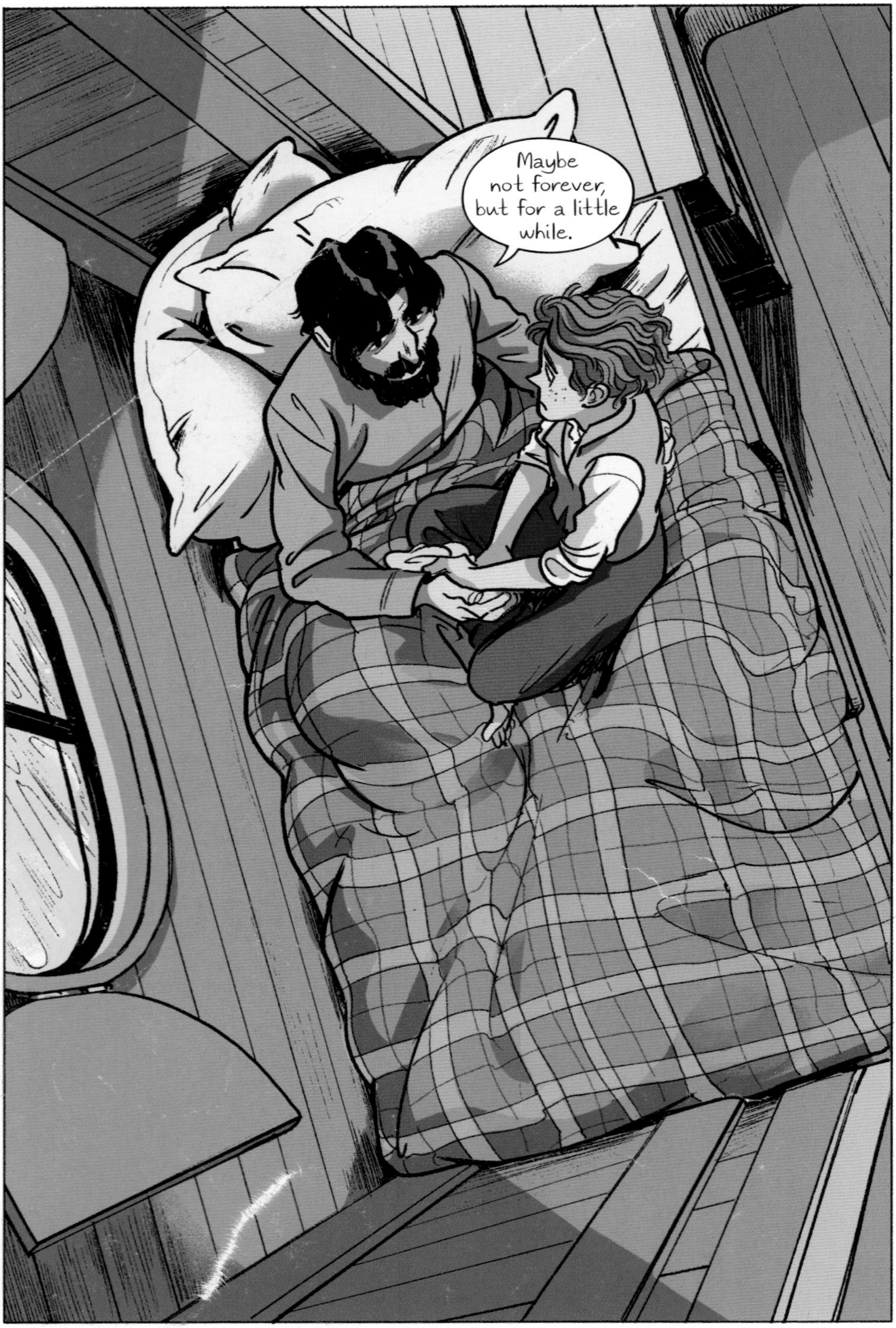
Maybe not forever, but for a little while.

CHAPTER THREE
B IS FOR BRANDEL

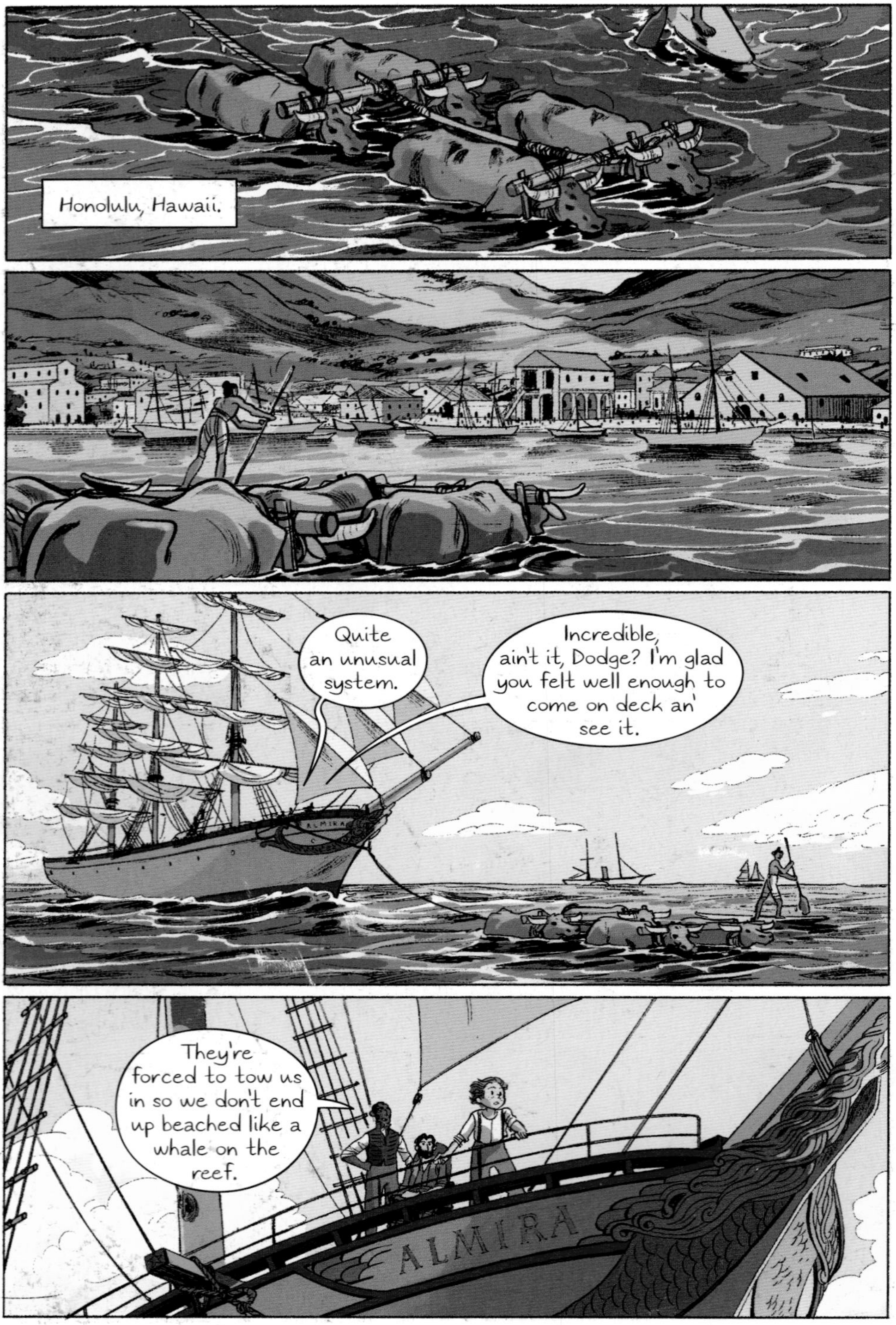

Honolulu, Hawaii.
Quite an unusual system.
Incredible, ain't it, Dodge? I'm glad you felt well enough to come on deck an' see it.
They're forced to tow us in so we don't end up beached like a whale on the reef.
ALMIRA

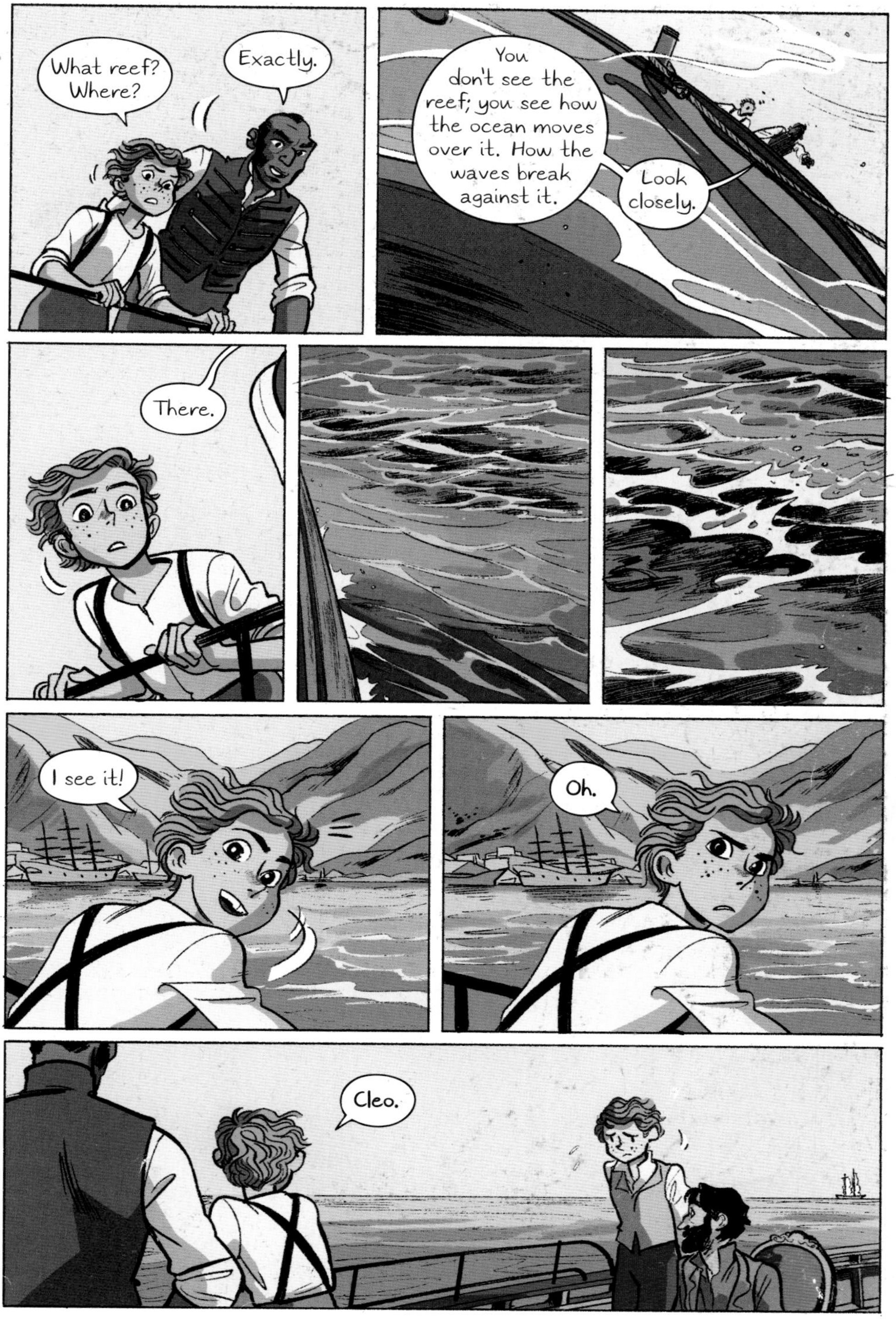
What reef? Where?
Exactly.
You don't see the reef; you see how the ocean moves over it. How the waves break against it.
Look closely.
There.
I see it!
Oh.
Cleo.

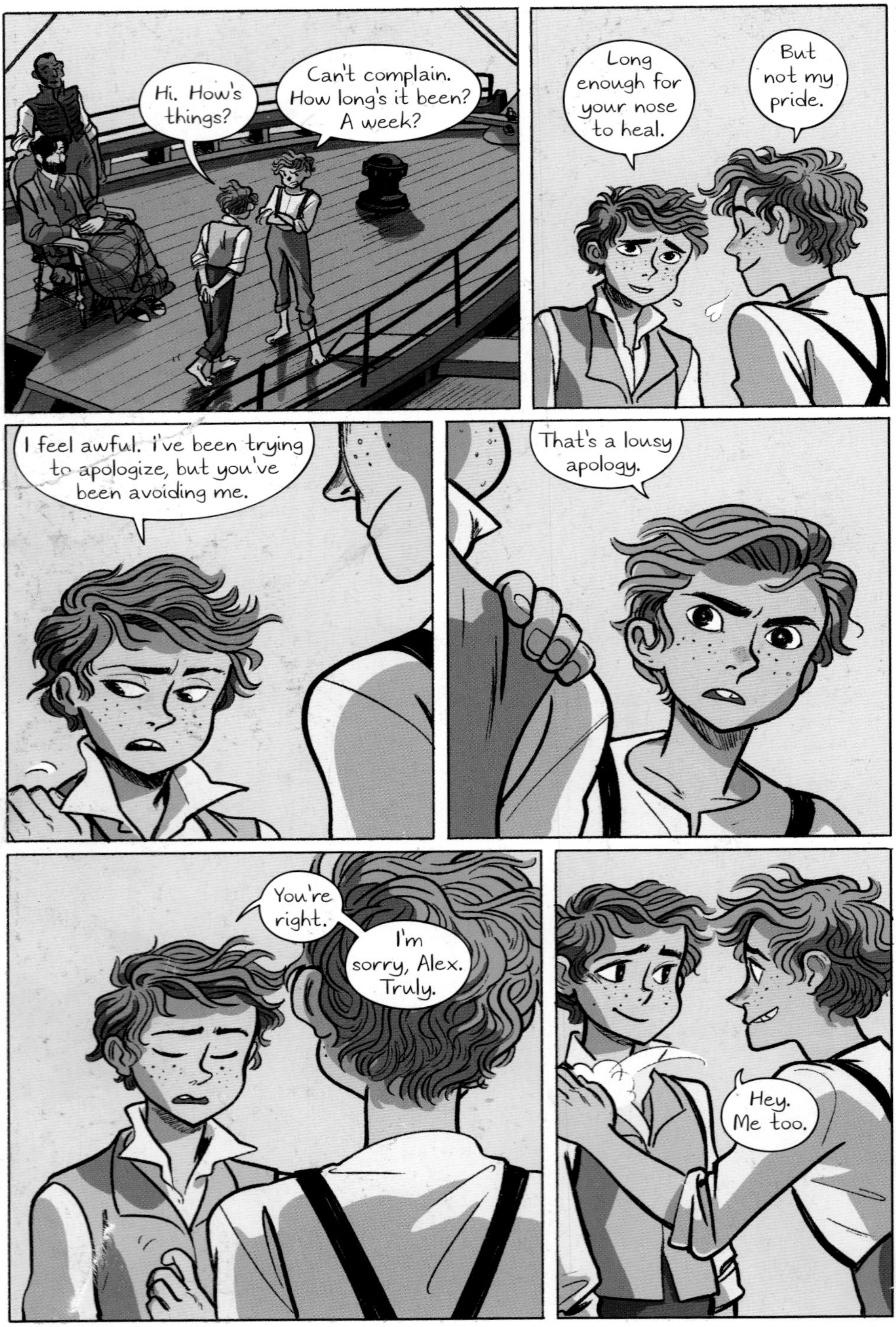
Hi. How's things?
Can't complain. How long's it been? A week?
Long enough for your nose to heal.
But not my pride.
I feel awful. I've been trying to apologize, but you've been avoiding me.
That's a lousy apology.
You're right.
I'm sorry, Alex. Truly.
Hey. Me too.

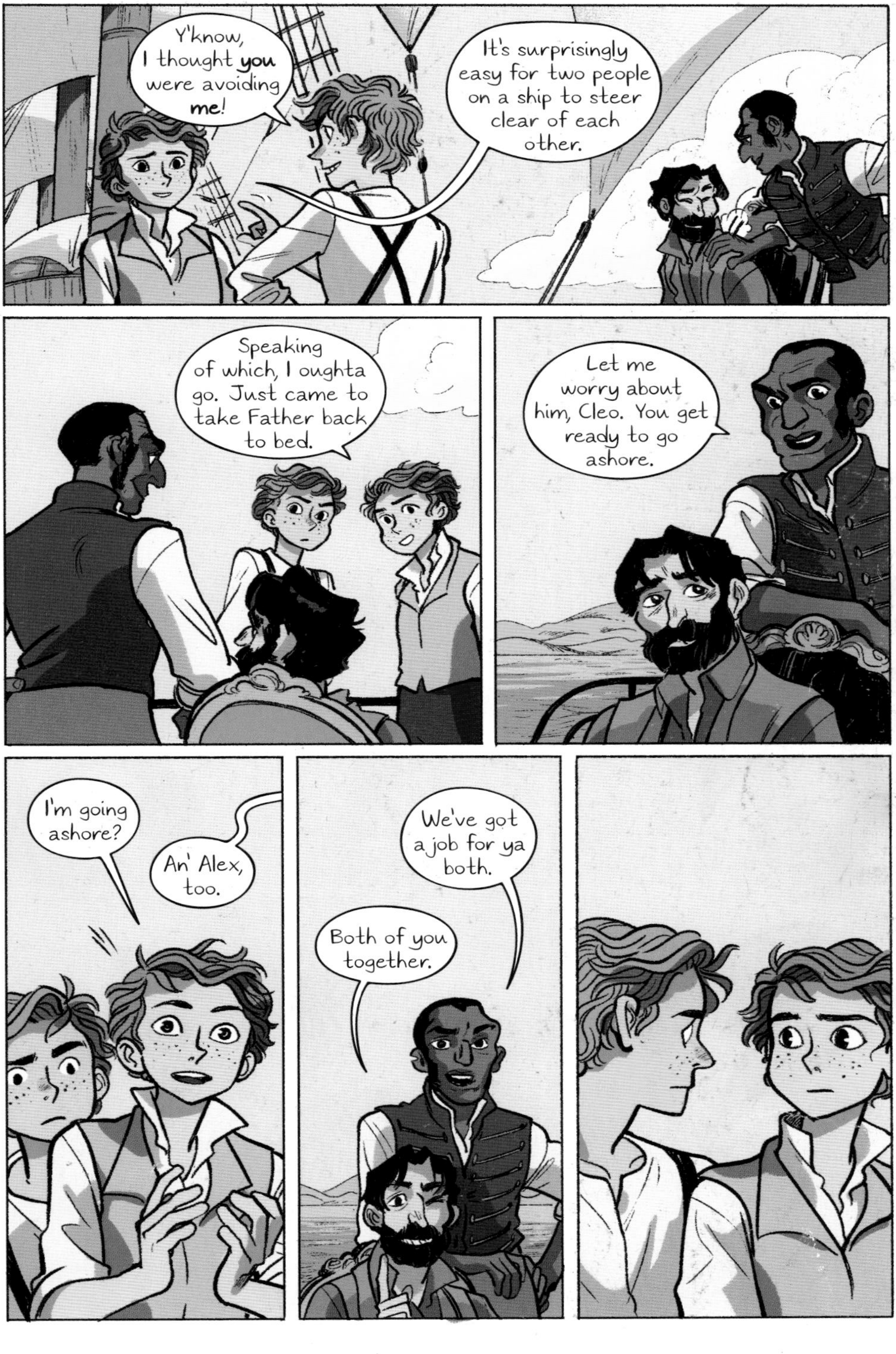
Y'know, I thought **you** were avoiding **me**!
It's surprisingly easy for two people on a ship to steer clear of each other.
Speaking of which, I oughta go. Just came to take Father back to bed.
Let me worry about him, Cleo. You get ready to go ashore.
I'm going ashore?
An' Alex, too.
We've got a job for ya both.
Both of you together.

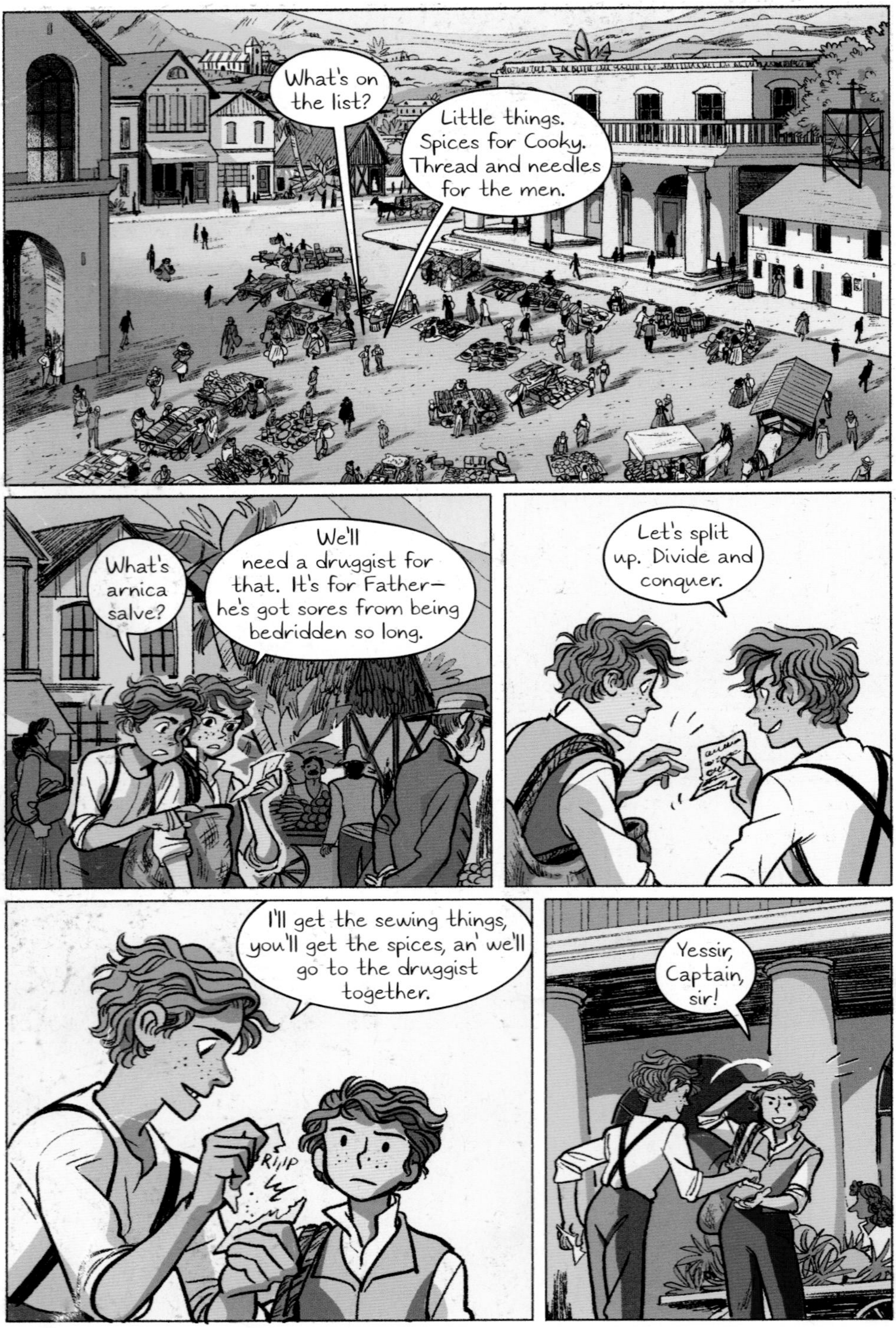
What's on the list?
Little things. Spices for Cooky. Thread and needles for the men.
What's arnica salve?
We'll need a druggist for that. It's for Father— he's got sores from being bedridden so long.
Let's split up. Divide and conquer.
I'll get the sewing things, you'll get the spices, an' we'll go to the druggist together.
RIIP
Yessir, Captain, sir!

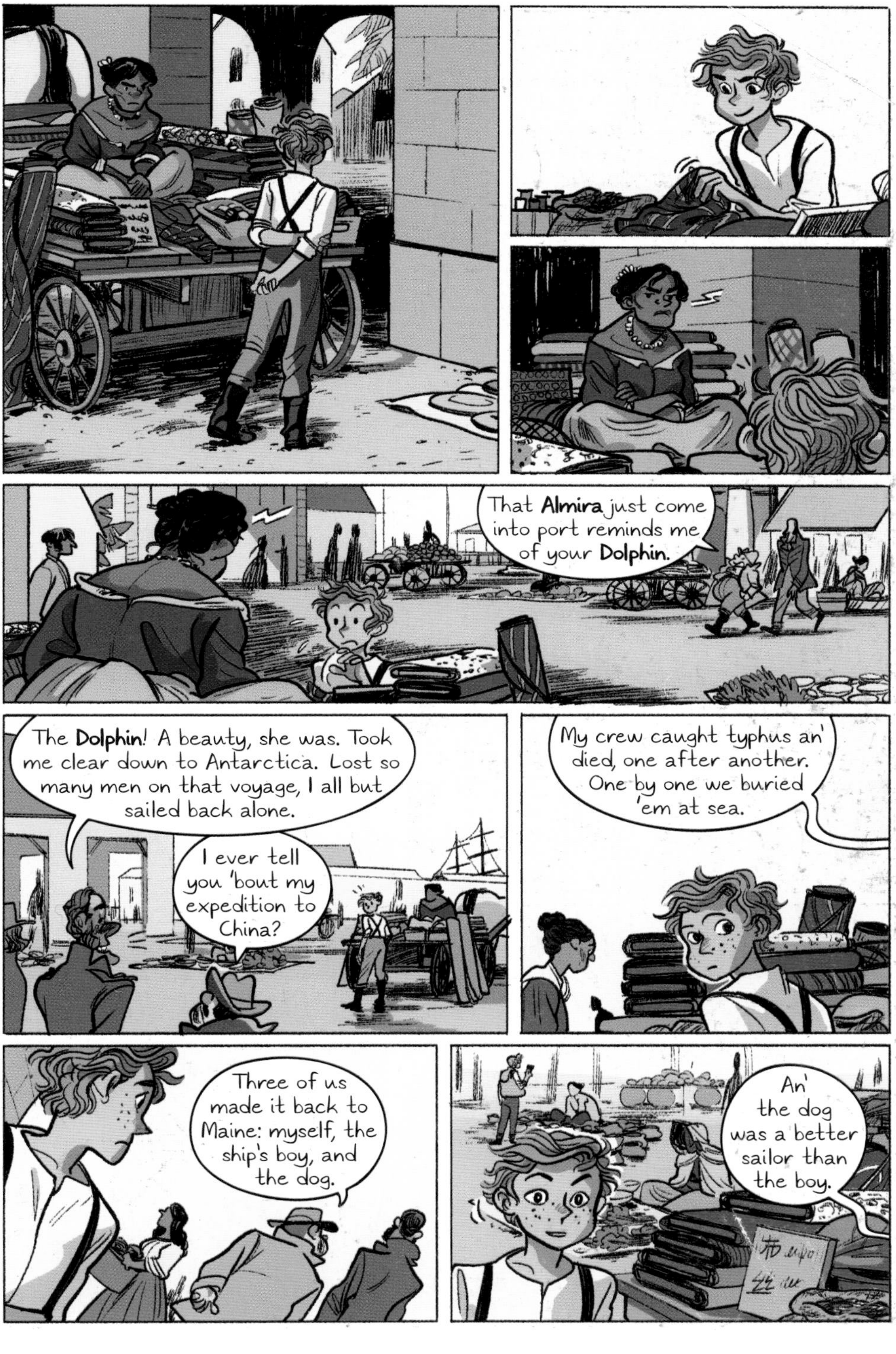

That **Almira** just come into port reminds me of your **Dolphin.**
The **Dolphin**! A beauty, she was. Took me clear down to Antarctica. Lost so many men on that voyage, I all but sailed back alone.
I ever tell you 'bout my expedition to China?
My crew caught typhus an' died, one after another. One by one we buried 'em at sea.
Three of us made it back to Maine: myself, the ship's boy, and the dog.
An' the dog was a better sailor than the boy.

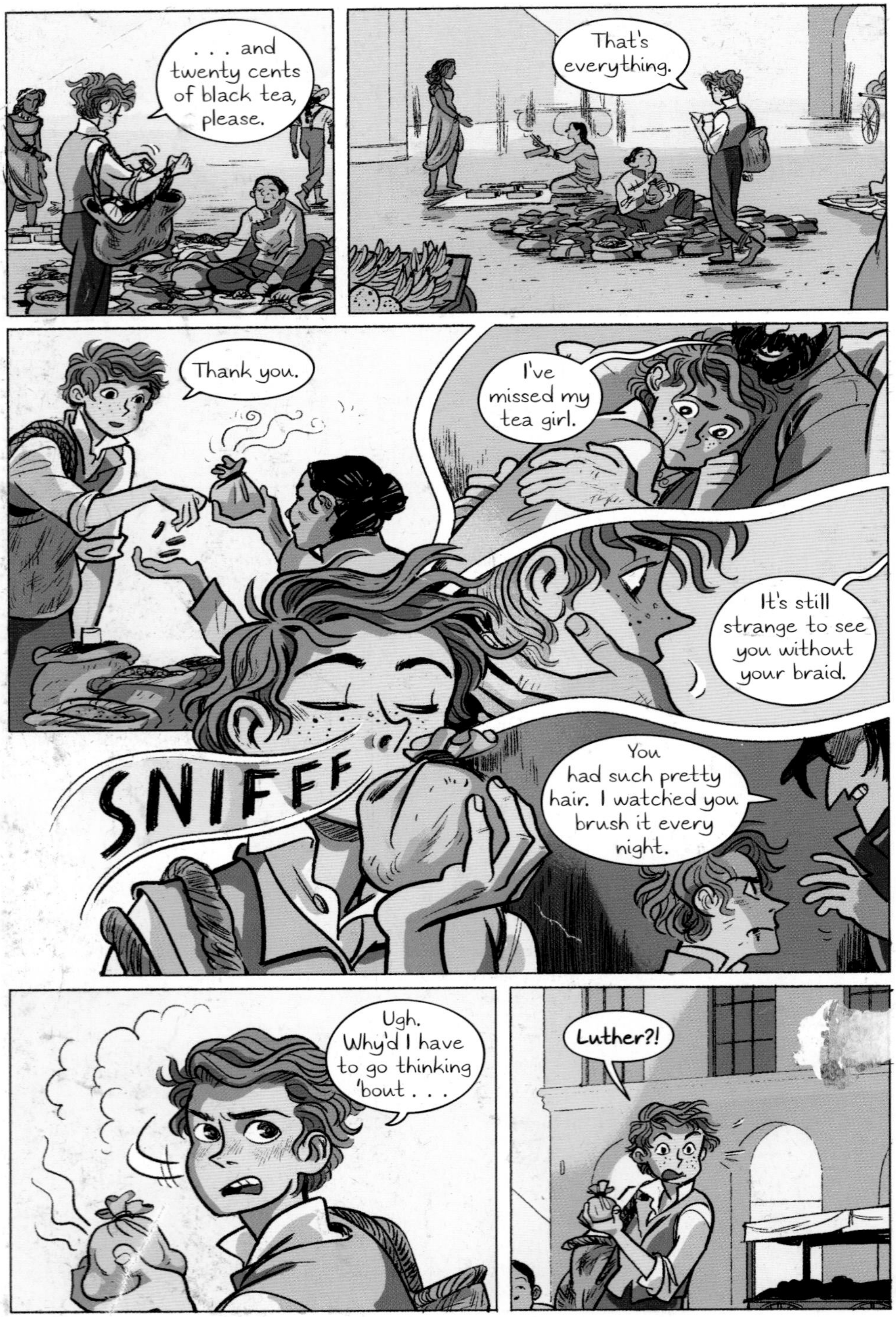
. . . and twenty cents of black tea, please.
That's everything.
Thank you.
I've missed my tea girl.
It's still strange to see you without your braid.
SNIFFF
You had such pretty hair. I watched you brush it every night.
Ugh. Why'd I have to go thinking 'bout . . .
Luther?!

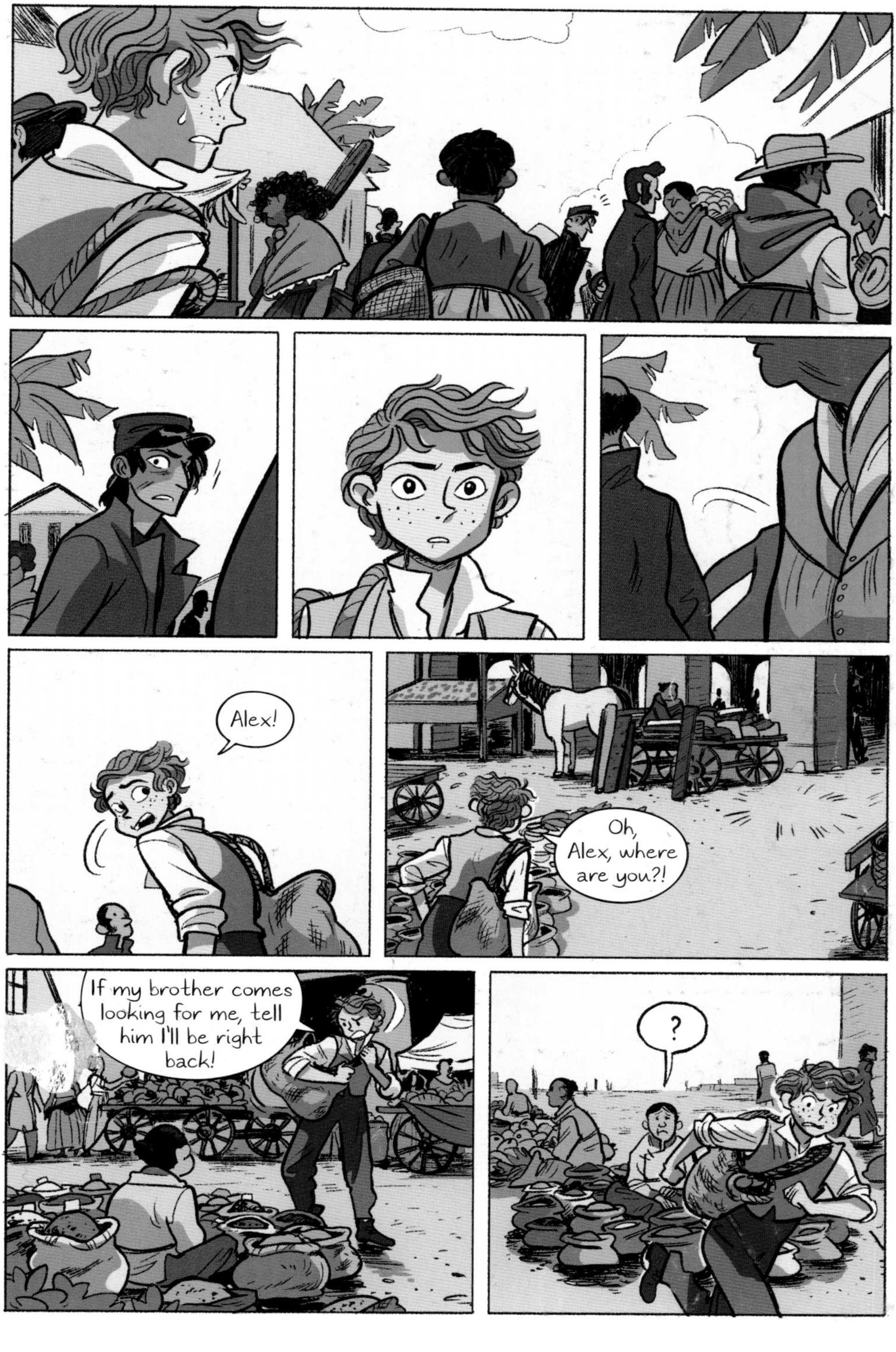
Alex!
Oh, Alex, where are you?!
If my brother comes looking for me, tell him I'll be right back!
?

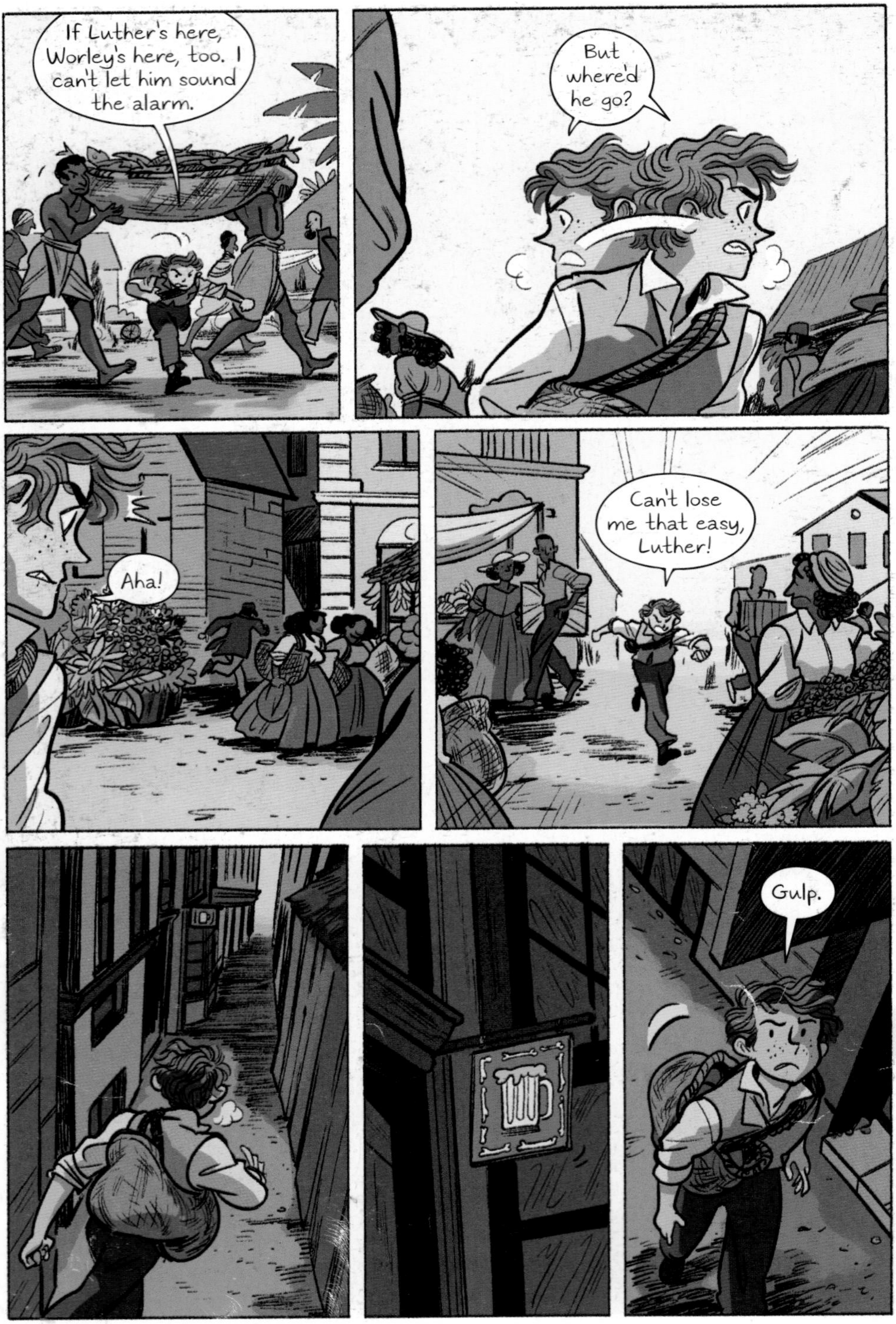
If Luther's here, Worley's here, too. I can't let him sound the alarm.
But where'd he go?
Aha!
Can't lose me that easy, Luther!
Gulp.

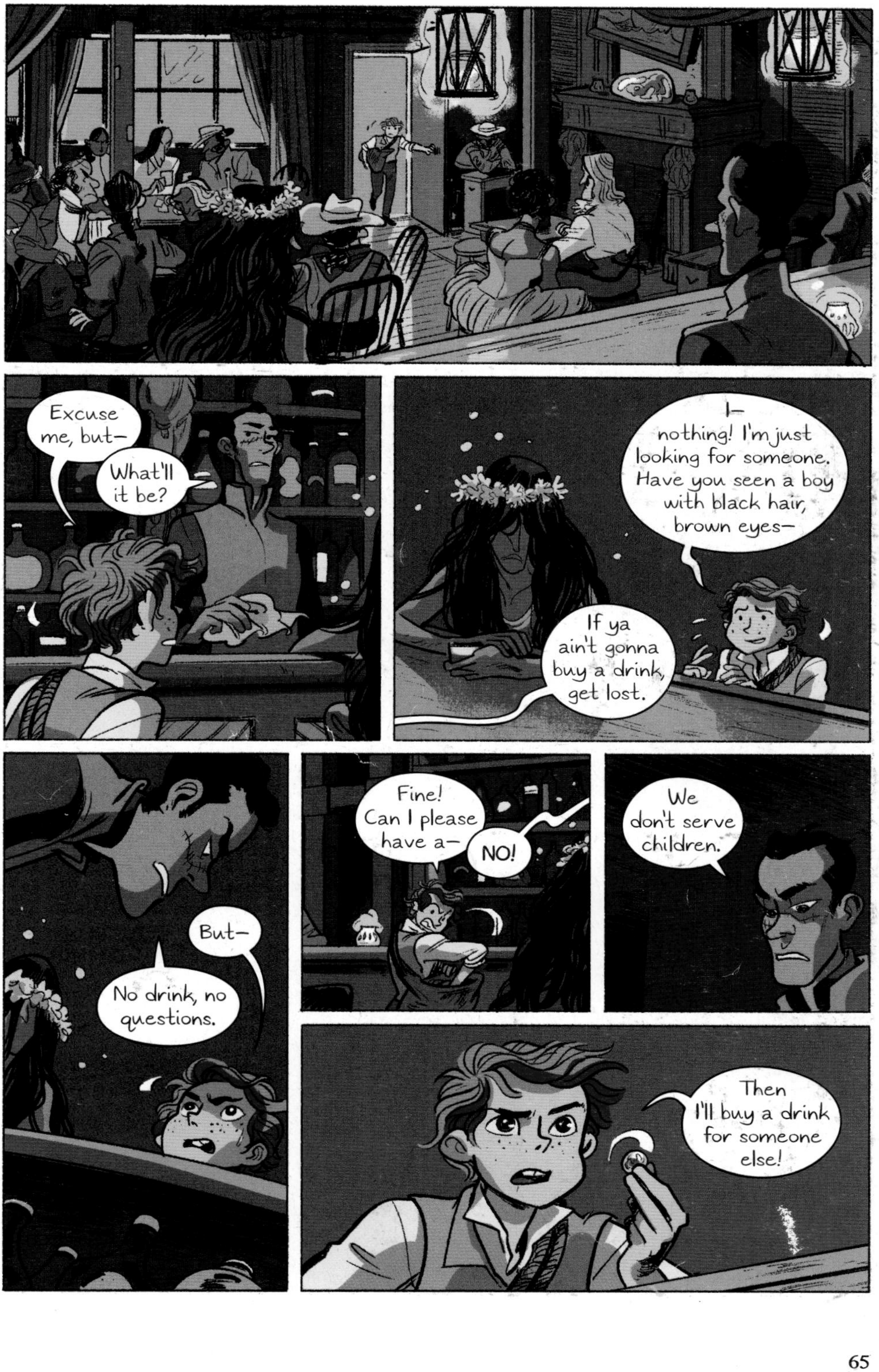
Excuse me, but—
What'll it be?
I—
nothing! I'm just looking for someone. Have you seen a boy with black hair, brown eyes—
If ya ain't gonna buy a drink, get lost.
But—
No drink, no questions.
Fine! Can I please have a—
NO!
We don't serve children.
Then I'll buy a drink for someone else!

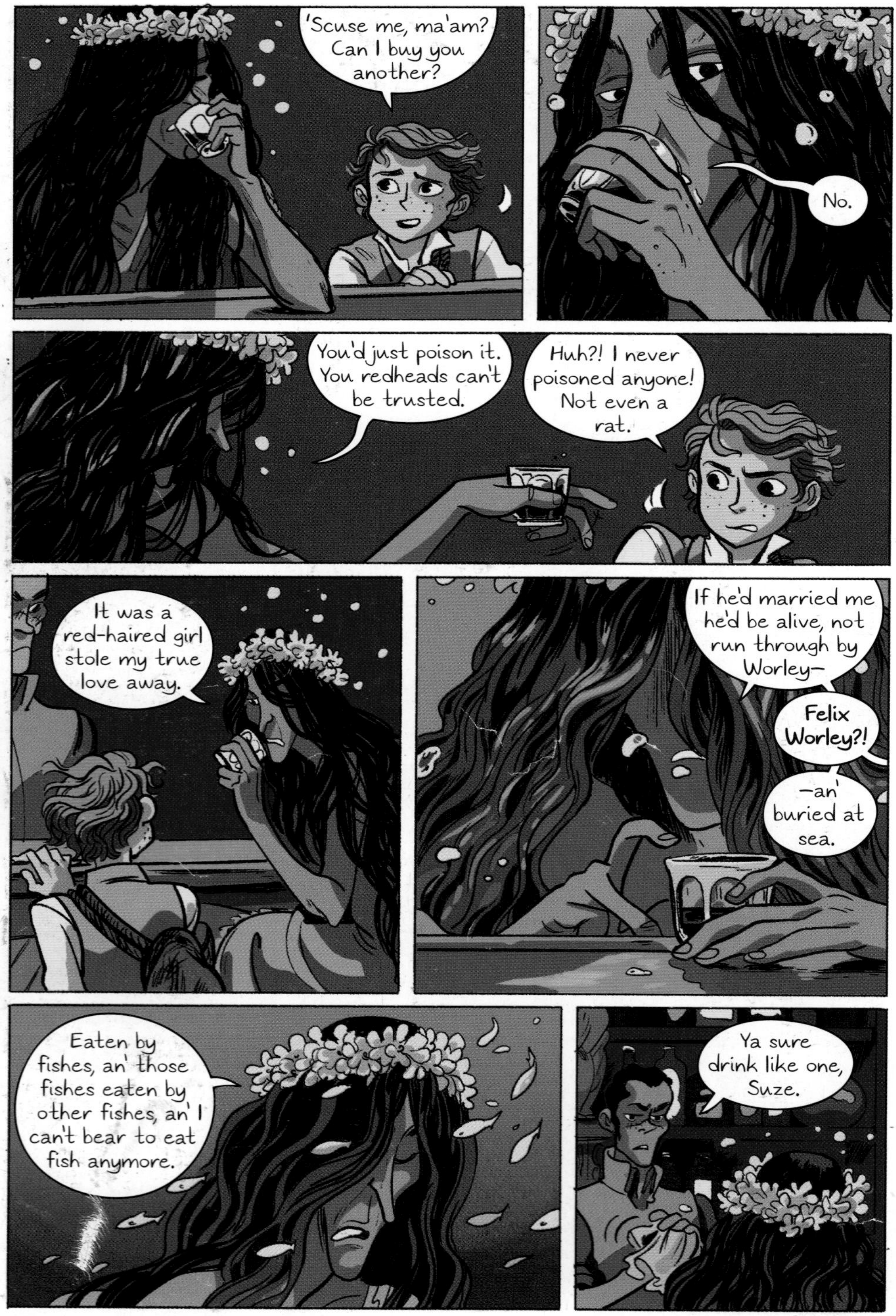
'Scuse me, ma'am? Can I buy you another?
No.
You'd just poison it. You redheads can't be trusted.
Huh?! I never poisoned anyone! Not even a rat.
It was a red-haired girl stole my true love away.
If he'd married me he'd be alive, not run through by Worley—
Felix Worley?!
—an' buried at sea.
Eaten by fishes, an' those fishes eaten by other fishes, an' I can't bear to eat fish anymore.
Ya sure drink like one, Suze.

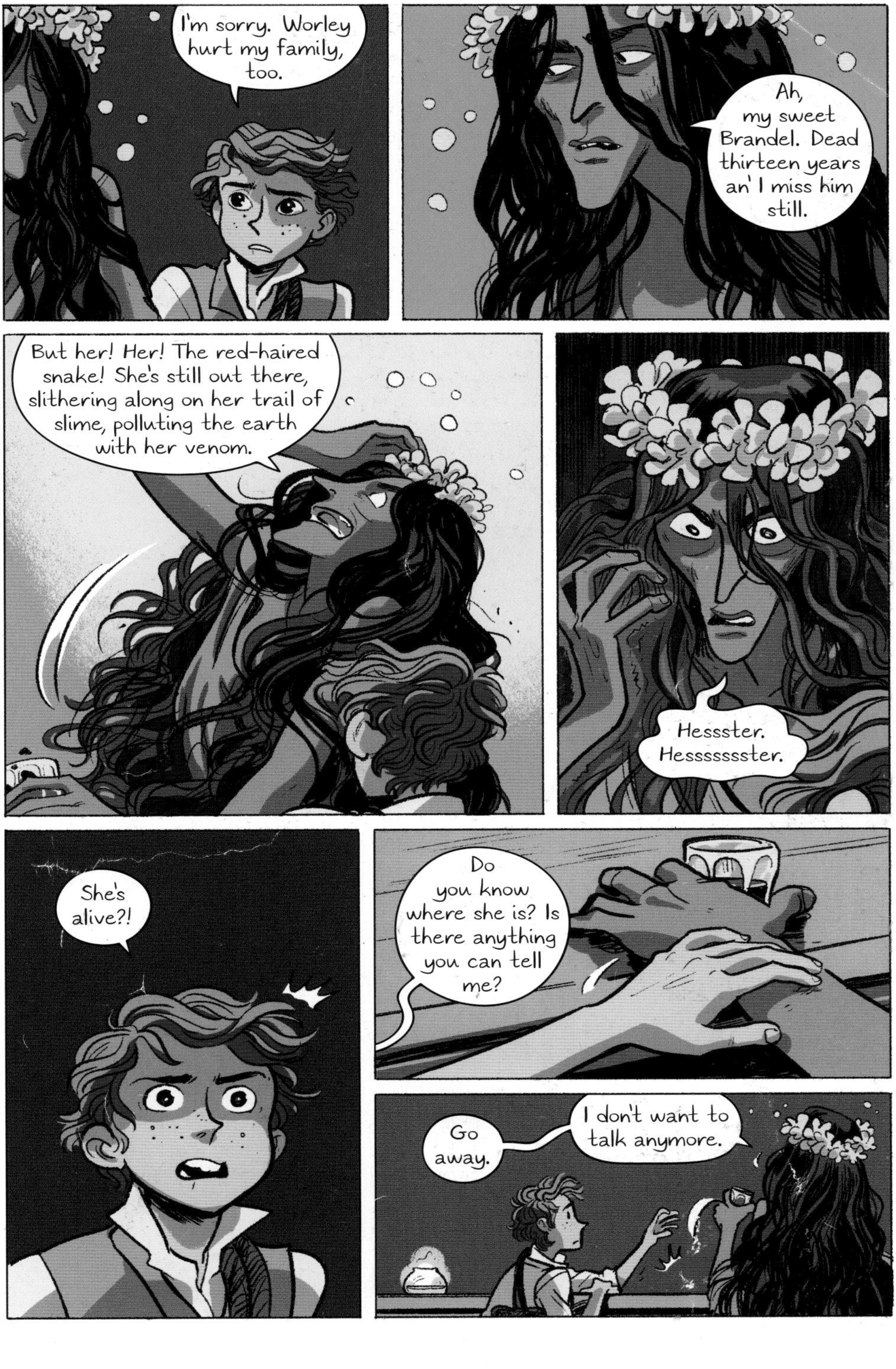
I'm sorry. Worley hurt my family, too.
Ah, my sweet Brandel. Dead thirteen years an' I miss him still.
But her! Her! The red-haired snake! She's still out there, slithering along on her trail of slime, polluting the earth with her venom.
Hessster. Hesssssssster.
She's alive?!
Do you know where she is? Is there anything you can tell me?
Go away.
I don't want to talk anymore.

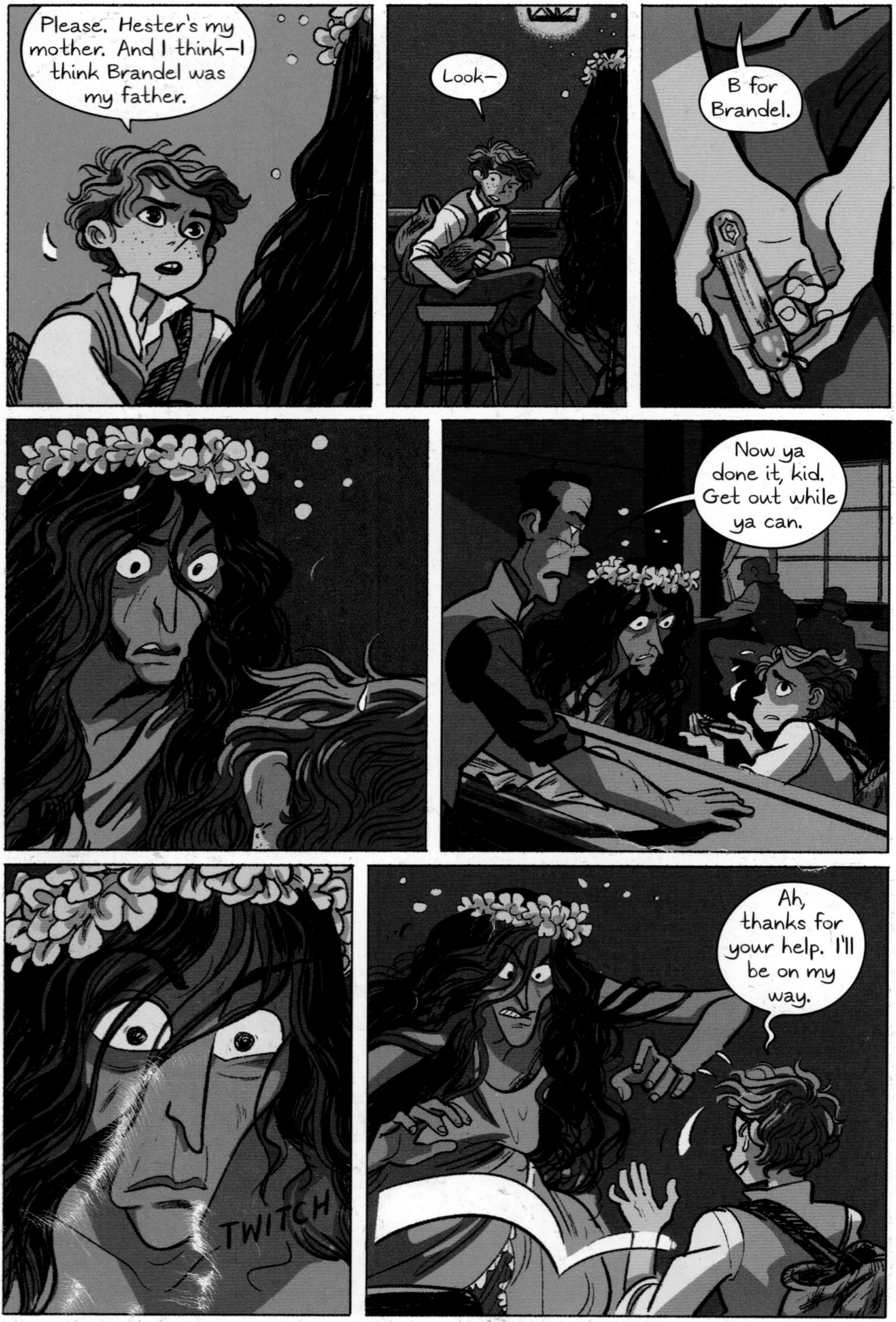
Please. Hester's my mother. And I think—I think Brandel was my father.
Look—
B for Brandel.
Now ya done it, kid. Get out while ya can.
TWITCH
Ah, thanks for your help. I'll be on my way.

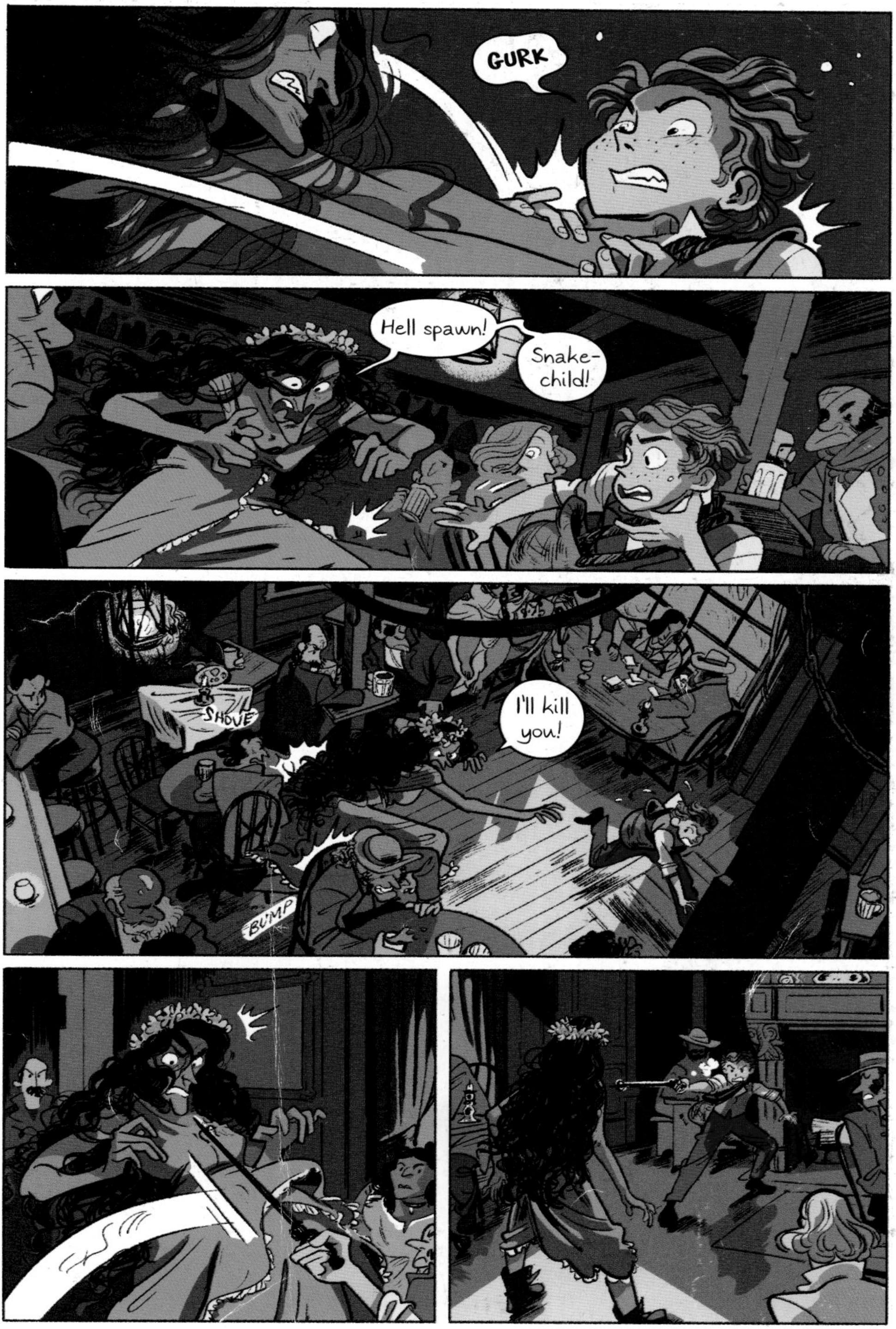
GURK
Hell spawn!
Snake-child!
SHOVE
I'll kill you!
BUMP

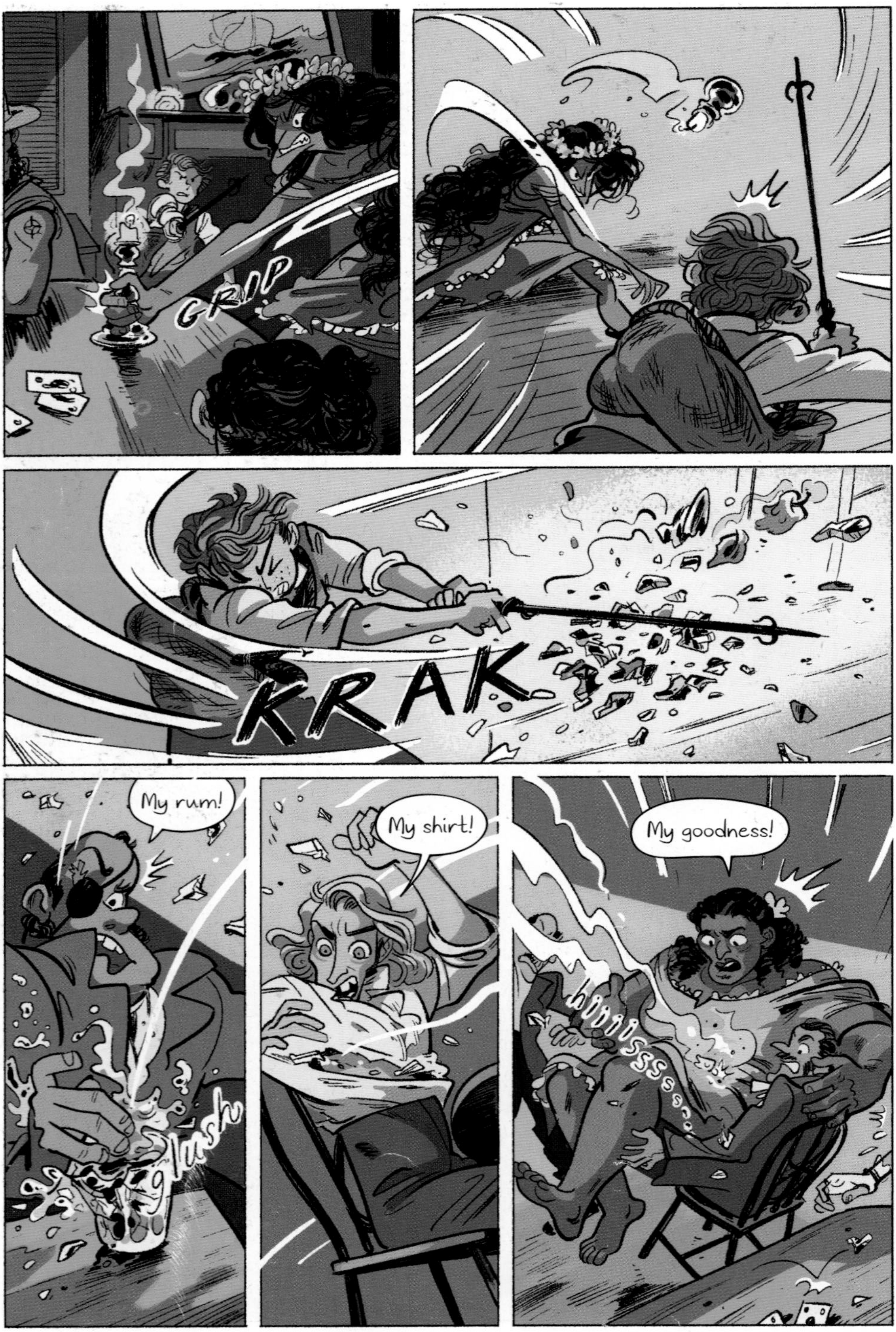
GRIP
KRAK
My rum!
glush
My shirt!
My goodness!
hiiiissssss

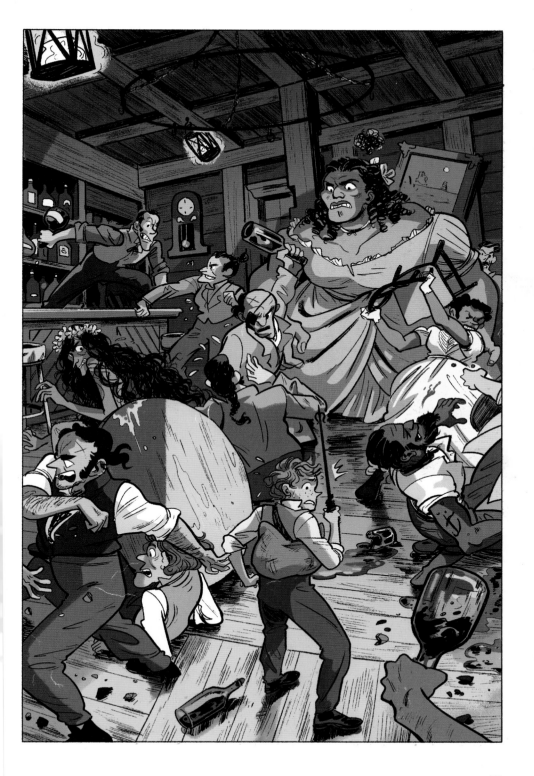

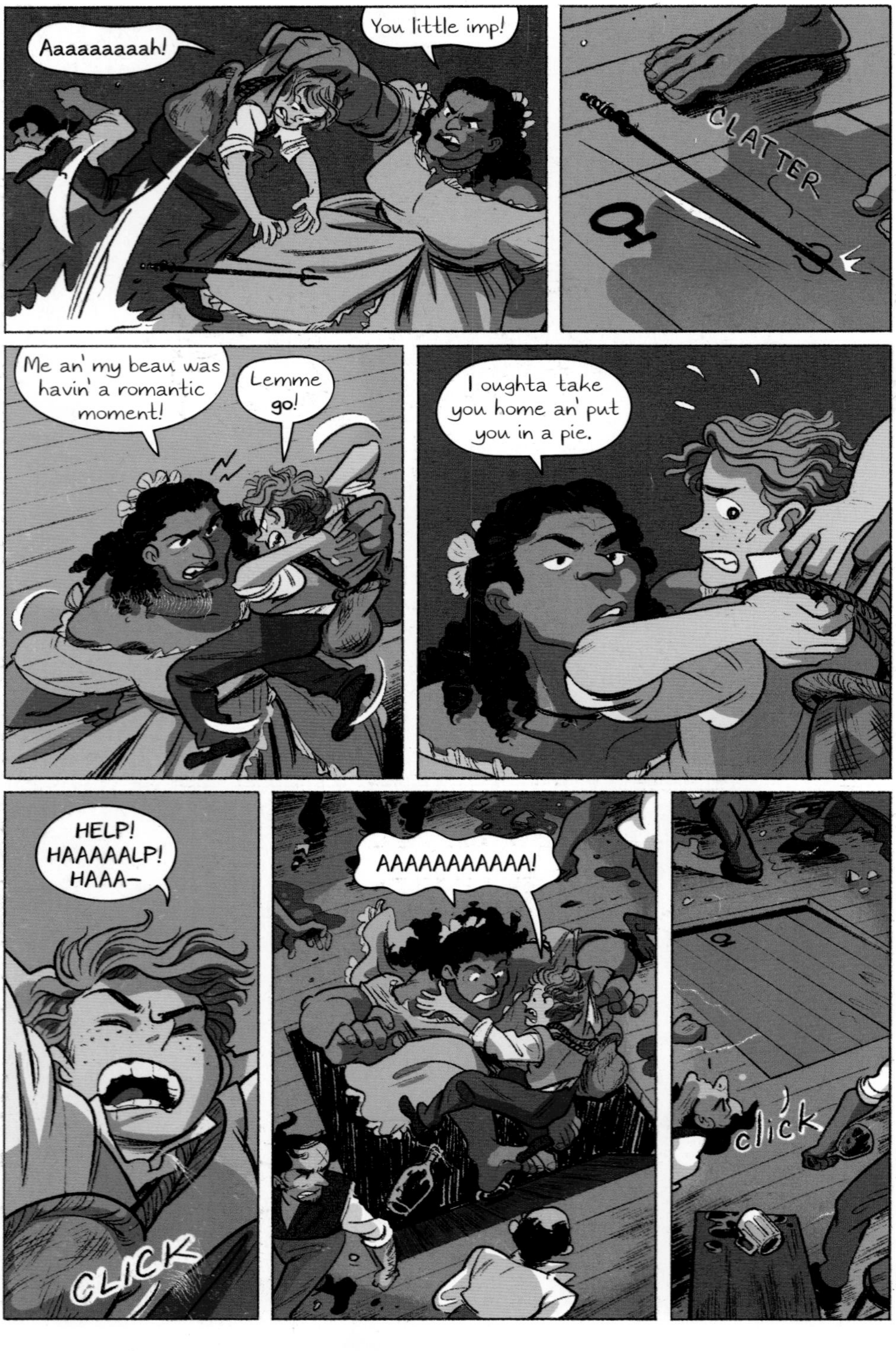

Aaaaaaaaah!
You little imp!
CLATTER
Me an' my beau was havin' a romantic moment!
Lemme go!
I oughta take you home an' put you in a pie.
HELP! HAAAAALP! HAAA—
CLICK
AAAAAAAAAAA!
click

CHAPTER FOUR
A MARKED MAN

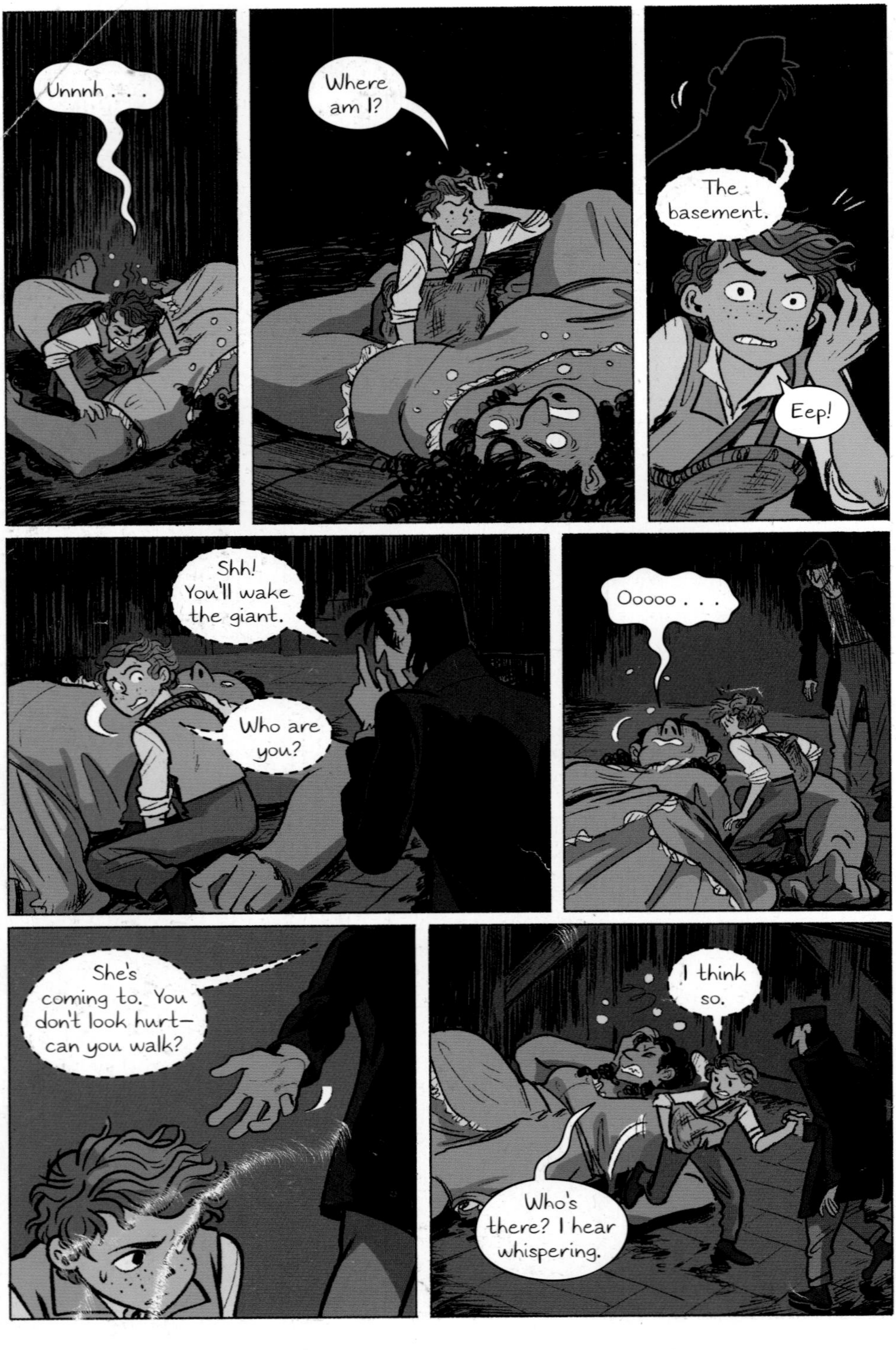

Unnnh . . .
Where am I?
The basement.
Eep!
Shh! You'll wake the giant.
Who are you?
Ooooo . . .
She's coming to. You don't look hurt— can you walk?
I think so.
Who's there? I hear whispering.

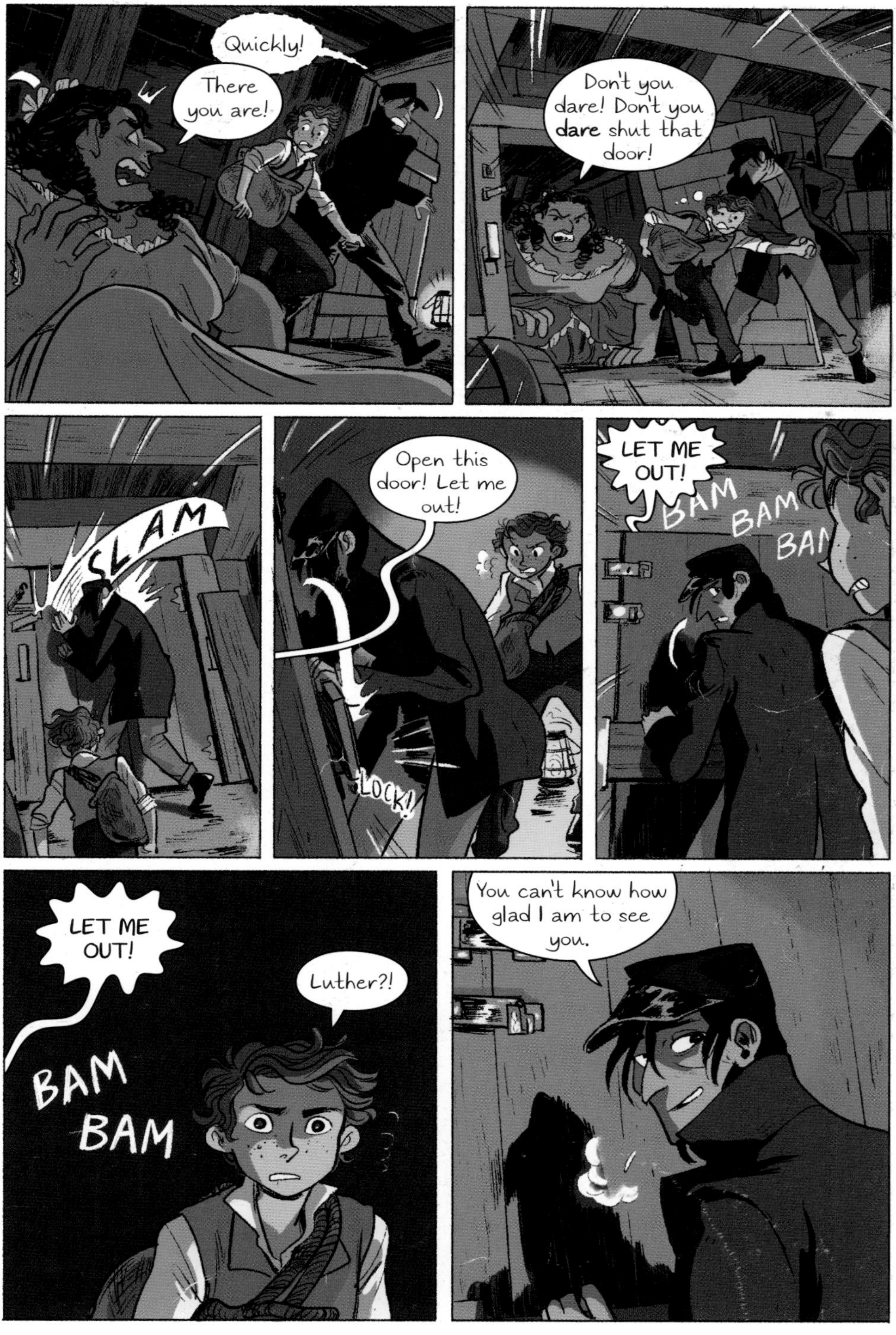
Quickly!
There you are!
Don't you dare! Don't you **dare** shut that door!
SLAM
Open this door! Let me out!
LOCK!
LET ME OUT!
BAM
BAM
BAM
LET ME OUT!
Luther?!
BAM
BAM
You can't know how glad I am to see you.

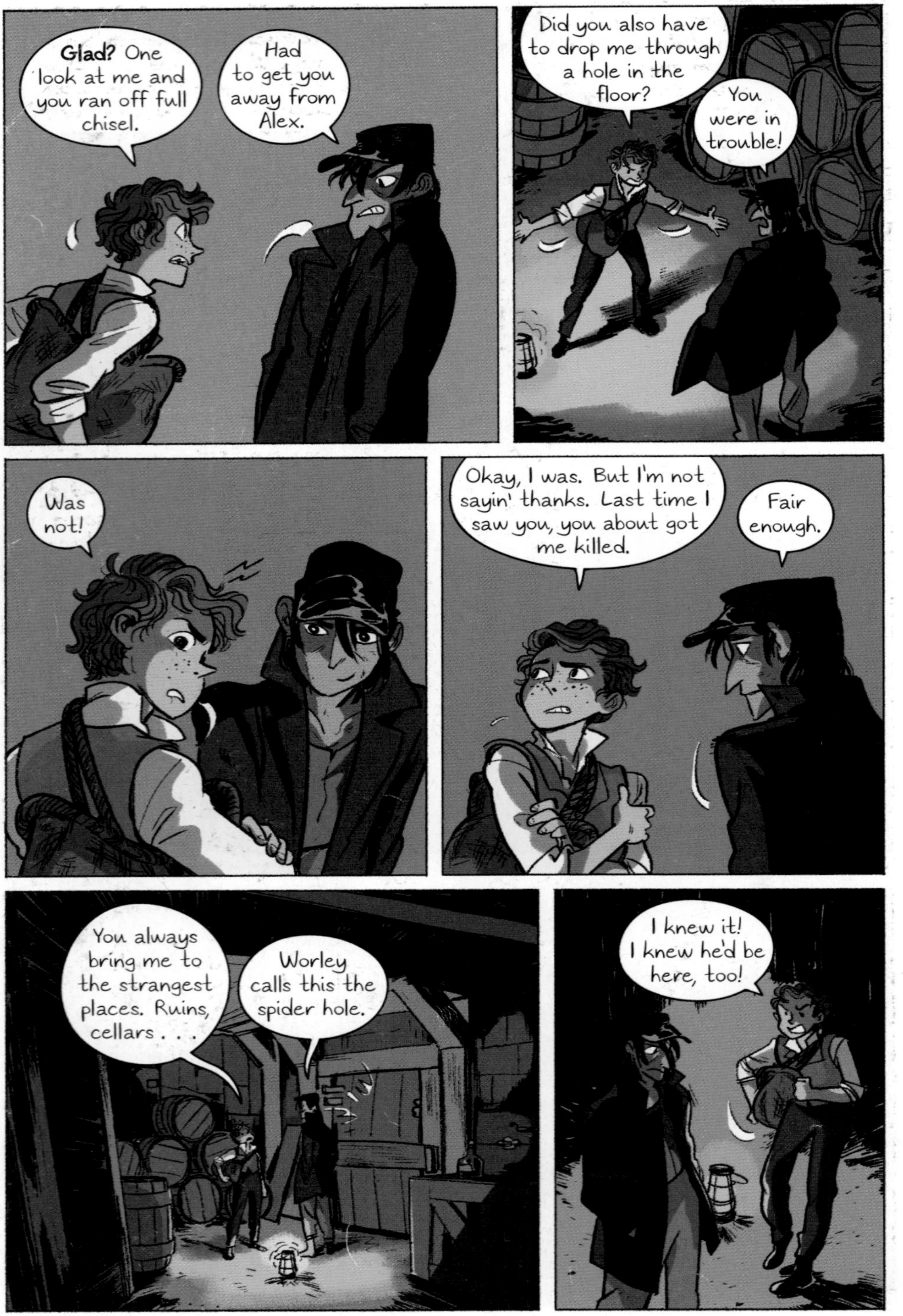
Glad? One look at me and you ran off full chisel.
Had to get you away from Alex.
Did you also have to drop me through a hole in the floor?
You were in trouble!
Was not!
Okay, I was. But I'm not sayin' thanks. Last time I saw you, you about got me killed.
Fair enough.
You always bring me to the strangest places. Ruins, cellars . . .
Worley calls this the spider hole.
I knew it! I knew he'd be here, too!

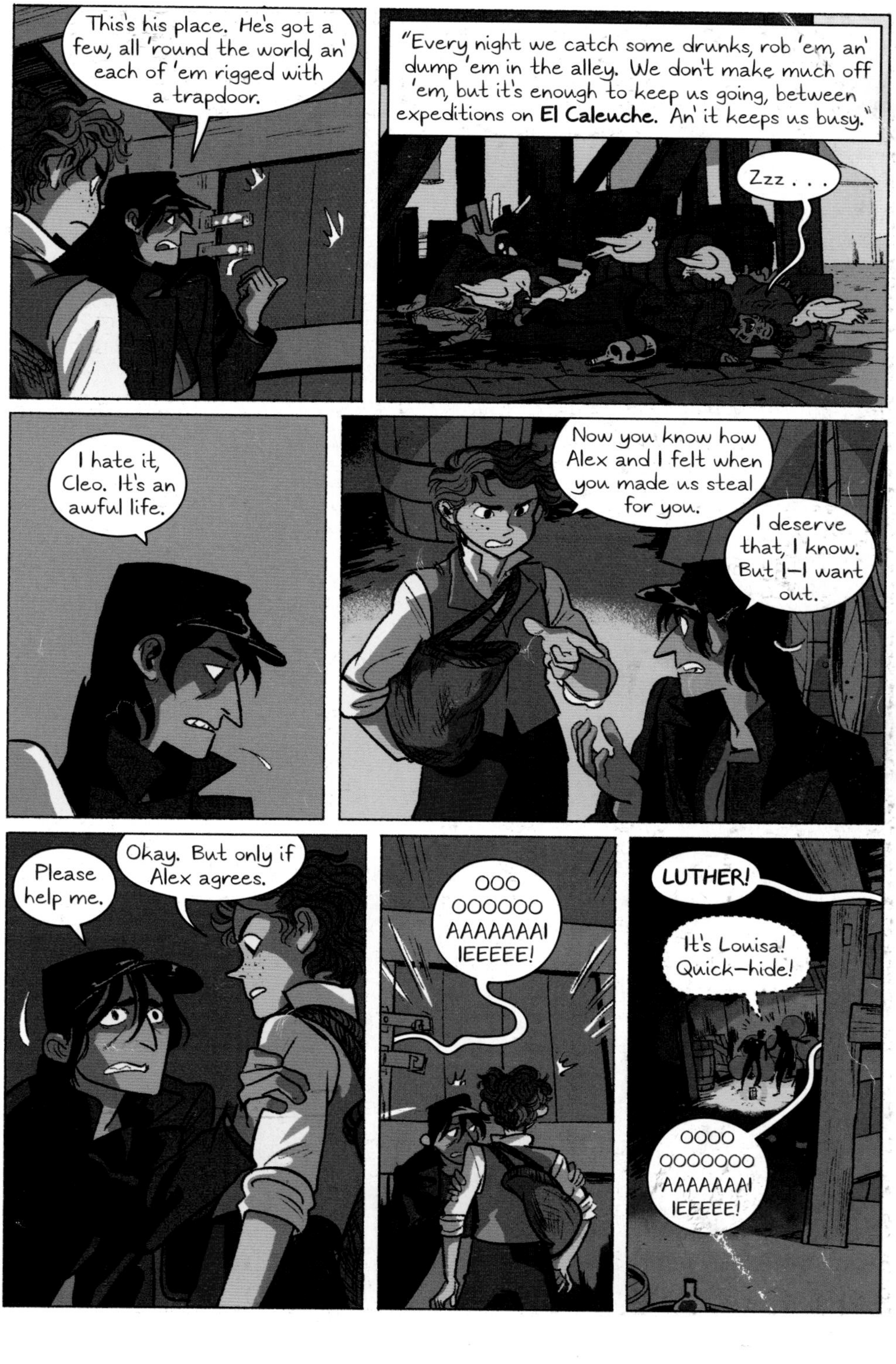
This's his place. He's got a few, all 'round the world, an' each of 'em rigged with a trapdoor.
"Every night we catch some drunks, rob 'em, an' dump 'em in the alley. We don't make much off 'em, but it's enough to keep us going, between expeditions on El Caleuche. An' it keeps us busy."
Zzz . . .
I hate it, Cleo. It's an awful life.
Now you know how Alex and I felt when you made us steal for you.
I deserve that, I know. But I—I want out.
Please help me.
Okay. But only if Alex agrees.
OOO OOOOOO AAAAAAAI IEEEEE!
LUTHER!
It's Louisa! Quick—hide!
OOOO OOOOOOO AAAAAAAI IEEEEE!

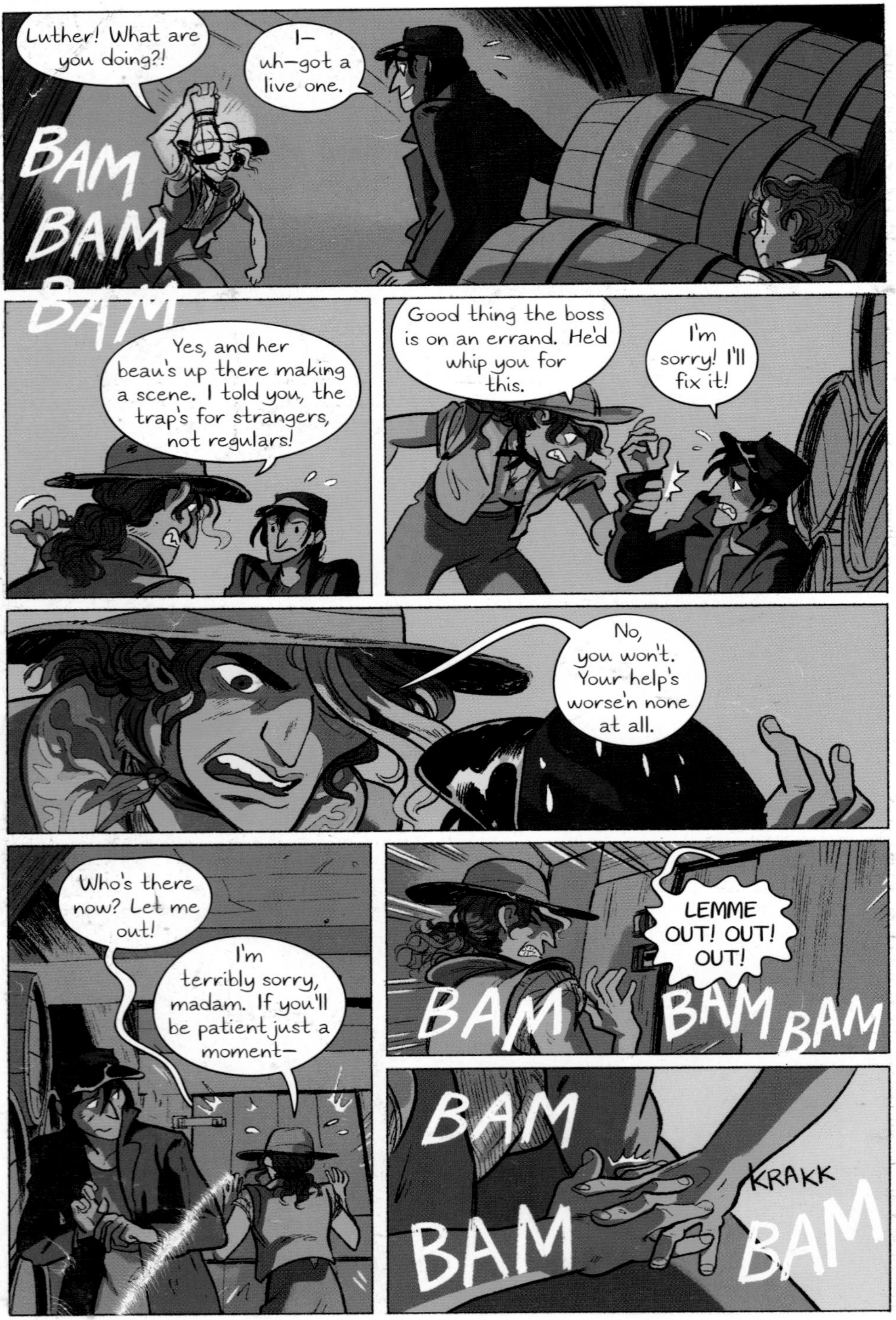
Luther! What are you doing?!
I— uh—got a live one.
BAM BAM BAM
Yes, and her beau's up there making a scene. I told you, the trap's for strangers, not regulars!
Good thing the boss is on an errand. He'd whip you for this.
I'm sorry! I'll fix it!
No, you won't. Your help's worse'n none at all.
Who's there now? Let me out!
I'm terribly sorry, madam. If you'll be patient just a moment—
LEMME OUT! OUT! OUT!
BAM BAM BAM
BAM BAM
KRAKK
BAM

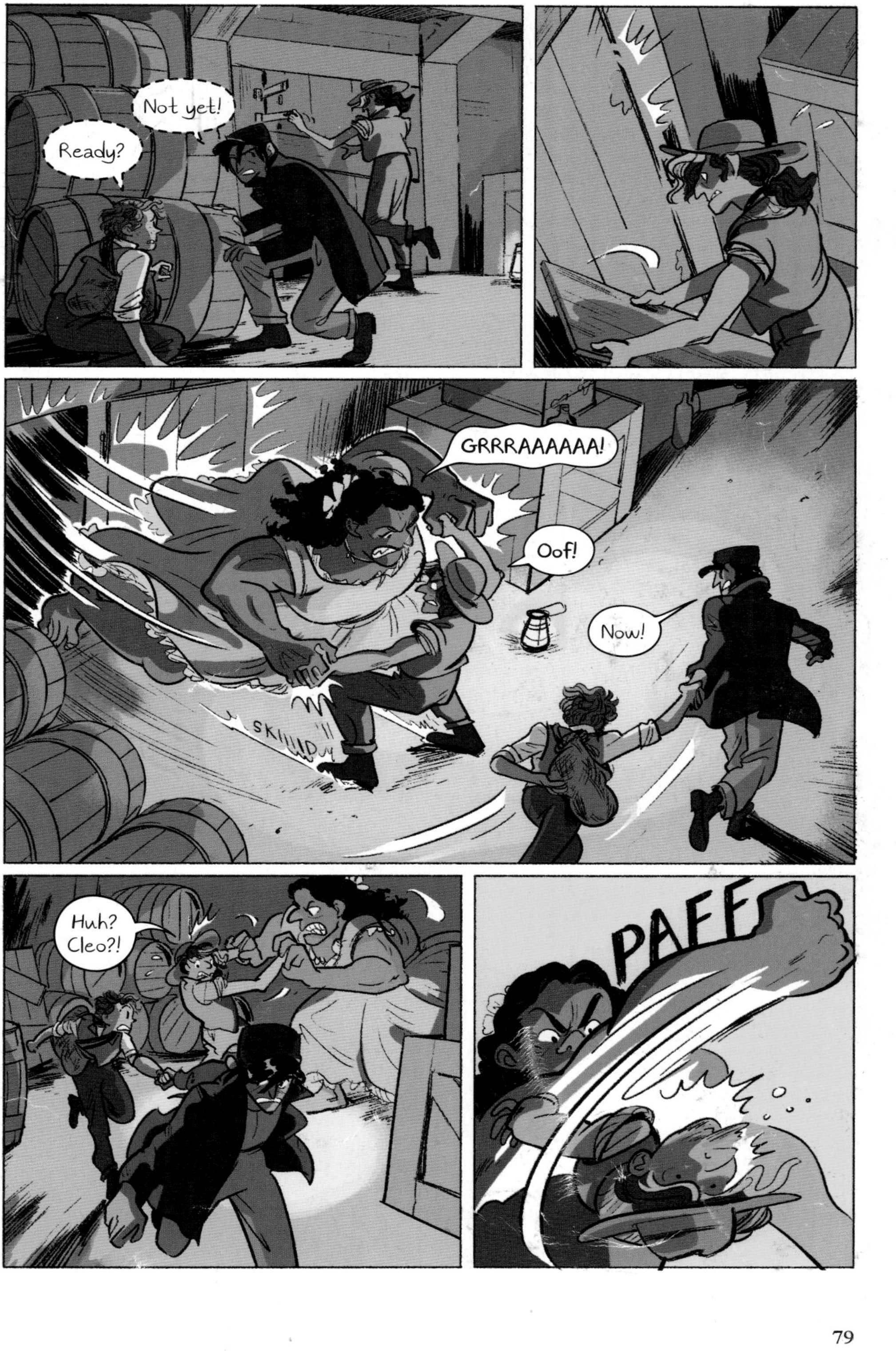
Ready?
Not yet!
GRRRAAAAAA!
Oof!
SKIIIID
Now!
Huh?
Cleo?!
PAFF

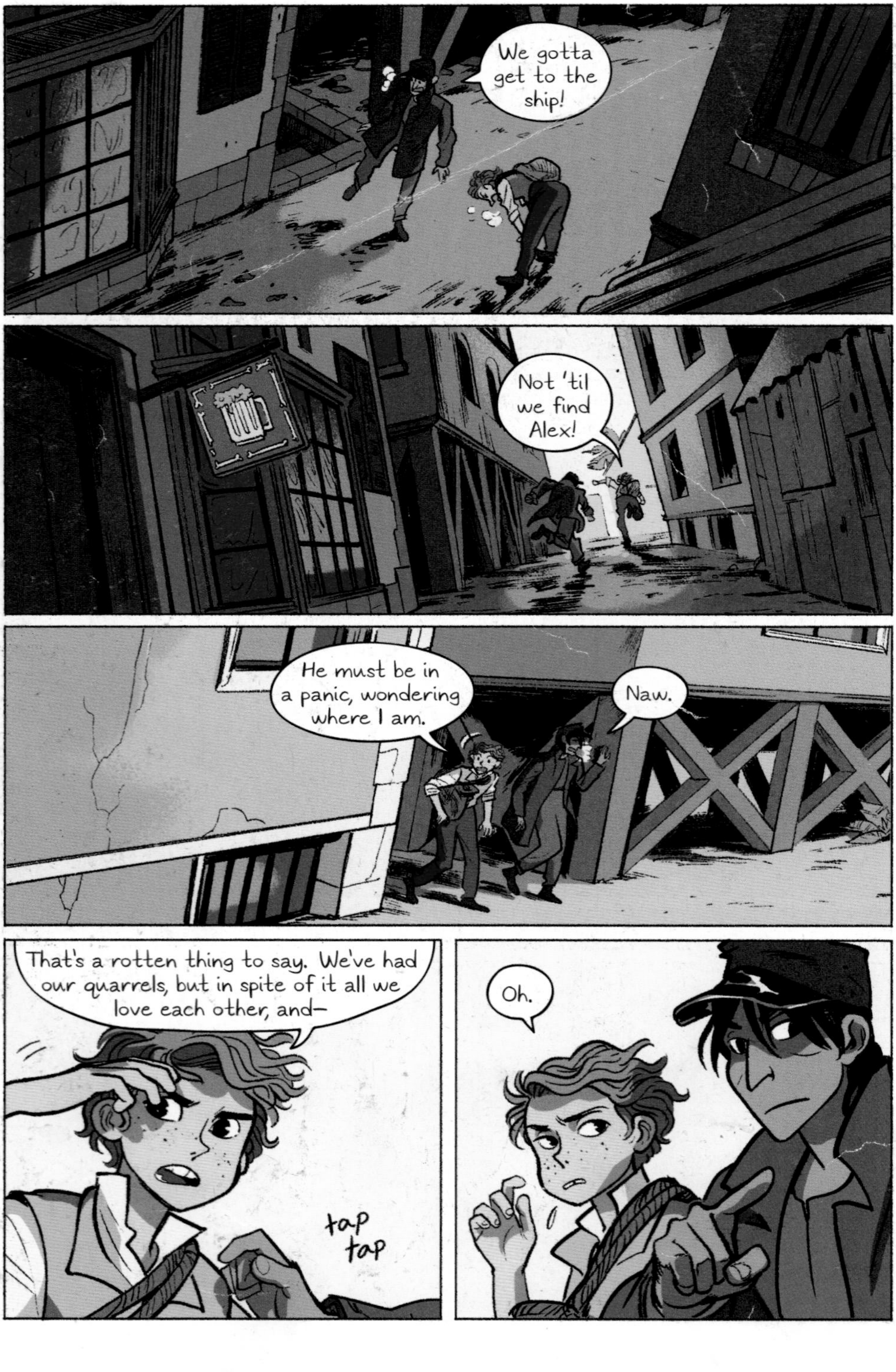
We gotta get to the ship!
Not 'til we find Alex!
He must be in a panic, wondering where I am.
Naw.
That's a rotten thing to say. We've had our quarrels, but in spite of it all we love each other, and—
tap tap
Oh.

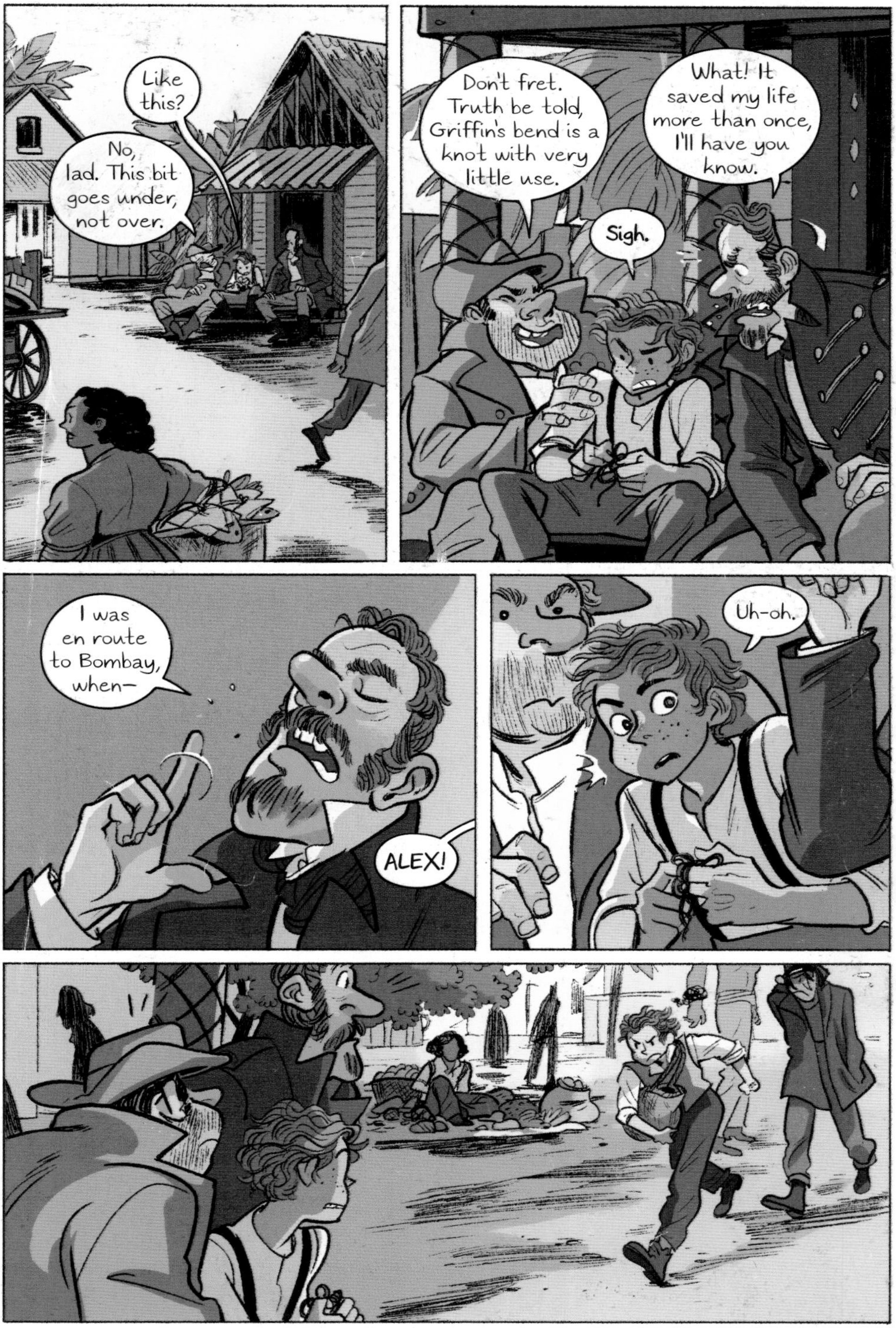
Like this?
No, lad. This bit goes under, not over.
Don't fret. Truth be told, Griffin's bend is a knot with very little use.
What! It saved my life more than once, I'll have you know.
Sigh.
I was en route to Bombay, when—
ALEX!
Uh-oh.

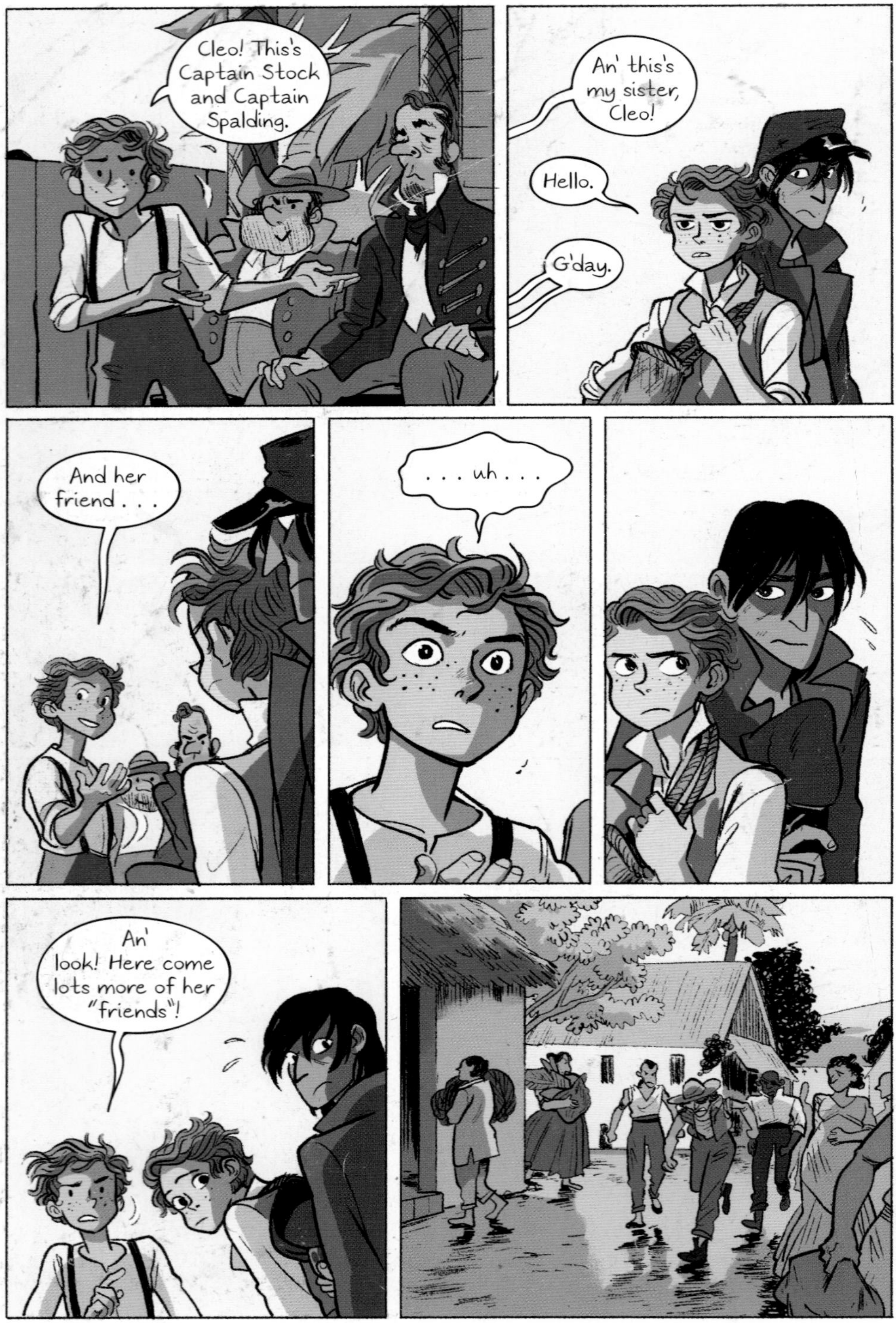
Cleo! This's Captain Stock and Captain Spalding.
An' this's my sister, Cleo!
Hello.
G'day.
And her friend . . .
. . . uh . . .
An' look! Here come lots more of her "friends"!

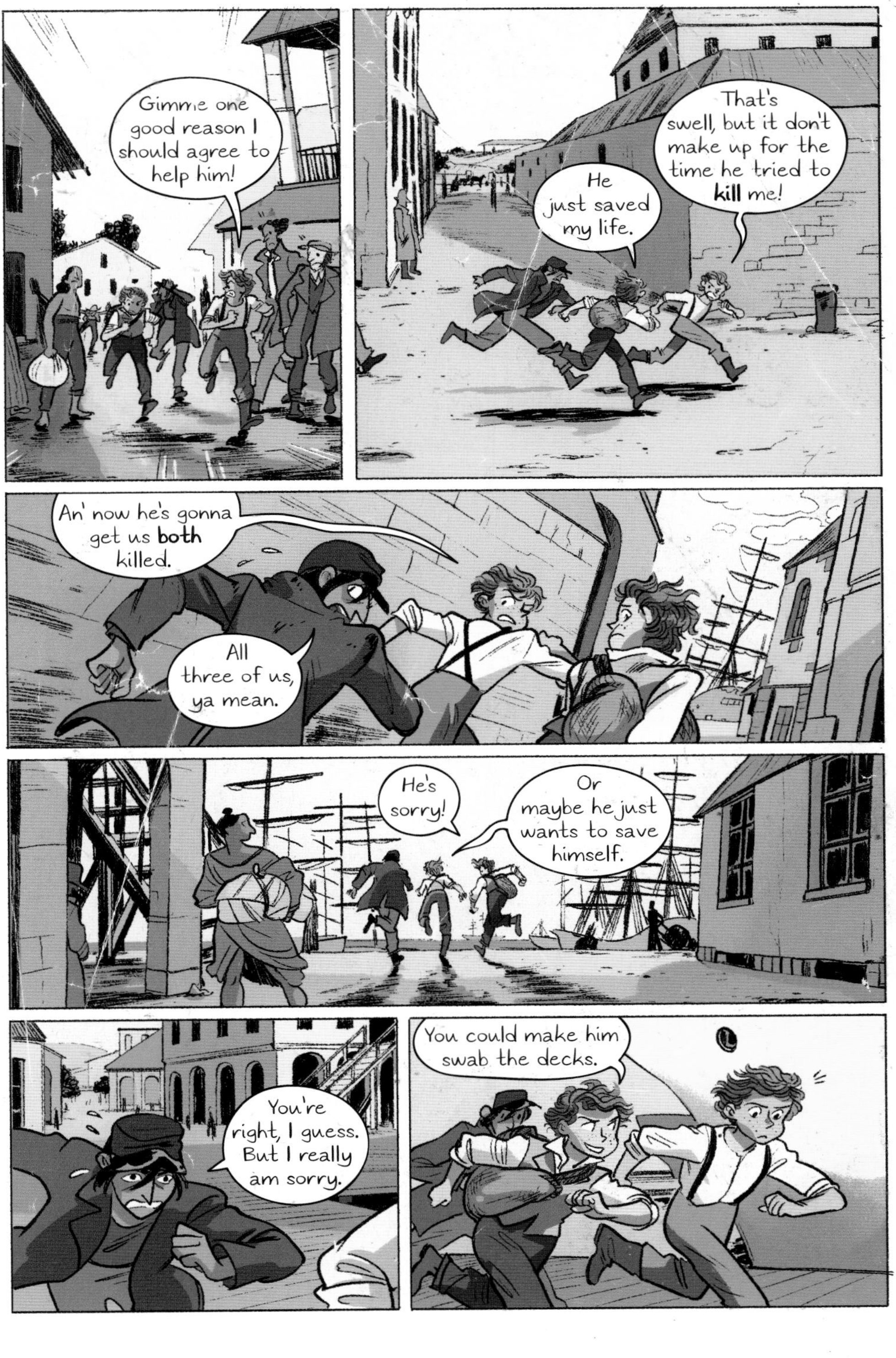
Gimme one good reason I should agree to help him!
He just saved my life.
That's swell, but it don't make up for the time he tried to **kill** me!
An' now he's gonna get us **both** killed.
All three of us, ya mean.
He's sorry!
Or maybe he just wants to save himself.
You're right, I guess. But I really am sorry.
You could make him swab the decks.

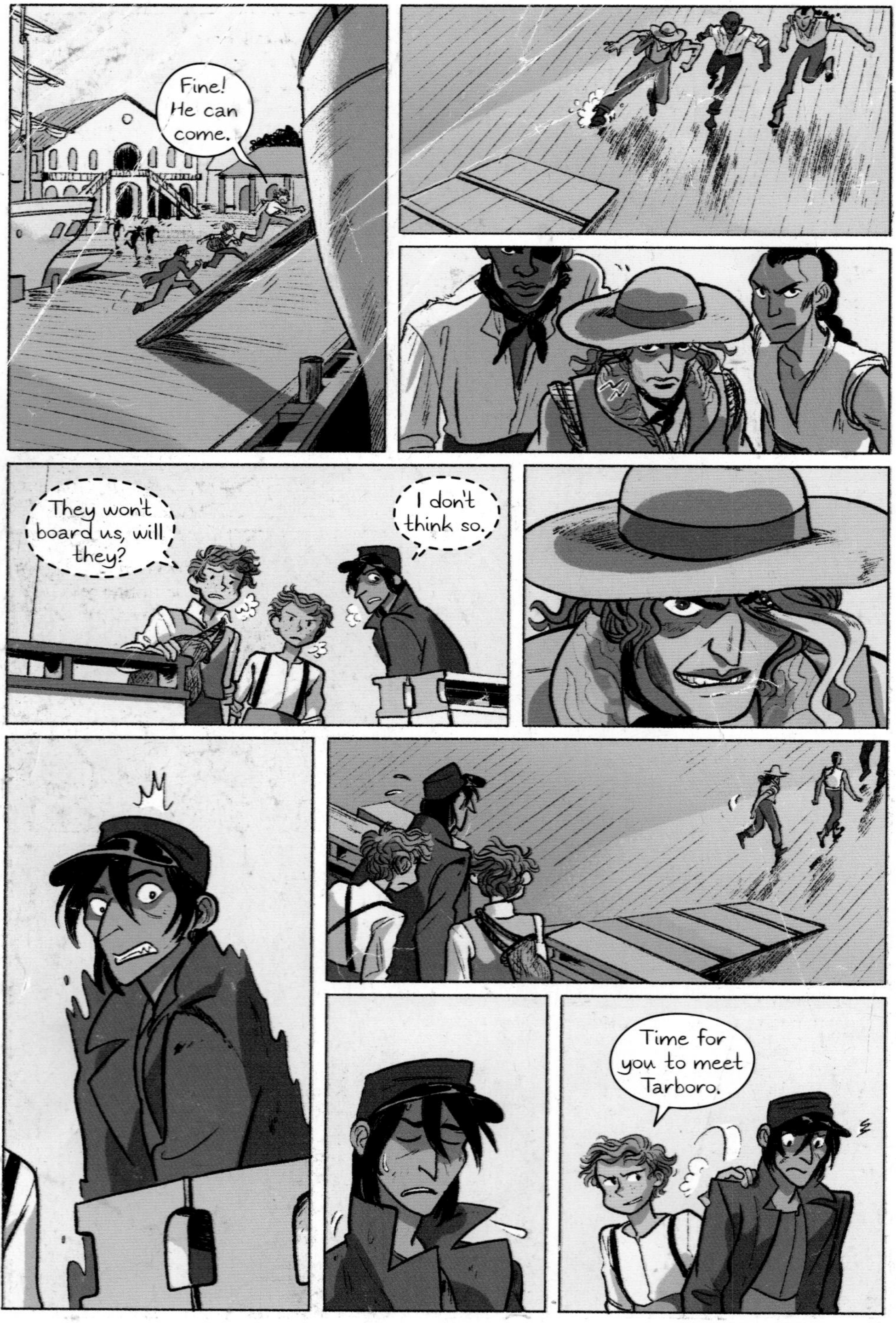
Fine! He can come.
They won't board us, will they?
I don't think so.
Time for you to meet Tarboro.

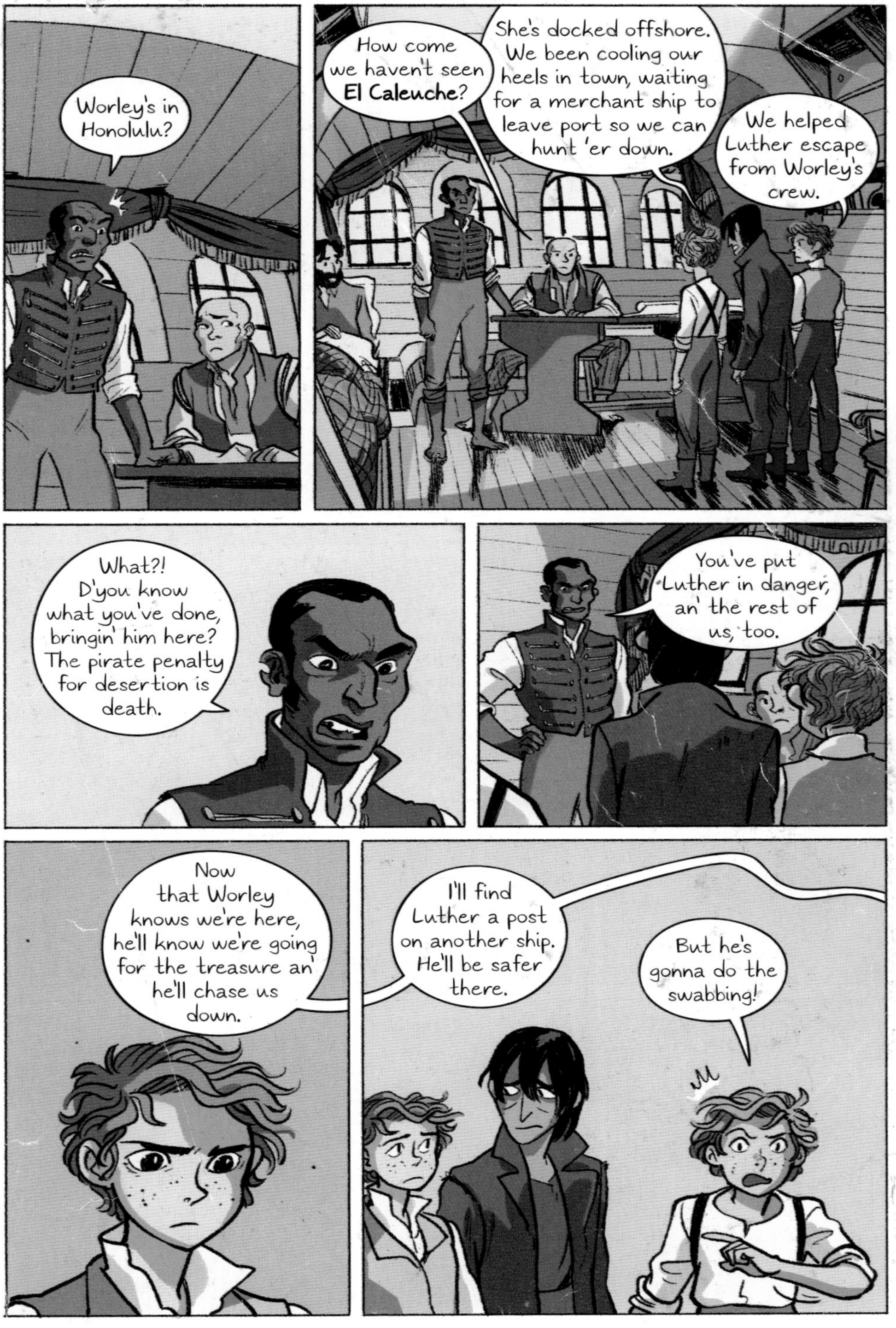
Worley's in Honolulu?
How come we haven't seen **El Caleuche**?
She's docked offshore. We been cooling our heels in town, waiting for a merchant ship to leave port so we can hunt 'er down.
We helped Luther escape from Worley's crew.
What?! D'you know what you've done, bringin' him here? The pirate penalty for desertion is death.
You've put Luther in danger, an' the rest of us, too.
Now that Worley knows we're here, he'll know we're going for the treasure an' he'll chase us down.
I'll find Luther a post on another ship. He'll be safer there.
But he's gonna do the swabbing!

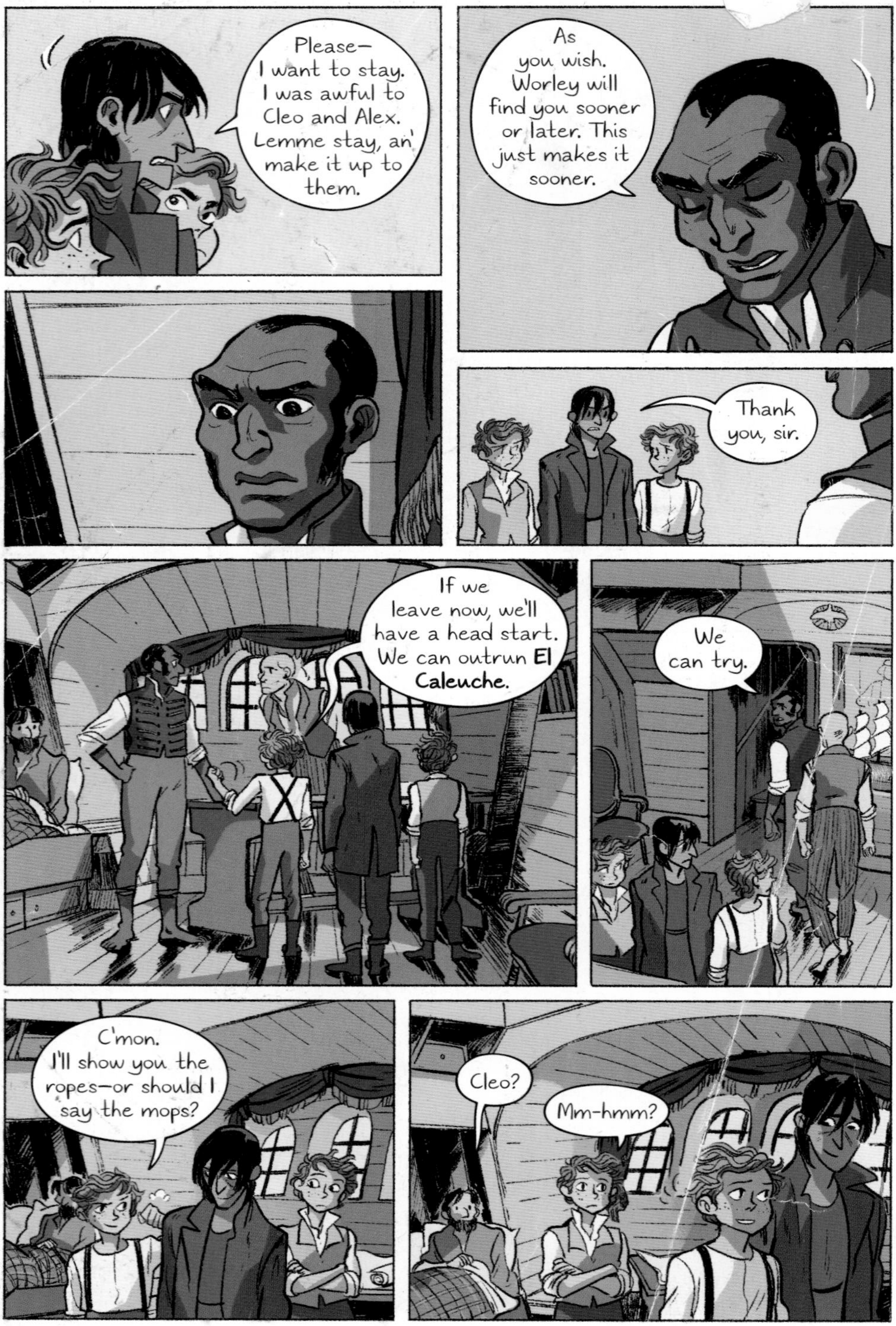
Please— I want to stay. I was awful to Cleo and Alex. Lemme stay, an' make it up to them.
As you wish. Worley will find you sooner or later. This just makes it sooner.
Thank you, sir.
If we leave now, we'll have a head start. We can outrun **El Caleuche.**
We can try.
C'mon. I'll show you the ropes—or should I say the mops?
Cleo?
Mm-hmm?

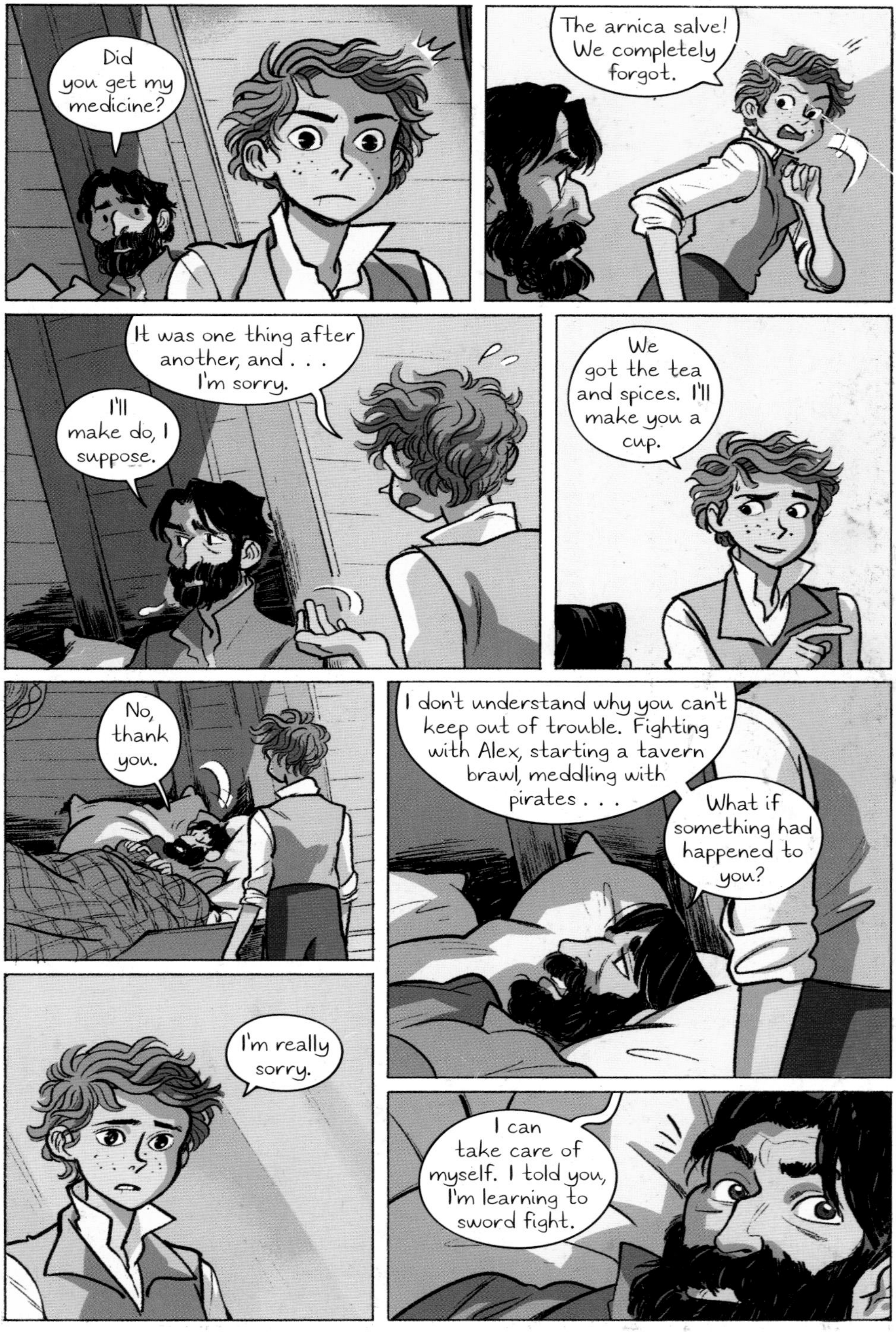
Did you get my medicine?
The arnica salve! We completely forgot.
It was one thing after another, and . . . I'm sorry.
I'll make do, I suppose.
We got the tea and spices. I'll make you a cup.
No, thank you.
I don't understand why you can't keep out of trouble. Fighting with Alex, starting a tavern brawl, meddling with pirates . . .
What if something had happened to you?
I'm really sorry.
I can take care of myself. I told you, I'm learning to sword fight.

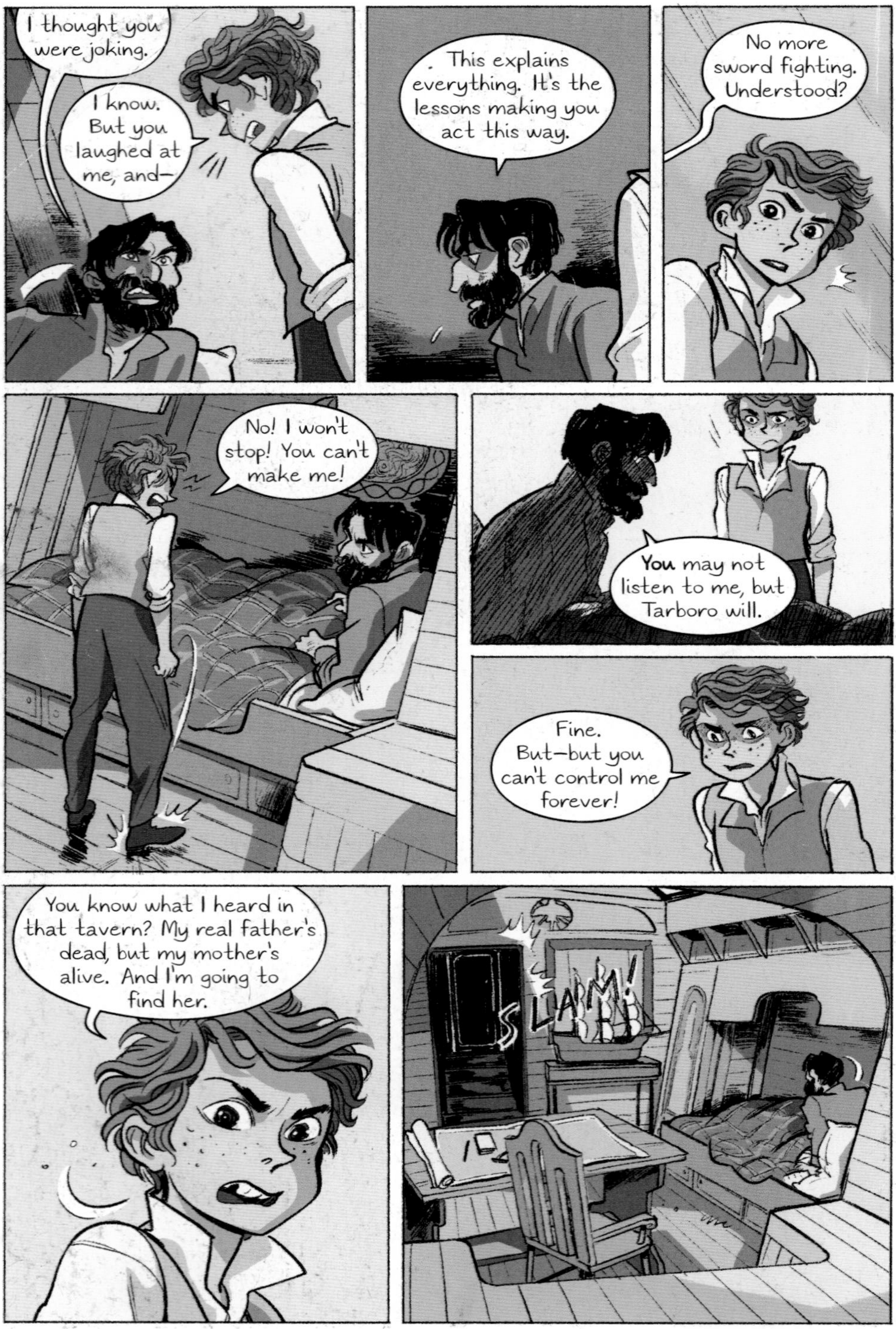
I thought you were joking.
I know. But you laughed at me, and—
This explains everything. It's the lessons making you act this way.
No more sword fighting. Understood?
No! I won't stop! You can't make me!
You may not listen to me, but Tarboro will.
Fine. But—but you can't control me forever!
You know what I heard in that tavern? My real father's dead, but my mother's alive. And I'm going to find her.
SLAM!

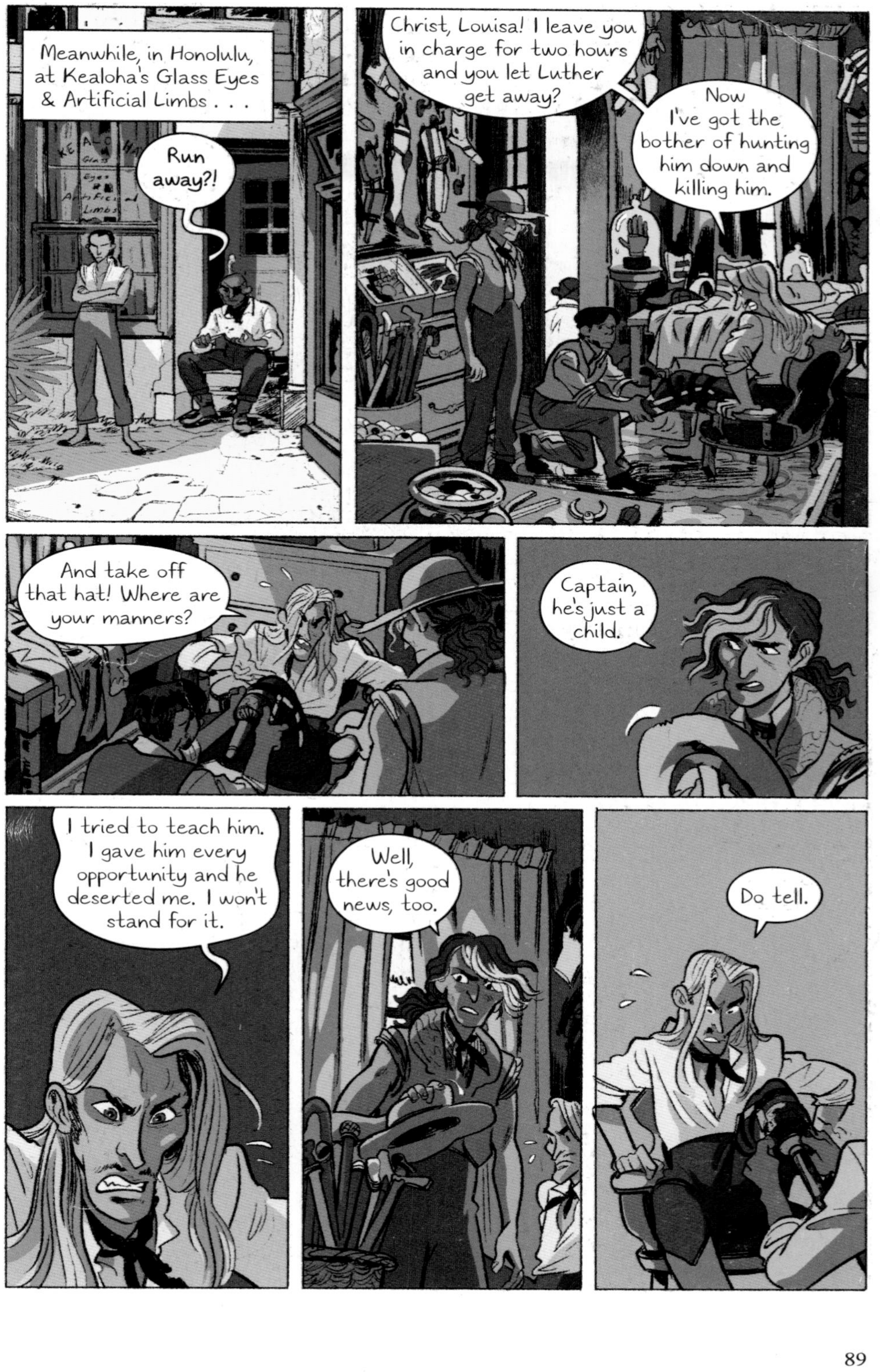
Meanwhile, in Honolulu, at Kealoha's Glass Eyes & Artificial Limbs . . .
Run away?!
Christ, Louisa! I leave you in charge for two hours and you let Luther get away?
Now I've got the bother of hunting him down and killing him.
And take off that hat! Where are your manners?
Captain, he's just a child.
I tried to teach him. I gave him every opportunity and he deserted me. I won't stand for it.
Well, there's good news, too.
Do tell.

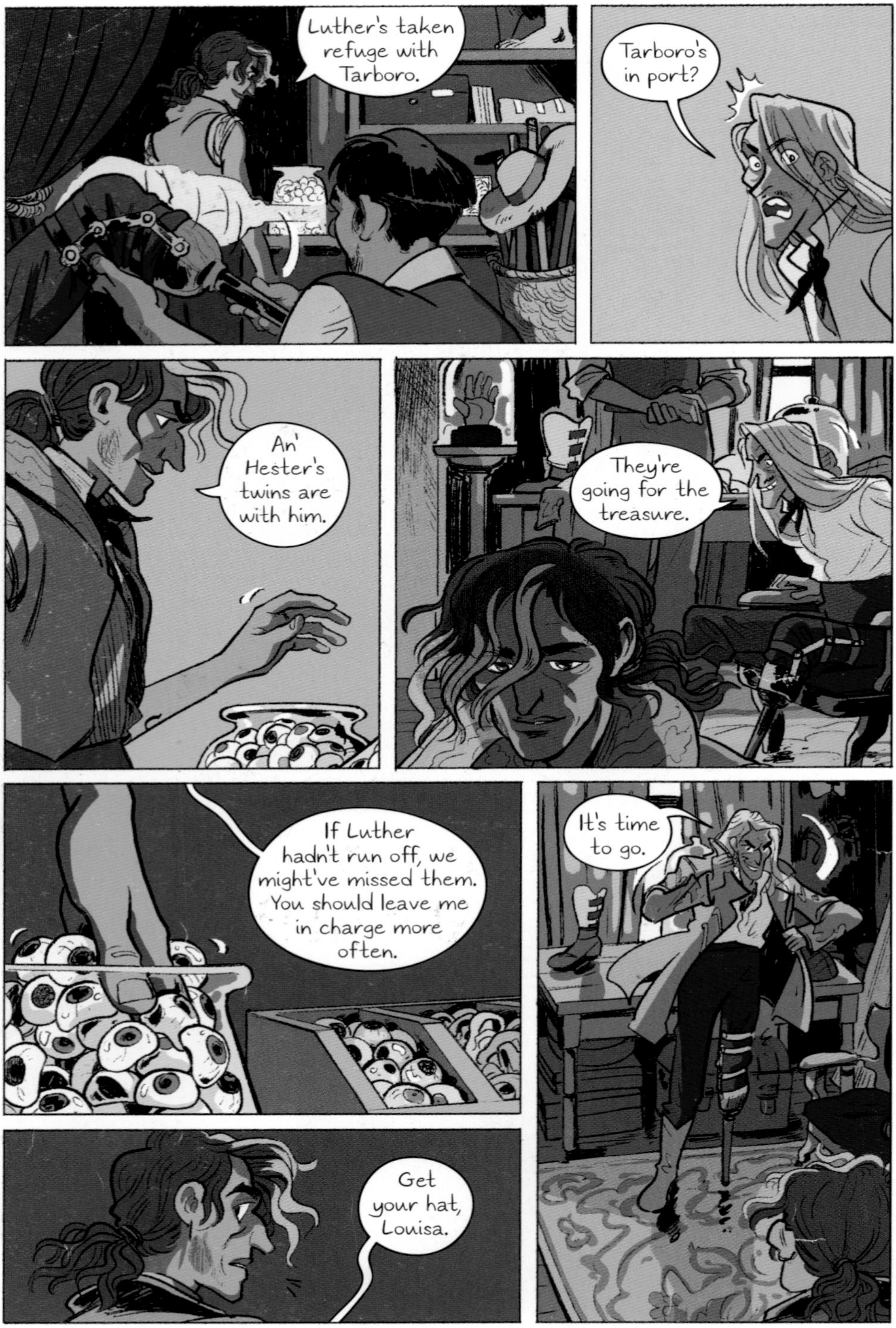
Luther's taken refuge with Tarboro.
Tarboro's in port?
An' Hester's twins are with him.
They're going for the treasure.
If Luther hadn't run off, we might've missed them. You should leave me in charge more often.
It's time to go.
Get your hat, Louisa.

CHAPTER FIVE
THE SHIP AND HER MASTER

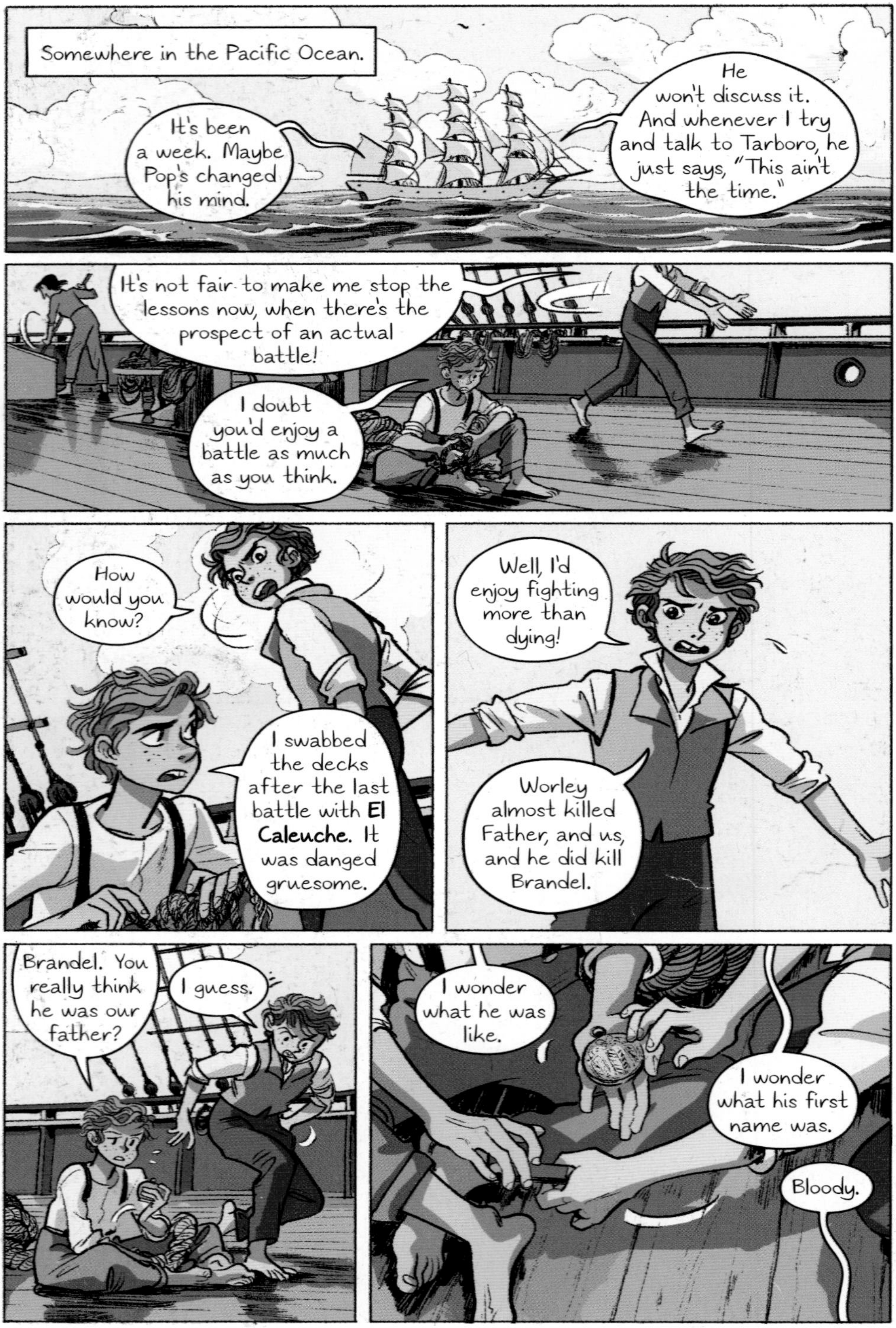
Somewhere in the Pacific Ocean.
It's been a week. Maybe Pop's changed his mind.
He won't discuss it. And whenever I try and talk to Tarboro, he just says, "This ain't the time."
It's not fair to make me stop the lessons now, when there's the prospect of an actual battle!
I doubt you'd enjoy a battle as much as you think.
How would you know?
I swabbed the decks after the last battle with **El Caleuche**. It was danged gruesome.
Well, I'd enjoy fighting more than dying!
Worley almost killed Father, and us, and he did kill Brandel.
Brandel. You really think he was our father?
I guess.
I wonder what he was like.
I wonder what his first name was.
Bloody.

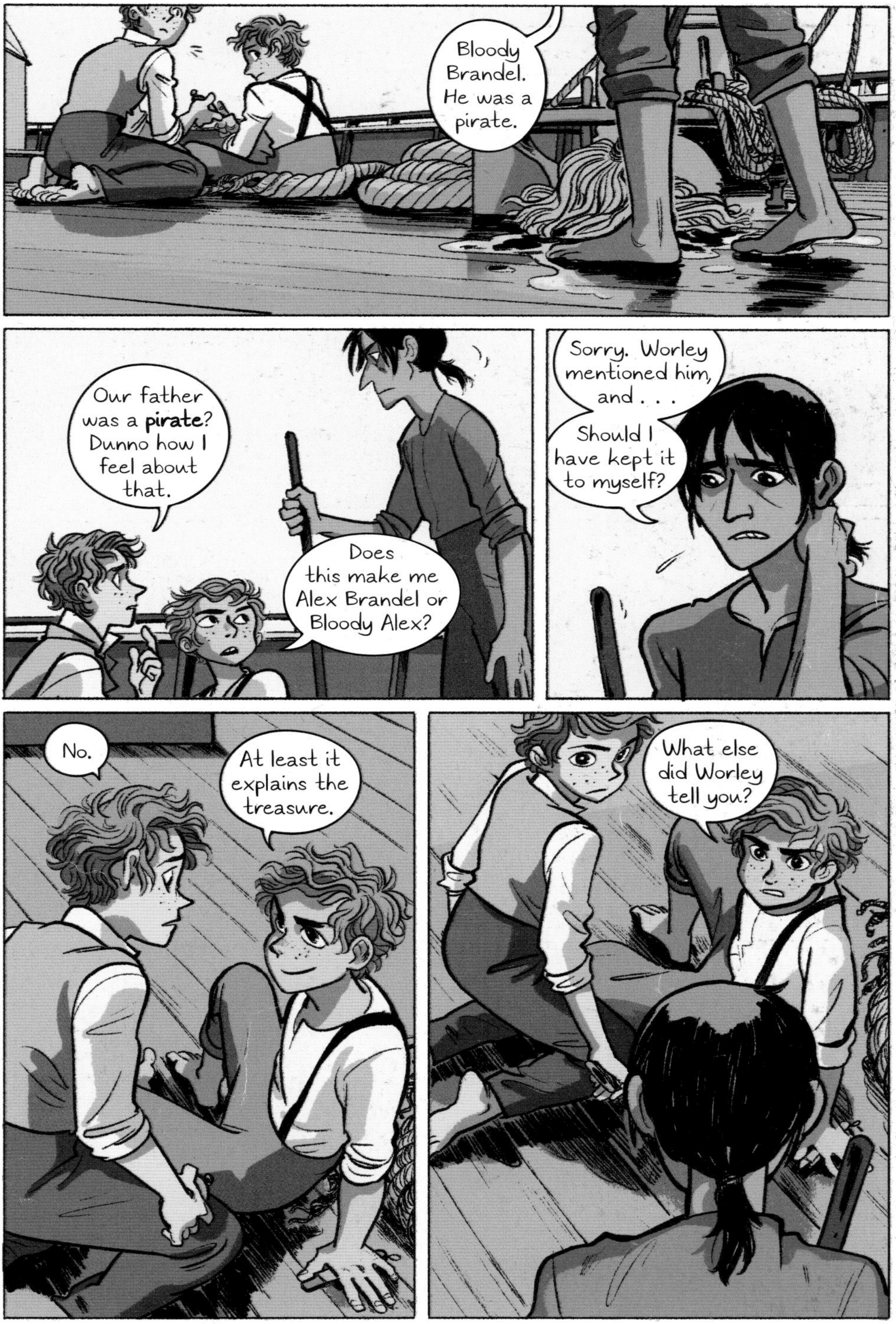
Bloody Brandel. He was a pirate.
Our father was a **pirate**? Dunno how I feel about that.
Does this make me Alex Brandel or Bloody Alex?
Sorry. Worley mentioned him, and . . .
Should I have kept it to myself?
No.
At least it explains the treasure.
What else did Worley tell you?

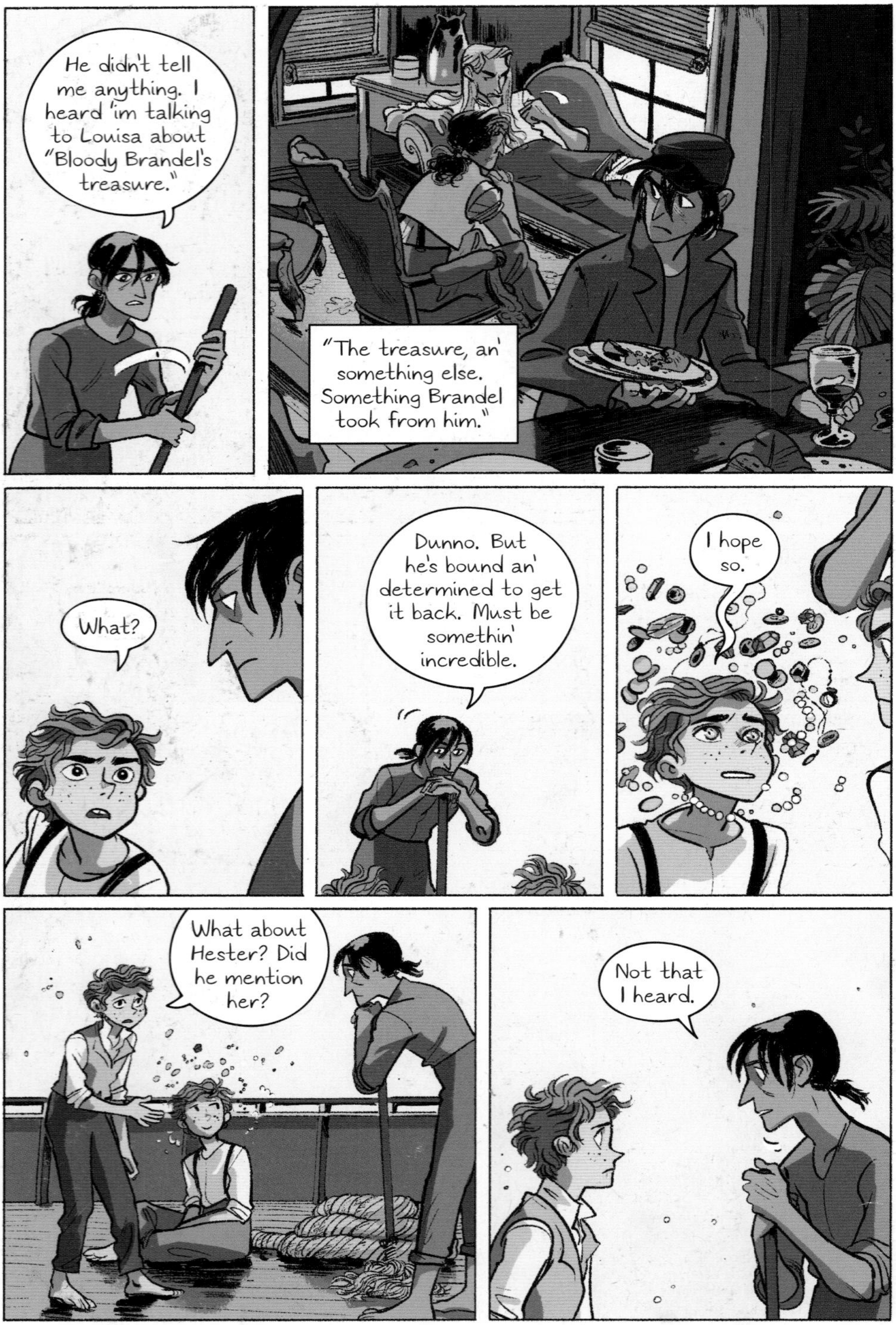
He didn't tell me anything. I heard 'im talking to Louisa about "Bloody Brandel's treasure."
"The treasure, an' something else. Something Brandel took from him."
What?
Dunno. But he's bound an' determined to get it back. Must be somethin' incredible.
I hope so.
What about Hester? Did he mention her?
Not that I heard.

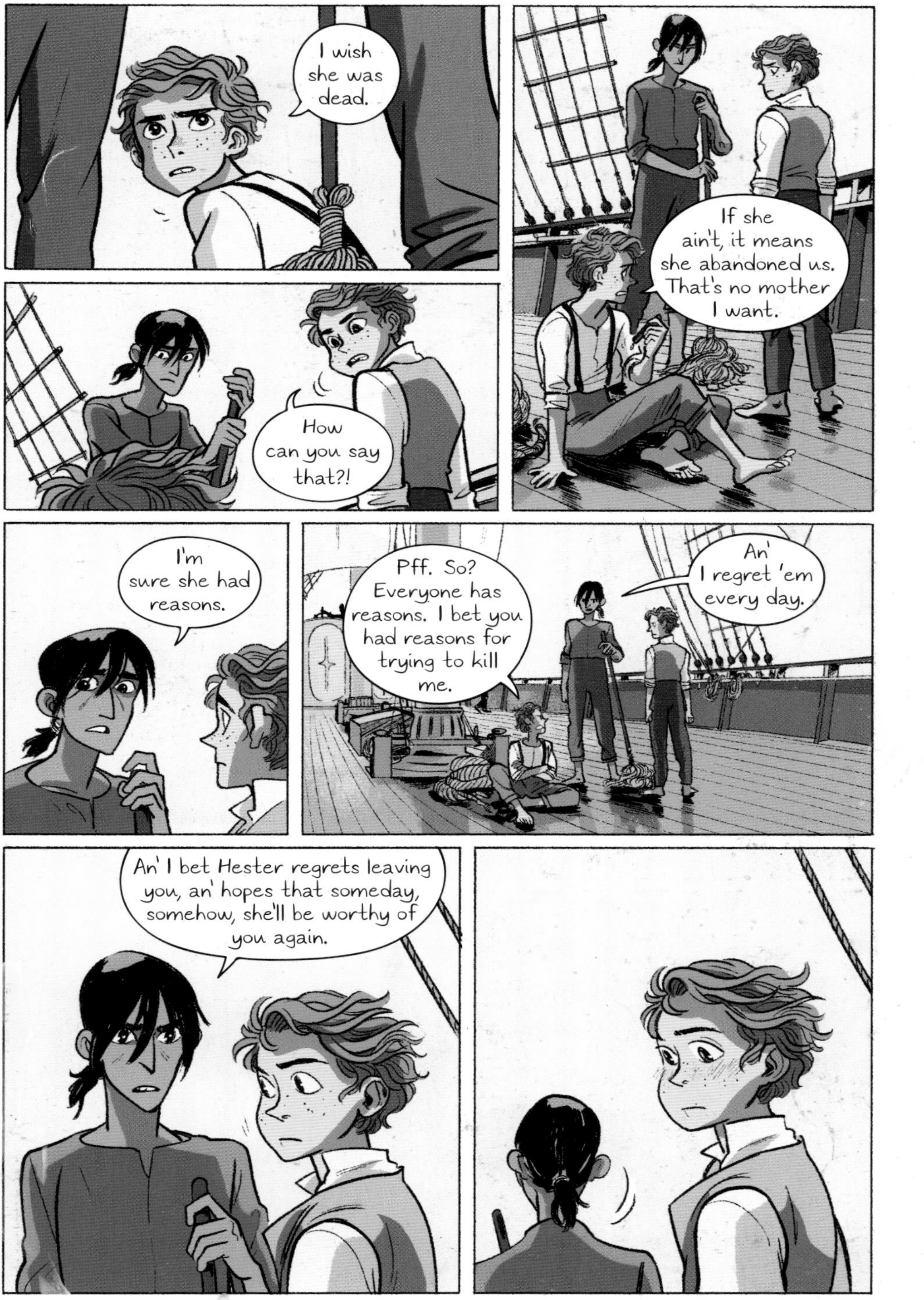
I wish she was dead.
If she ain't, it means she abandoned us. That's no mother I want.
How can you say that?!
I'm sure she had reasons.
Pff. So? Everyone has reasons. I bet you had reasons for trying to kill me.
An' I regret 'em every day.
An' I bet Hester regrets leaving you, an' hopes that someday, somehow, she'll be worthy of you again.

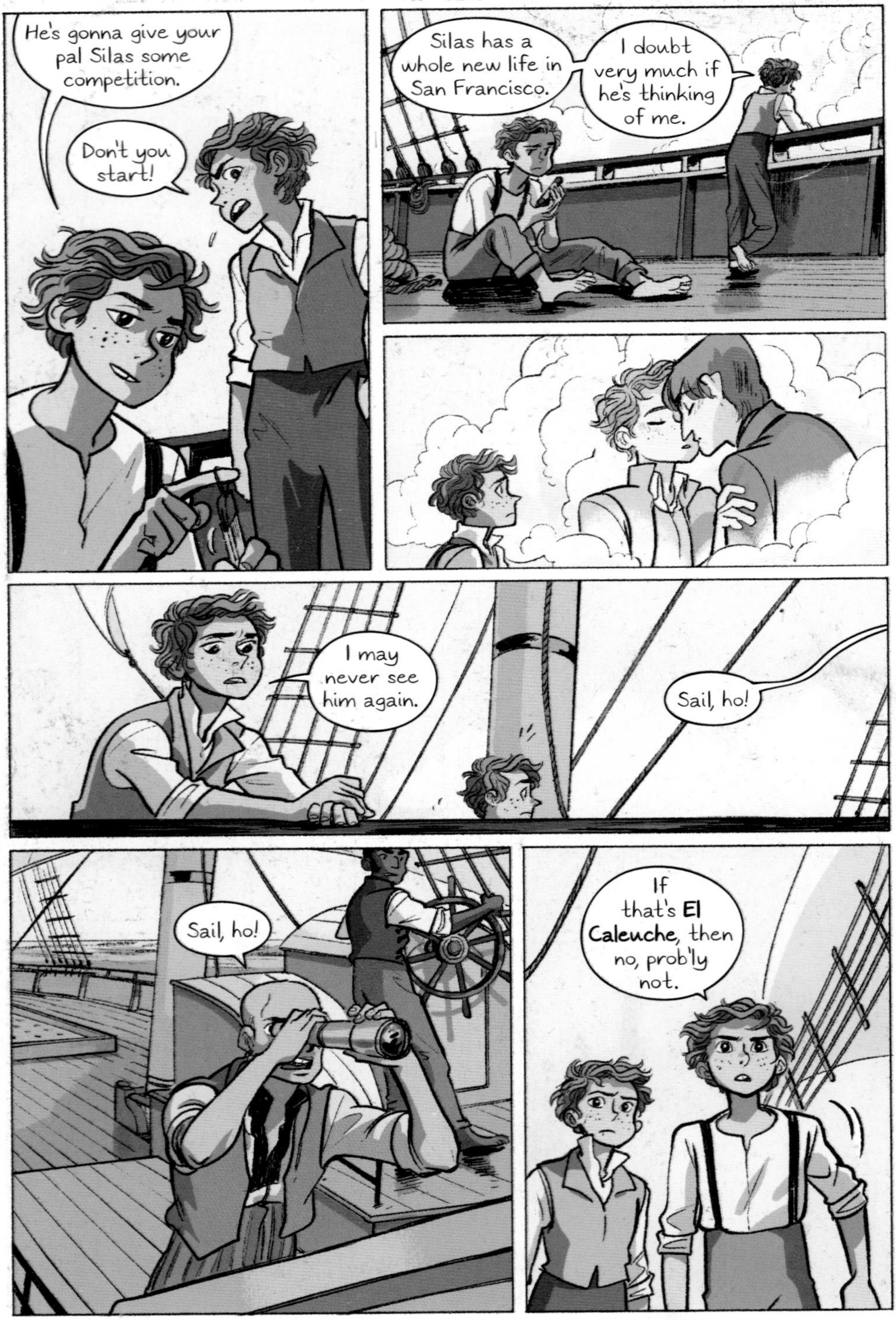
He's gonna give your pal Silas some competition.
Don't you start!
Silas has a whole new life in San Francisco.
I doubt very much if he's thinking of me.
I may never see him again.
Sail, ho!
Sail, ho!
If that's **El Caleuche**, then no, prob'ly not.

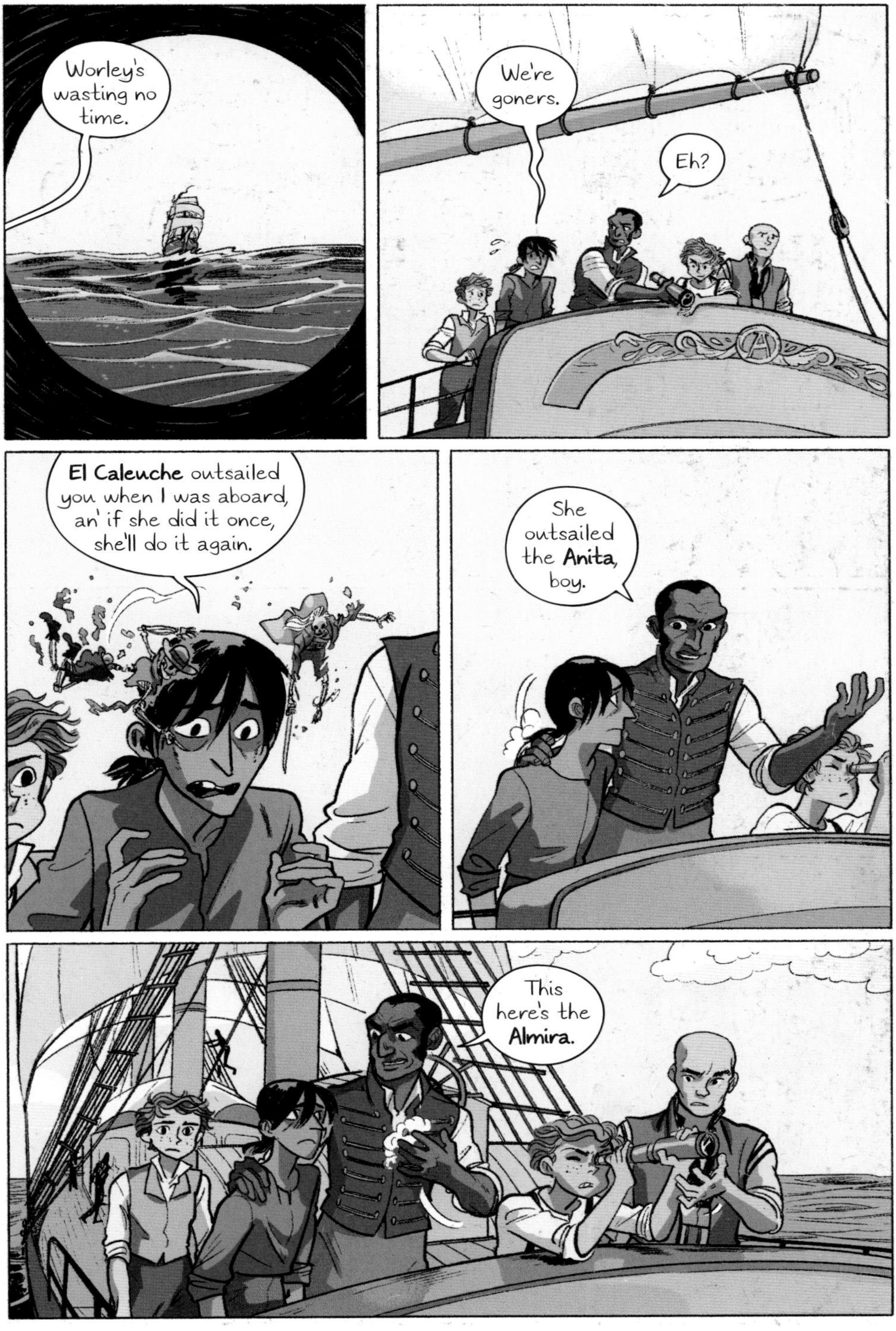
Worley's wasting no time.
We're goners.
Eh?
El Caleuche outsailed you when I was aboard, an' if she did it once, she'll do it again.
She outsailed the Anita, boy.
This here's the Almira.

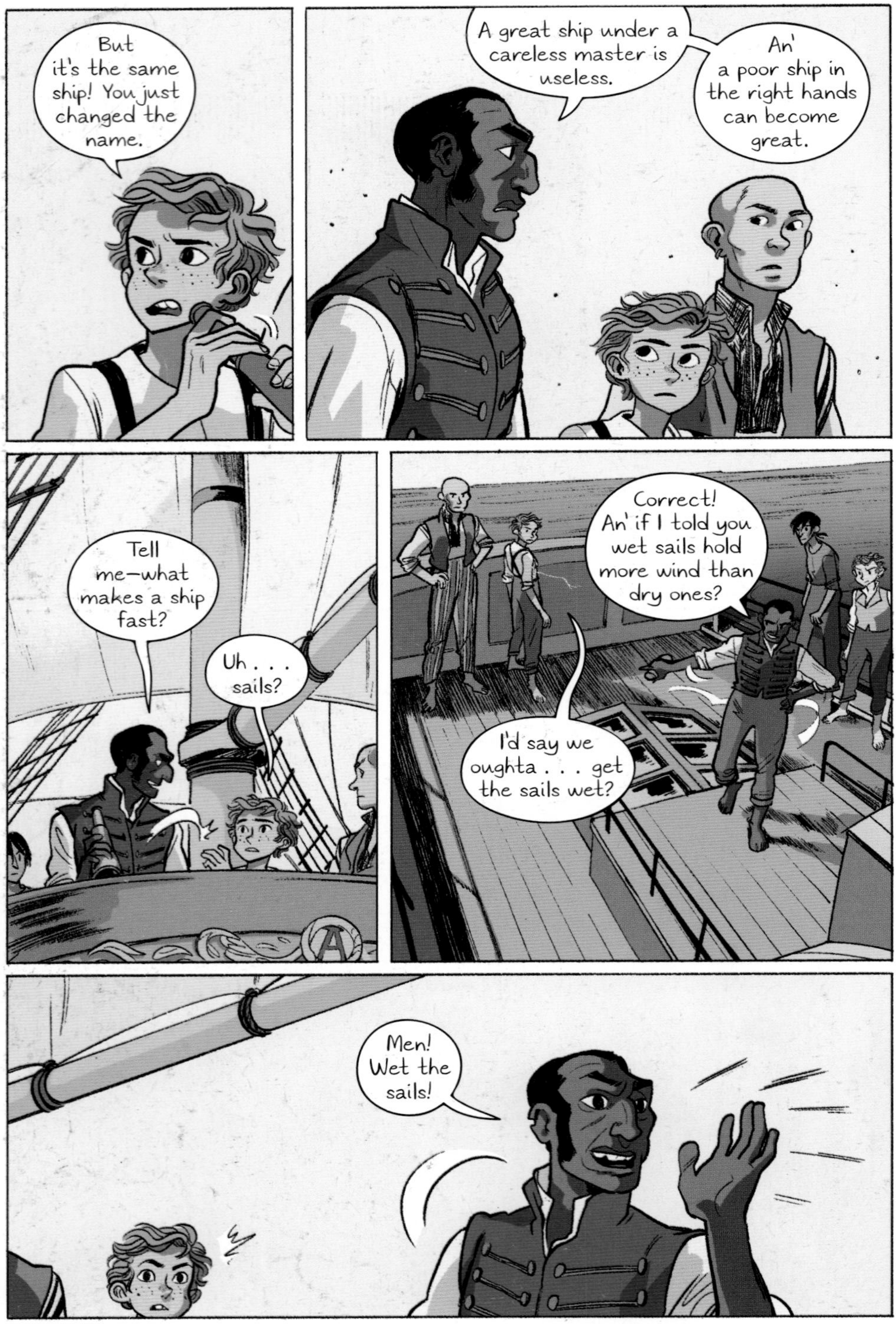
But it's the same ship! You just changed the name.
A great ship under a careless master is useless.
An' a poor ship in the right hands can become great.
Tell me—what makes a ship fast?
Uh . . . sails?
Correct! An' if I told you wet sails hold more wind than dry ones?
I'd say we oughta . . . get the sails wet?
Men! Wet the sails!

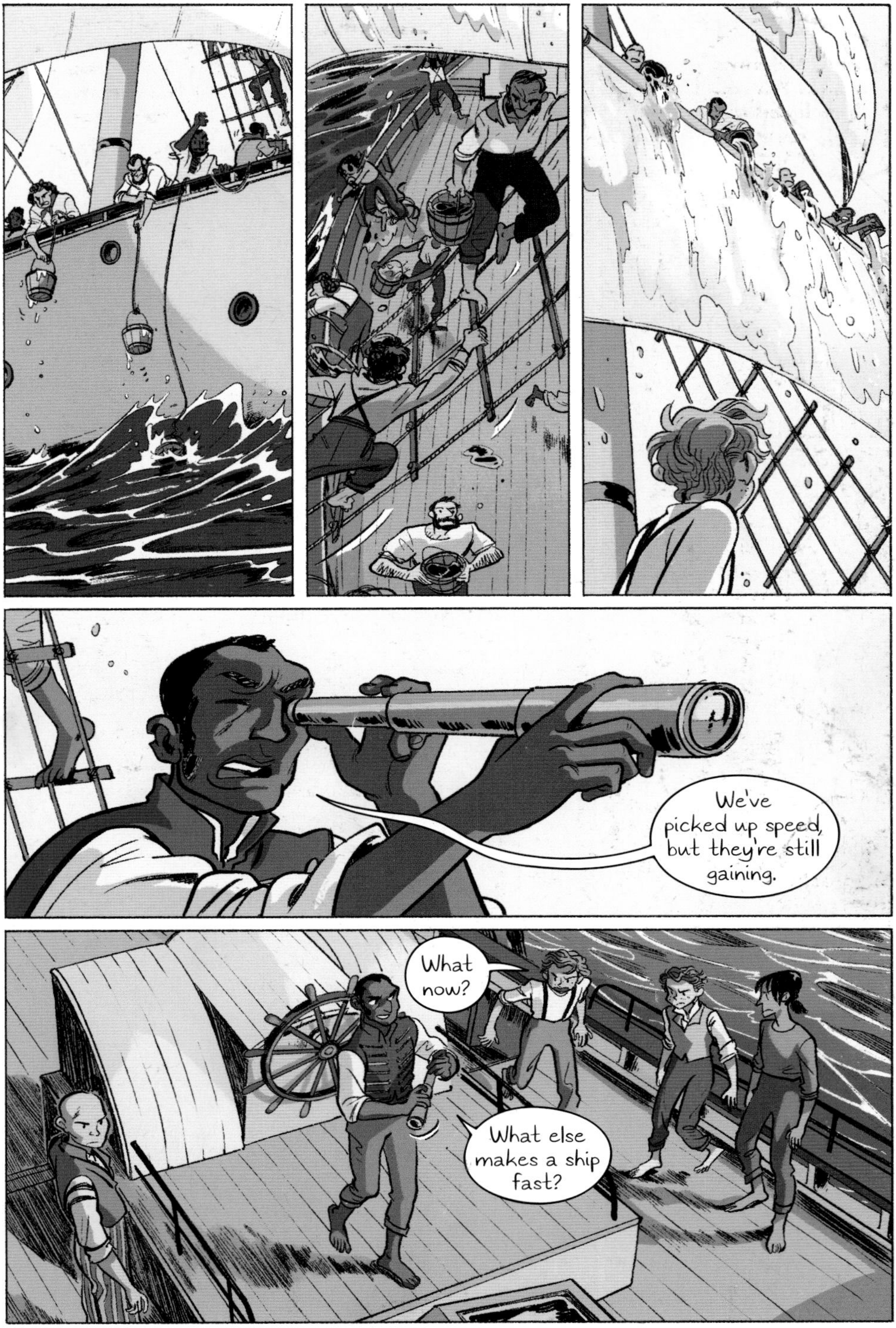
We've picked up speed, but they're still gaining.
What now?
What else makes a ship fast?

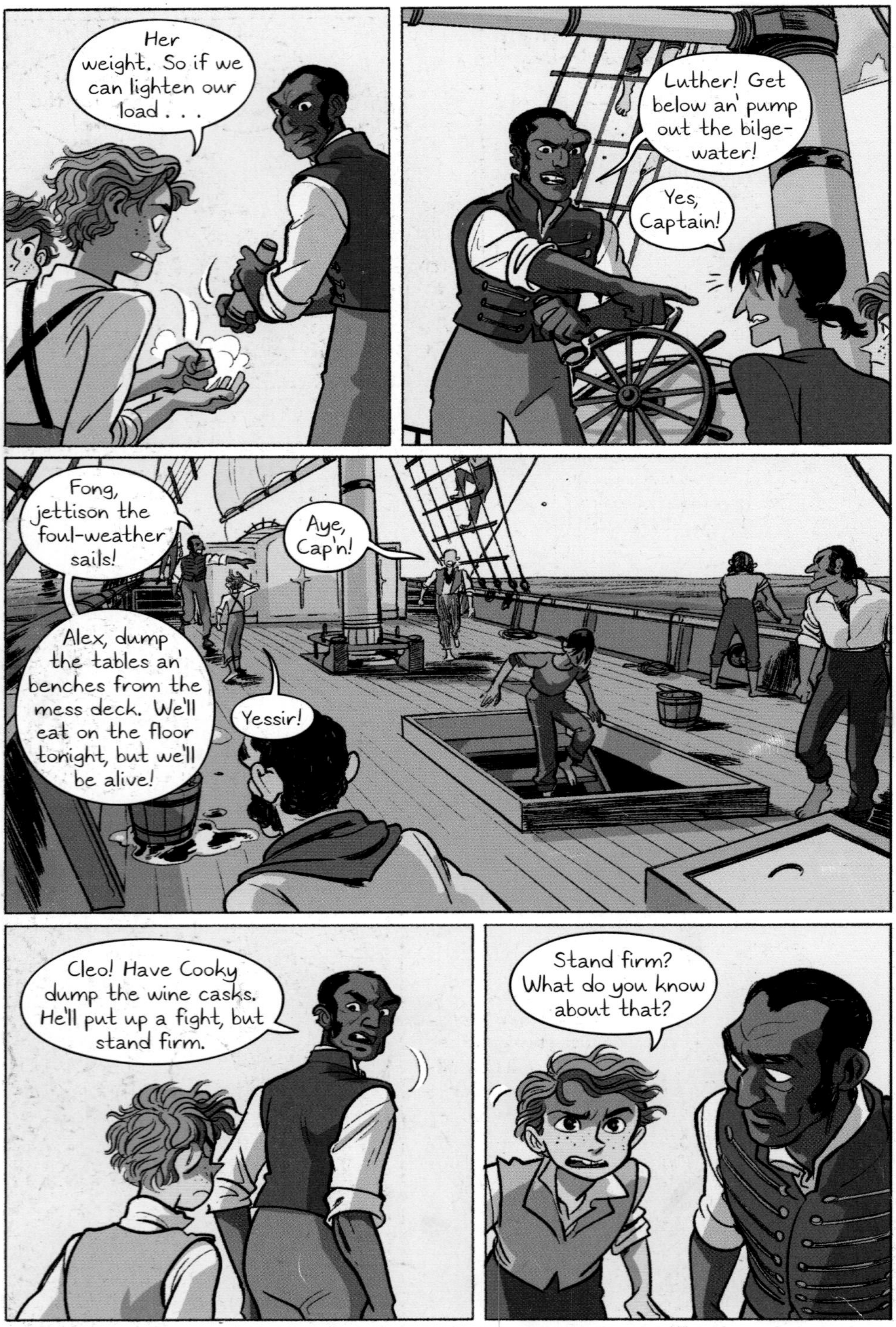
Her weight. So if we can lighten our load . . .
Luther! Get below an' pump out the bilge-water!
Yes, Captain!
Fong, jettison the foul-weather sails!
Aye, Cap'n!
Alex, dump the tables an' benches from the mess deck. We'll eat on the floor tonight, but we'll be alive!
Yessir!
Cleo! Have Cooky dump the wine casks. He'll put up a fight, but stand firm.
Stand firm? What do you know about that?

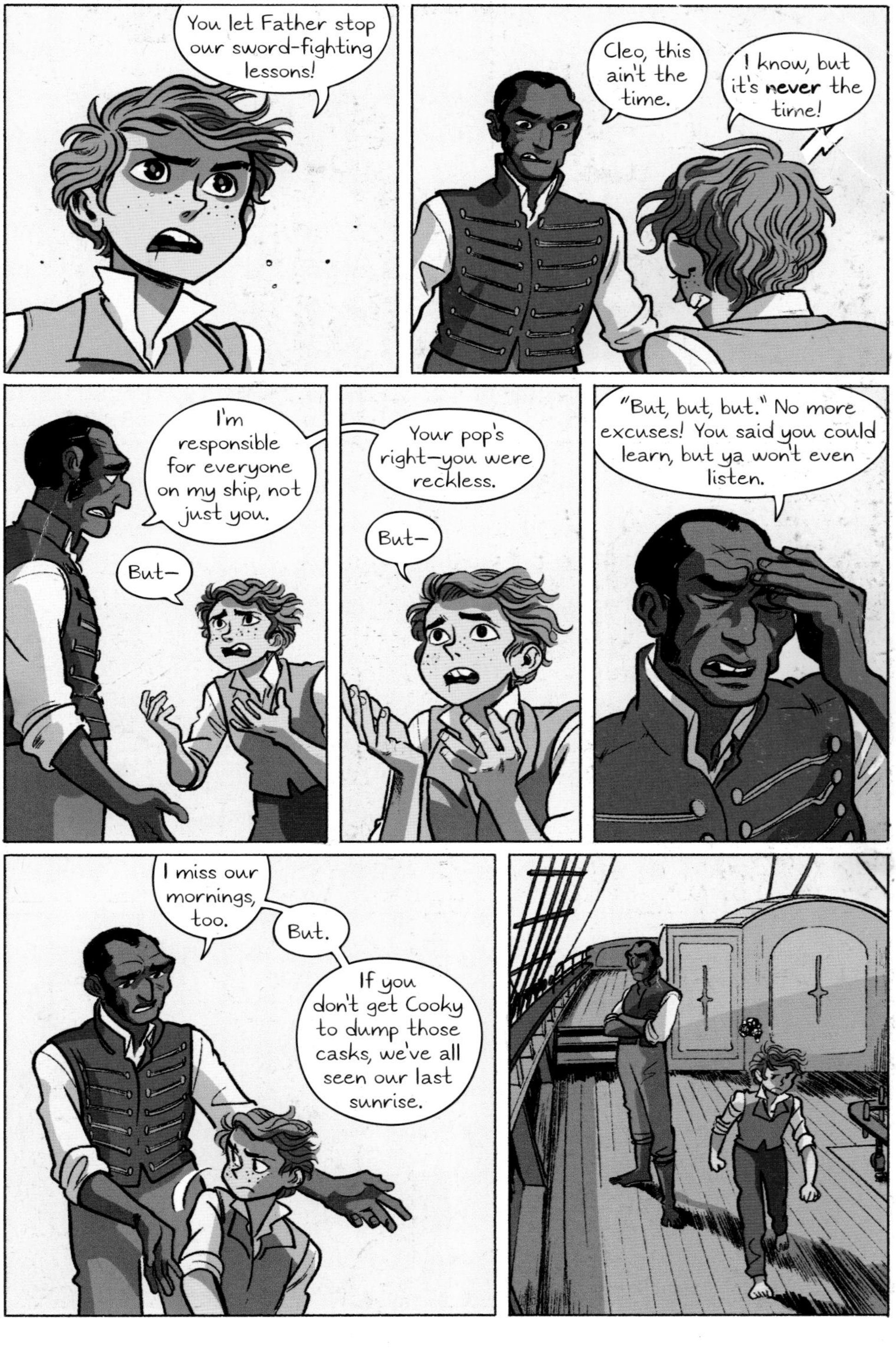
You let Father stop our sword-fighting lessons!
Cleo, this ain't the time.
I know, but it's **never** the time!
I'm responsible for everyone on my ship, not just you.
But–
Your pop's right–you were reckless.
But–
"But, but, but." No more excuses! You said you could learn, but ya won't even listen.
I miss our mornings, too.
But.
If you don't get Cooky to dump those casks, we've all seen our last sunrise.

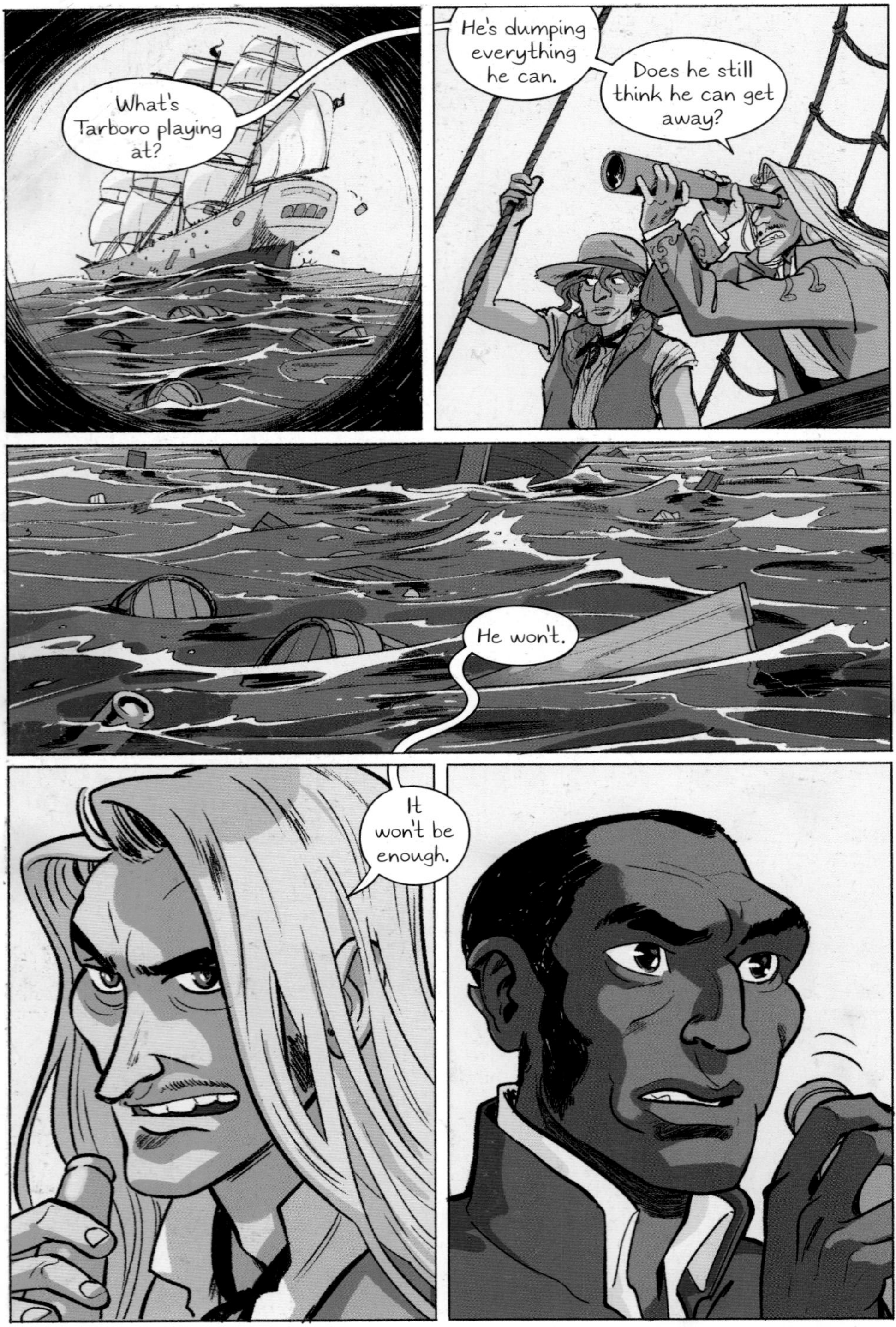
What's Tarboro playing at?
He's dumping everything he can.
Does he still think he can get away?
He won't.
It won't be enough.

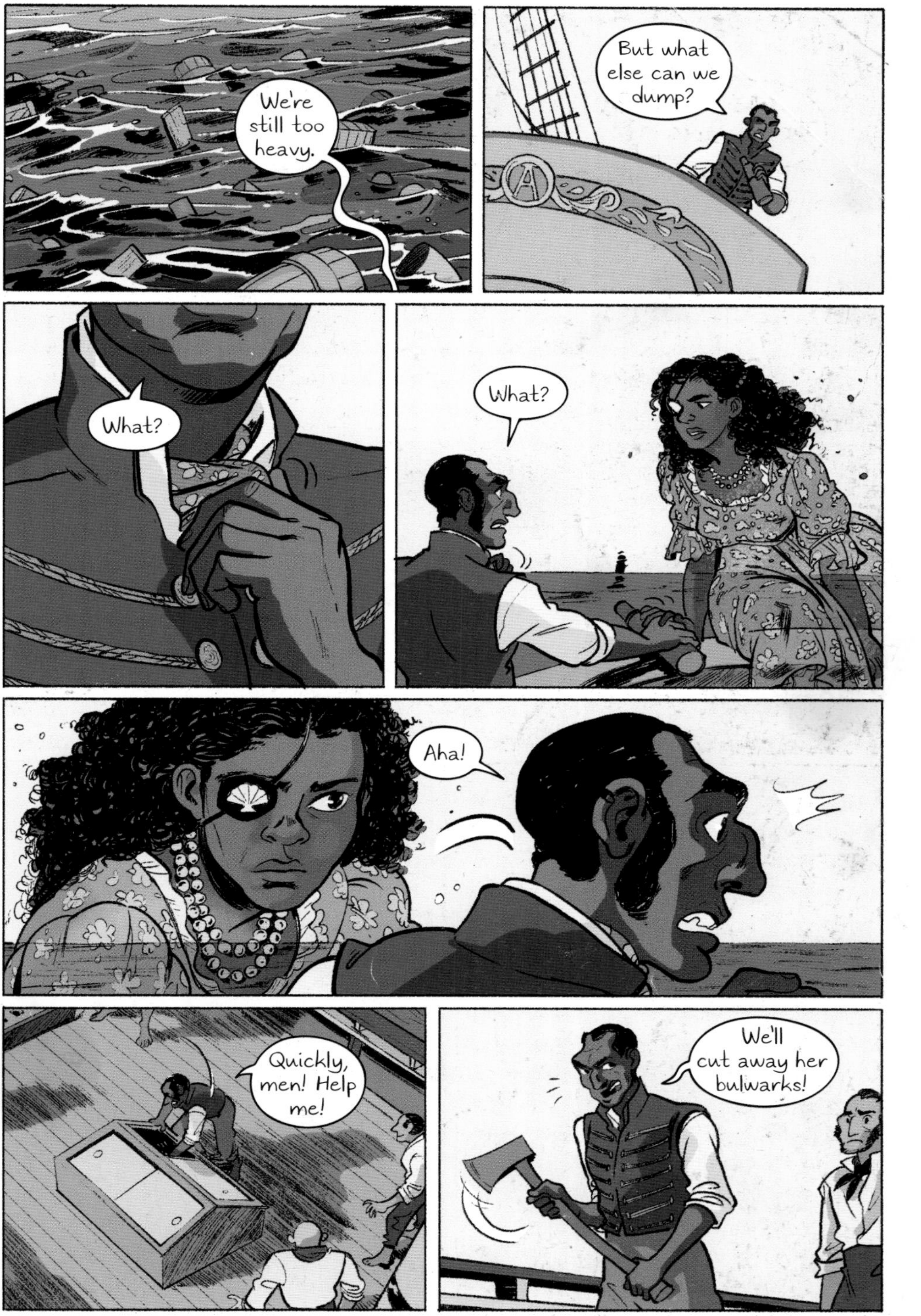
We're still too heavy.
But what else can we dump?
What?
What?
Aha!
Quickly, men! Help me!
We'll cut away her bulwarks!

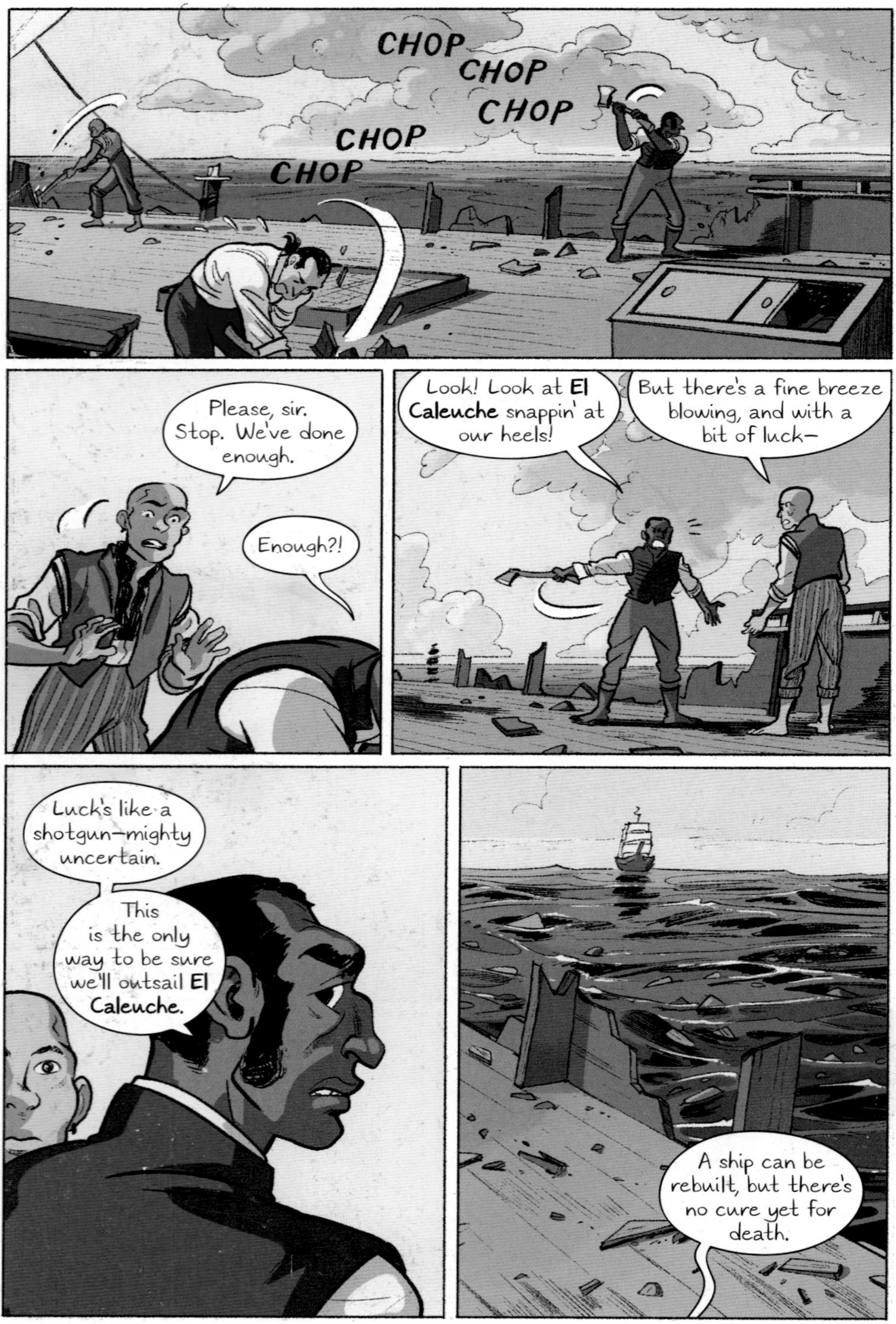
CHOP
CHOP
CHOP
CHOP
CHOP
Please, sir. Stop. We've done enough.
Enough?!
Look! Look at **El Caleuche** snappin' at our heels!
But there's a fine breeze blowing, and with a bit of luck—
Luck's like a shotgun—mighty uncertain.
This is the only way to be sure we'll outsail **El Caleuche.**
A ship can be rebuilt, but there's no cure yet for death.

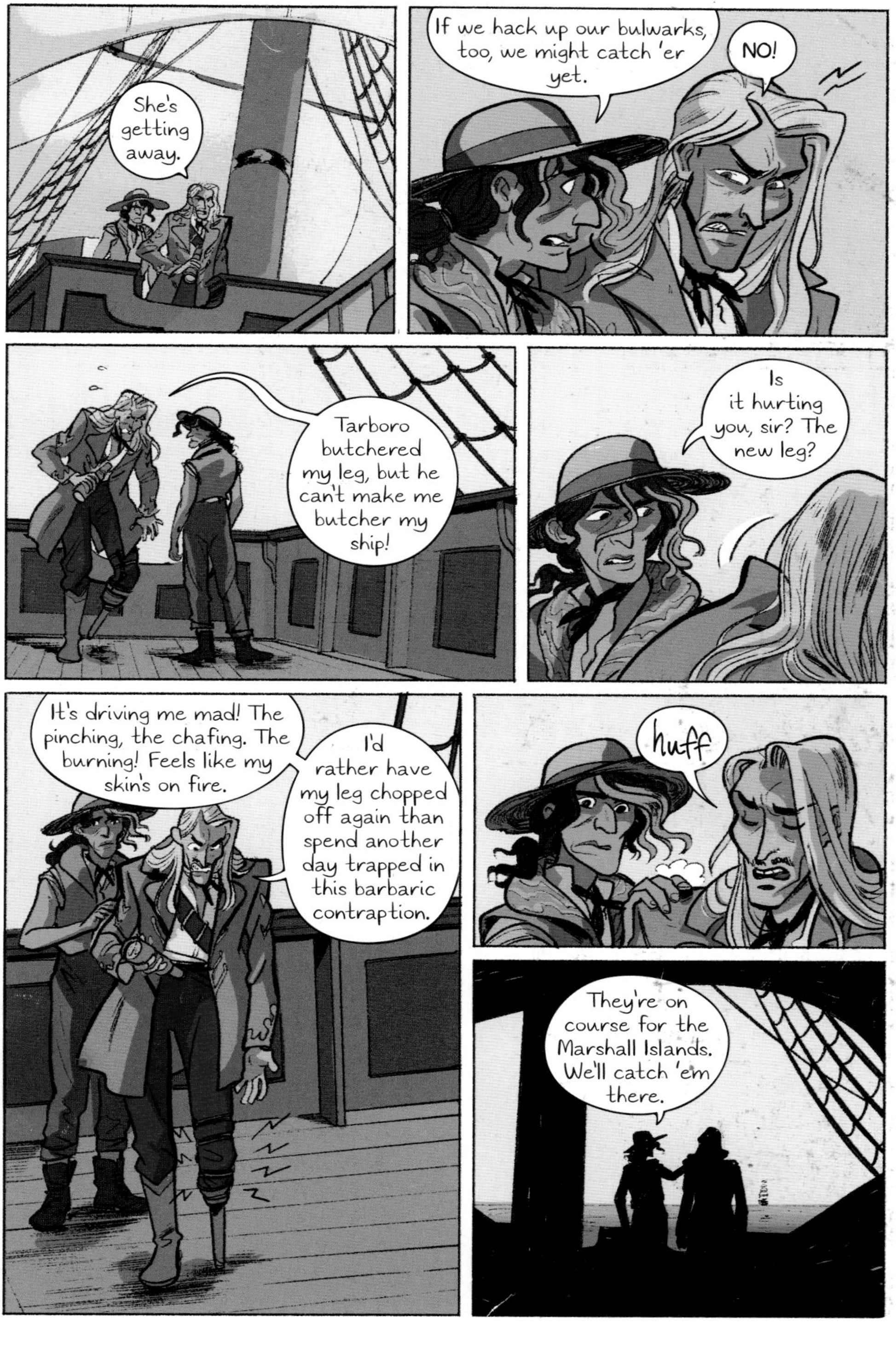
She's getting away.
If we hack up our bulwarks, too, we might catch 'er yet.
NO!
Tarboro butchered my leg, but he can't make me butcher my ship!
Is it hurting you, sir? The new leg?
It's driving me mad! The pinching, the chafing. The burning! Feels like my skin's on fire.
I'd rather have my leg chopped off again than spend another day trapped in this barbaric contraption.
huff
They're on course for the Marshall Islands. We'll catch 'em there.

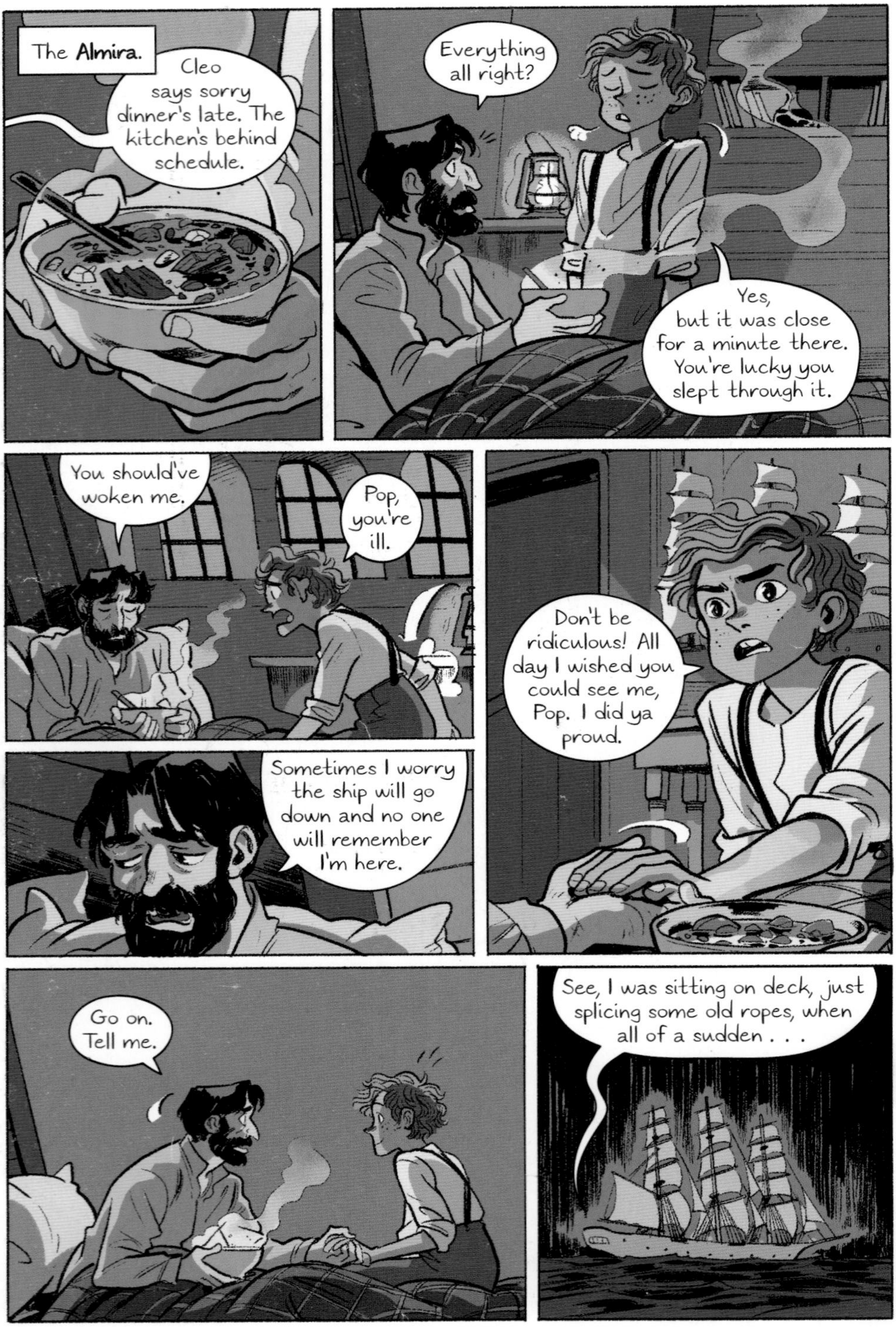
The Almira.
Cleo says sorry dinner's late. The kitchen's behind schedule.
Everything all right?
Yes, but it was close for a minute there. You're lucky you slept through it.
You should've woken me.
Pop, you're ill.
Don't be ridiculous! All day I wished you could see me, Pop. I did ya proud.
Sometimes I worry the ship will go down and no one will remember I'm here.
Go on. Tell me.
See, I was sitting on deck, just splicing some old ropes, when all of a sudden . . .

CHAPTER SIX
RECONSTRUCTION

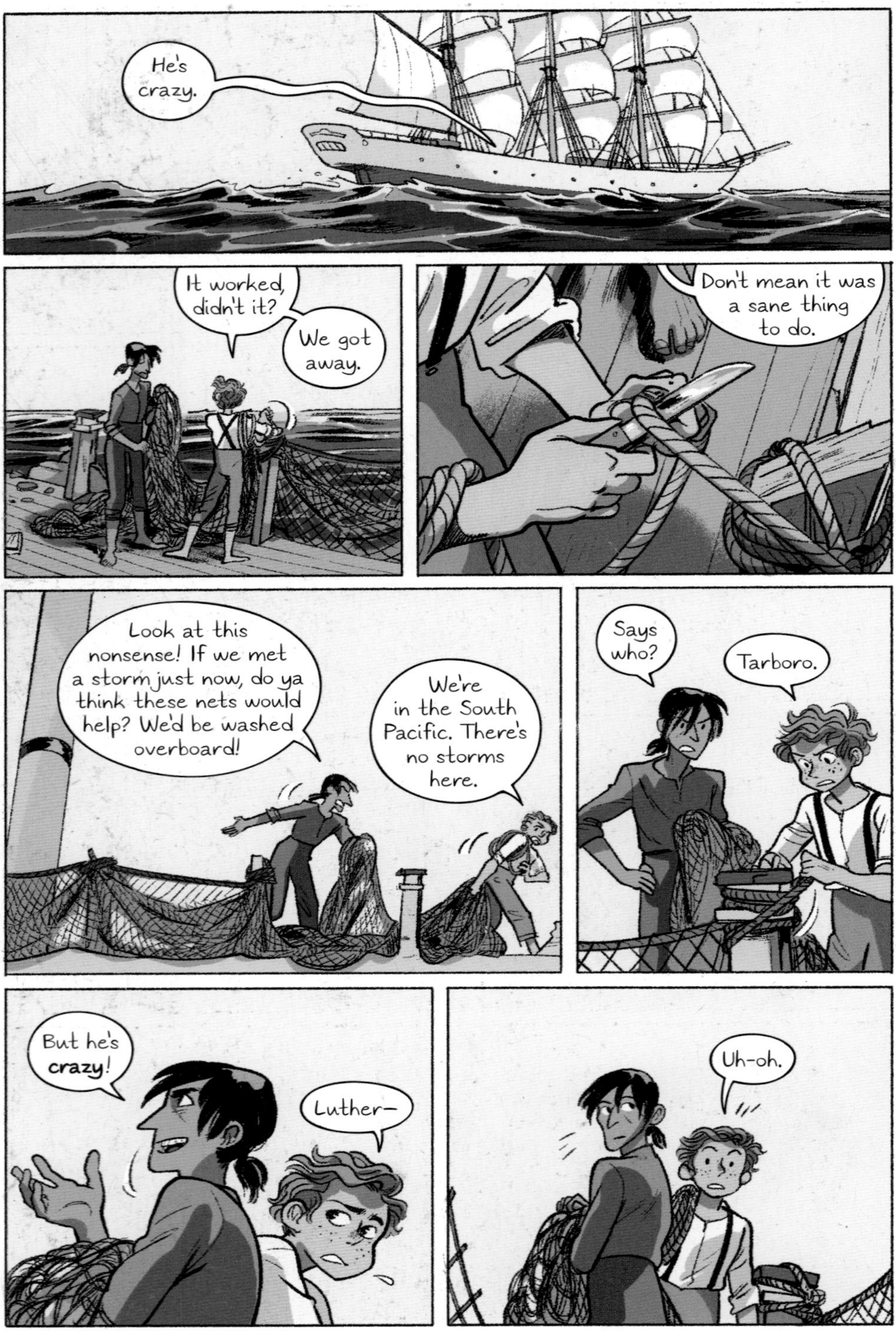
He's crazy.
It worked, didn't it?
We got away.
Don't mean it was a sane thing to do.
Look at this nonsense! If we met a storm just now, do ya think these nets would help? We'd be washed overboard!
We're in the South Pacific. There's no storms here.
Says who?
Tarboro.
But he's **crazy**!
Luther–
Uh-oh.

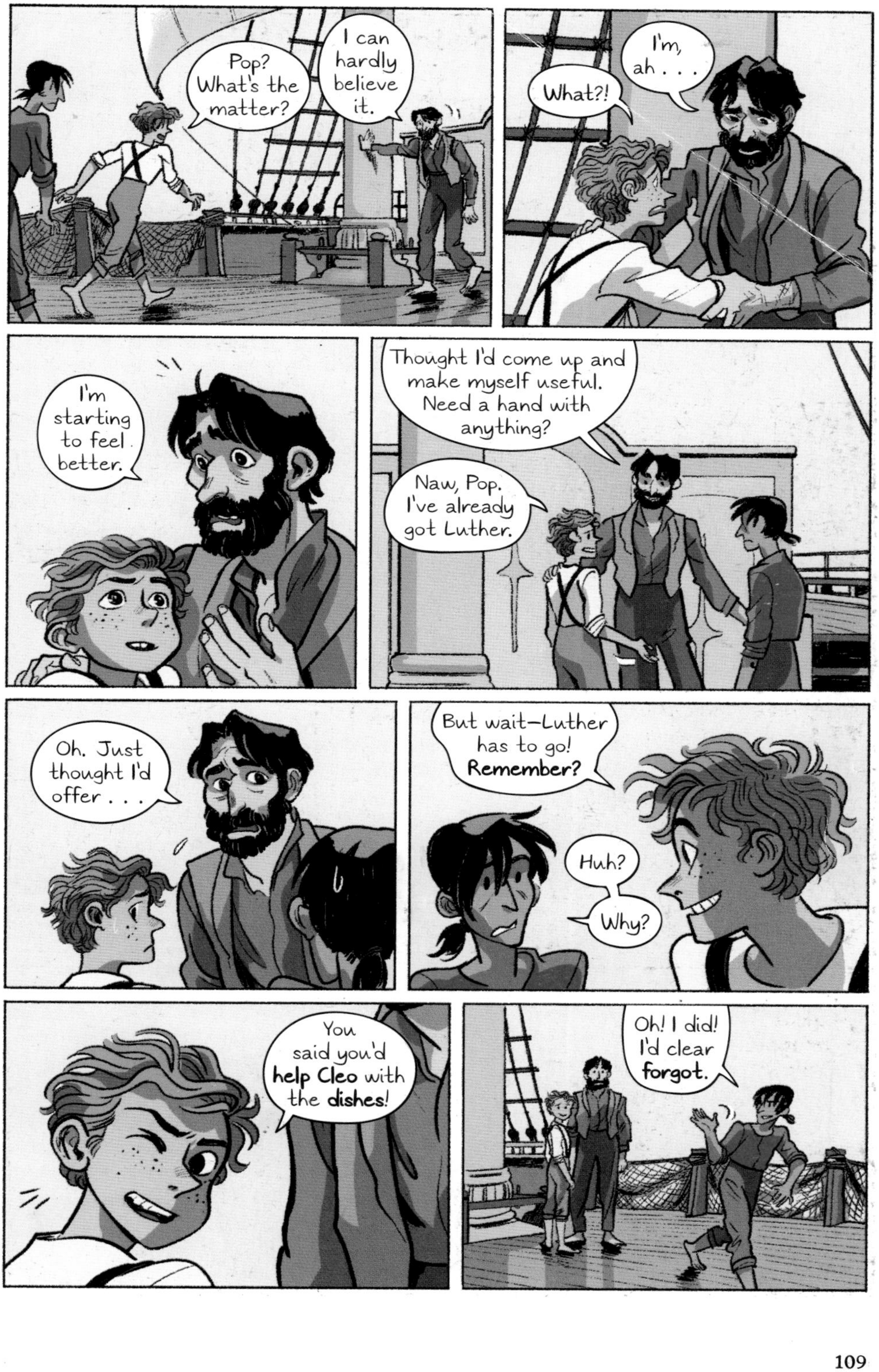

Pop? What's the matter?
I can hardly believe it.
I'm, ah . . .
What?!
I'm starting to feel better.
Thought I'd come up and make myself useful. Need a hand with anything?
Naw, Pop. I've already got Luther.
Oh. Just thought I'd offer . . .
But wait—Luther has to go! **Remember?**
Huh?
Why?
You said you'd **help Cleo** with the **dishes**!
Oh! I did! I'd clear **forgot**.

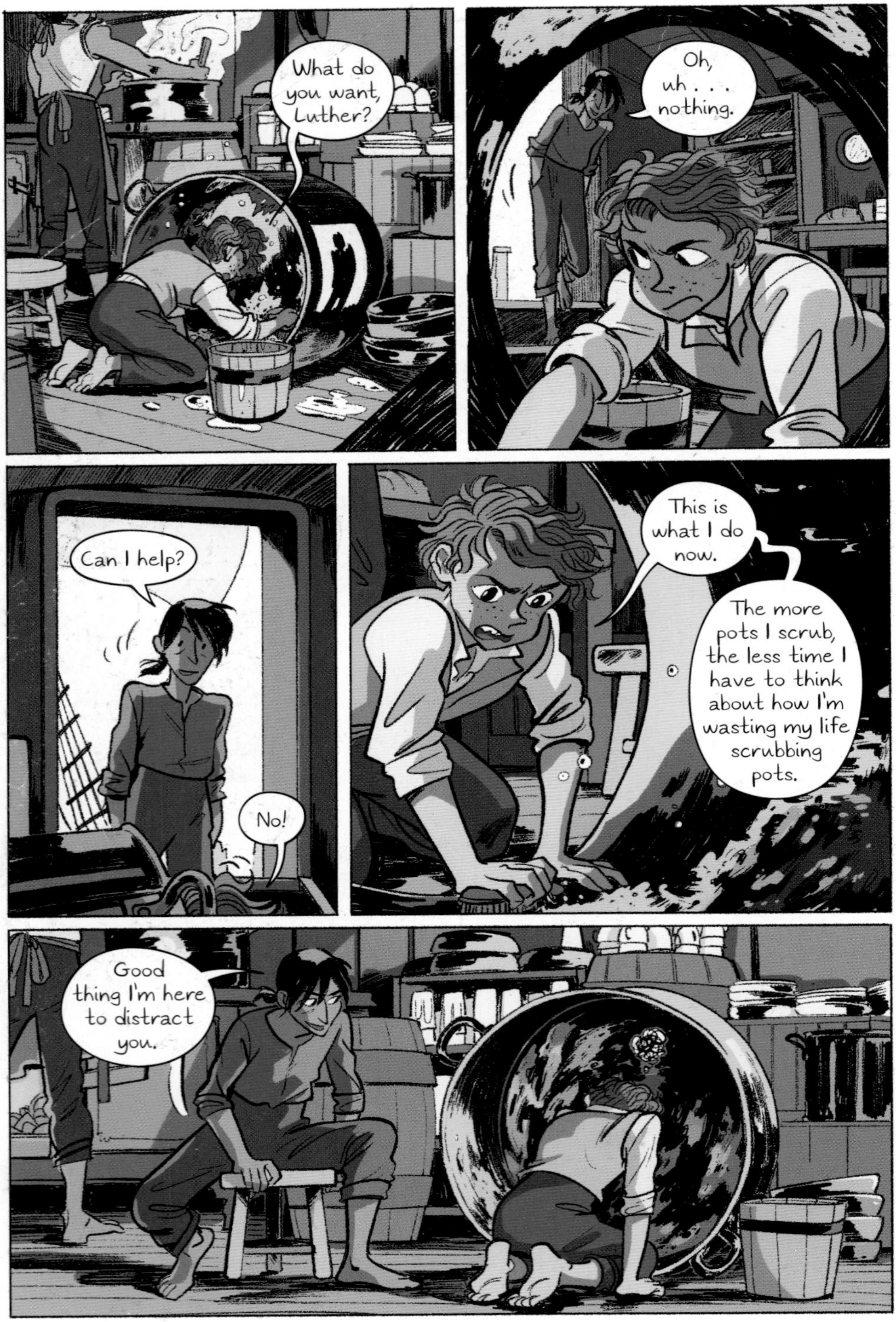
What do you want, Luther?
Oh, uh . . . nothing.
Can I help?
No!
This is what I do now.
The more pots I scrub, the less time I have to think about how I'm wasting my life scrubbing pots.
Good thing I'm here to distract you.

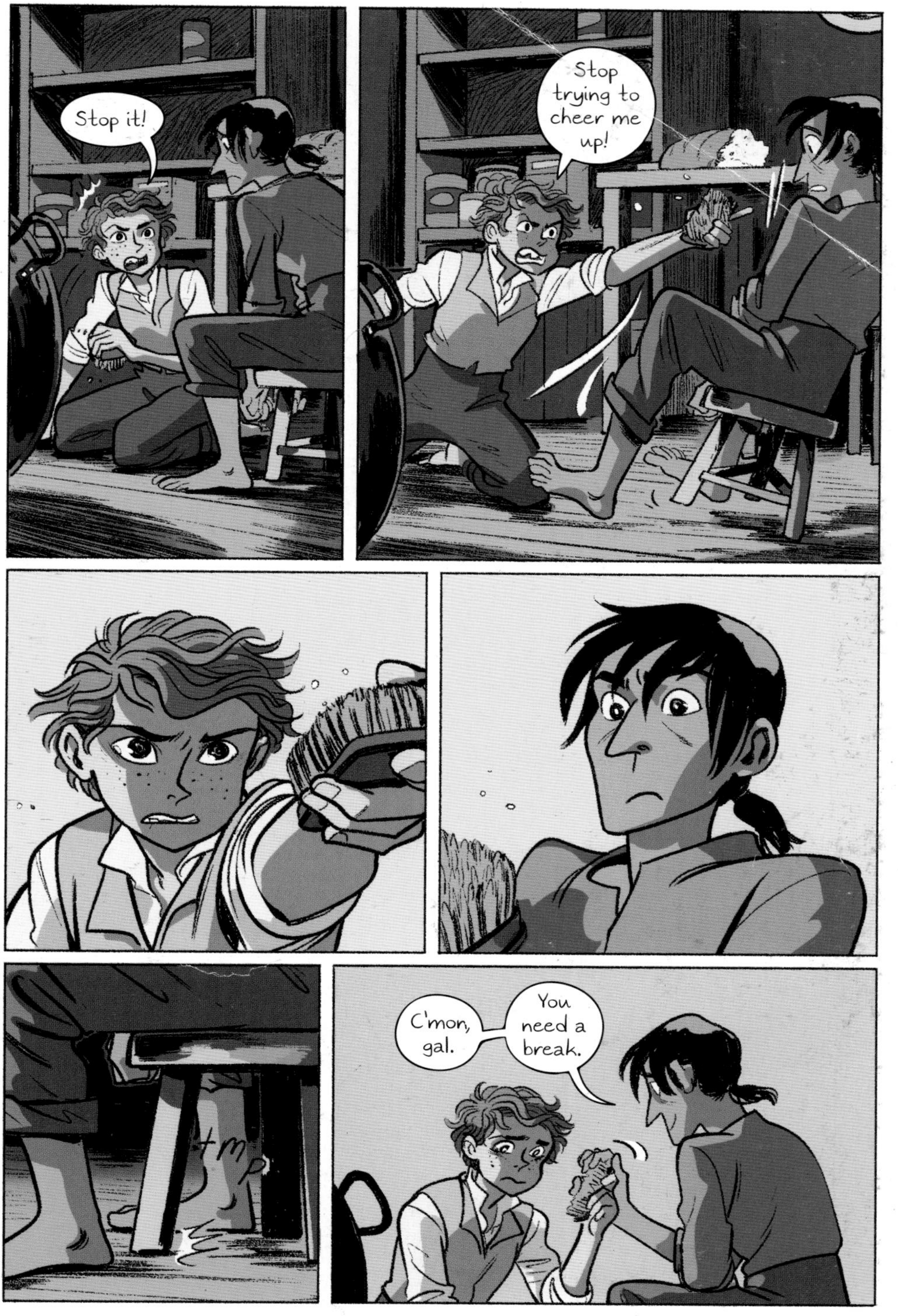

Stop it!
Stop trying to cheer me up!
C'mon, gal.
You need a break.

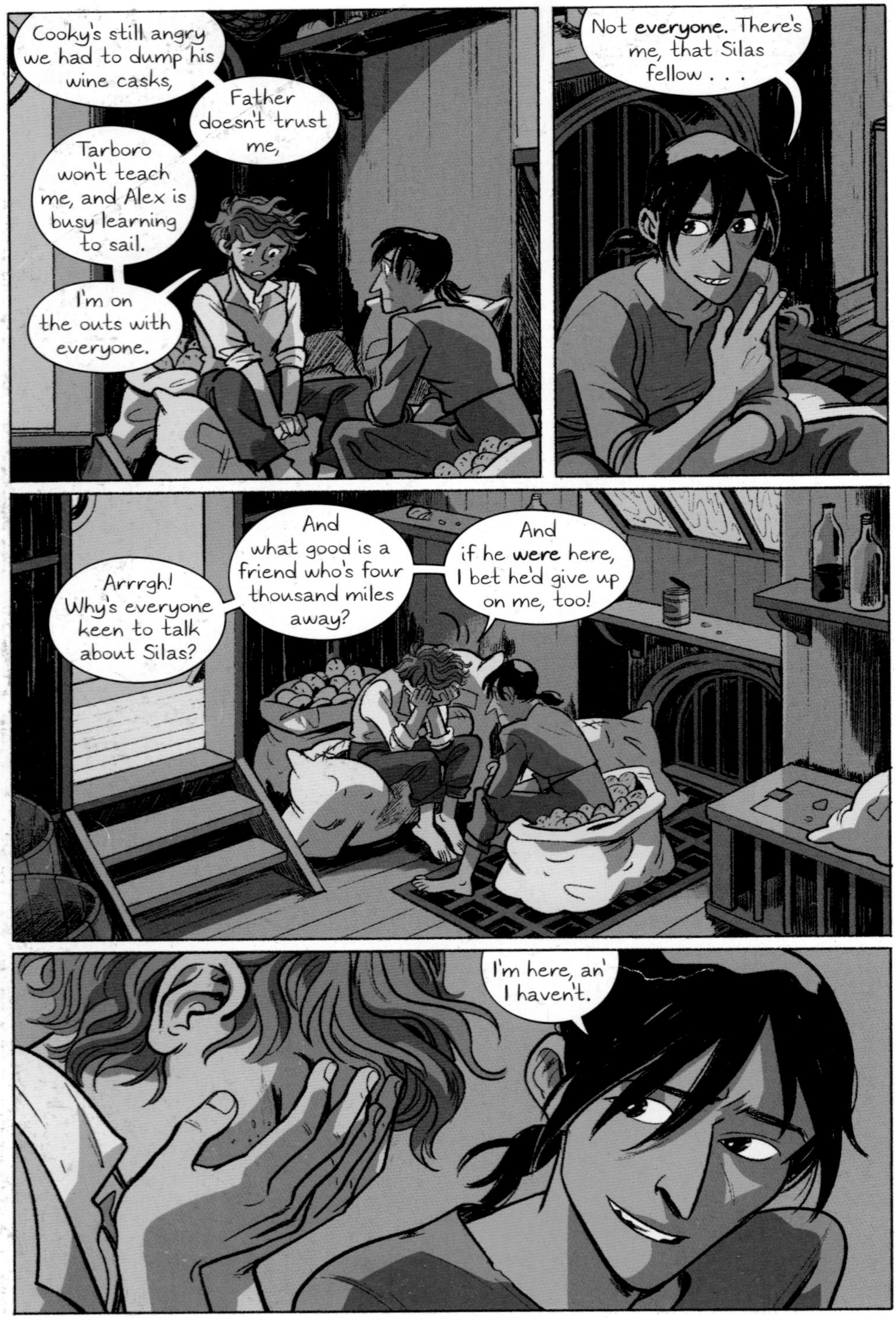
Cooky's still angry we had to dump his wine casks,
Father doesn't trust me,
Tarboro won't teach me, and Alex is busy learning to sail.
I'm on the outs with everyone.
Not **everyone.** There's me, that Silas fellow . . .
Arrrgh! Why's everyone keen to talk about Silas?
And what good is a friend who's four thousand miles away?
And if he **were** here, I bet he'd give up on me, too!
I'm here, an' I haven't.

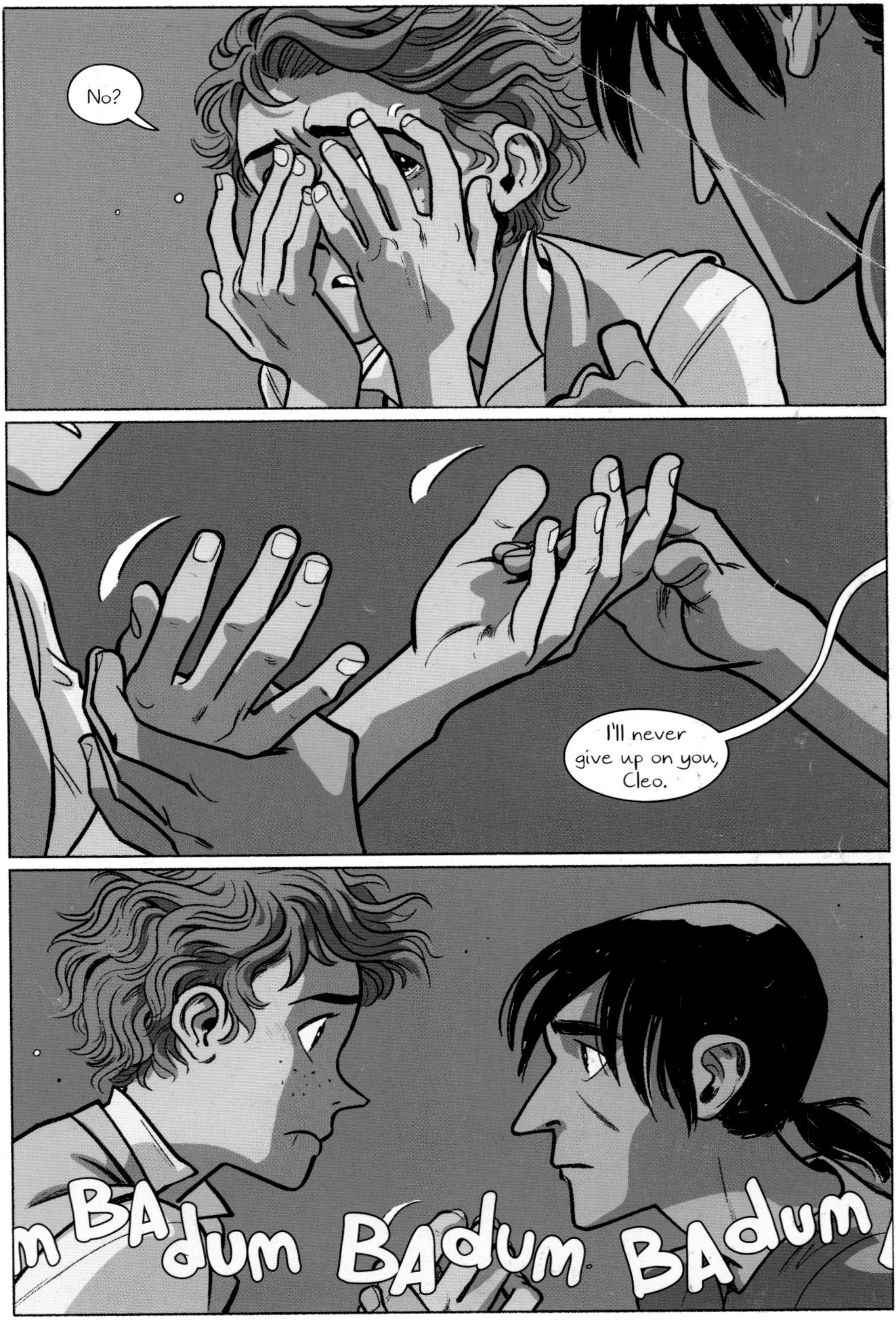
No?
I'll never give up on you, Cleo.
m BA dum BAdum BAdum

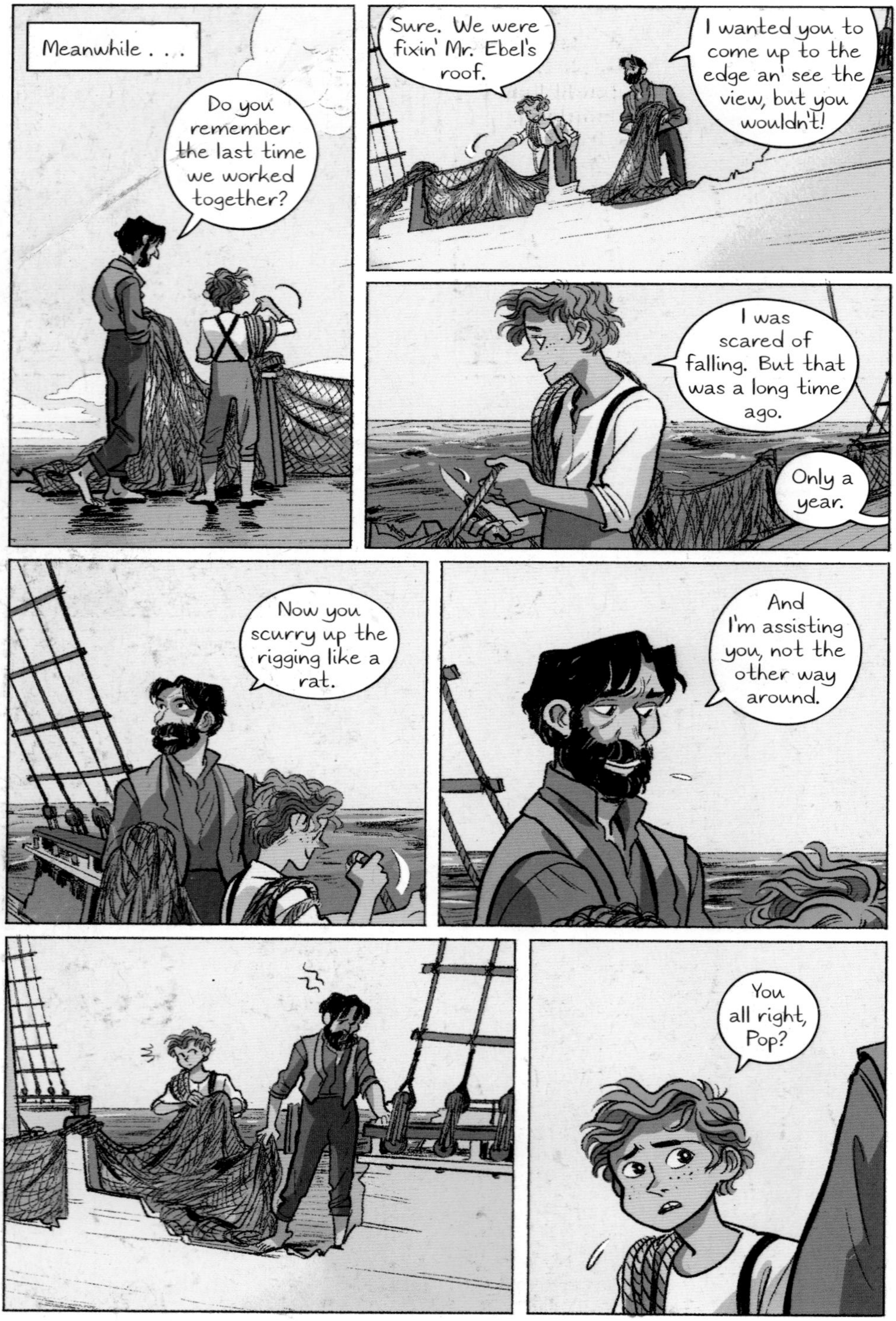
Meanwhile . . .
Do you remember the last time we worked together?
Sure. We were fixin' Mr. Ebel's roof.
I wanted you to come up to the edge an' see the view, but you wouldn't!
I was scared of falling. But that was a long time ago.
Only a year.
Now you scurry up the rigging like a rat.
And I'm assisting you, not the other way around.
You all right, Pop?

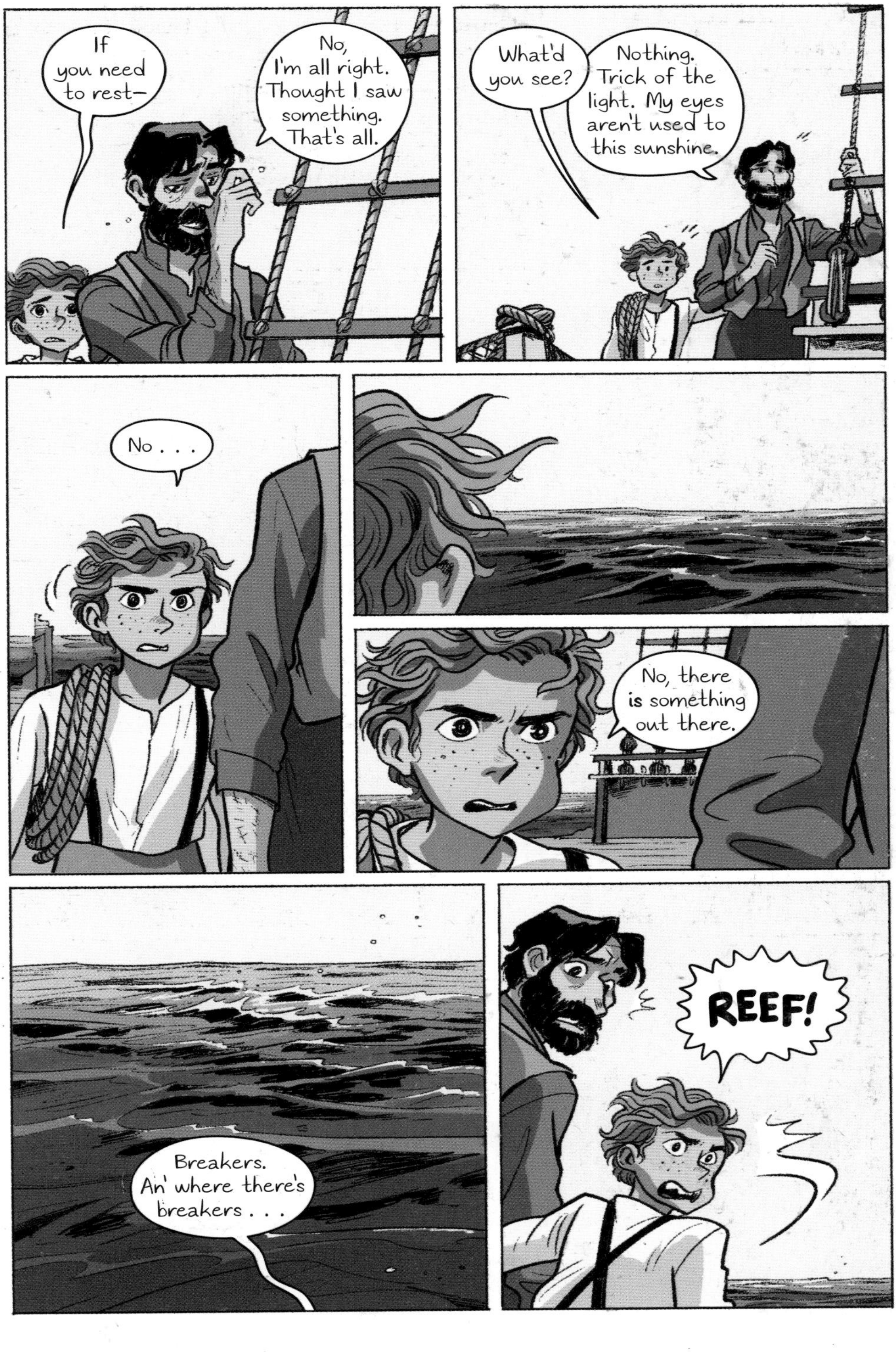
If you need to rest—
No, I'm all right. Thought I saw something. That's all.
What'd you see?
Nothing. Trick of the light. My eyes aren't used to this sunshine.
No . . .
No, there **is** something out there.
Breakers. An' where there's breakers . . .
REEF!

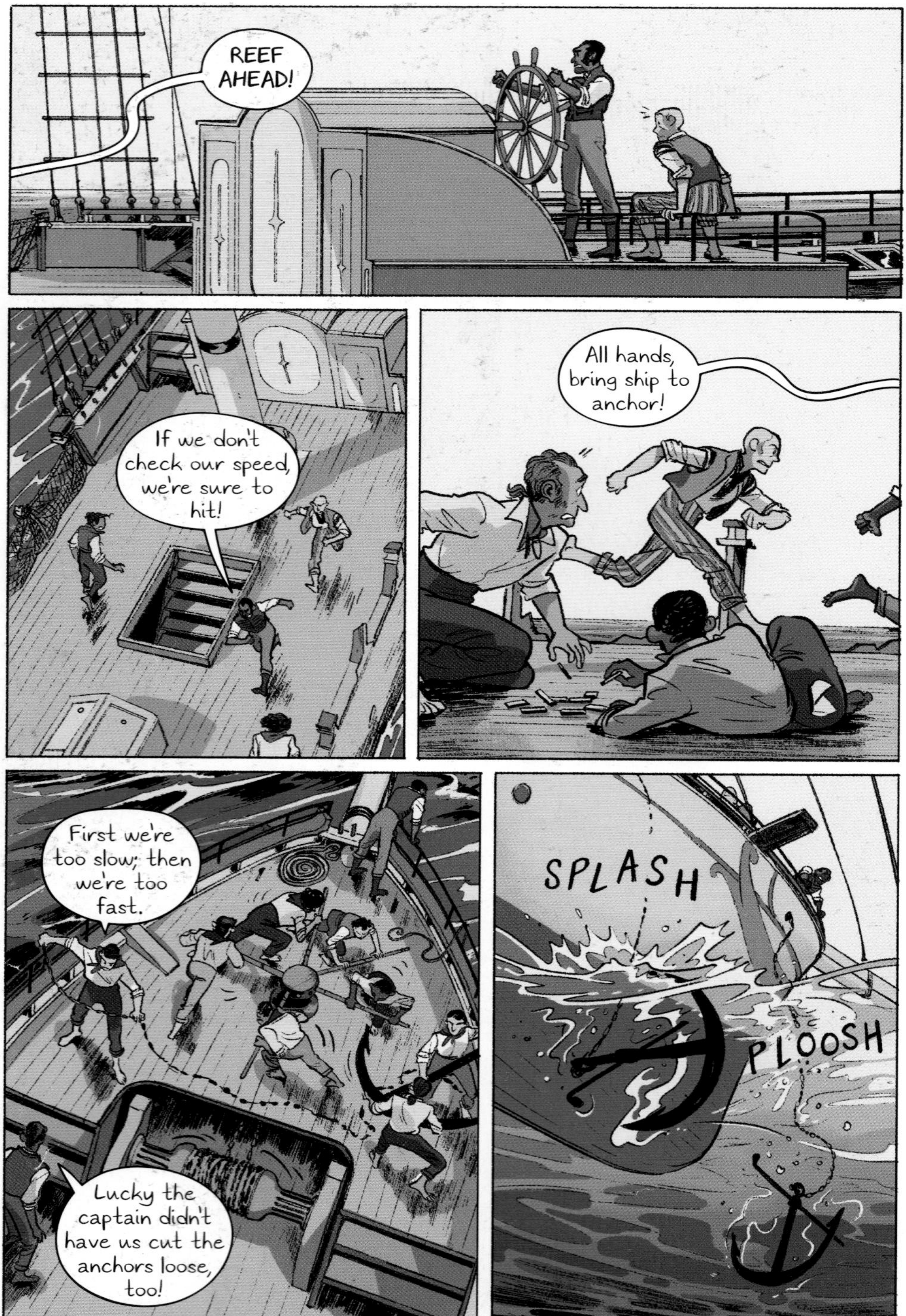
REEF AHEAD!
If we don't check our speed, we're sure to hit!
All hands, bring ship to anchor!
First we're too slow; then we're too fast.
Lucky the captain didn't have us cut the anchors loose, too!
SPLASH
PLOOSH

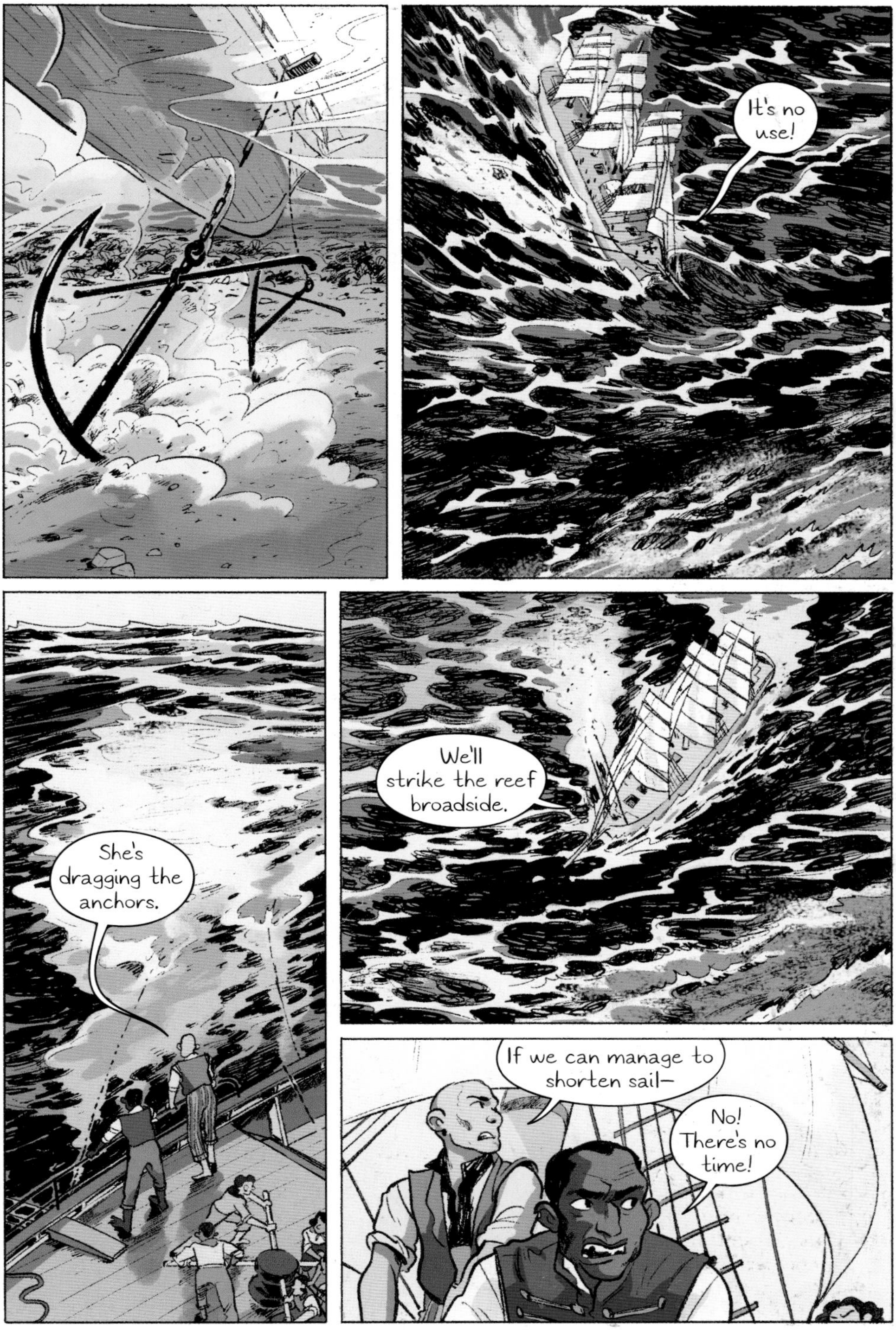
It's no use!
She's dragging the anchors.
We'll strike the reef broadside.
If we can manage to shorten sail—
No! There's no time!

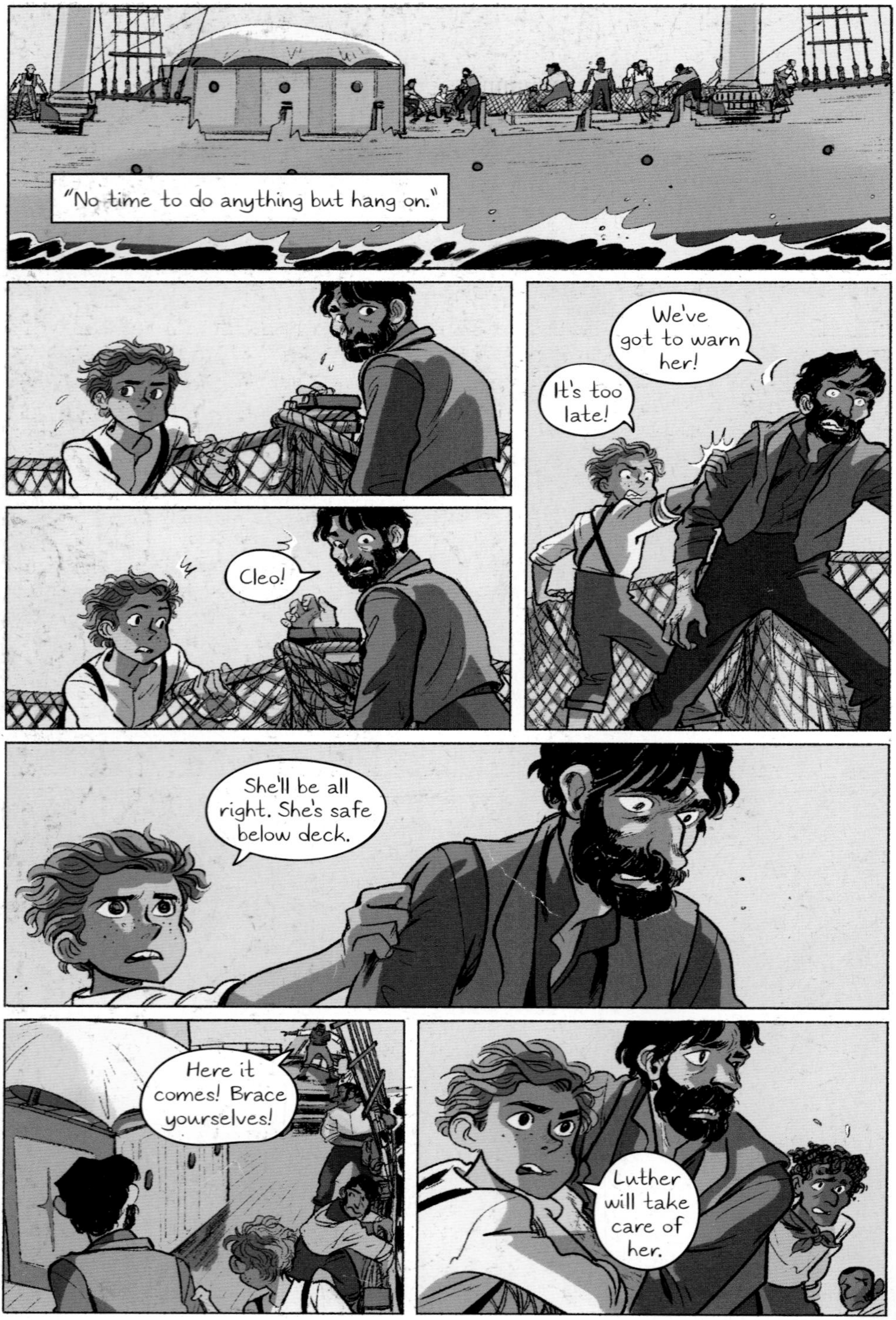
"No time to do anything but hang on."
Cleo!
We've got to warn her!
It's too late!
She'll be all right. She's safe below deck.
Here it comes! Brace yourselves!
Luther will take care of her.

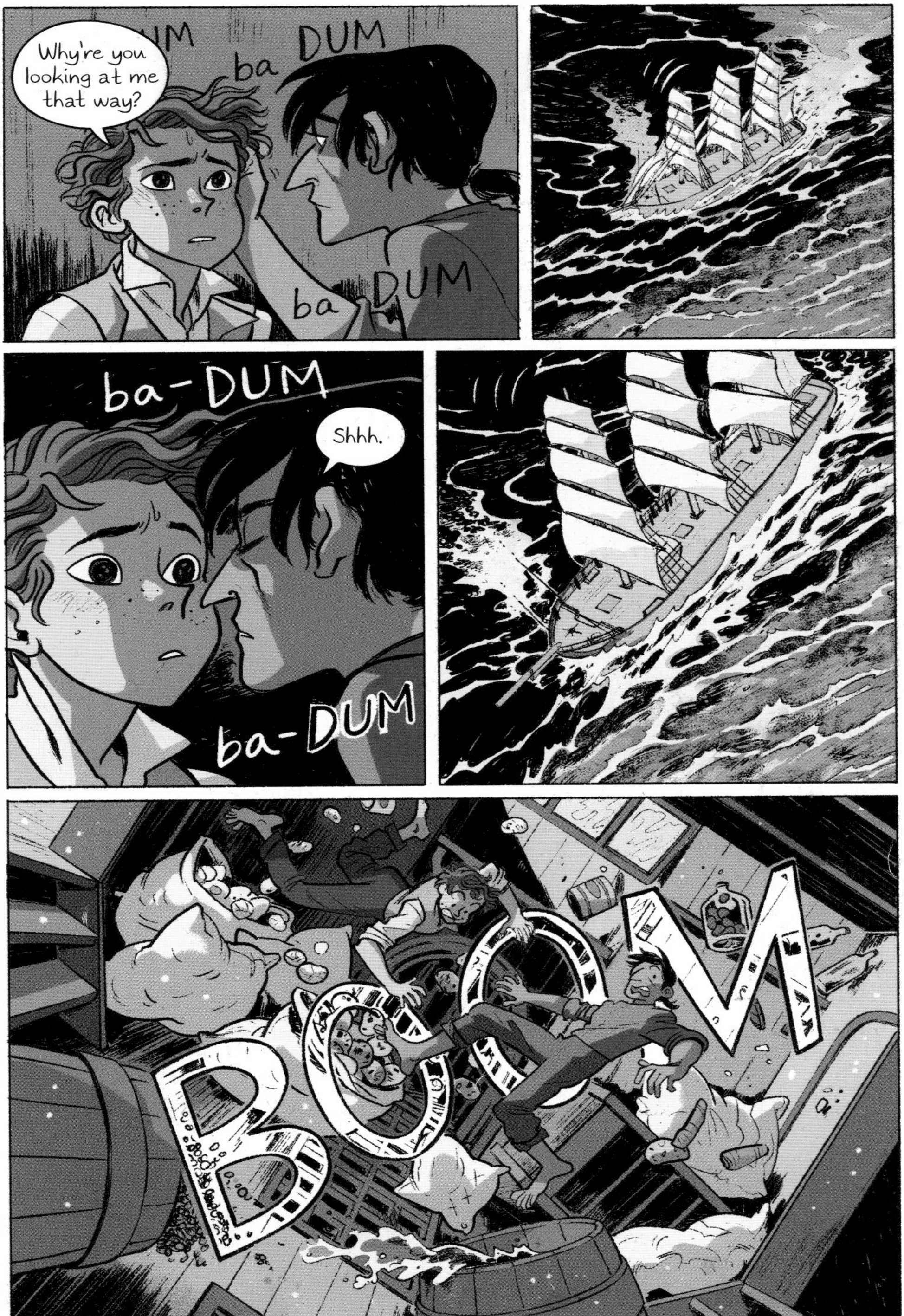
DUM
ba DUM
Why're you looking at me that way?
ba DUM
ba-DUM
Shhh.
ba-DUM
BOOM

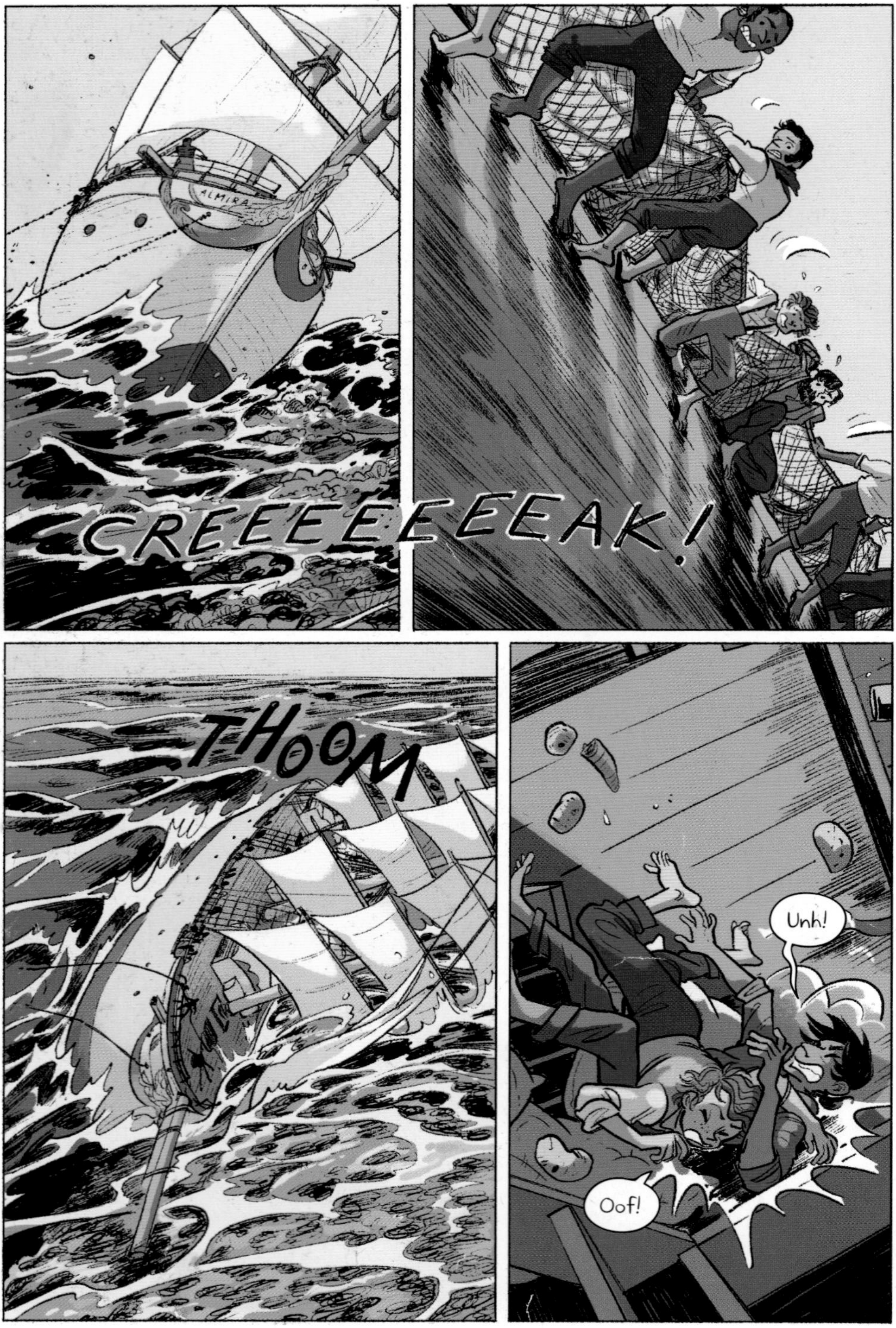

ALMIRA
CREEEEEEEAK!
THOOM
Unh!
Oof!

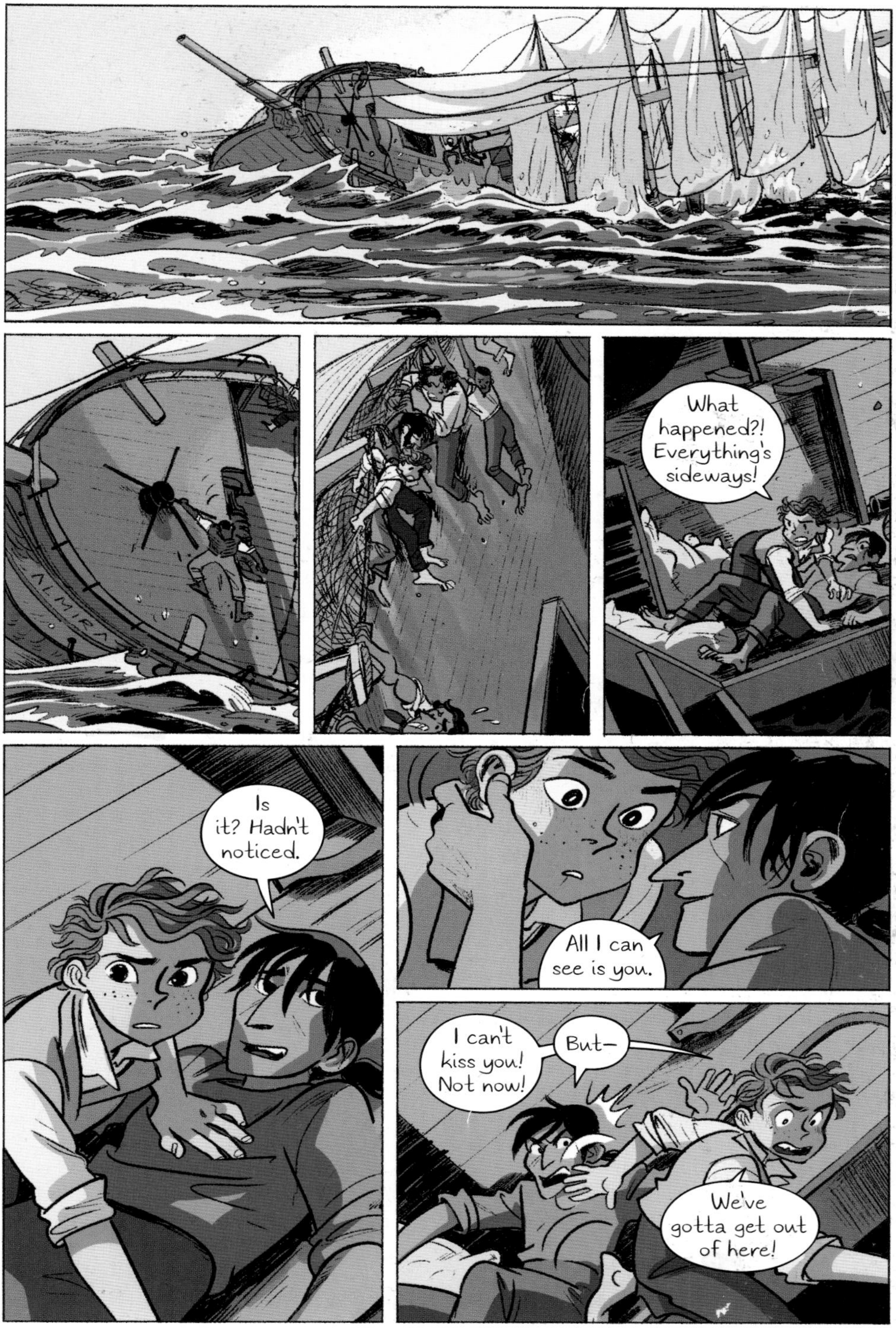
What happened?! Everything's sideways!
Is it? Hadn't noticed.
All I can see is you.
I can't kiss you! Not now!
But—
We've gotta get out of here!

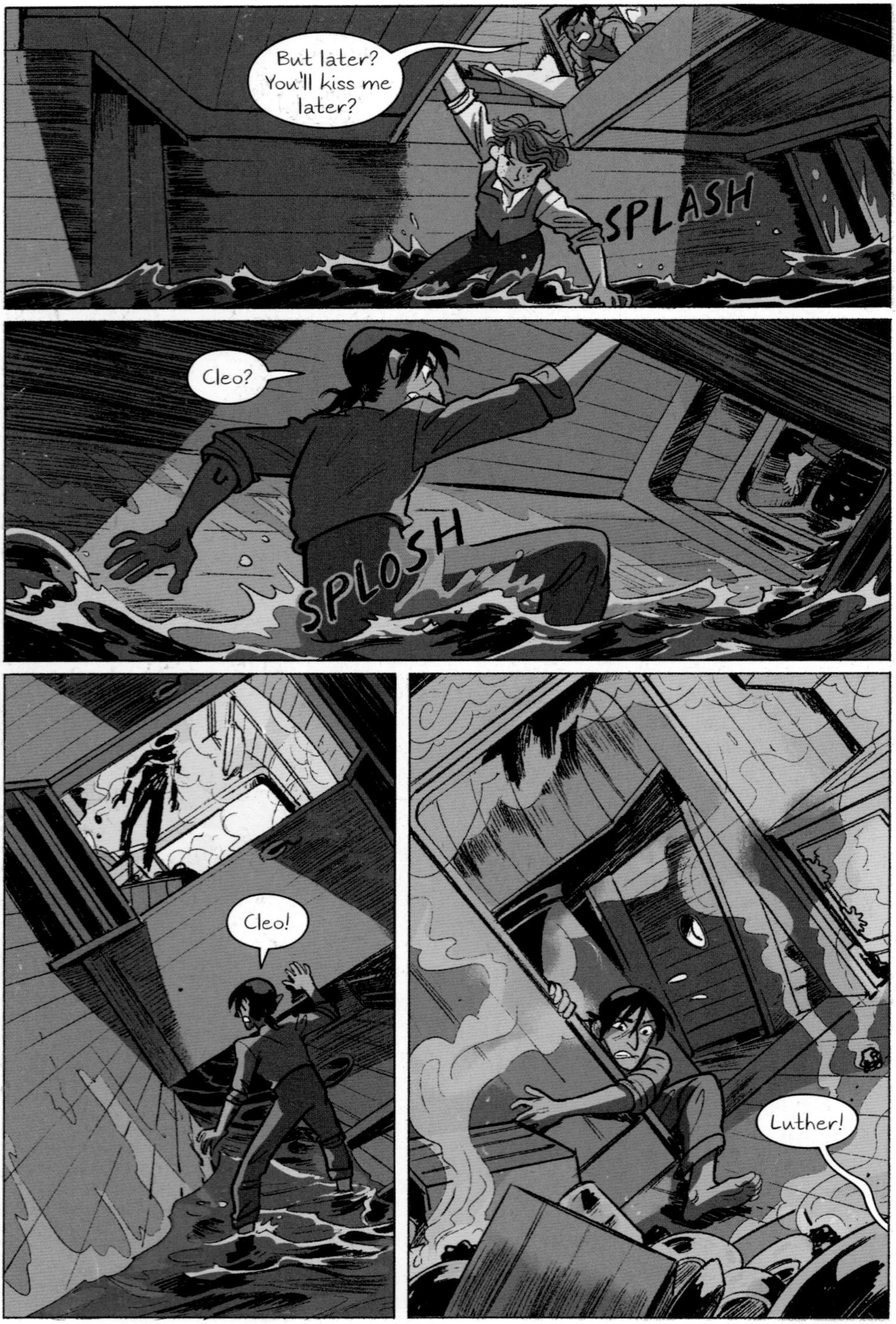
But later? You'll kiss me later?
SPLASH
Cleo?
SPLOSH
Cleo!
Luther!

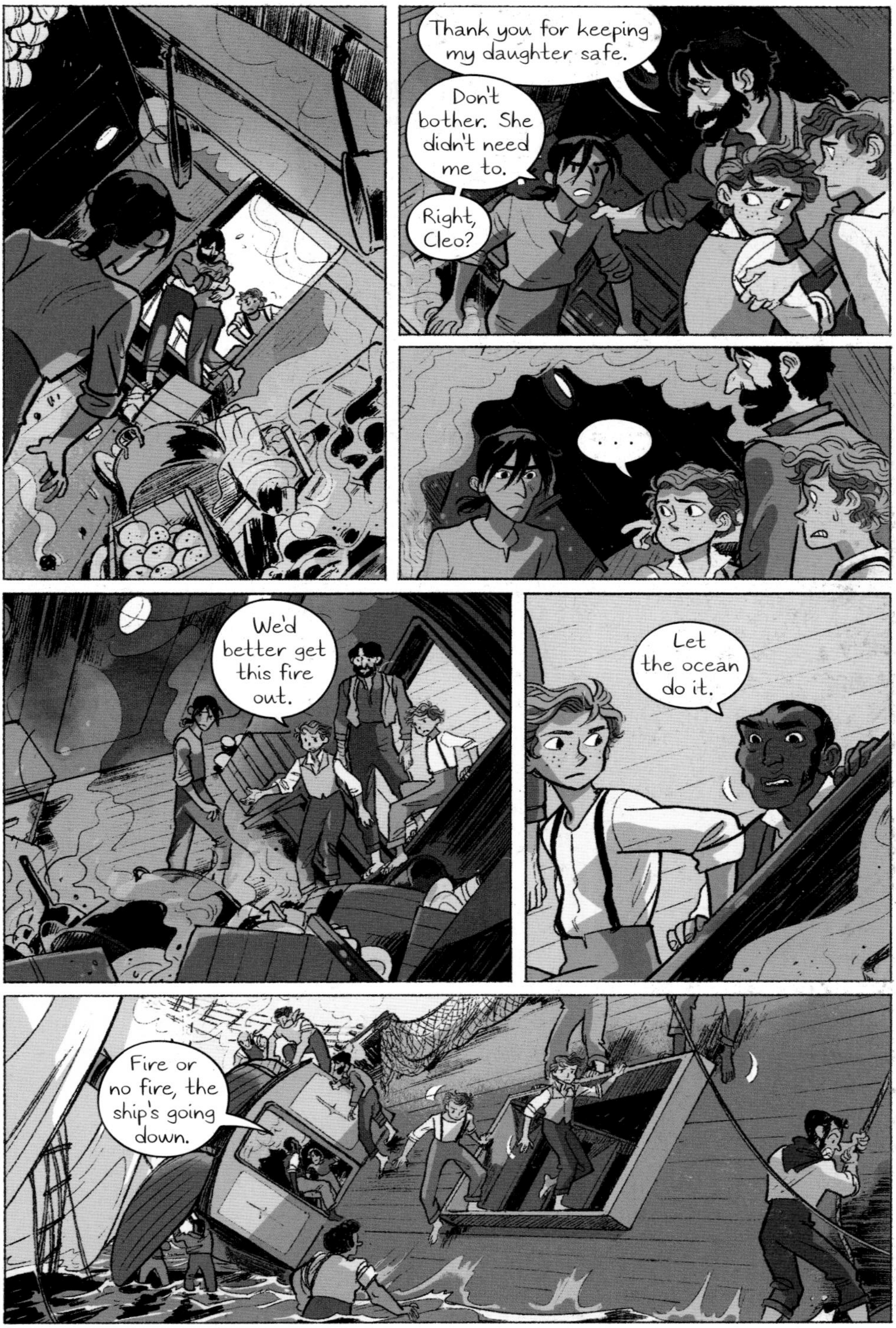
Thank you for keeping my daughter safe.
Don't bother. She didn't need me to.
Right, Cleo?
. . .
We'd better get this fire out.
Let the ocean do it.
Fire or no fire, the ship's going down.

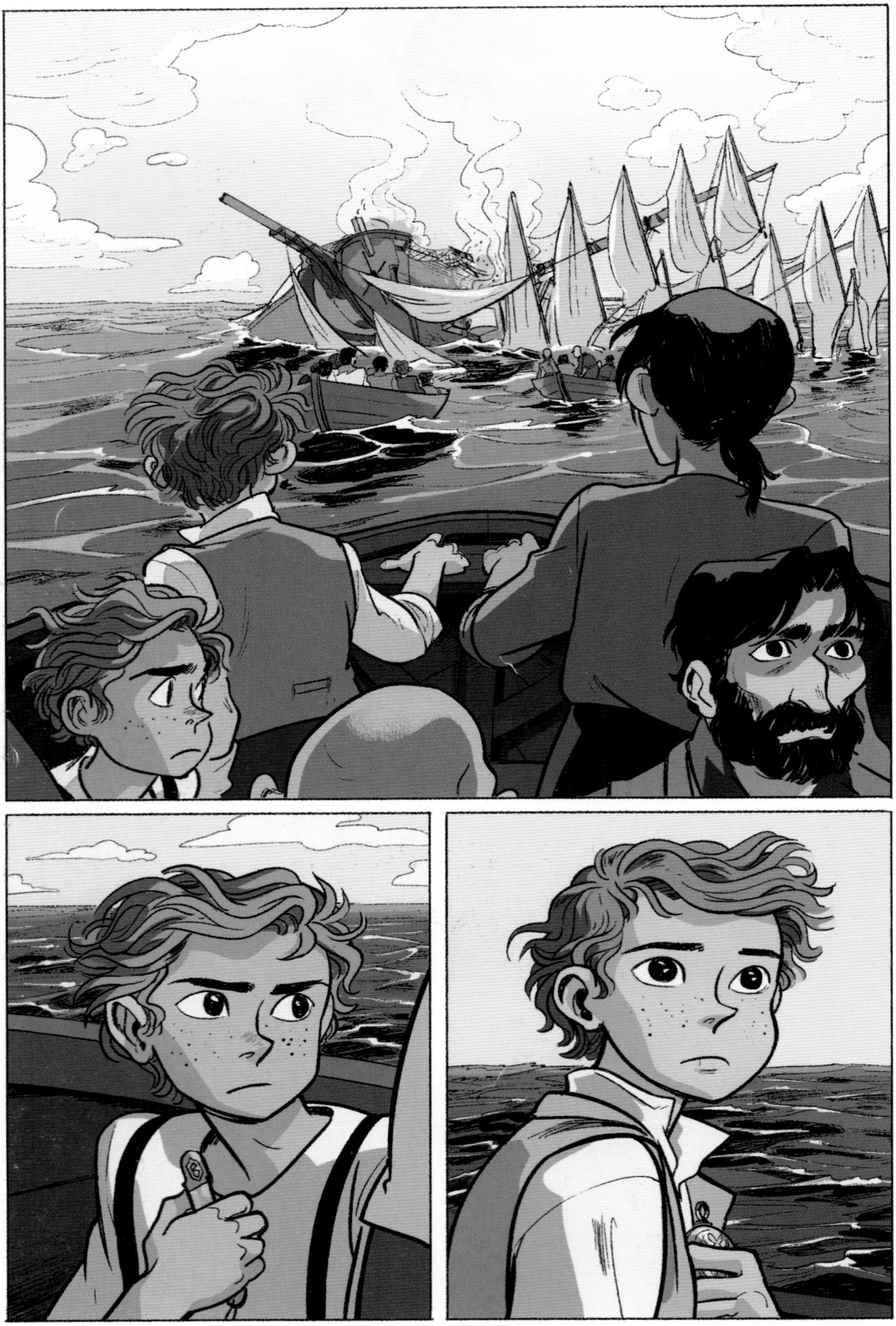

CHAPTER SEVEN
MONONO

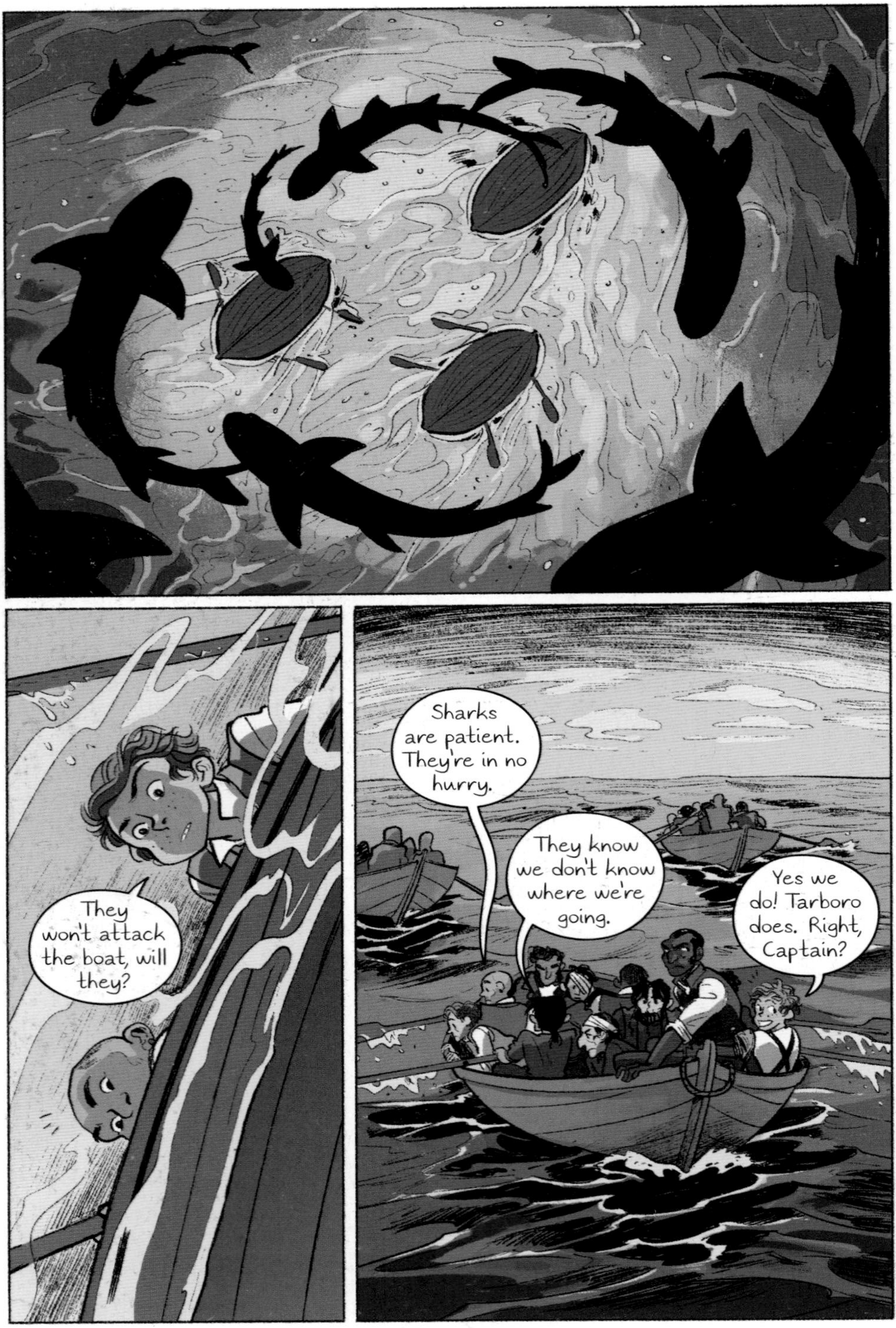
They won't attack the boat, will they?
Sharks are patient. They're in no hurry.
They know we don't know where we're going.
Yes we do! Tarboro does. Right, Captain?

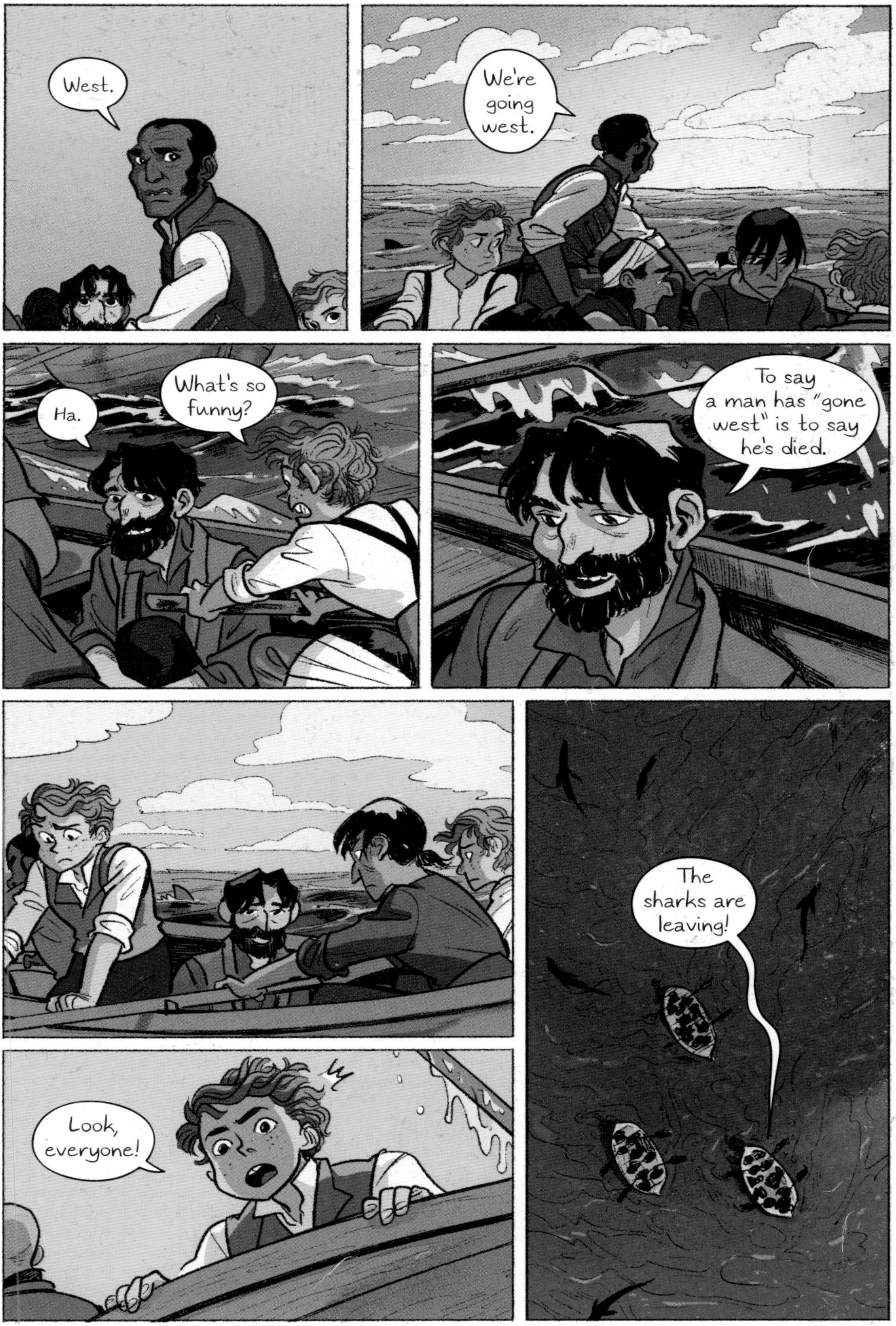
West.
We're going west.
Ha.
What's so funny?
To say a man has "gone west" is to say he's died.
Look, everyone!
The sharks are leaving!

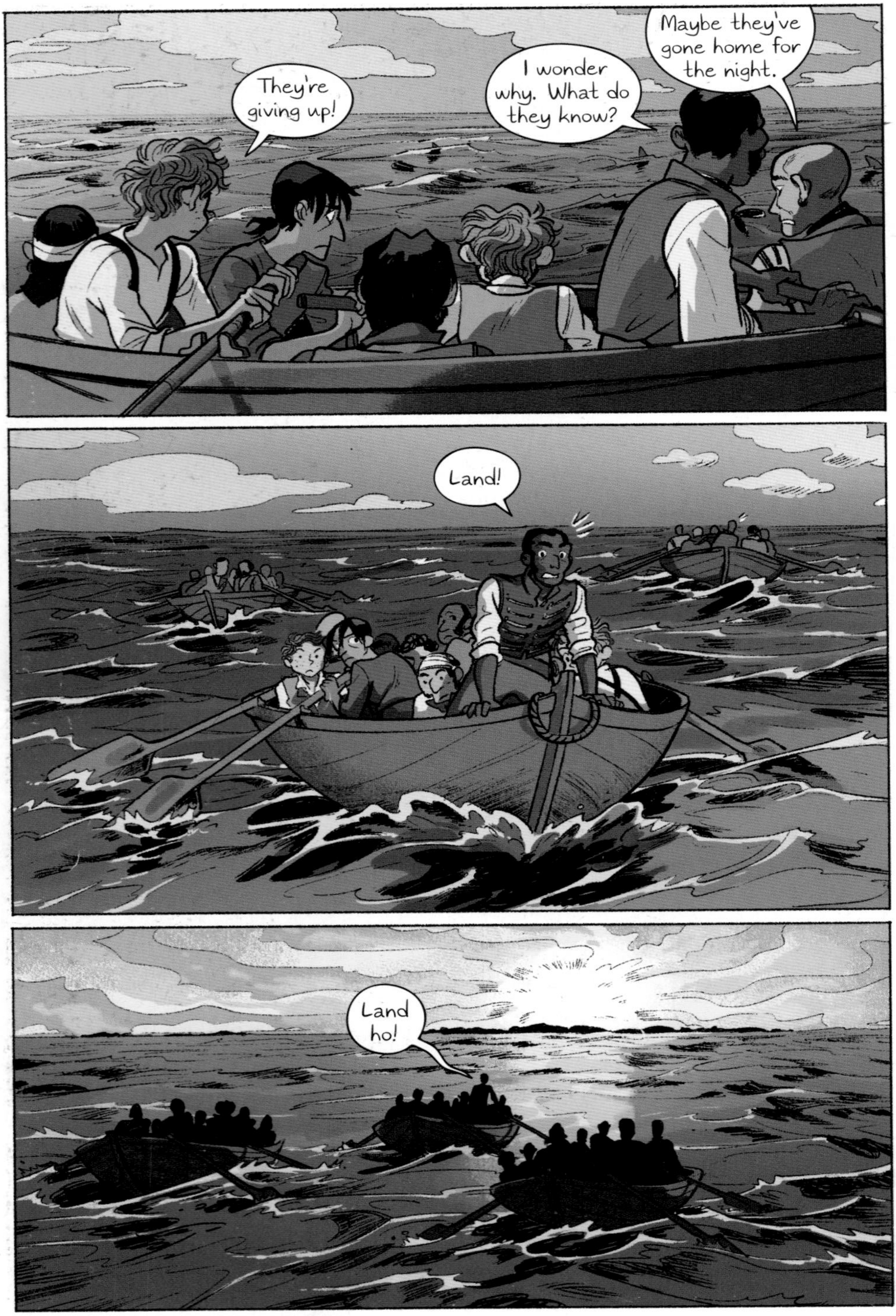
They're giving up!
I wonder why. What do they know?
Maybe they've gone home for the night.
Land!
Land ho!

We're saved!

Saved— or lost.

It depends on what we find there.

ping

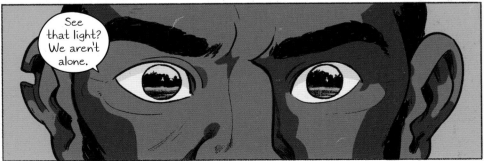

See that light? We aren't alone.

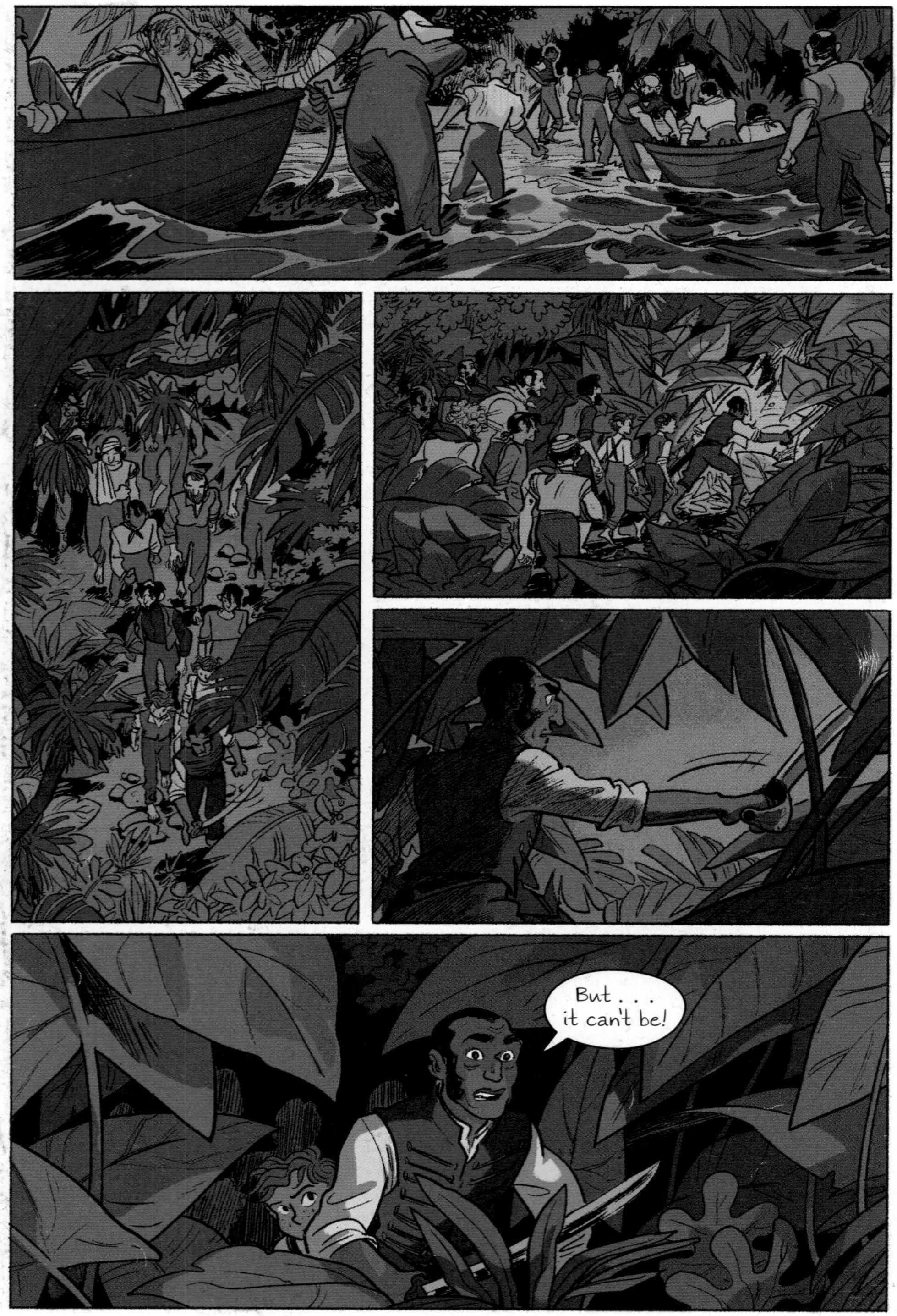
But . . .
it can't be!

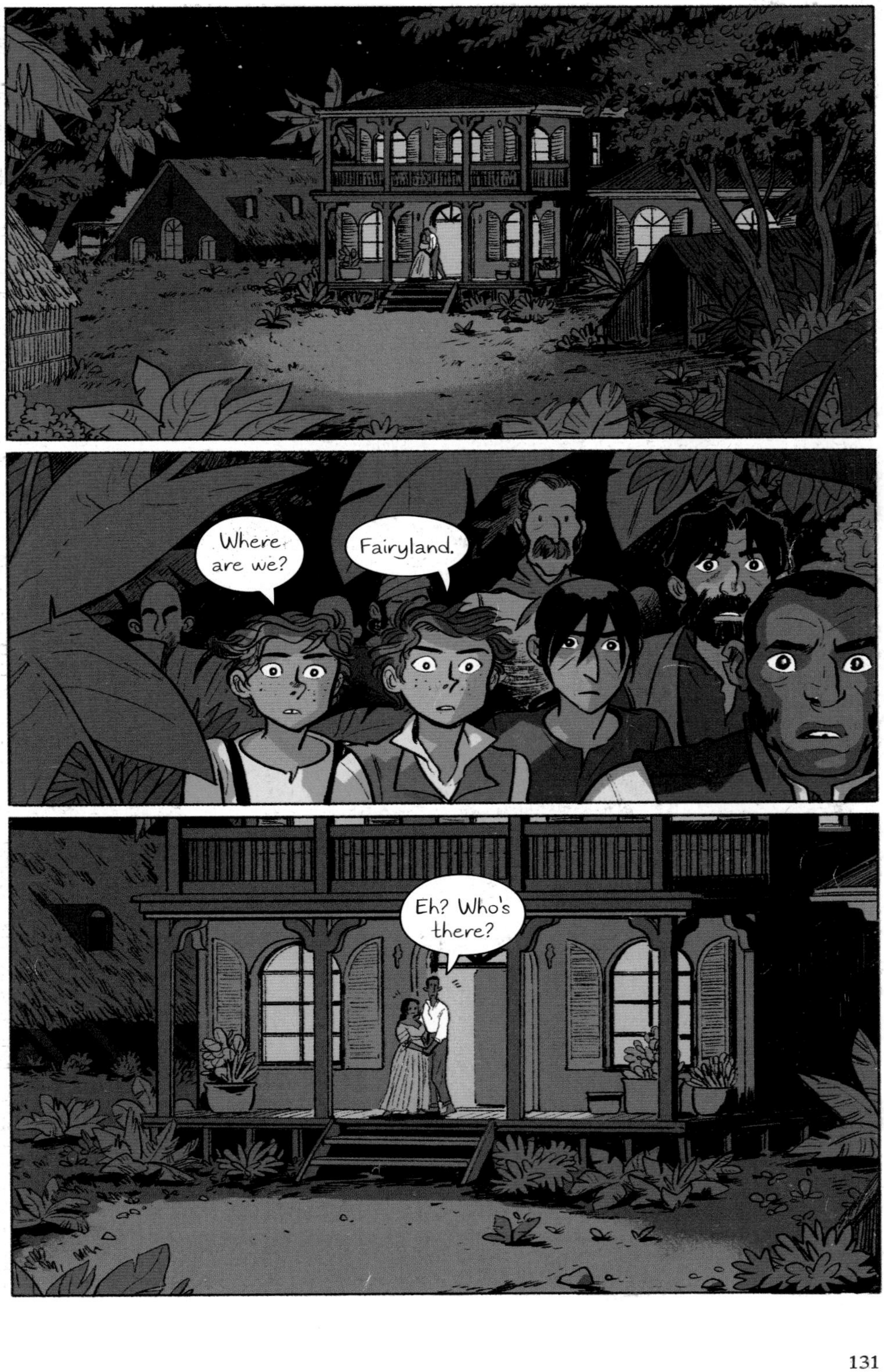
Where are we?
Fairyland.
Eh? Who's there?

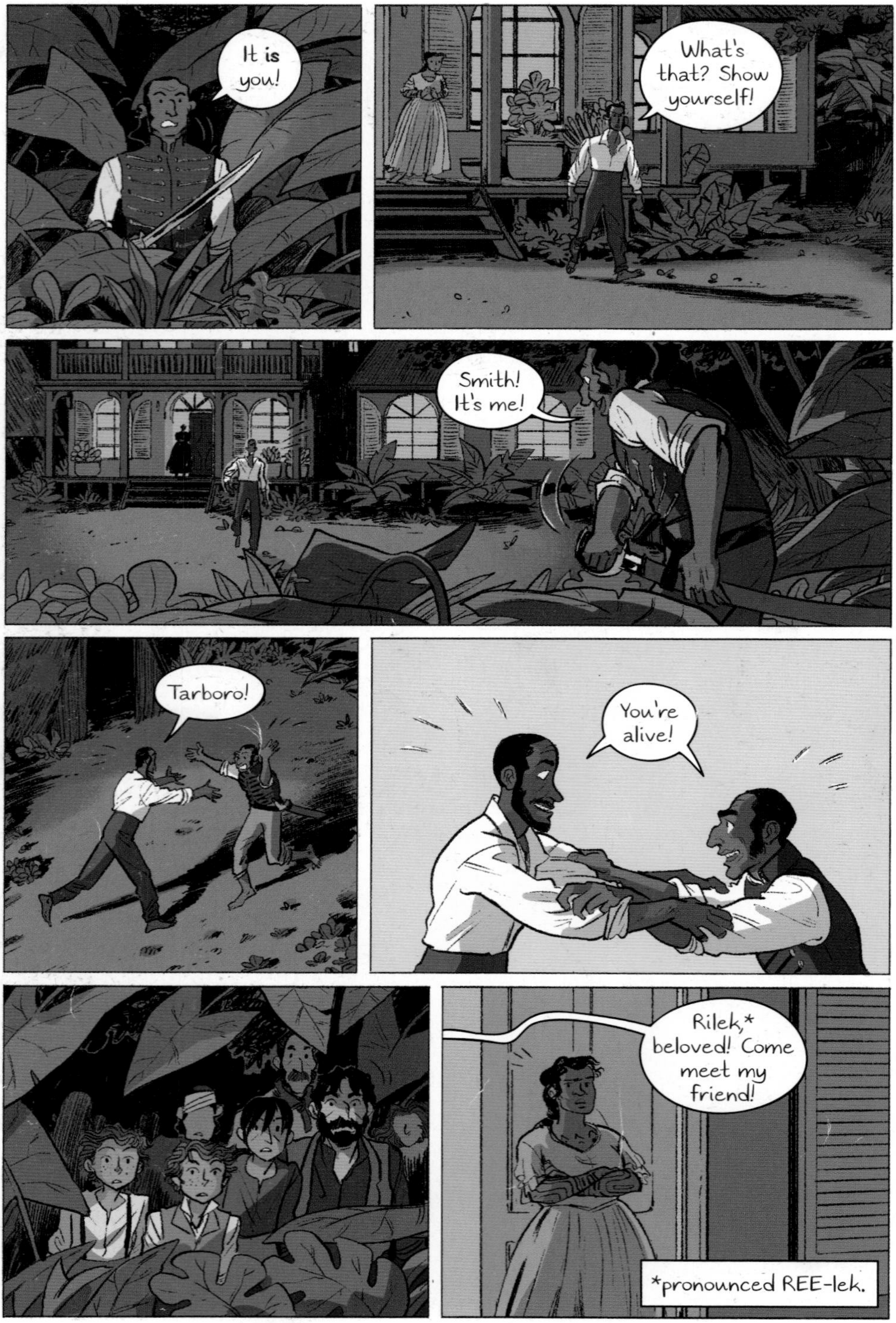
It is you!
What's that? Show yourself!
Smith! It's me!
Tarboro!
You're alive!
Rilek,* beloved! Come meet my friend!
*pronounced REE-lek.

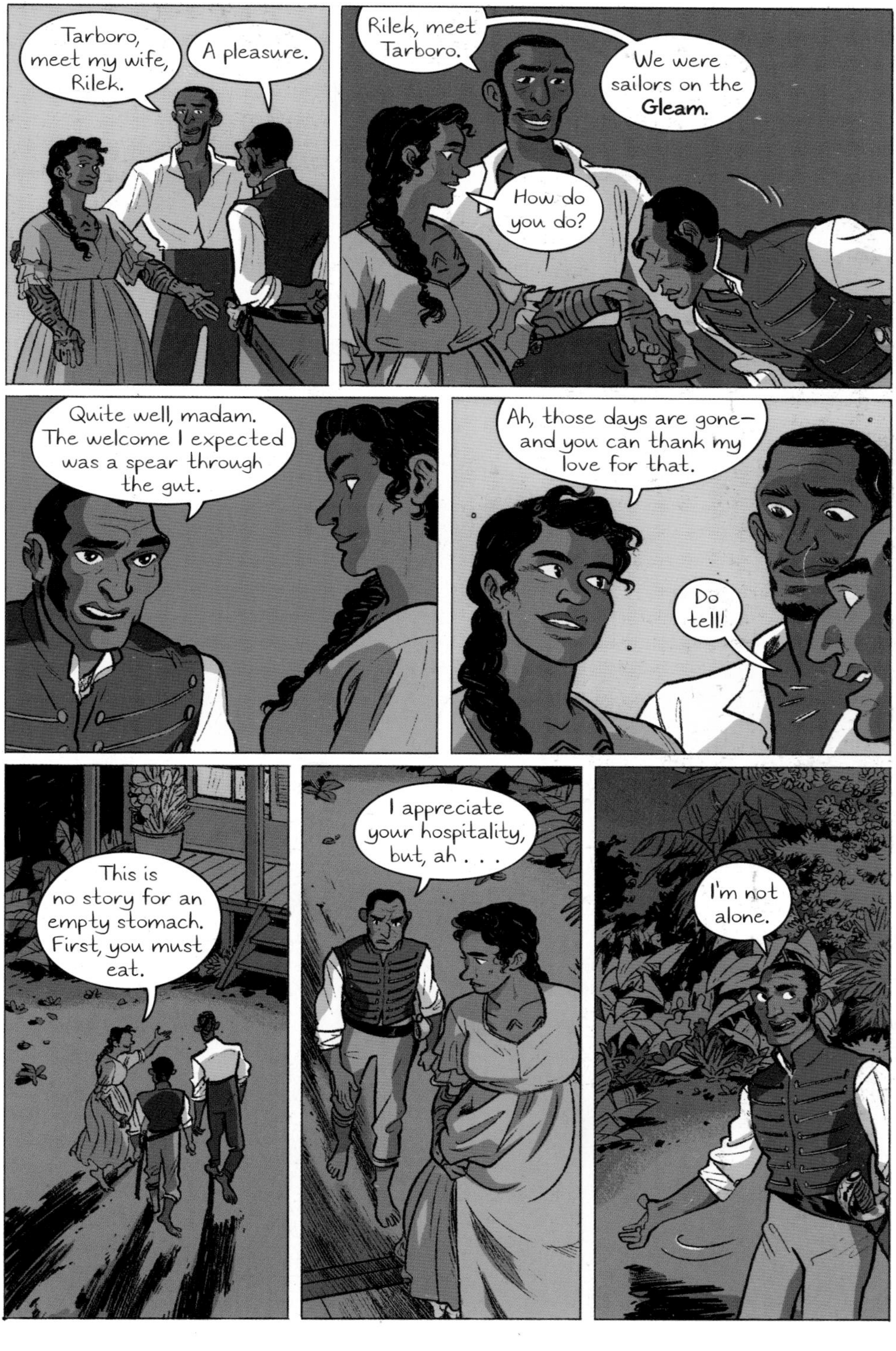
Tarboro, meet my wife, Rilek.
A pleasure.
Rilek, meet Tarboro.
We were sailors on the **Gleam**.
How do you do?
Quite well, madam. The welcome I expected was a spear through the gut.
Ah, those days are gone—and you can thank my love for that.
Do tell!
This is no story for an empty stomach. First, you must eat.
I appreciate your hospitality, but, ah . . .
I'm not alone.

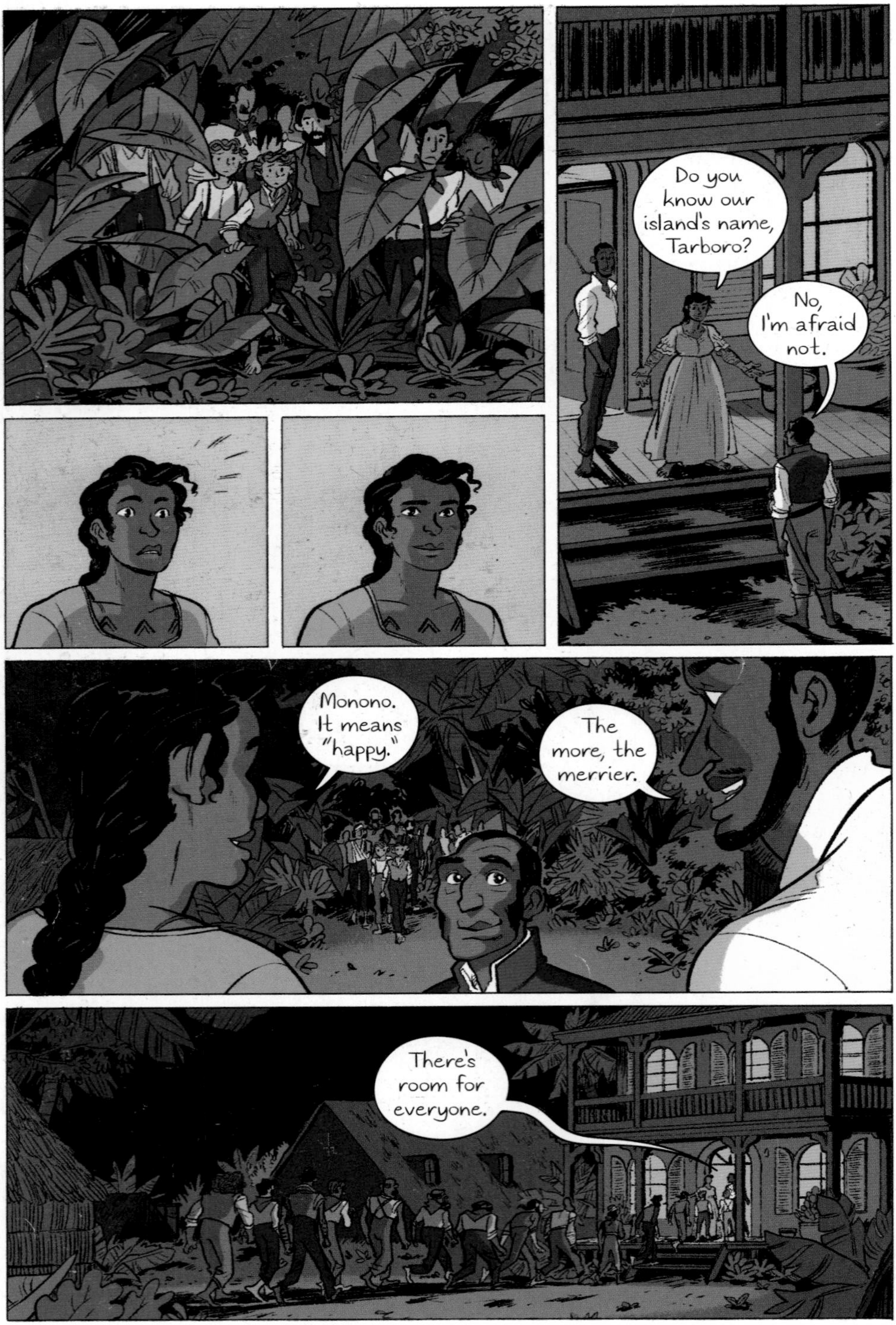

Do you know our island's name, Tarboro?
No, I'm afraid not.
Monono. It means "happy."
The more, the merrier.
There's room for everyone.

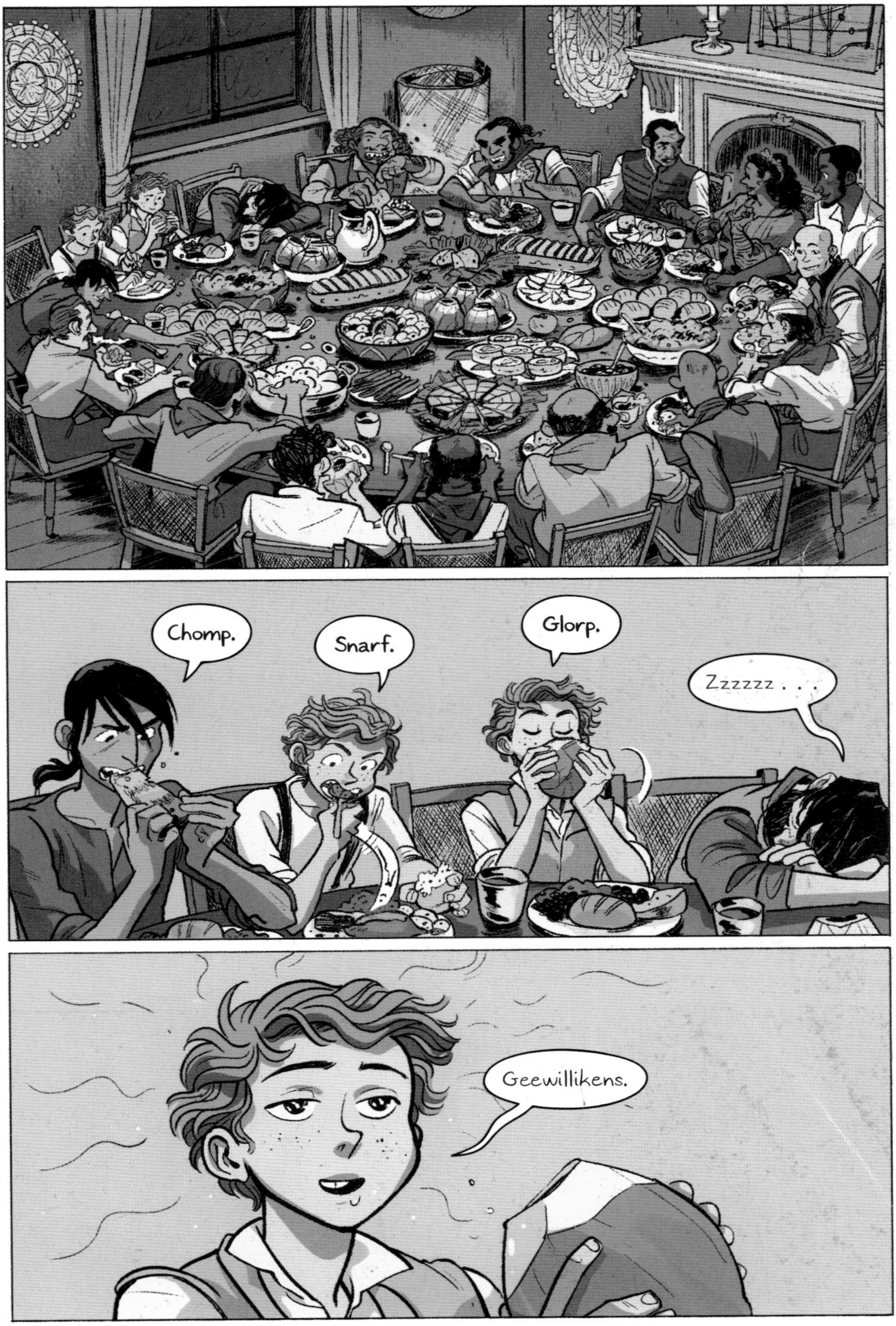
Chomp.
Snarf.
Glorp.
Zzzzzz . . .
Geewillikens.

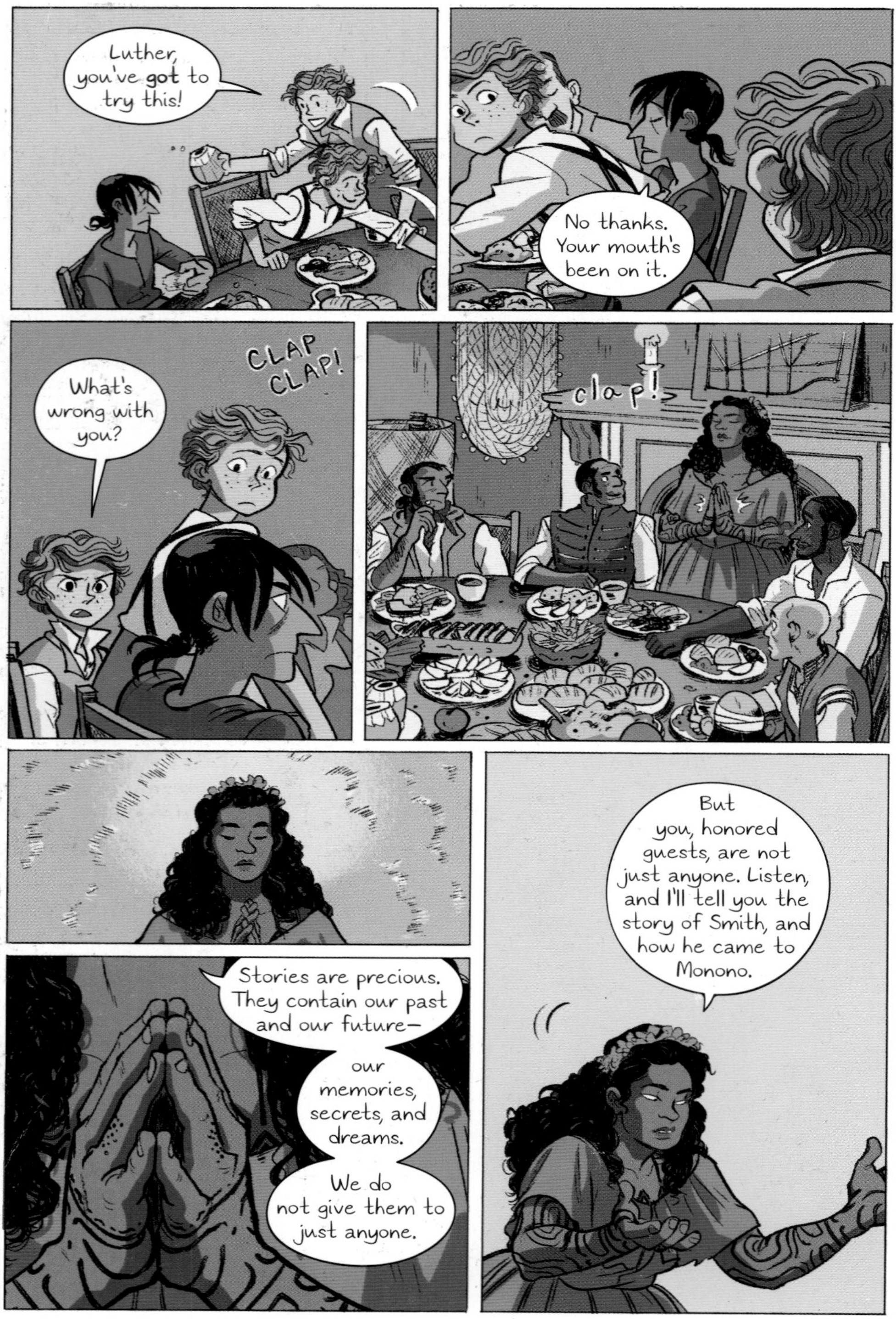
Luther, you've **got** to try this!
No thanks. Your mouth's been on it.
What's wrong with you?
CLAP CLAP!
clap!
Stories are precious. They contain our past and our future—
our memories, secrets, and dreams.
We do not give them to just anyone.
But you, honored guests, are not just anyone. Listen, and I'll tell you the story of Smith, and how he came to Monono.

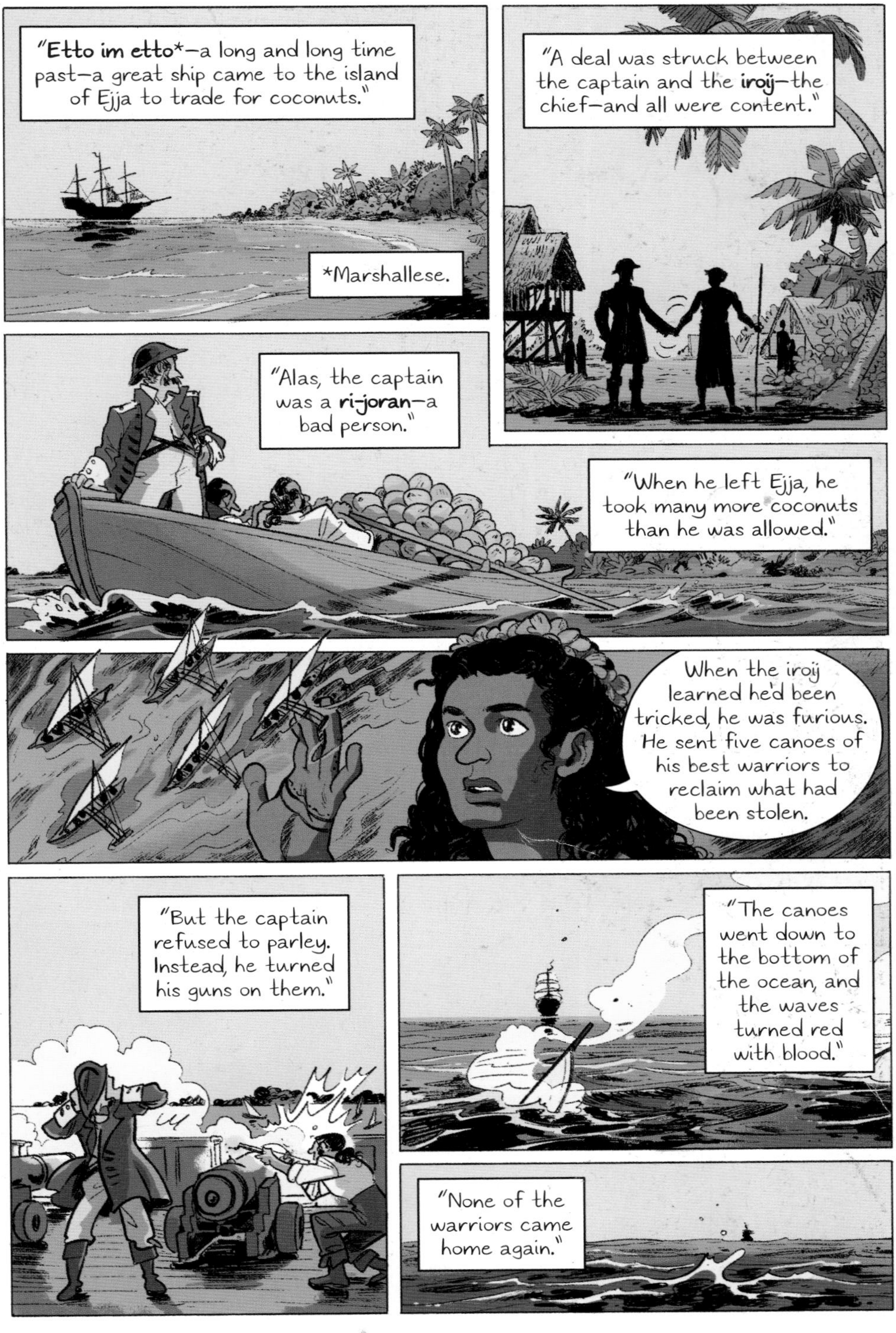
"Etto im etto*—a long and long time past—a great ship came to the island of Ejja to trade for coconuts."
*Marshallese.
"A deal was struck between the captain and the iroij—the chief—and all were content."
"Alas, the captain was a ri-joran—a bad person."
"When he left Ejja, he took many more coconuts than he was allowed."
When the iroij learned he'd been tricked, he was furious. He sent five canoes of his best warriors to reclaim what had been stolen.
"But the captain refused to parley. Instead, he turned his guns on them."
"The canoes went down to the bottom of the ocean, and the waves turned red with blood."
"None of the warriors came home again."

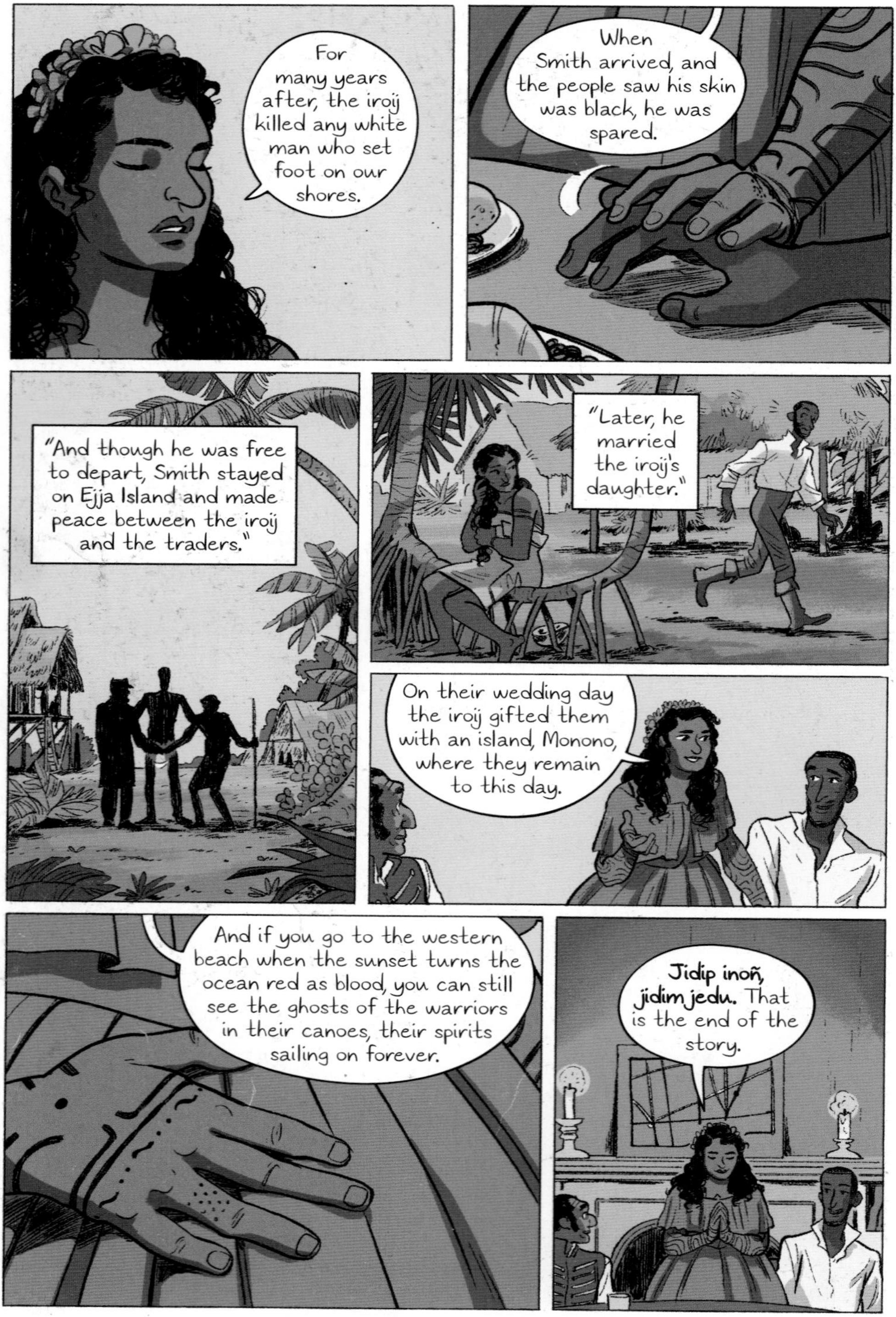
For many years after, the iroij killed any white man who set foot on our shores.
When Smith arrived, and the people saw his skin was black, he was spared.
"And though he was free to depart, Smith stayed on Ejja Island and made peace between the iroij and the traders."
"Later, he married the iroij's daughter."
On their wedding day the iroij gifted them with an island, Monono, where they remain to this day.
And if you go to the western beach when the sunset turns the ocean red as blood, you can still see the ghosts of the warriors in their canoes, their spirits sailing on forever.
Jidip inoñ, jidim jedu. That is the end of the story.

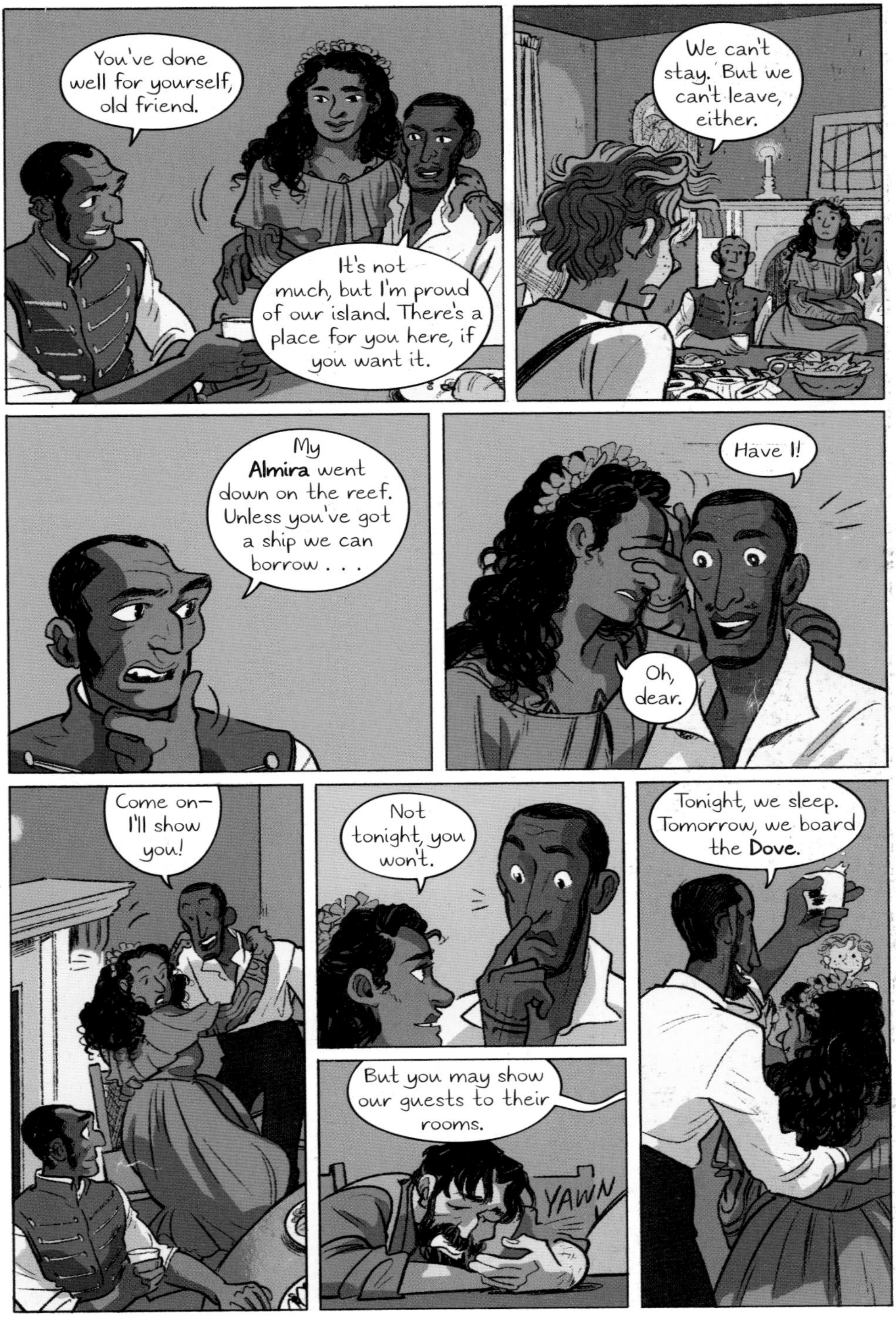
You've done well for yourself, old friend.
It's not much, but I'm proud of our island. There's a place for you here, if you want it.
We can't stay. But we can't leave, either.
My **Almira** went down on the reef. Unless you've got a ship we can borrow . . .
Have I!
Oh, dear.
Come on— I'll show you!
Not tonight, you won't.
But you may show our guests to their rooms.
YAWN
Tonight, we sleep. Tomorrow, we board the **Dove.**

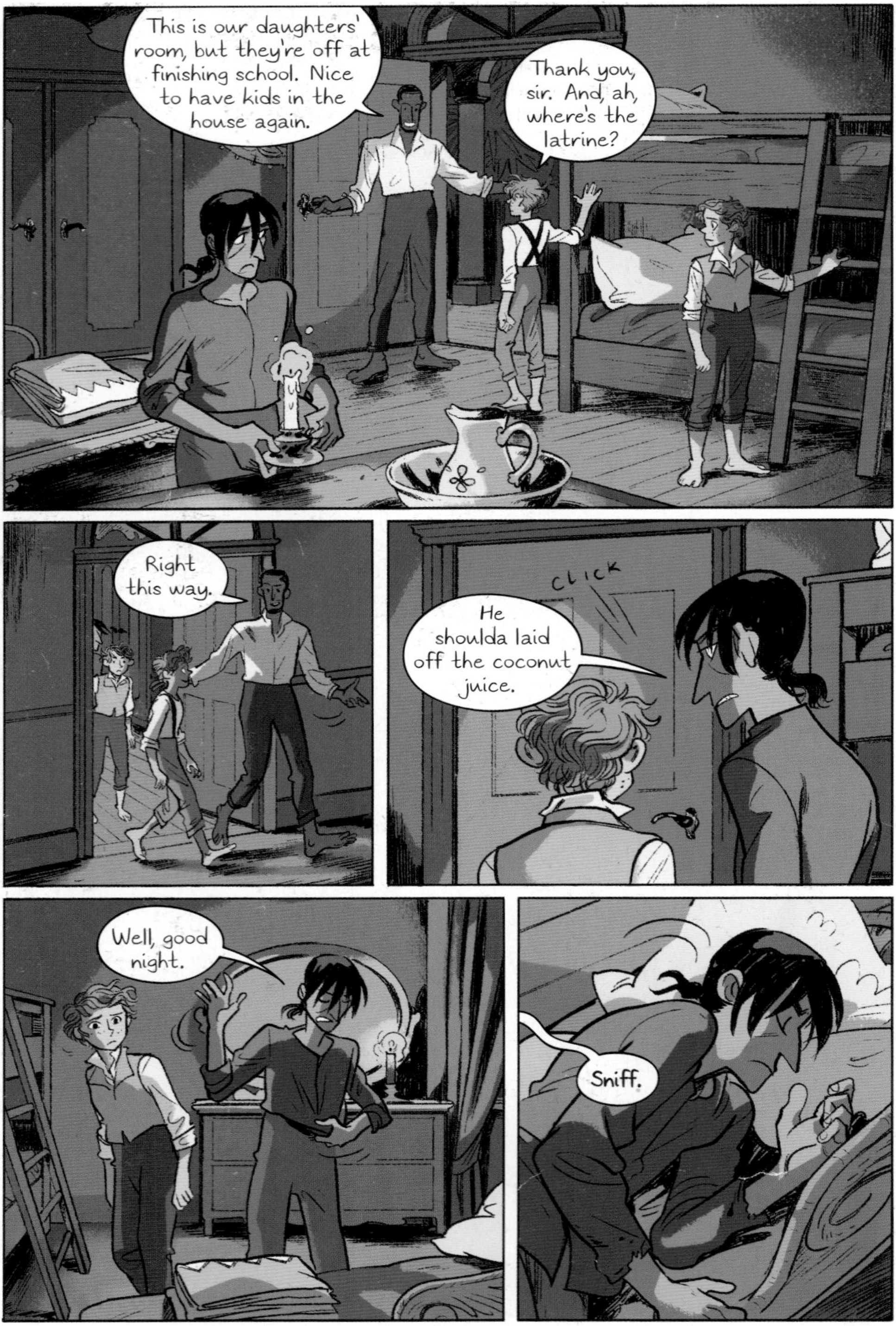
This is our daughters' room, but they're off at finishing school. Nice to have kids in the house again.
Thank you, sir. And, ah, where's the latrine?
Right this way.
CLICK
He shoulda laid off the coconut juice.
Well, good night.
Sniff.

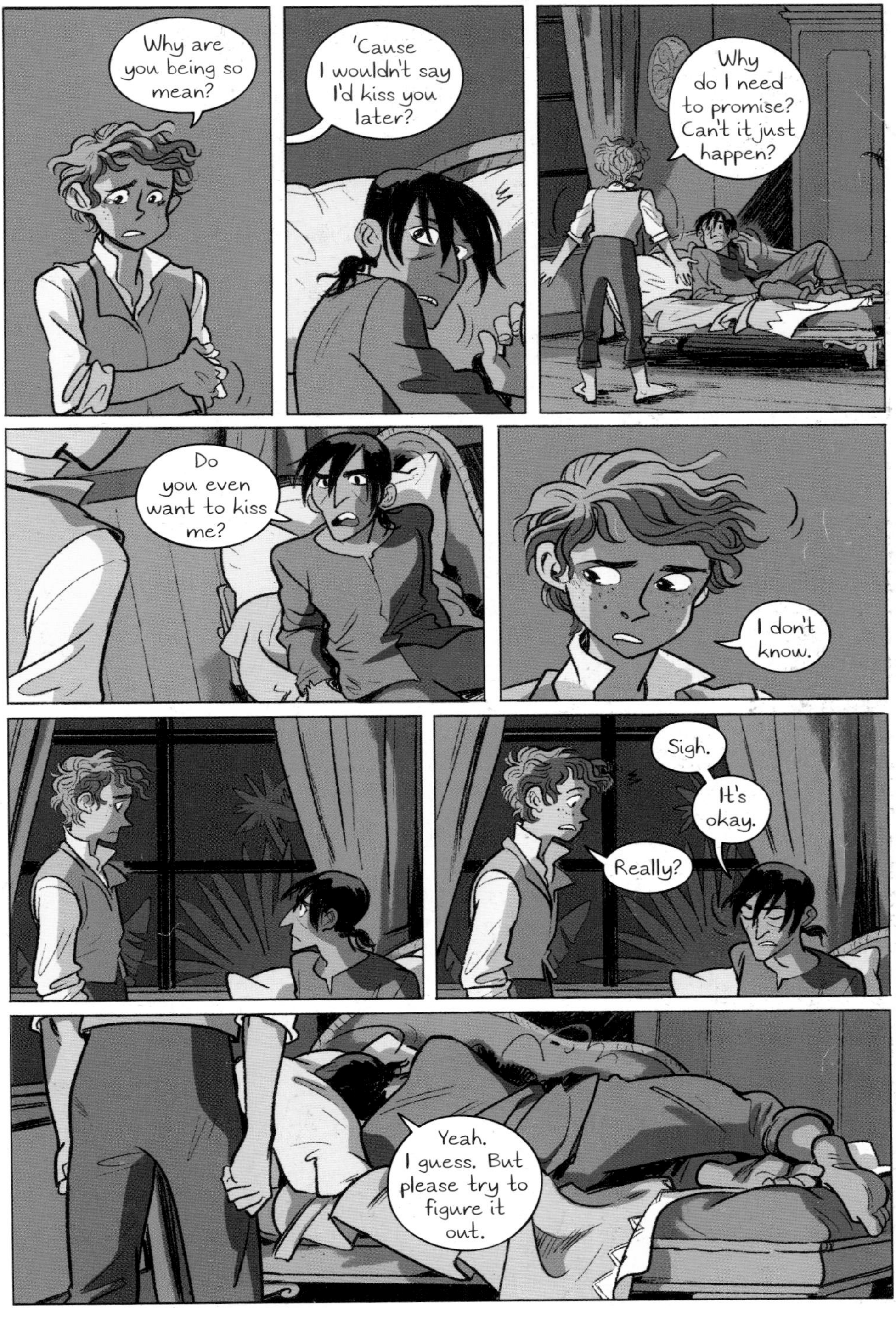
Why are you being so mean?
'Cause I wouldn't say I'd kiss you later?
Why do I need to promise? Can't it just happen?
Do you even want to kiss me?
I don't know.
Sigh.
It's okay.
Really?
Yeah. I guess. But please try to figure it out.

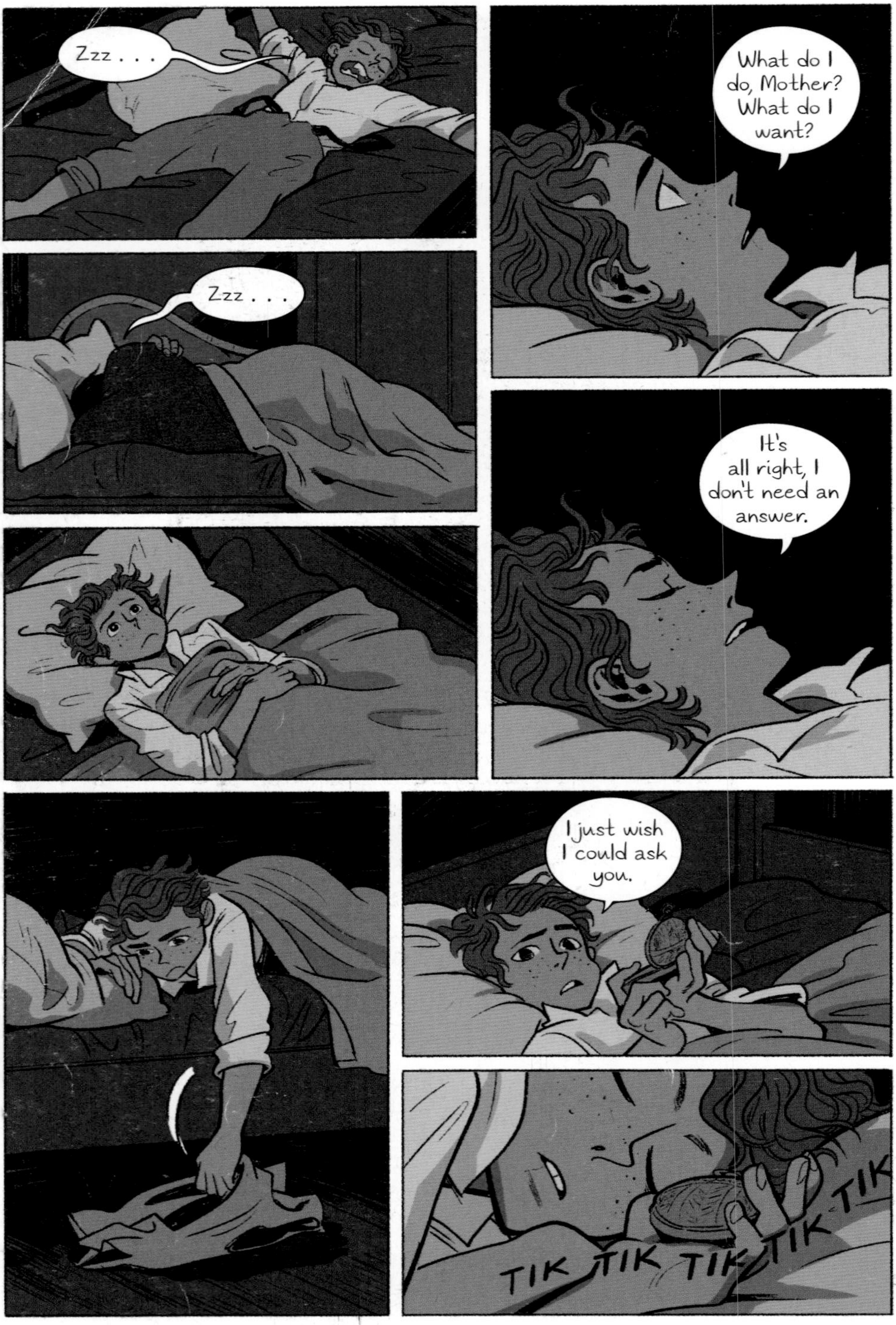
Zzz . . .
What do I do, Mother? What do I want?
Zzz . . .
It's all right, I don't need an answer.
I just wish I could ask you.
TIK TIK TIK TIK TIK

CHAPTER EIGHT
TRUCE

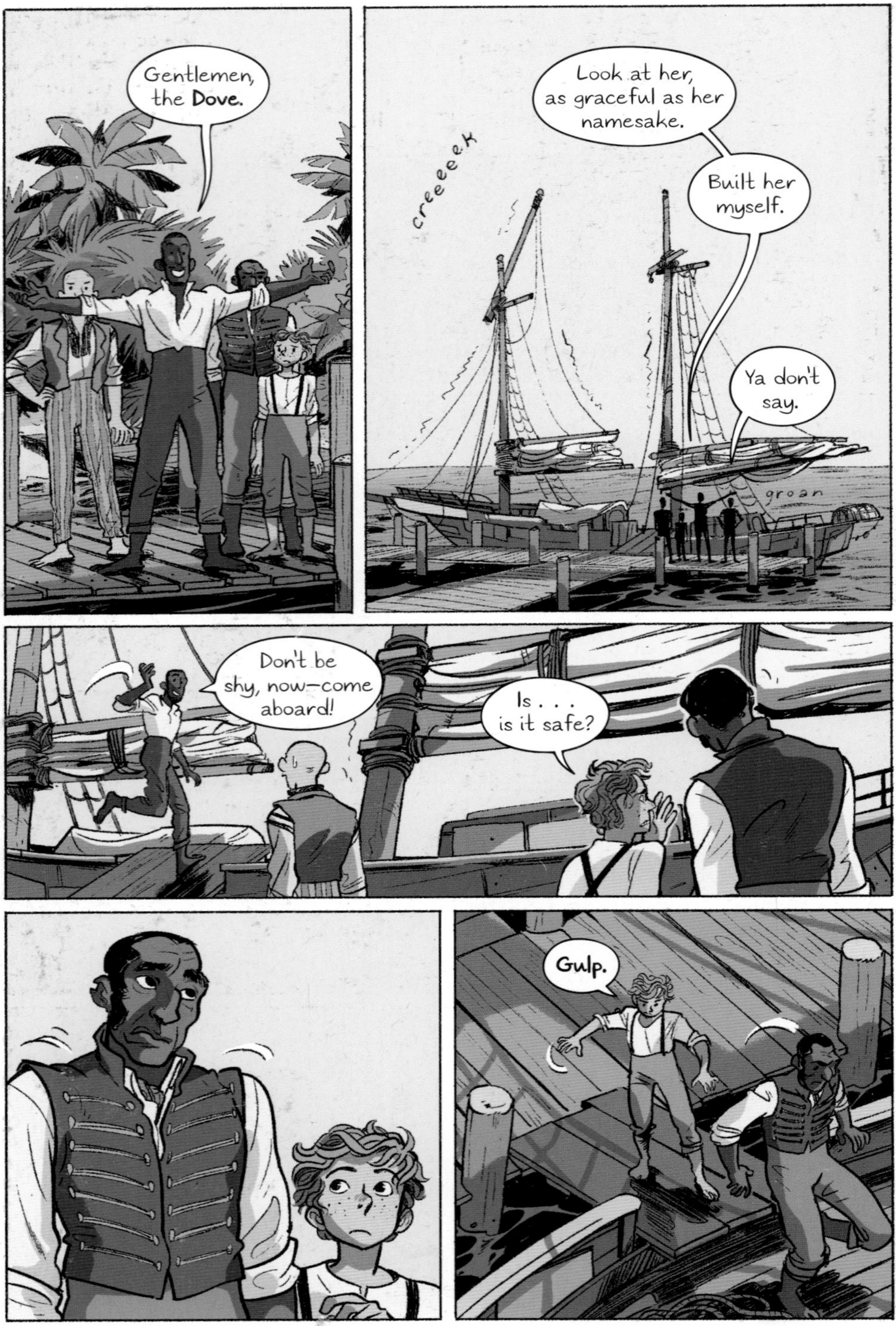
Gentlemen, the **Dove.**
Look at her, as graceful as her namesake.
creeeeek
Built her myself.
Ya don't say.
groan
Don't be shy, now—come aboard!
Is . . . is it safe?
Gulp.

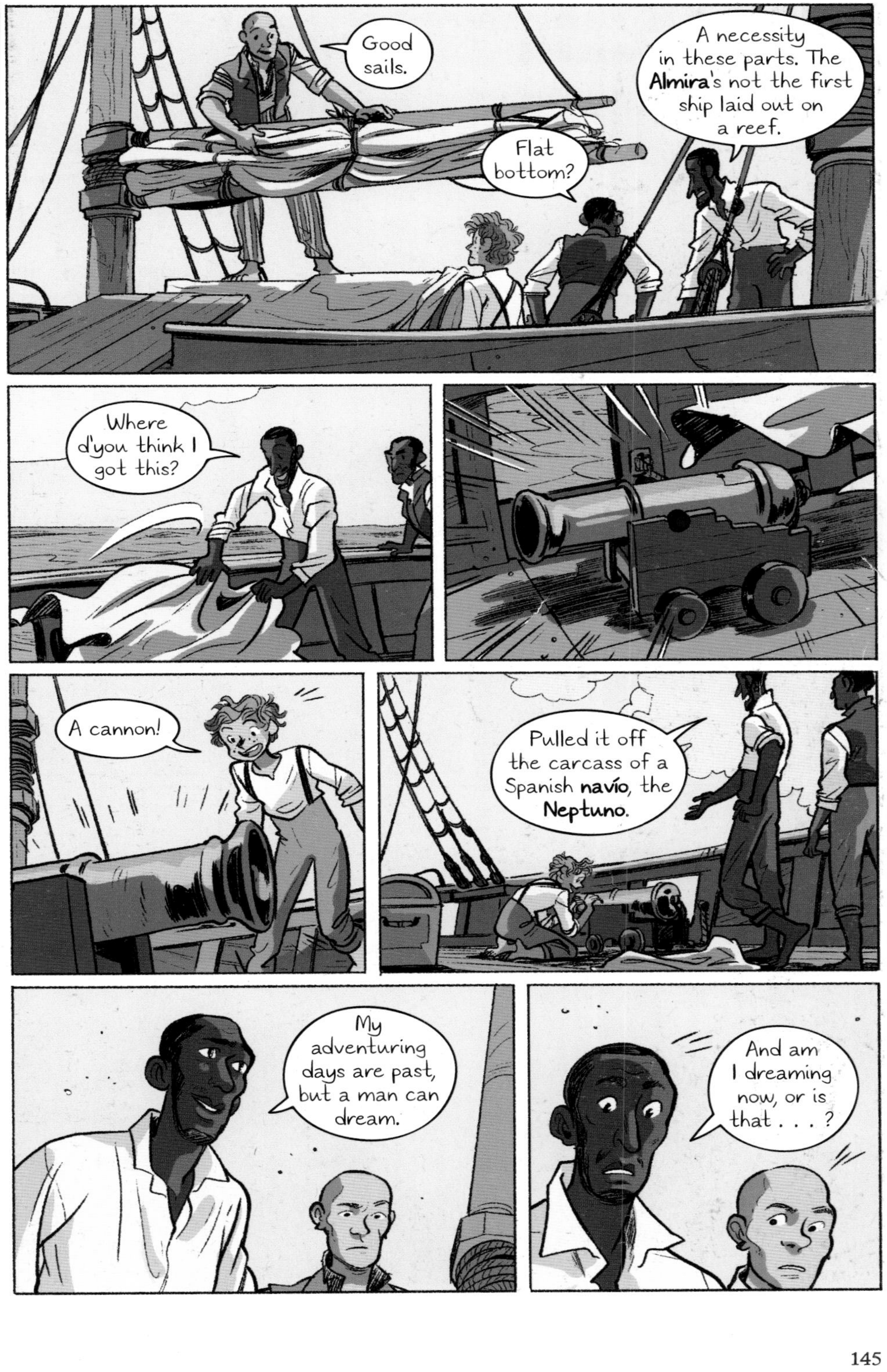
Good sails.
A necessity in these parts. The Almira's not the first ship laid out on a reef.
Flat bottom?
Where d'you think I got this?
A cannon!
Pulled it off the carcass of a Spanish navío, the Neptuno.
My adventuring days are past, but a man can dream.
And am I dreaming now, or is that . . . ?

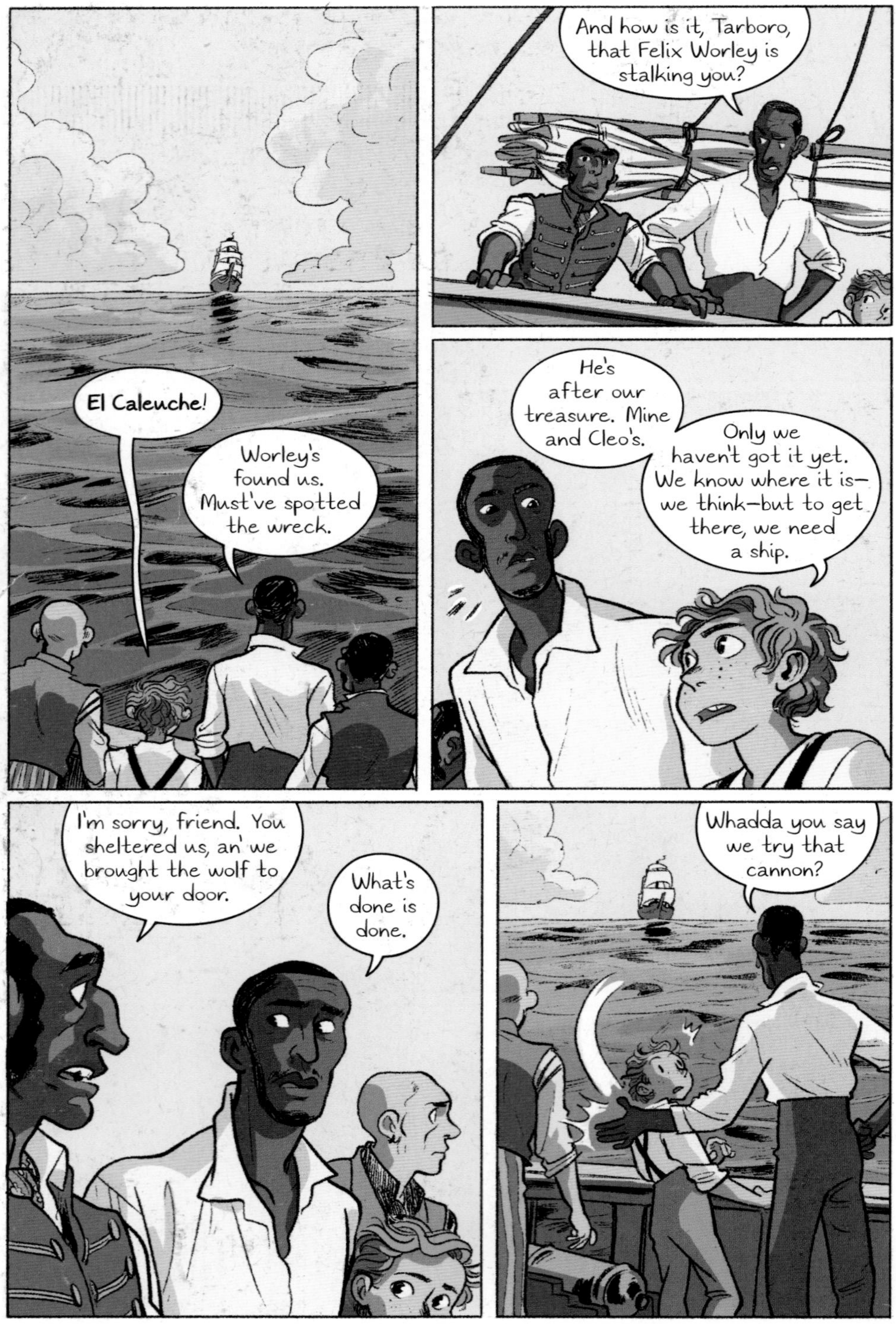
And how is it, Tarboro, that Felix Worley is stalking you?
El Caleuche!
Worley's found us. Must've spotted the wreck.
He's after our treasure. Mine and Cleo's.
Only we haven't got it yet. We know where it is—we think—but to get there, we need a ship.
I'm sorry, friend. You sheltered us, an' we brought the wolf to your door.
What's done is done.
Whadda you say we try that cannon?

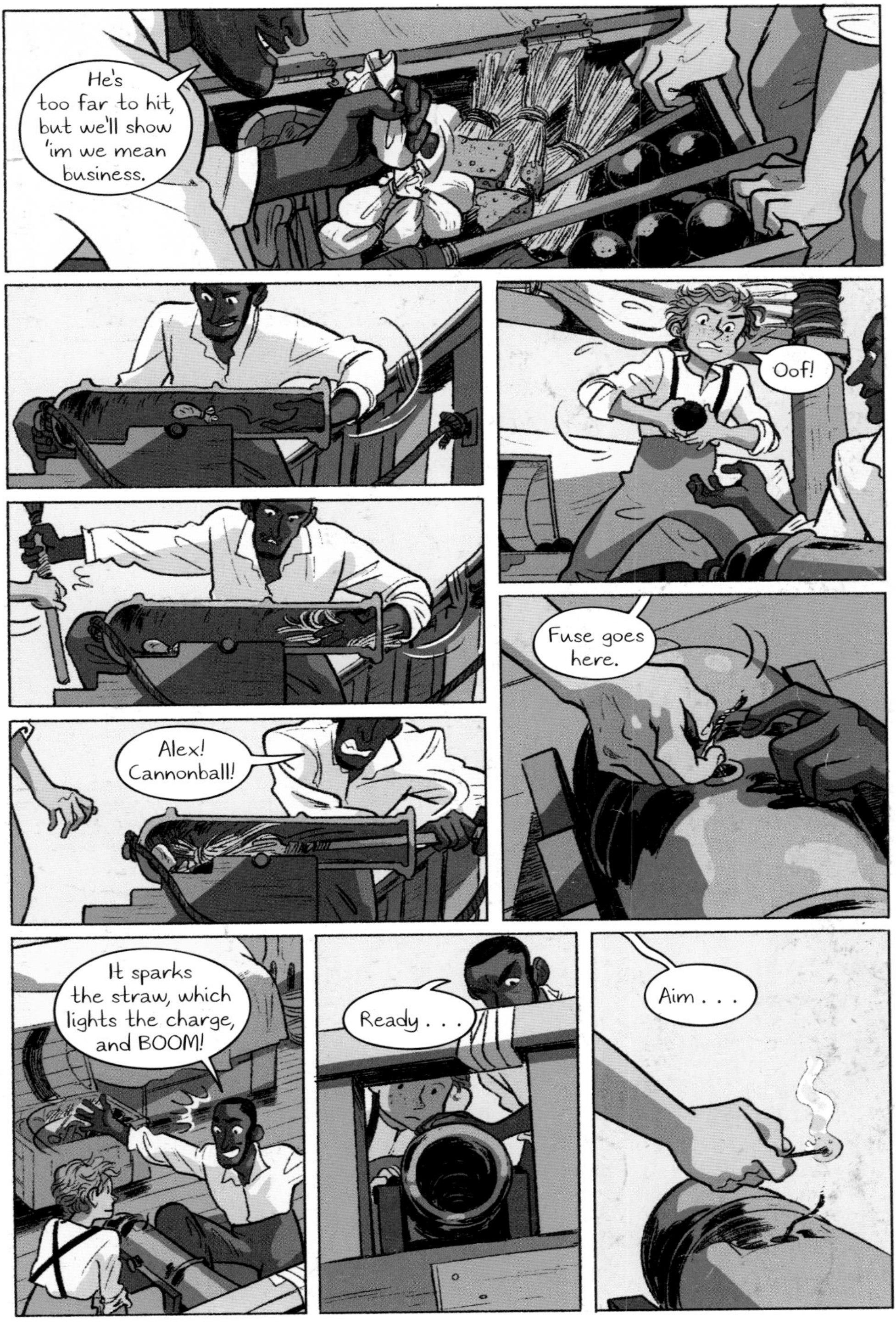
He's too far to hit, but we'll show 'im we mean business.
Oof!
Fuse goes here.
Alex! Cannonball!
It sparks the straw, which lights the charge, and BOOM!
Ready . . .
Aim . . .

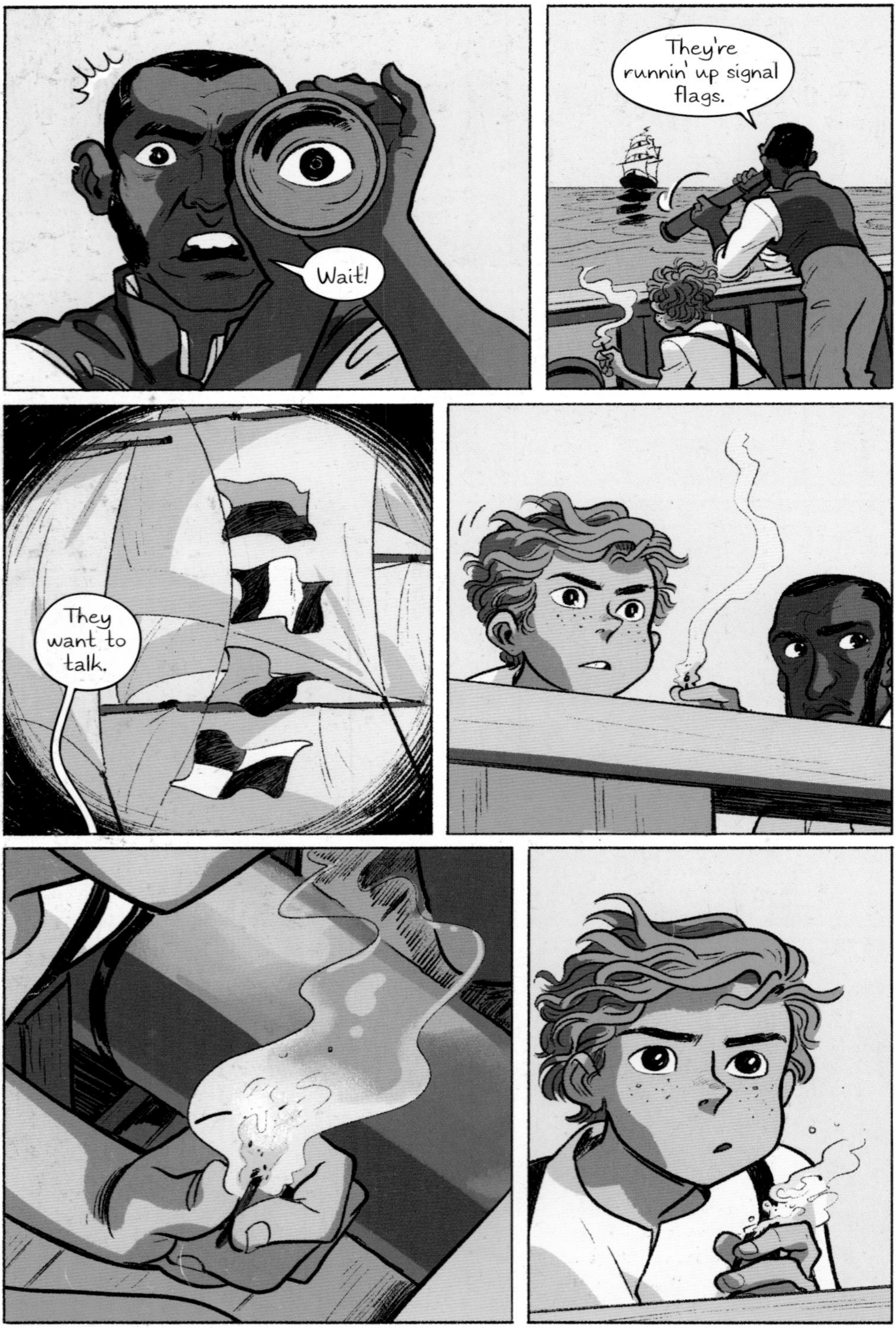
Wait!
They're runnin' up signal flags.
They want to talk.

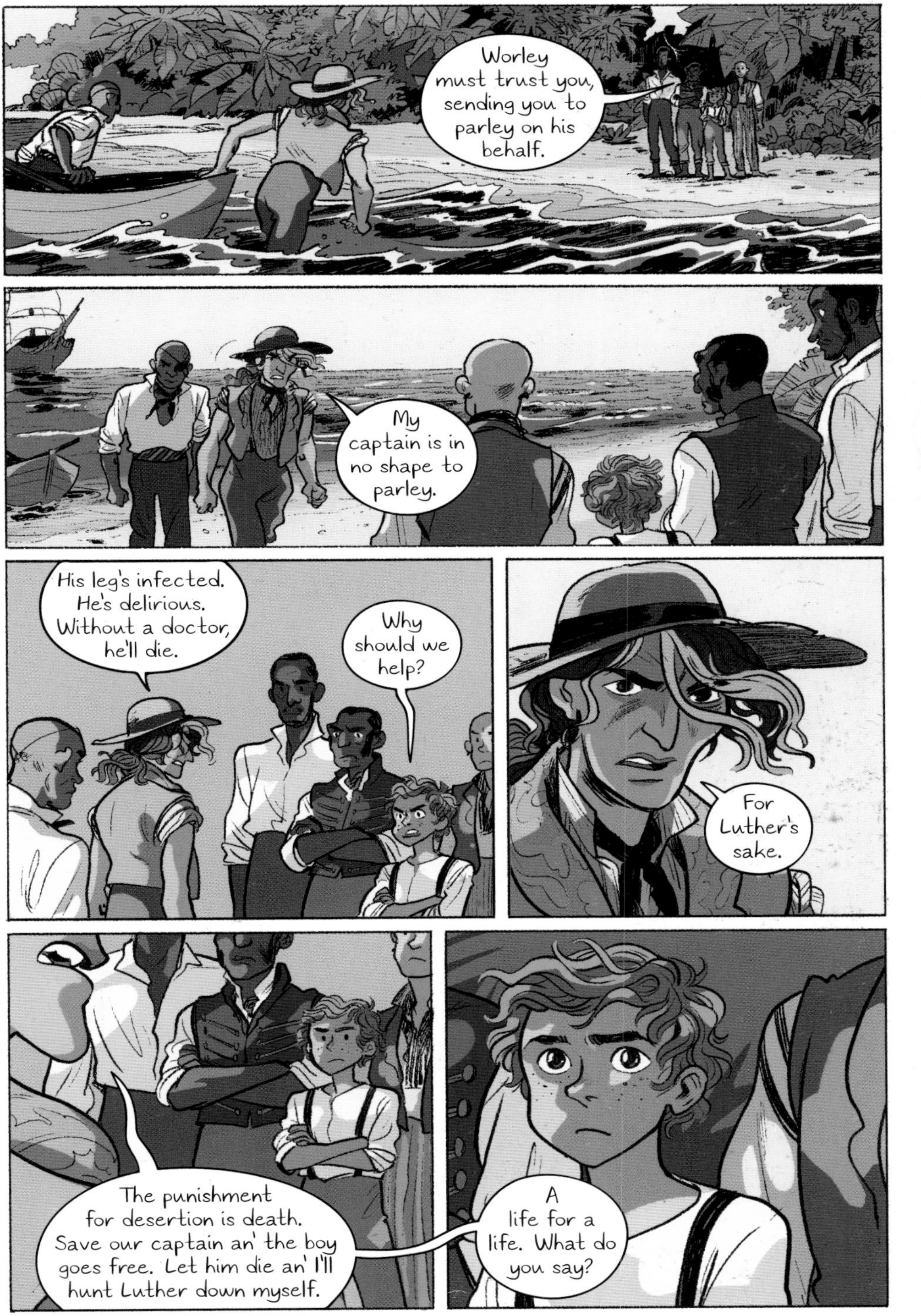
Worley must trust you, sending you to parley on his behalf.
My captain is in no shape to parley.
His leg's infected. He's delirious. Without a doctor, he'll die.
Why should we help?
For Luther's sake.
The punishment for desertion is death. Save our captain an' the boy goes free. Let him die an' I'll hunt Luther down myself.
A life for a life. What do you say?

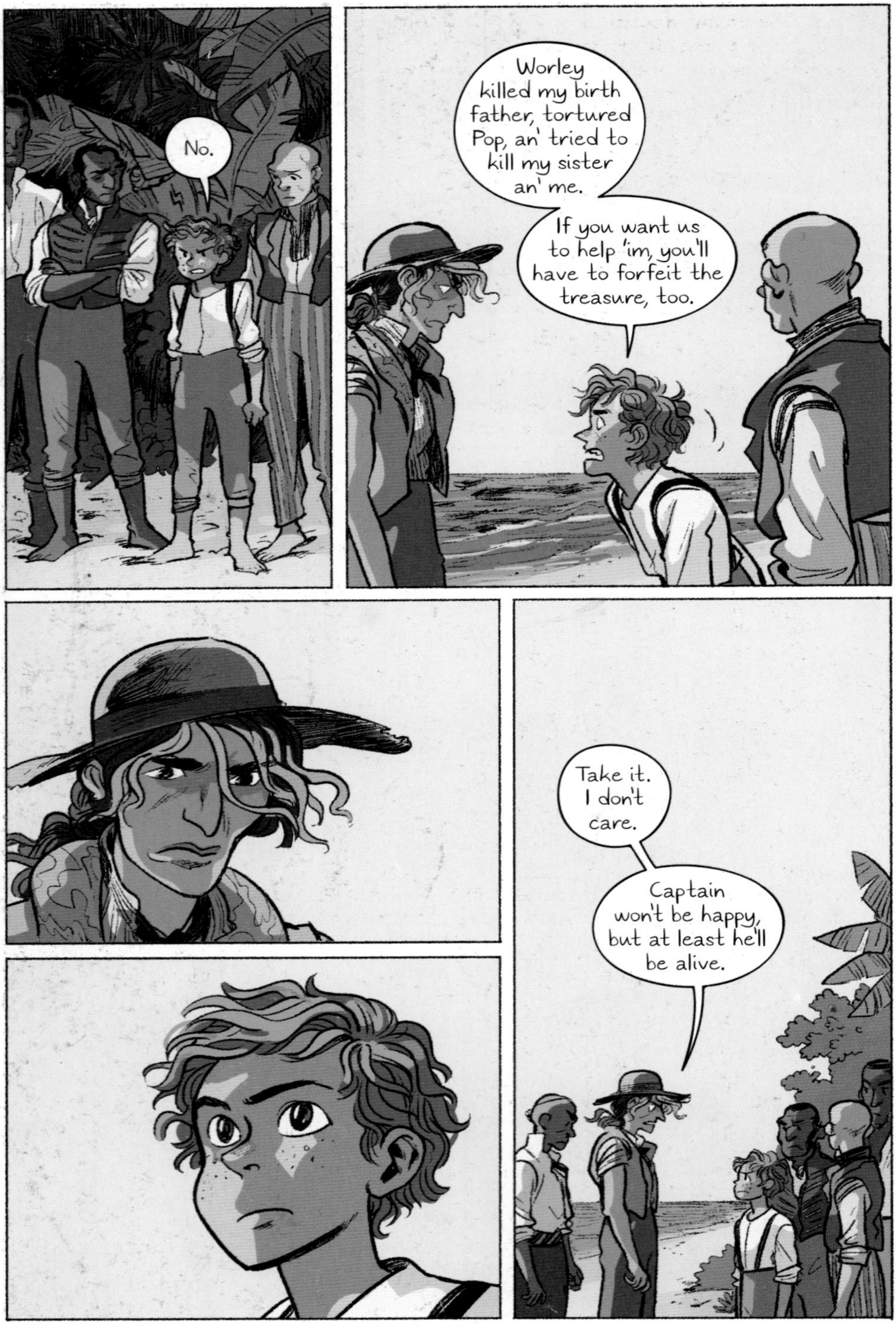
No.
Worley killed my birth father, tortured Pop, an' tried to kill my sister an' me.
If you want us to help 'im, you'll have to forfeit the treasure, too.
Take it. I don't care.
Captain won't be happy, but at least he'll be alive.

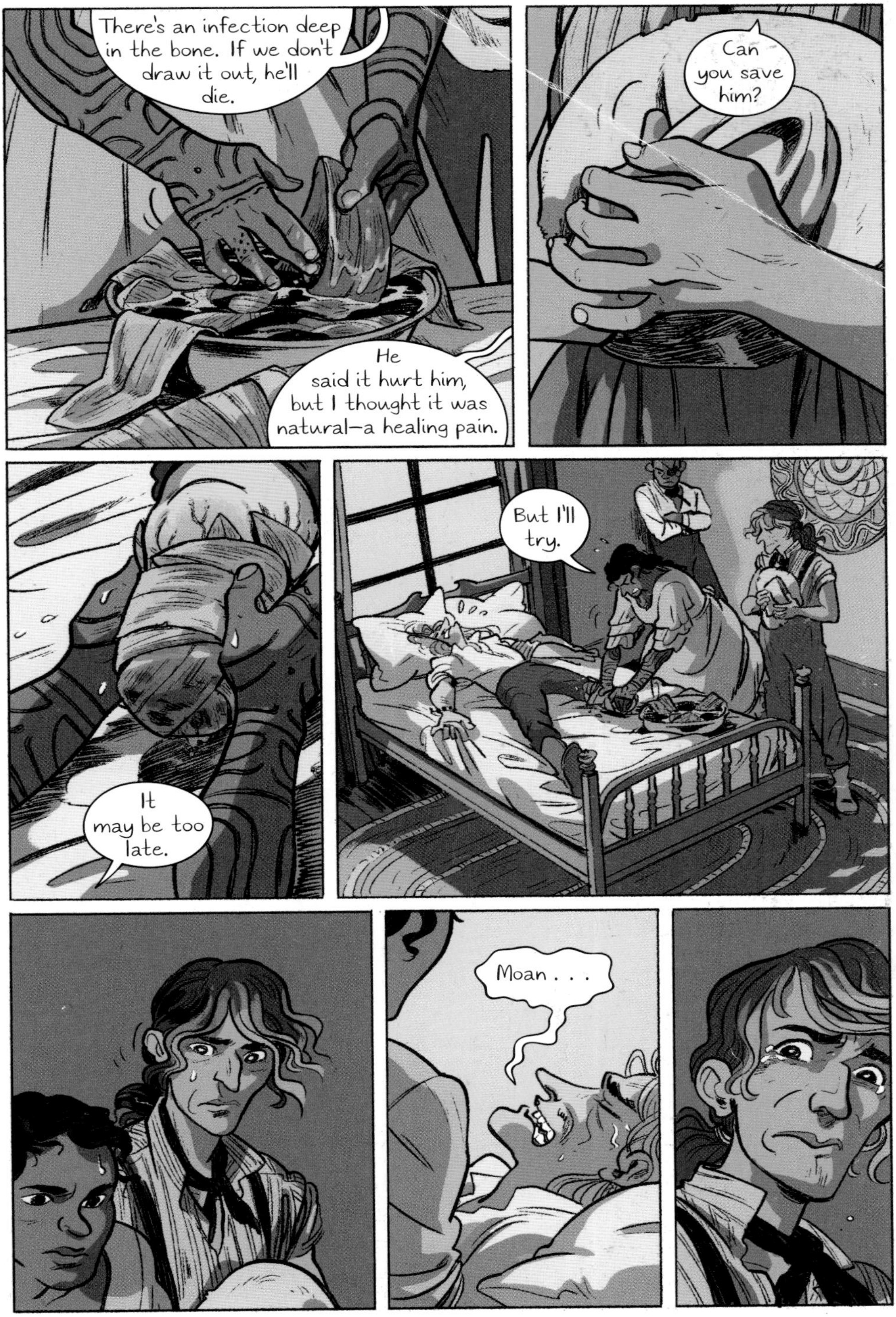
There's an infection deep in the bone. If we don't draw it out, he'll die.
Can you save him?
He said it hurt him, but I thought it was natural—a healing pain.
It may be too late.
But I'll try.
Moan . . .

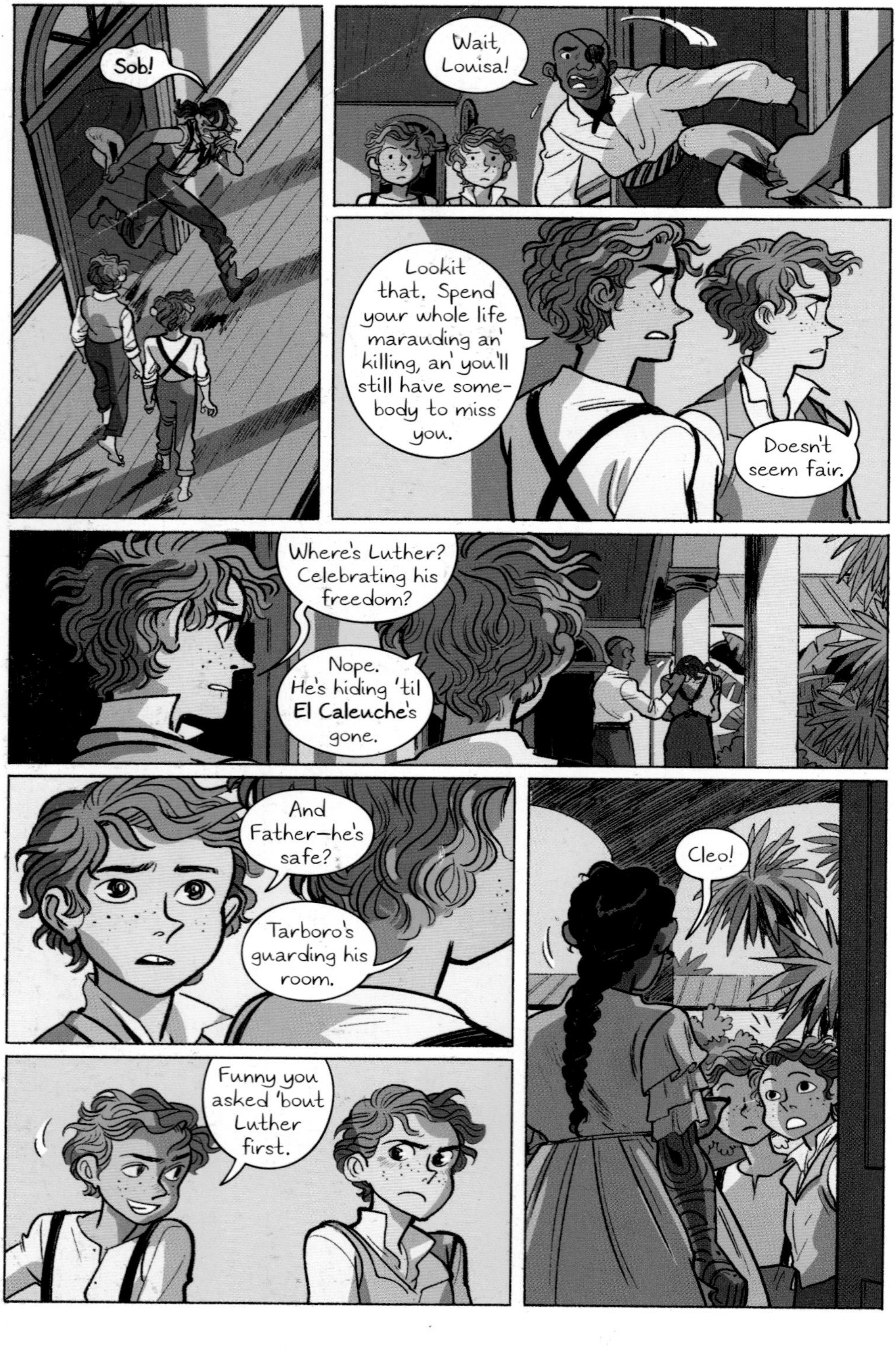
Sob!
Wait, Louisa!
Lookit that. Spend your whole life marauding an' killing, an' you'll still have some-body to miss you.
Doesn't seem fair.
Where's Luther? Celebrating his freedom?
Nope. He's hiding 'til El Caleuche's gone.
And Father—he's safe?
Tarboro's guarding his room.
Funny you asked 'bout Luther first.
Cleo!

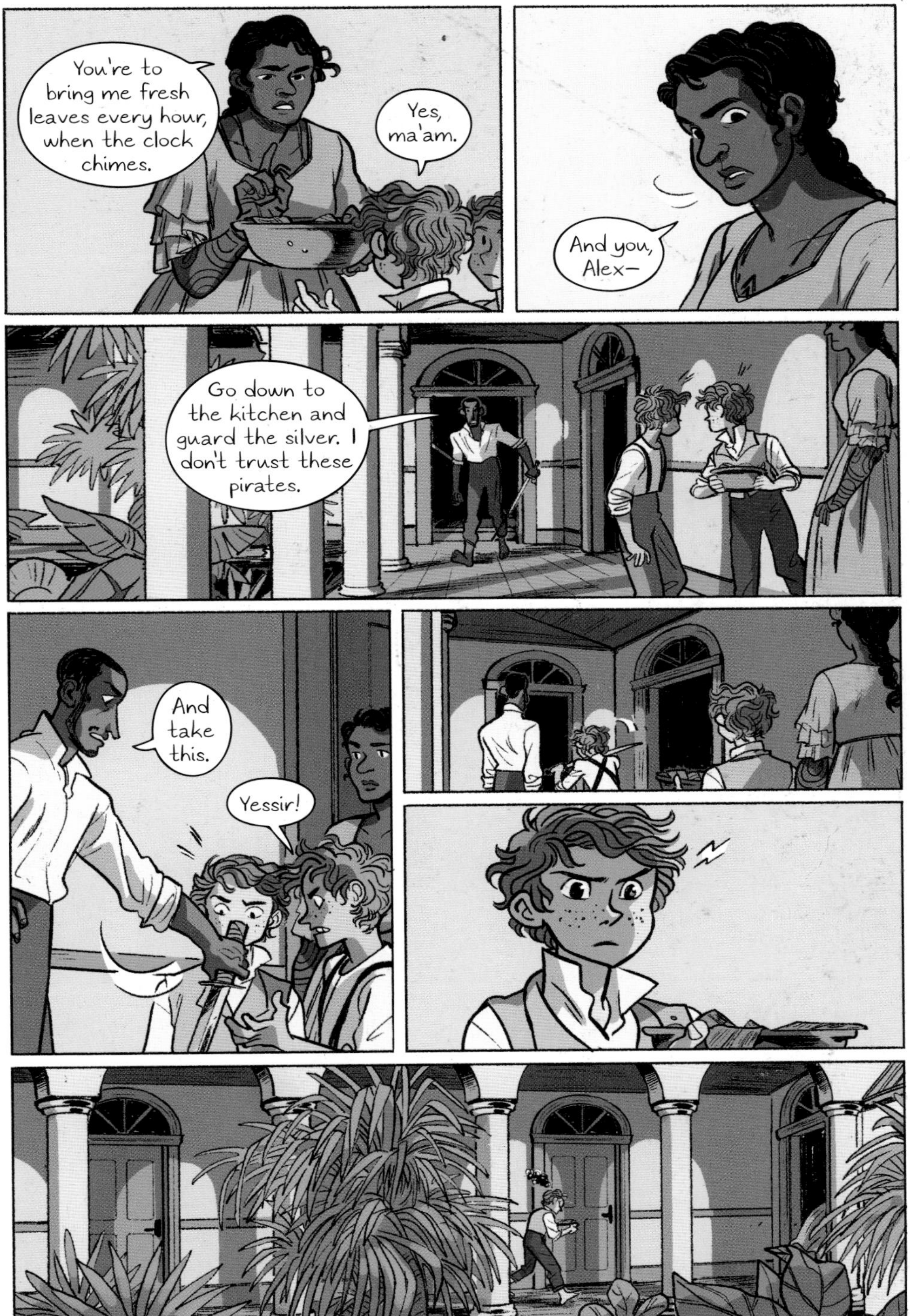
You're to bring me fresh leaves every hour, when the clock chimes.
Yes, ma'am.
And you, Alex—
Go down to the kitchen and guard the silver. I don't trust these pirates.
And take this.
Yessir!

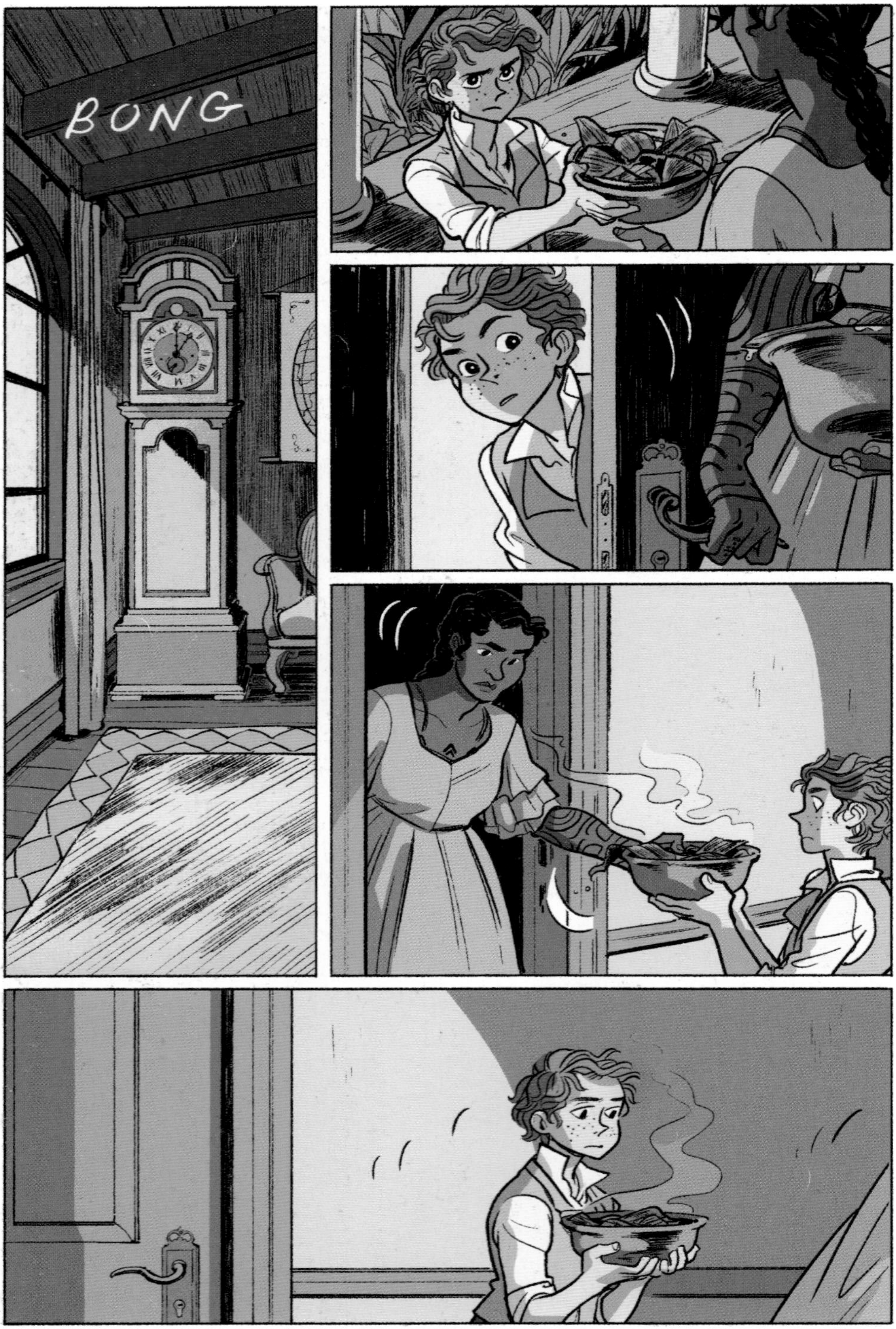
BONG

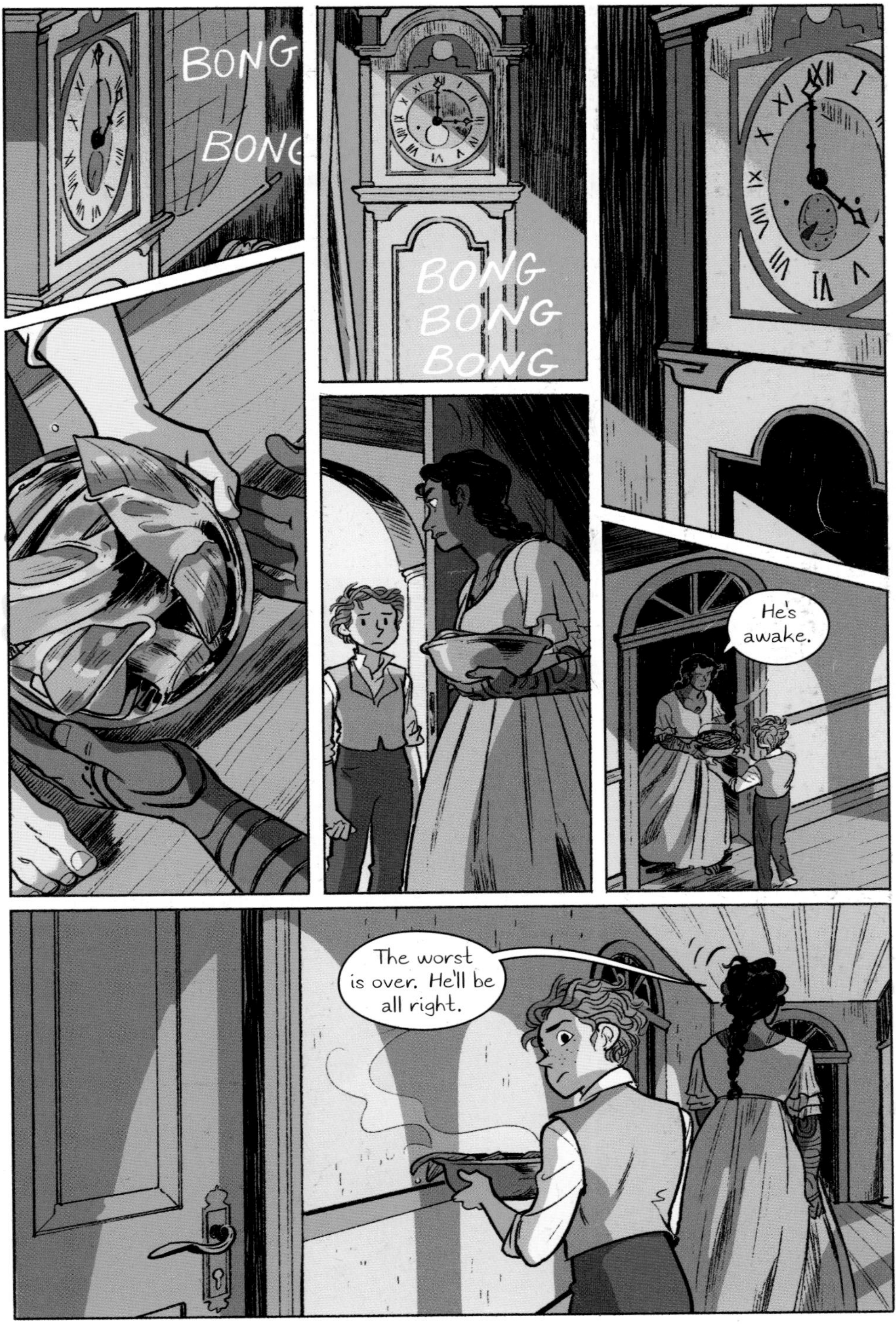
BONG
BONG
BONG
BONG
BONG
He's awake.
The worst is over. He'll be all right.

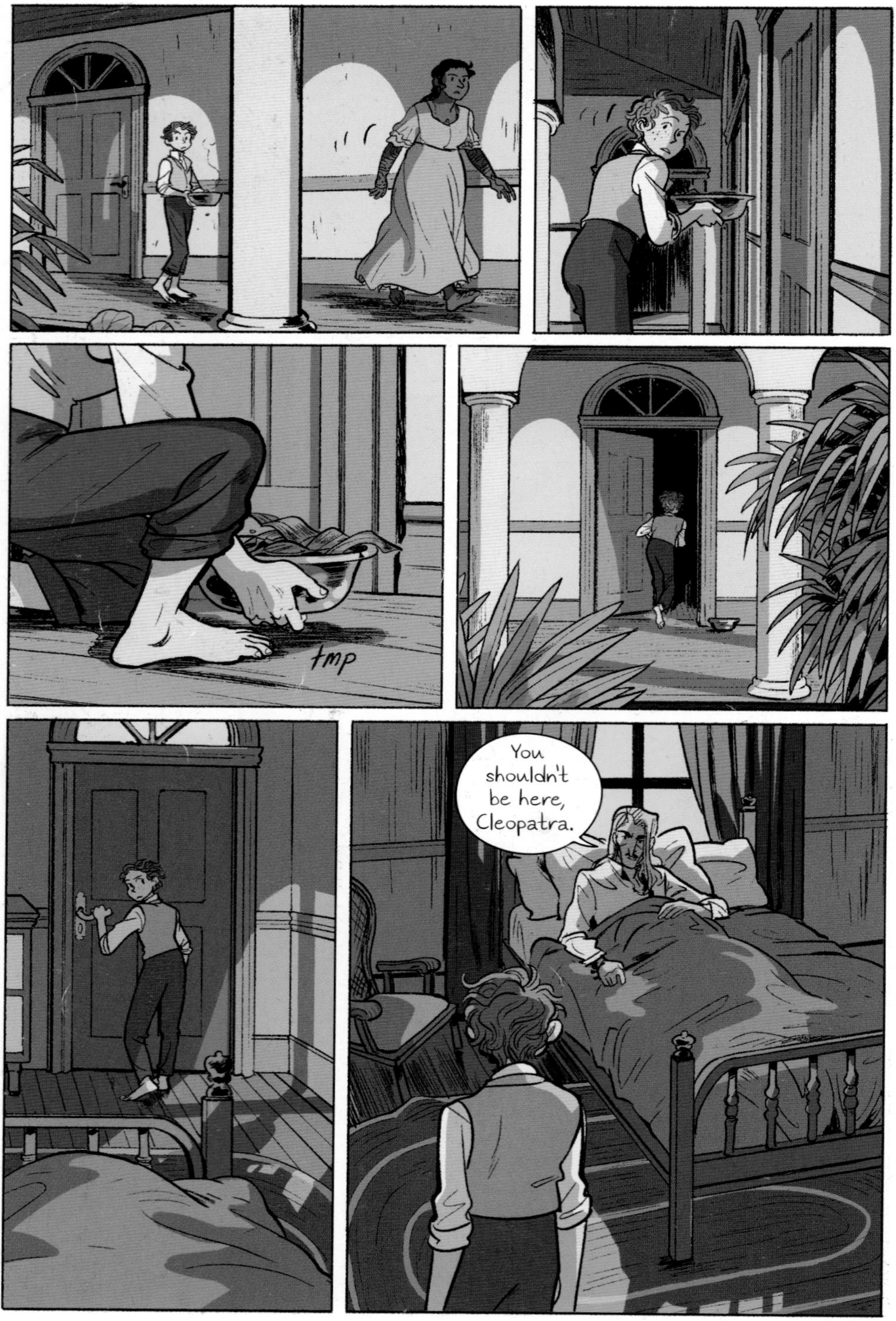
tmp
You shouldn't be here, Cleopatra.

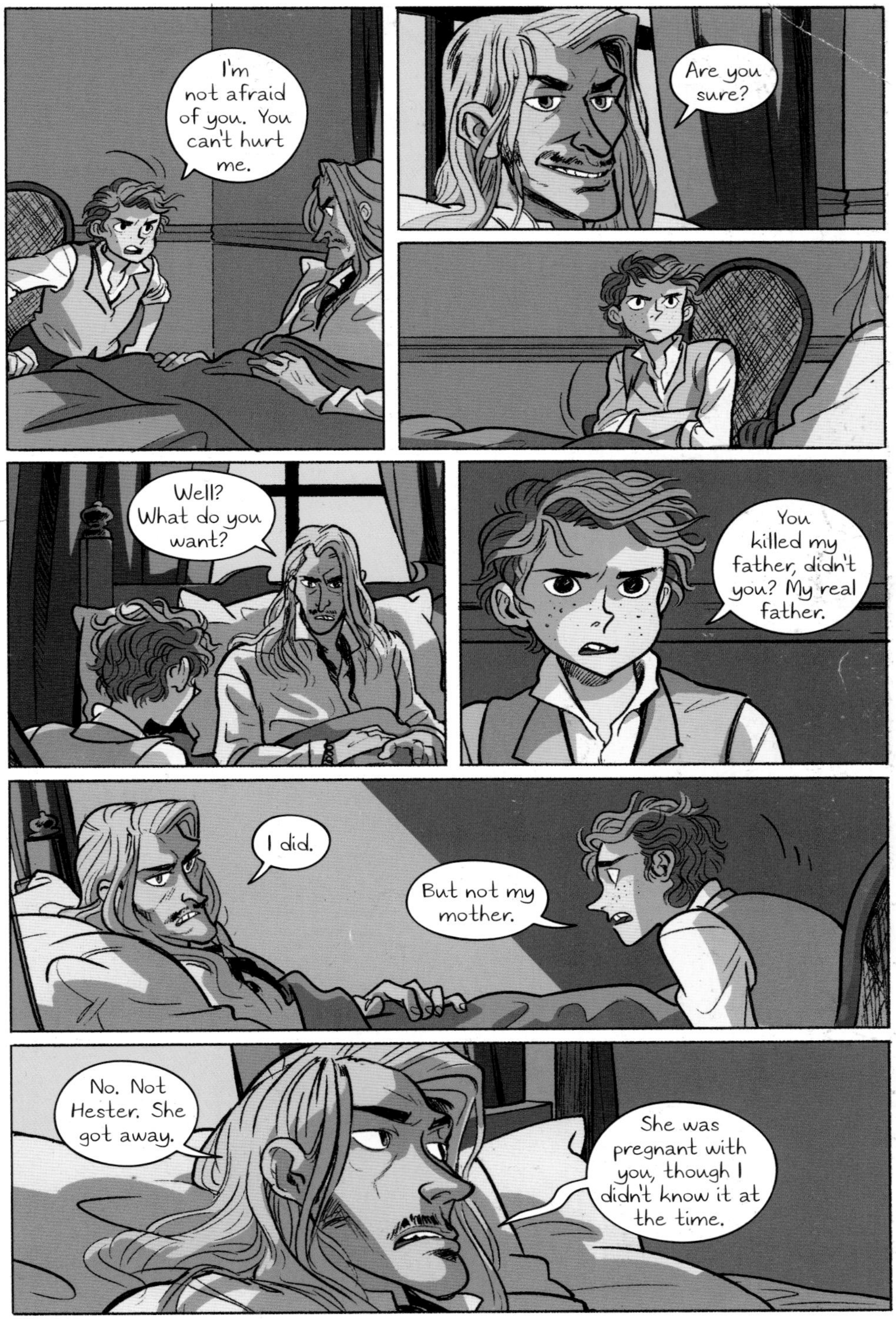
I'm not afraid of you. You can't hurt me.
Are you sure?
Well? What do you want?
You killed my father, didn't you? My real father.
I did.
But not my mother.
No. Not Hester. She got away.
She was pregnant with you, though I didn't know it at the time.

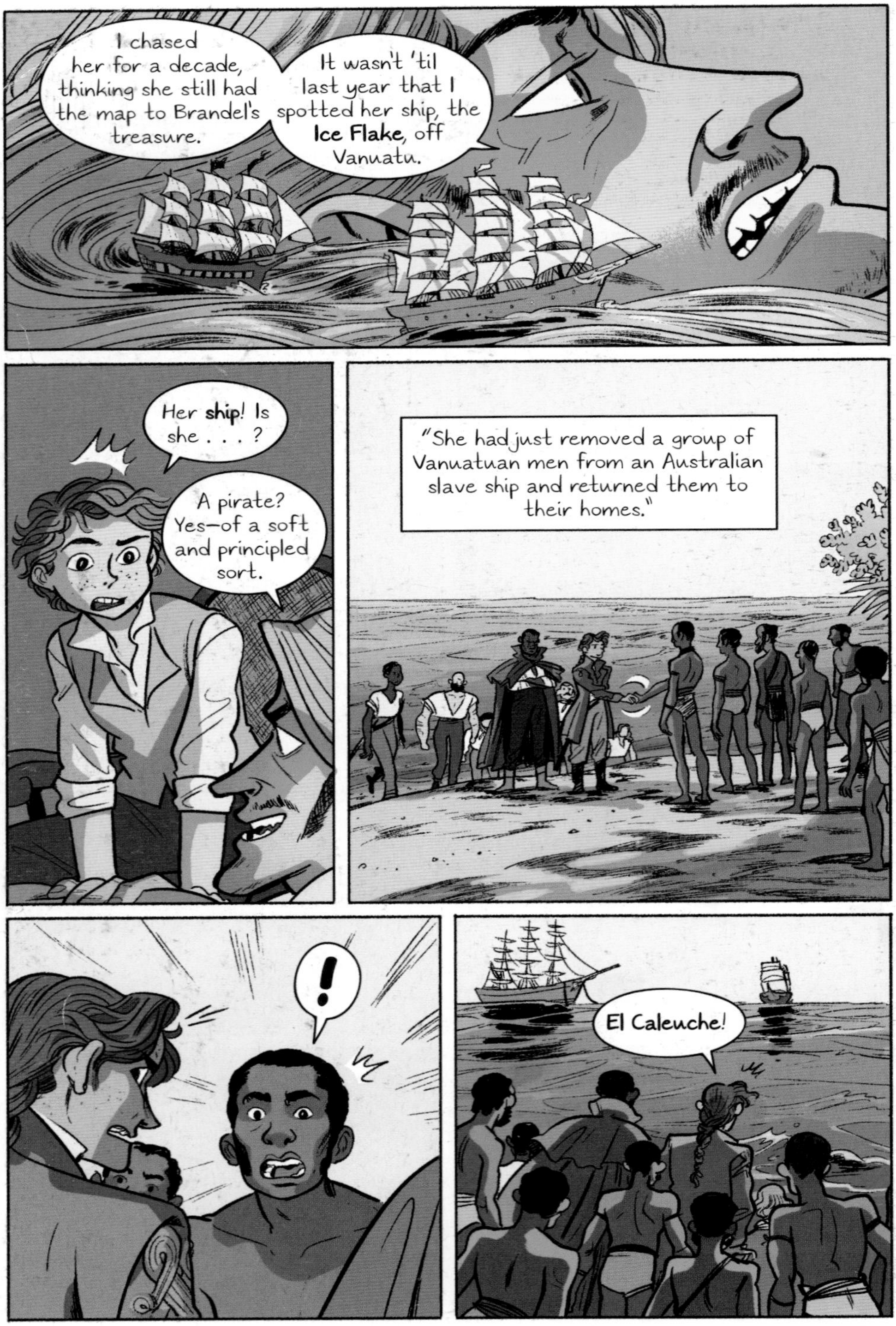
I chased her for a decade, thinking she still had the map to Brandel's treasure.
It wasn't 'til last year that I spotted her ship, the **Ice Flake**, off Vanuatu.
Her **ship**! Is she . . . ?
A pirate? Yes—of a soft and principled sort.
"She had just removed a group of Vanuatuan men from an Australian slave ship and returned them to their homes."
!
El Caleuche!

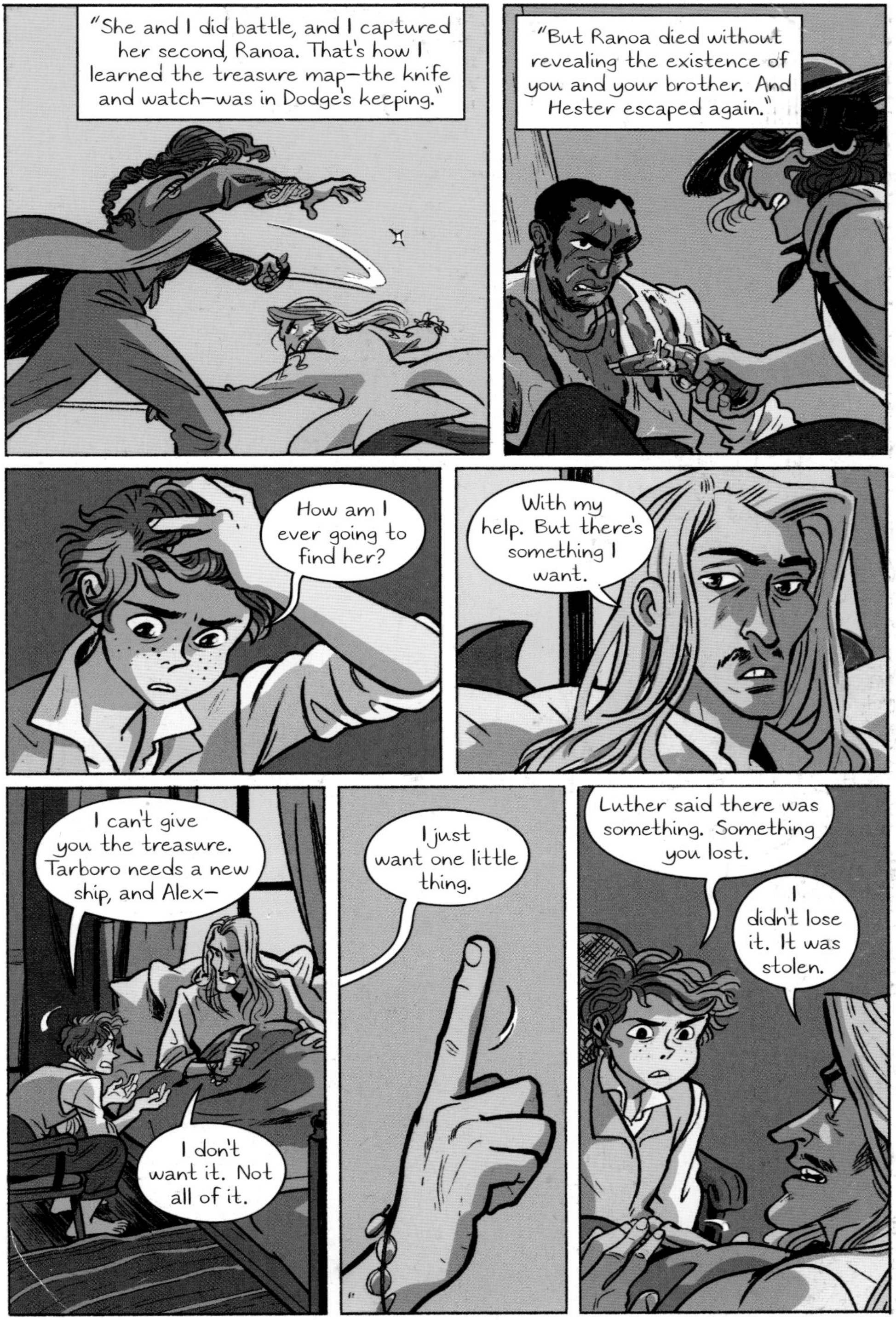
"She and I did battle, and I captured her second, Ranoa. That's how I learned the treasure map—the knife and watch—was in Dodge's keeping."
"But Ranoa died without revealing the existence of you and your brother. And Hester escaped again."
How am I ever going to find her?
With my help. But there's something I want.
I can't give you the treasure. Tarboro needs a new ship, and Alex—
I don't want it. Not all of it.
I just want one little thing.
Luther said there was something. Something you lost.
I didn't lose it. It was stolen.

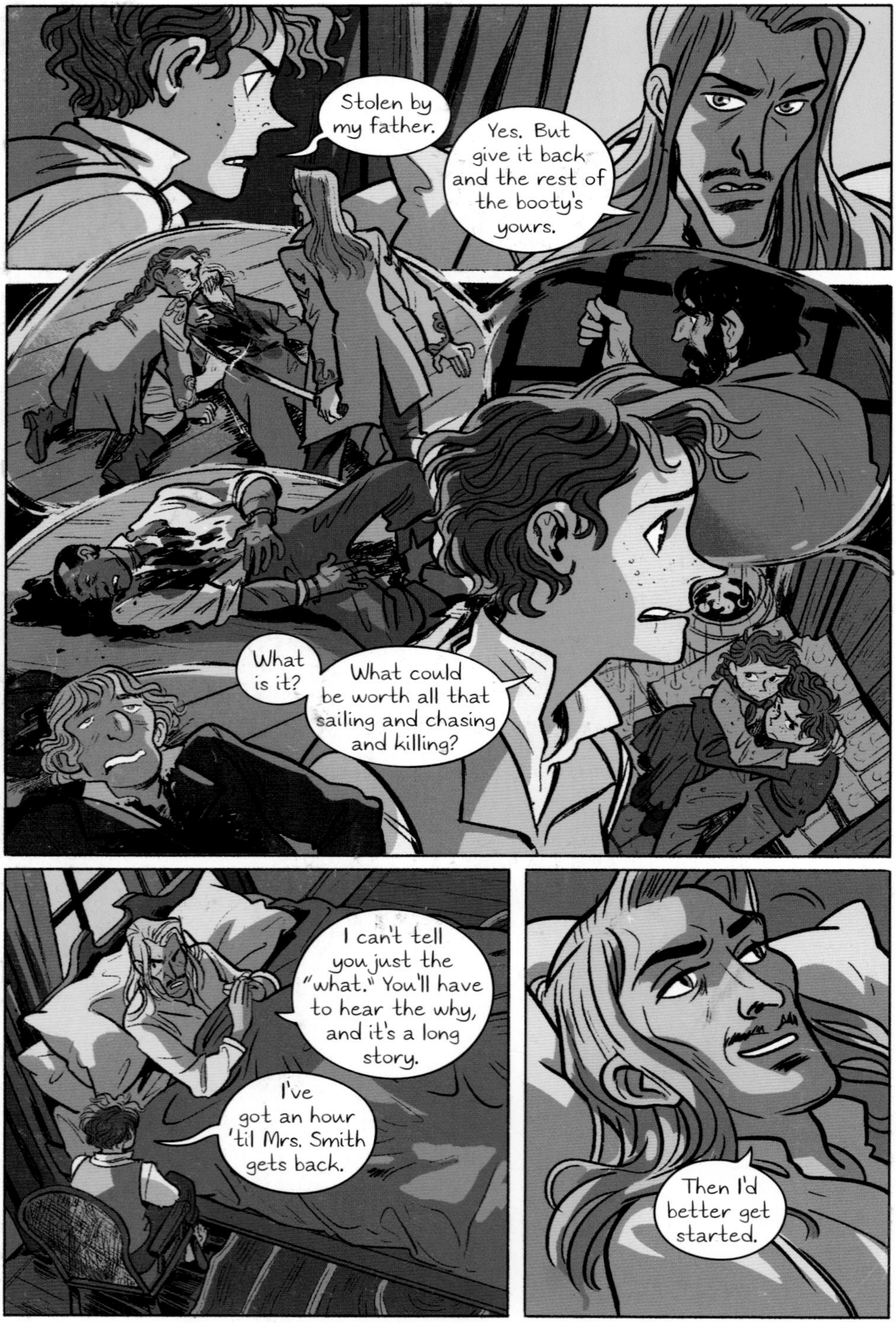
Stolen by my father.
Yes. But give it back and the rest of the booty's yours.
What is it?
What could be worth all that sailing and chasing and killing?
I can't tell you just the "what." You'll have to hear the why, and it's a long story.
I've got an hour 'til Mrs. Smith gets back.
Then I'd better get started.

CHAPTER NINE
A TASTE OF SUNSHINE

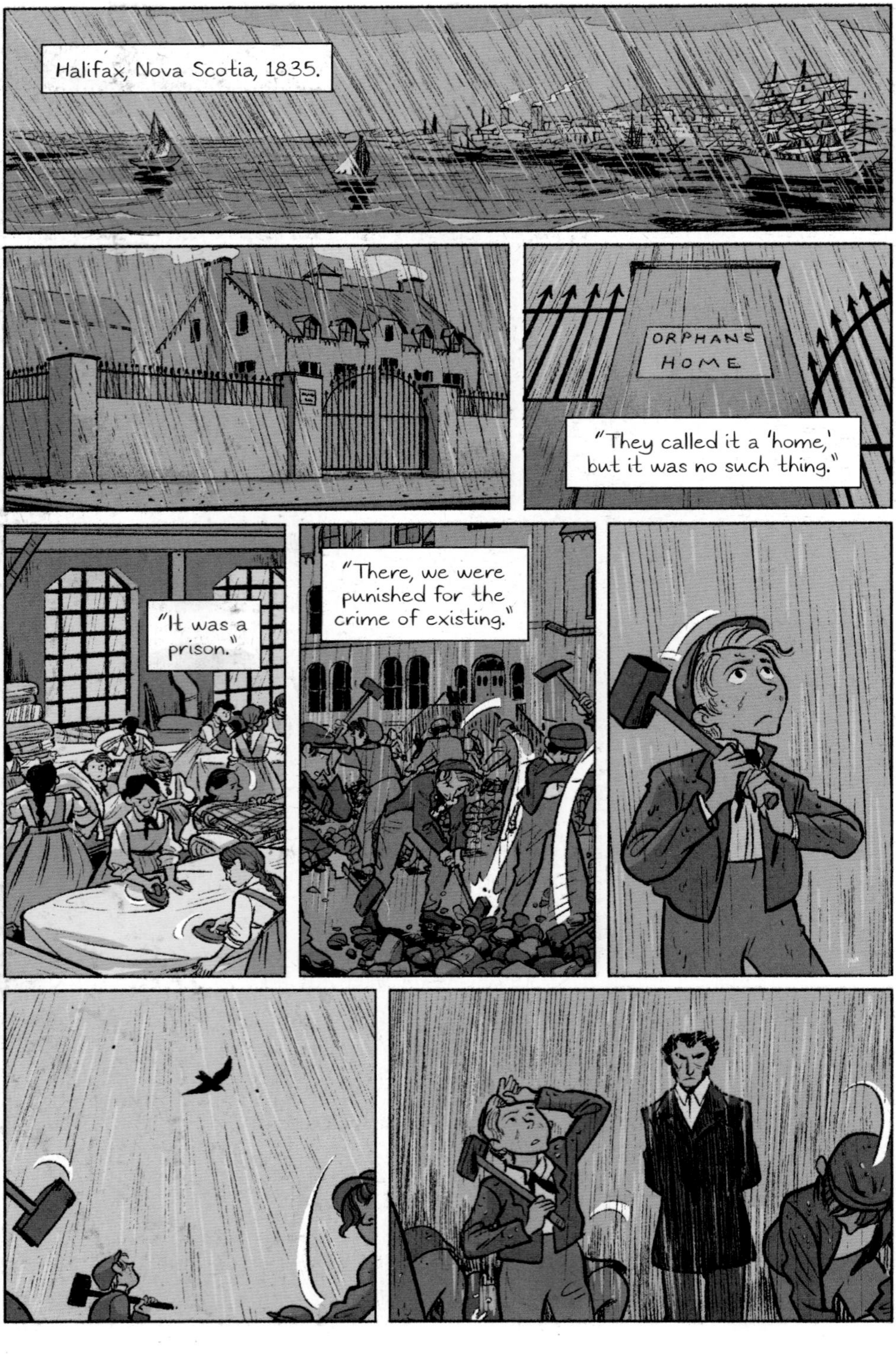

Halifax, Nova Scotia, 1835.
ORPHANS HOME
"They called it a 'home,' but it was no such thing."
"It was a prison."
"There, we were punished for the crime of existing."

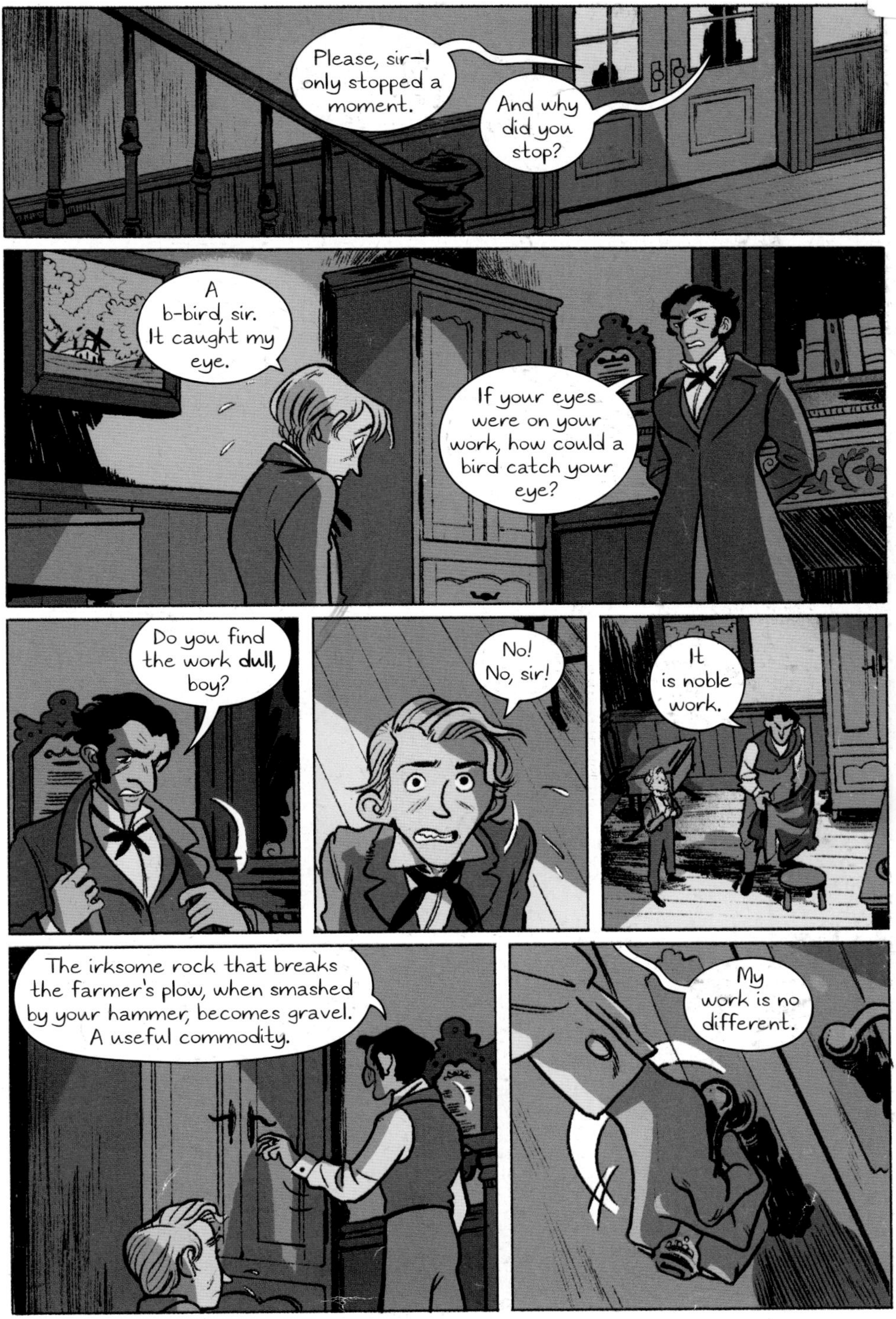
Please, sir—I only stopped a moment.
And why did you stop?
A b-bird, sir. It caught my eye.
If your eyes were on your work, how could a bird catch your eye?
Do you find the work **dull**, boy?
No! No, sir!
It is noble work.
The irksome rock that breaks the farmer's plow, when smashed by your hammer, becomes gravel. A useful commodity.
My work is no different.

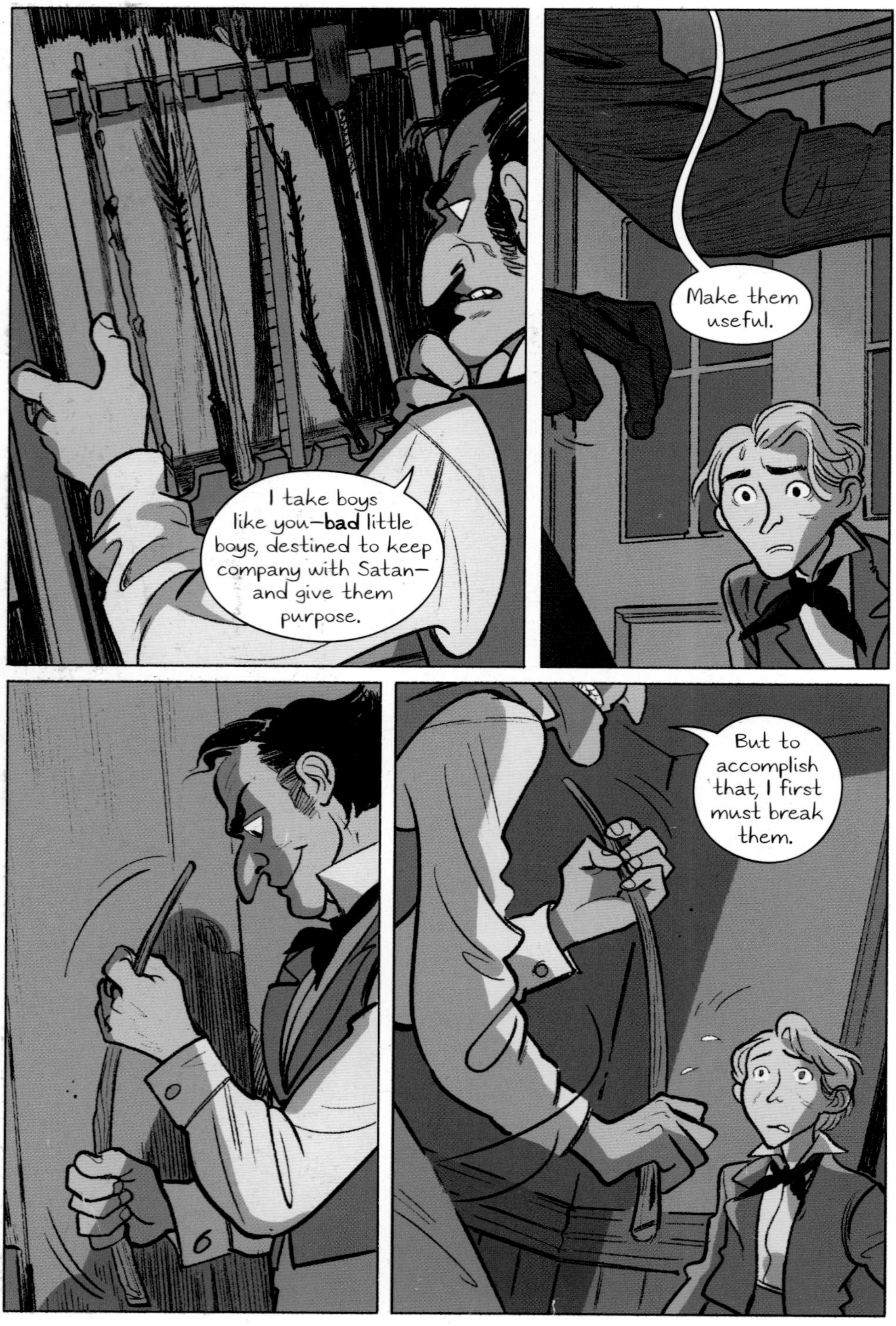
I take boys like you—**bad** little boys, destined to keep company with Satan—and give them purpose.
Make them useful.
But to accomplish that, I first must break them.

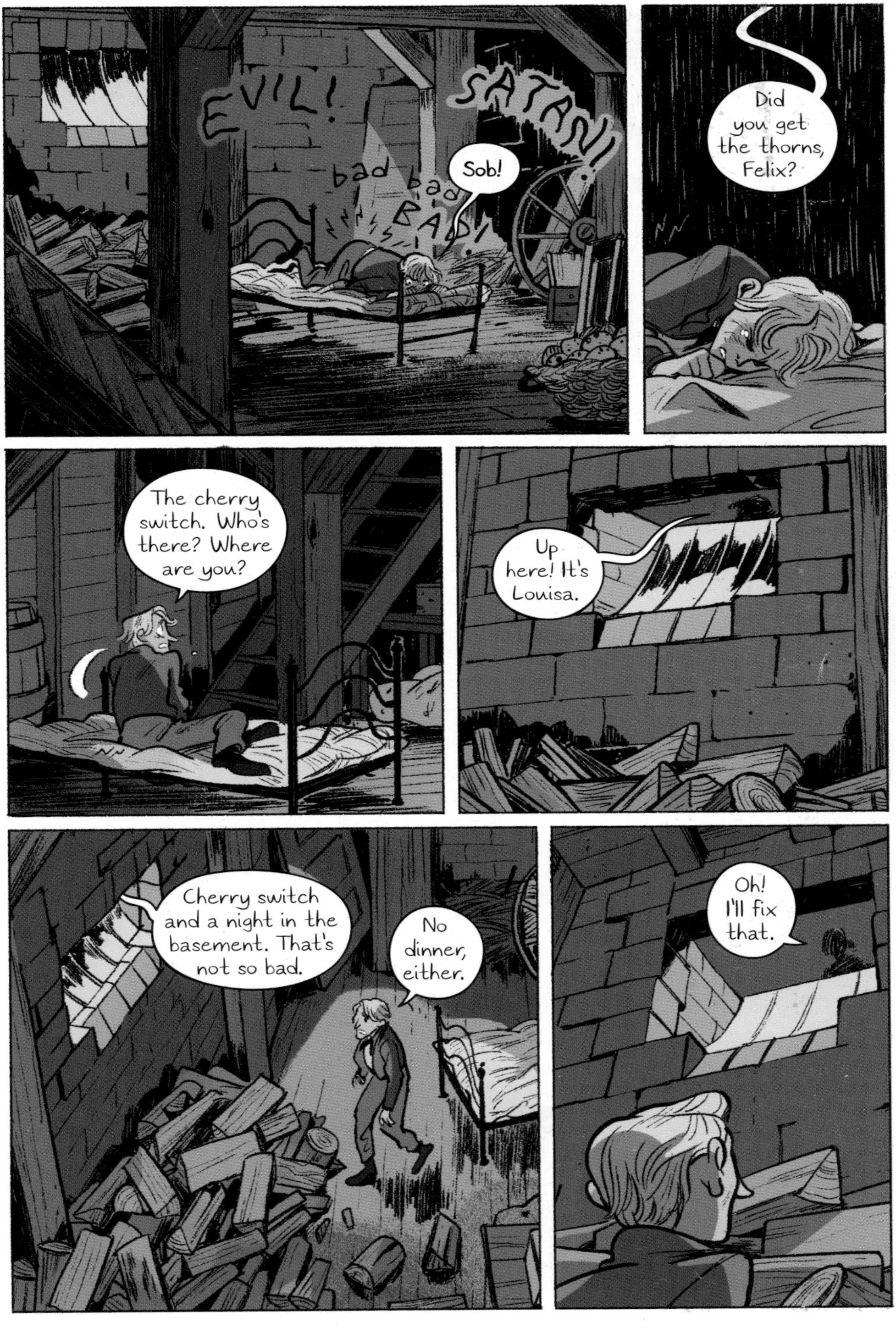
EVIL!
SATAN!
bad bad BAD!
Sob!
Did you get the thorns, Felix?
The cherry switch. Who's there? Where are you?
Up here! It's Louisa.
Cherry switch and a night in the basement. That's not so bad.
No dinner, either.
Oh! I'll fix that.

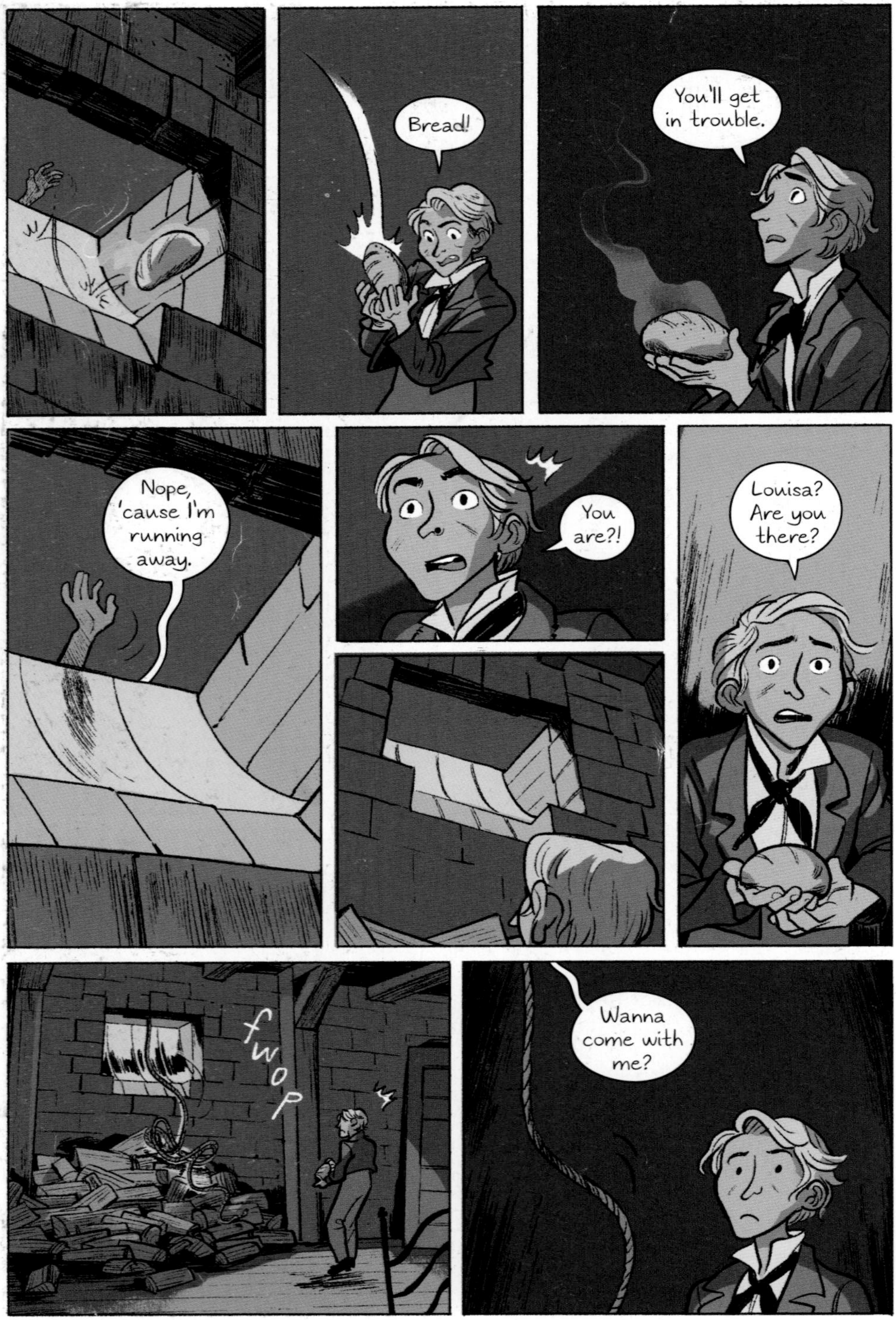
Bread!
You'll get in trouble.
Nope, 'cause I'm running away.
You are?!
Louisa? Are you there?
fwop
Wanna come with me?

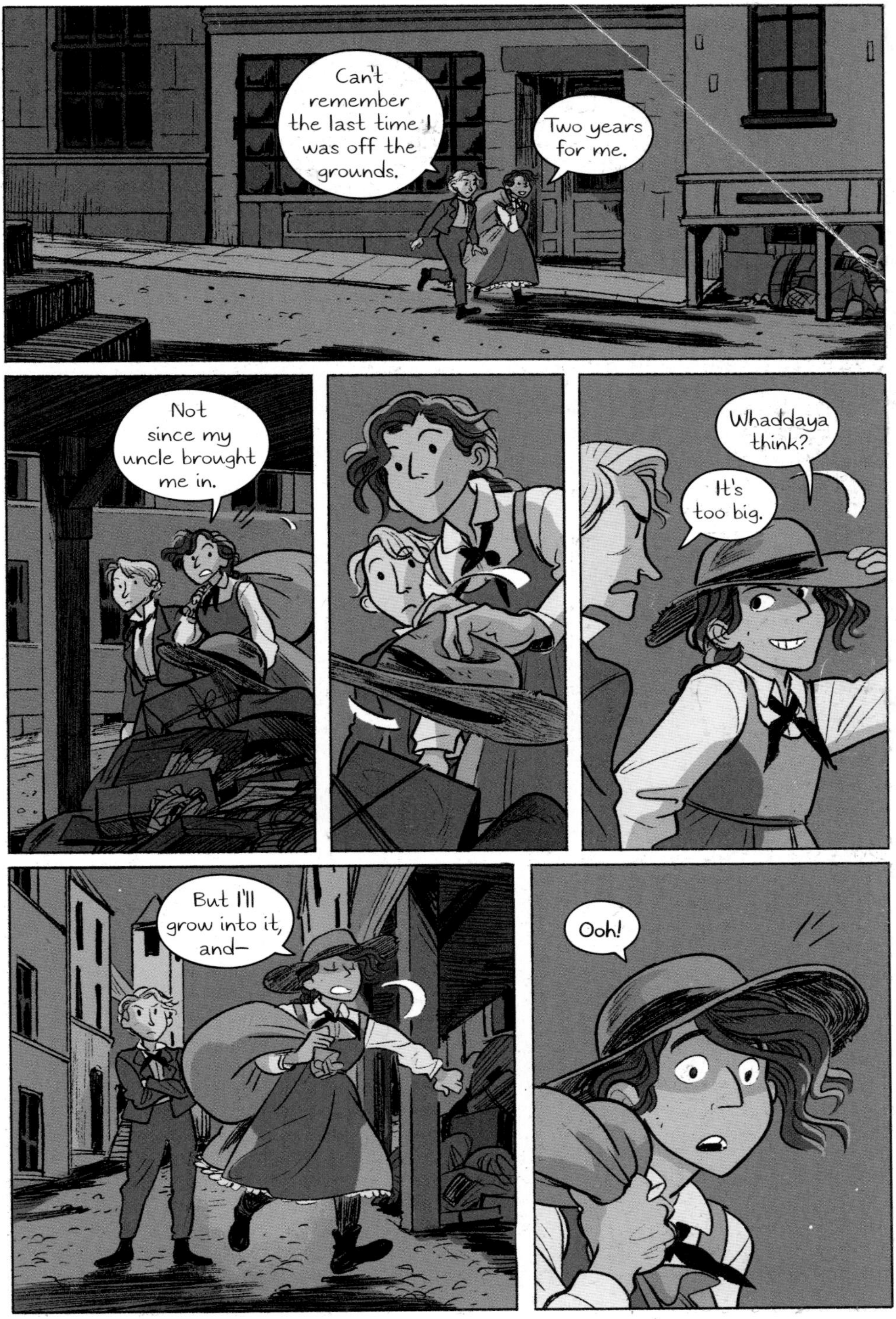
Can't remember the last time I was off the grounds.
Two years for me.
Not since my uncle brought me in.
Whaddaya think?
It's too big.
But I'll grow into it, and—
Ooh!

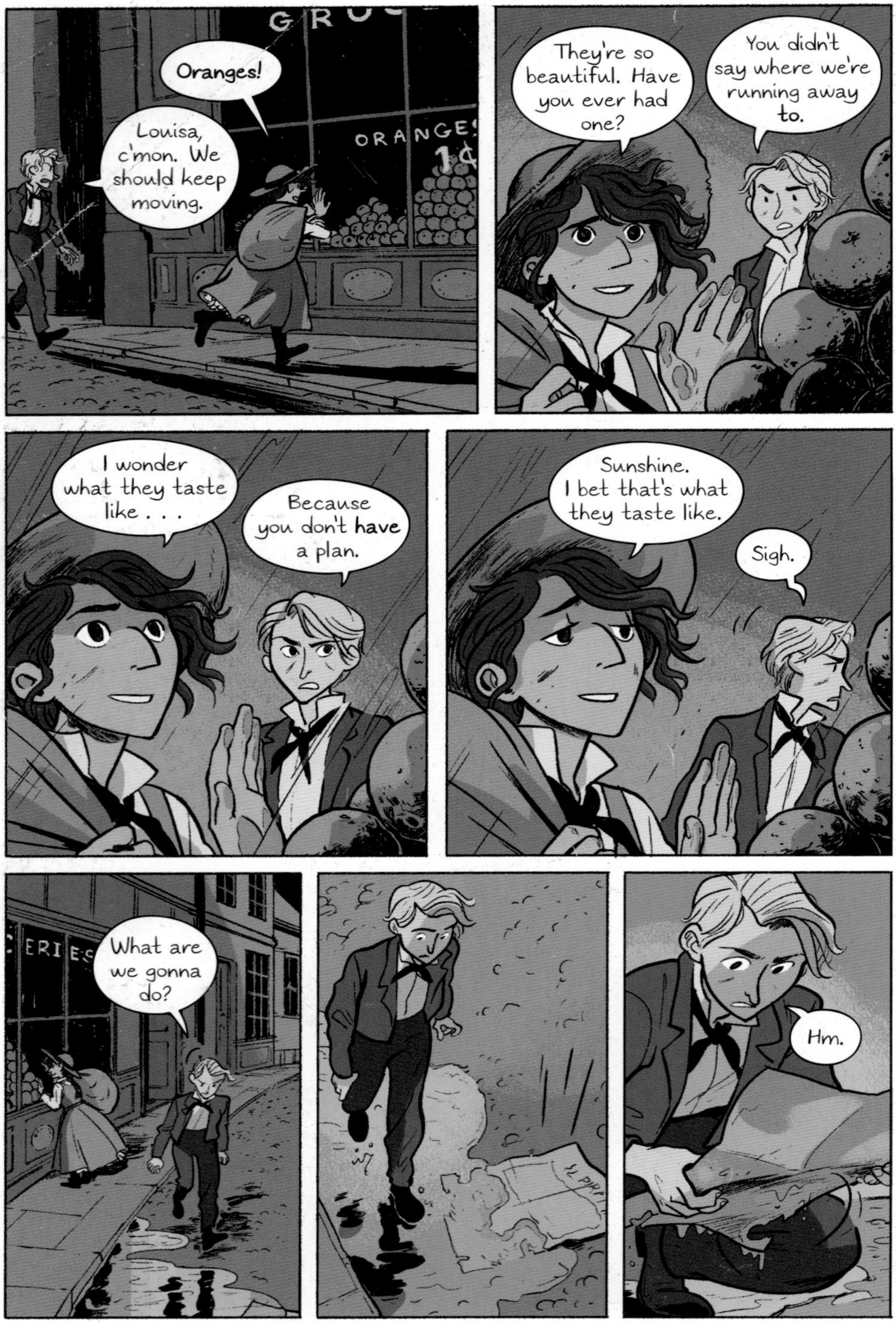
GROC
ORANGES 1¢
Oranges!
Louisa, c'mon. We should keep moving.
They're so beautiful. Have you ever had one?
You didn't say where we're running away to.
I wonder what they taste like . . .
Because you don't have a plan.
Sunshine. I bet that's what they taste like.
Sigh.
ERIES
What are we gonna do?
Hm.

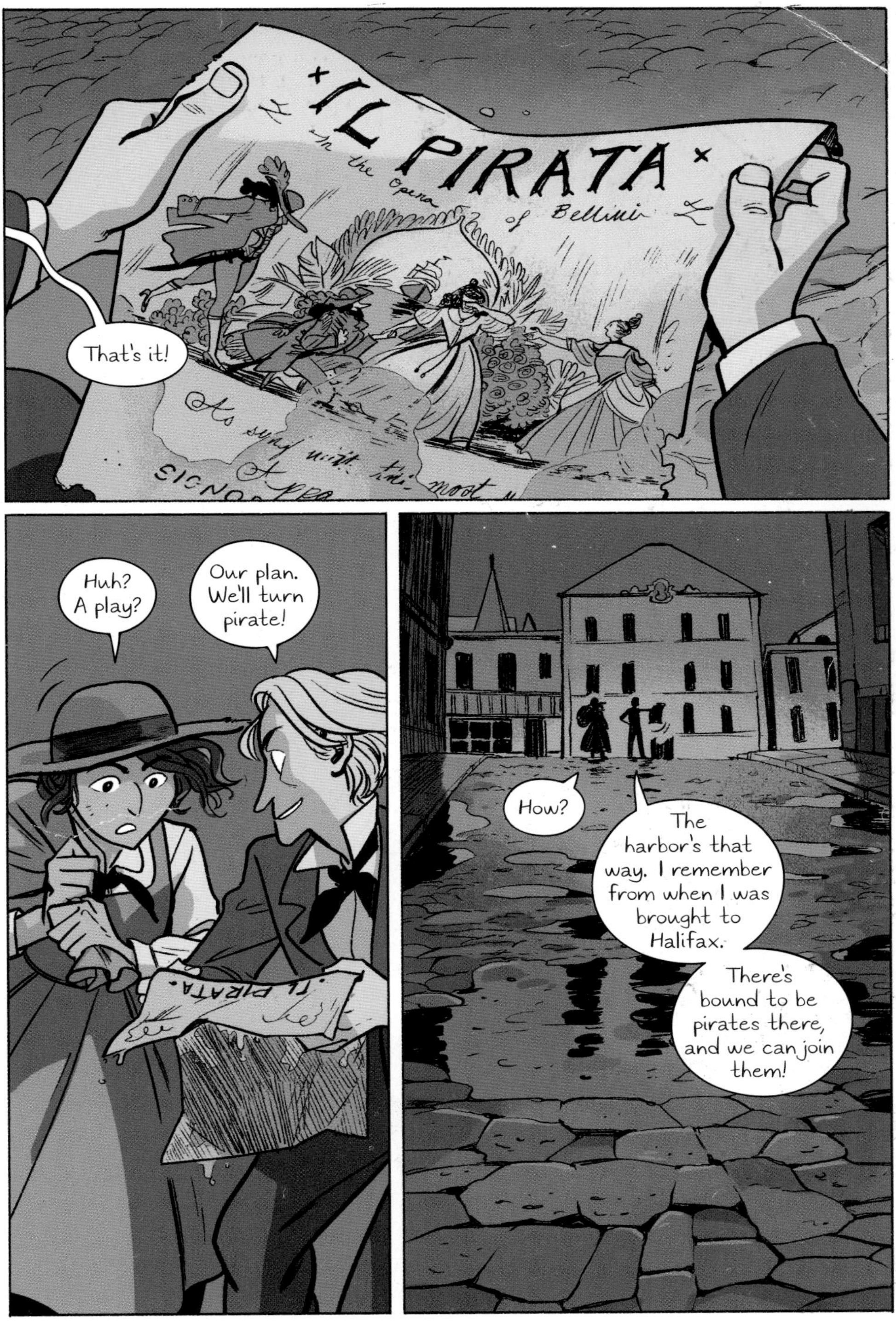
IL PIRATA
In the Opera of Bellini
That's it!
Huh? A play?
Our plan. We'll turn pirate!
IL PIRATA
How?
The harbor's that way. I remember from when I was brought to Halifax.
There's bound to be pirates there, and we can join them!

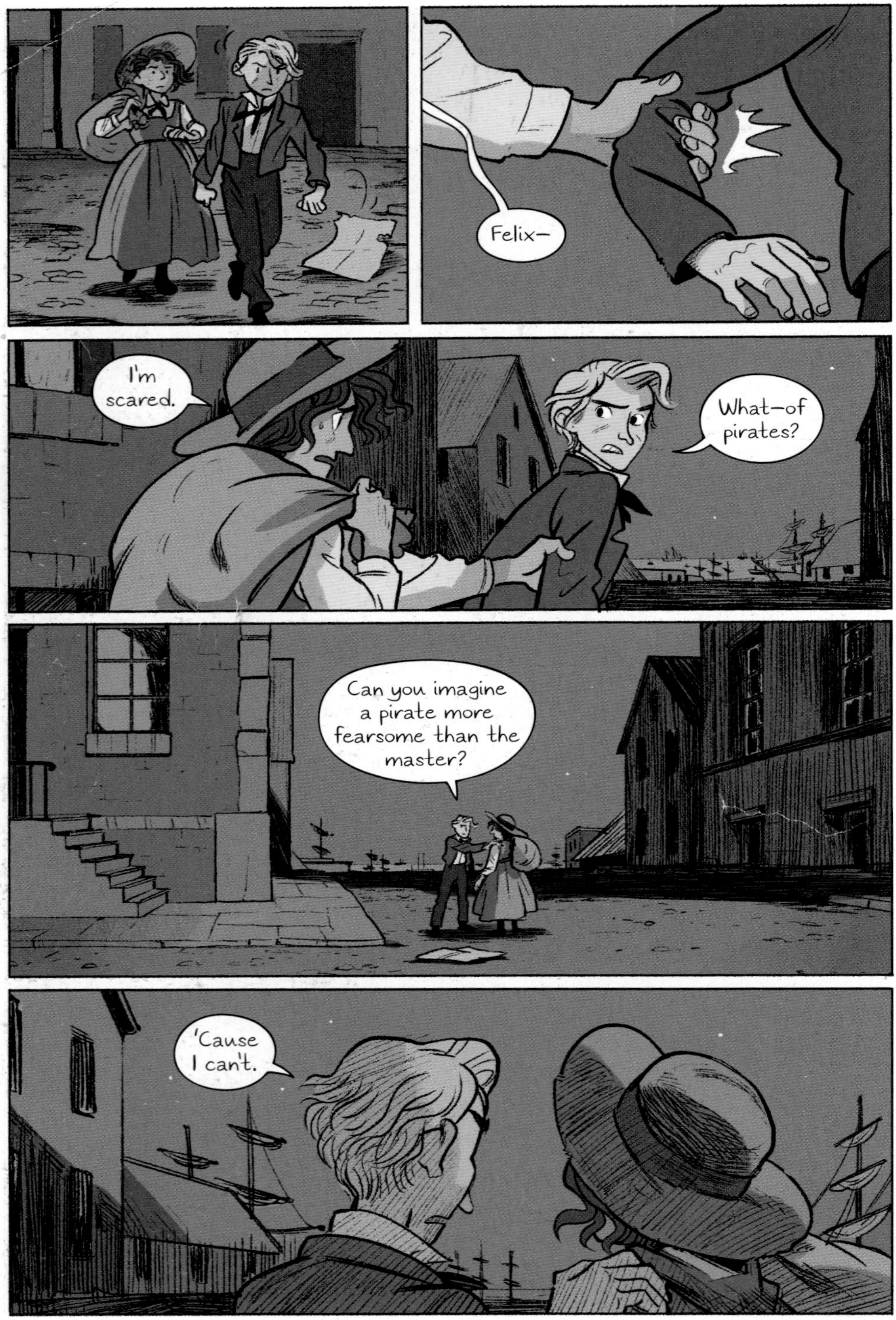

Felix—
I'm scared.
What—of pirates?
Can you imagine a pirate more fearsome than the master?
'Cause I can't.

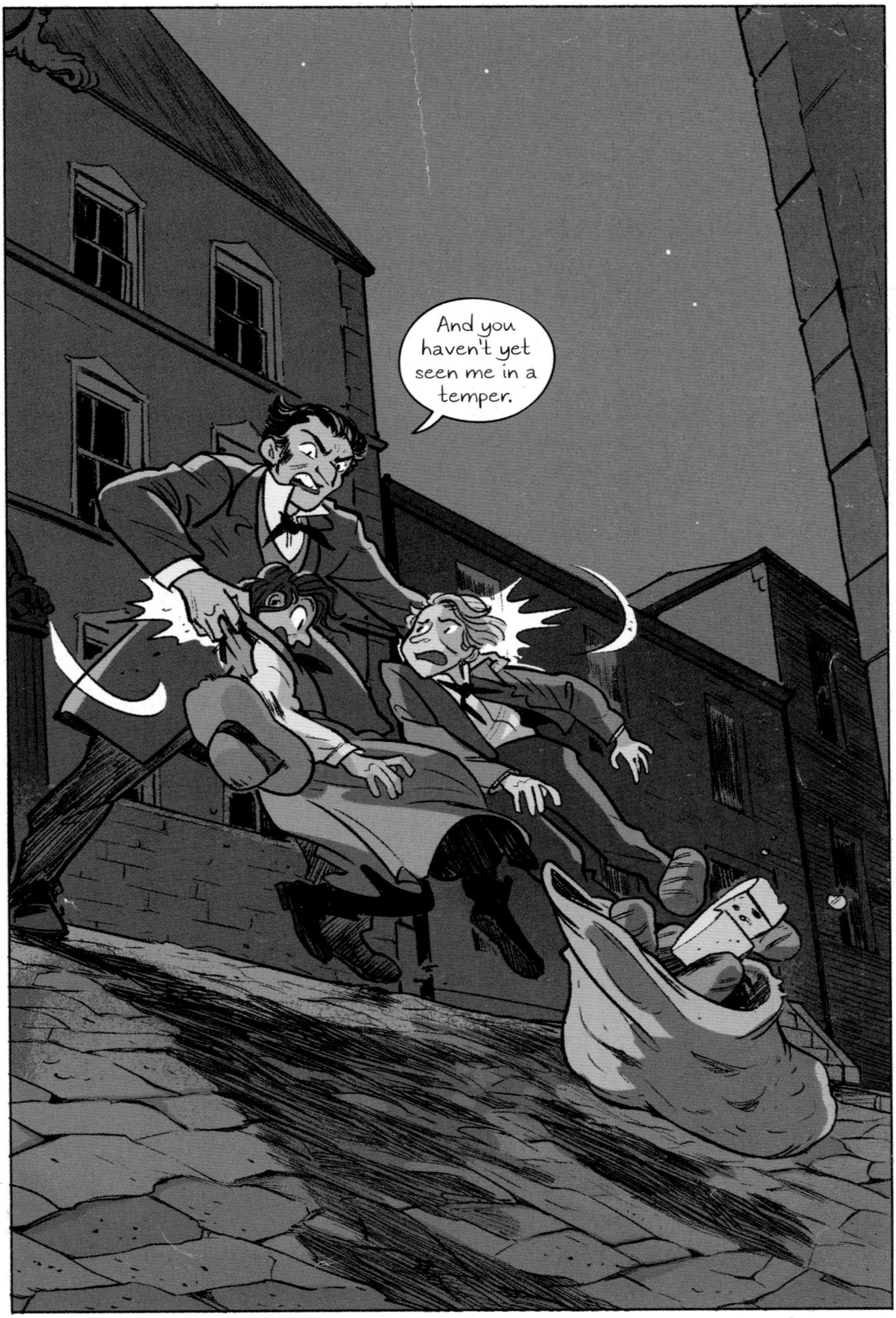
And you haven't yet seen me in a temper.

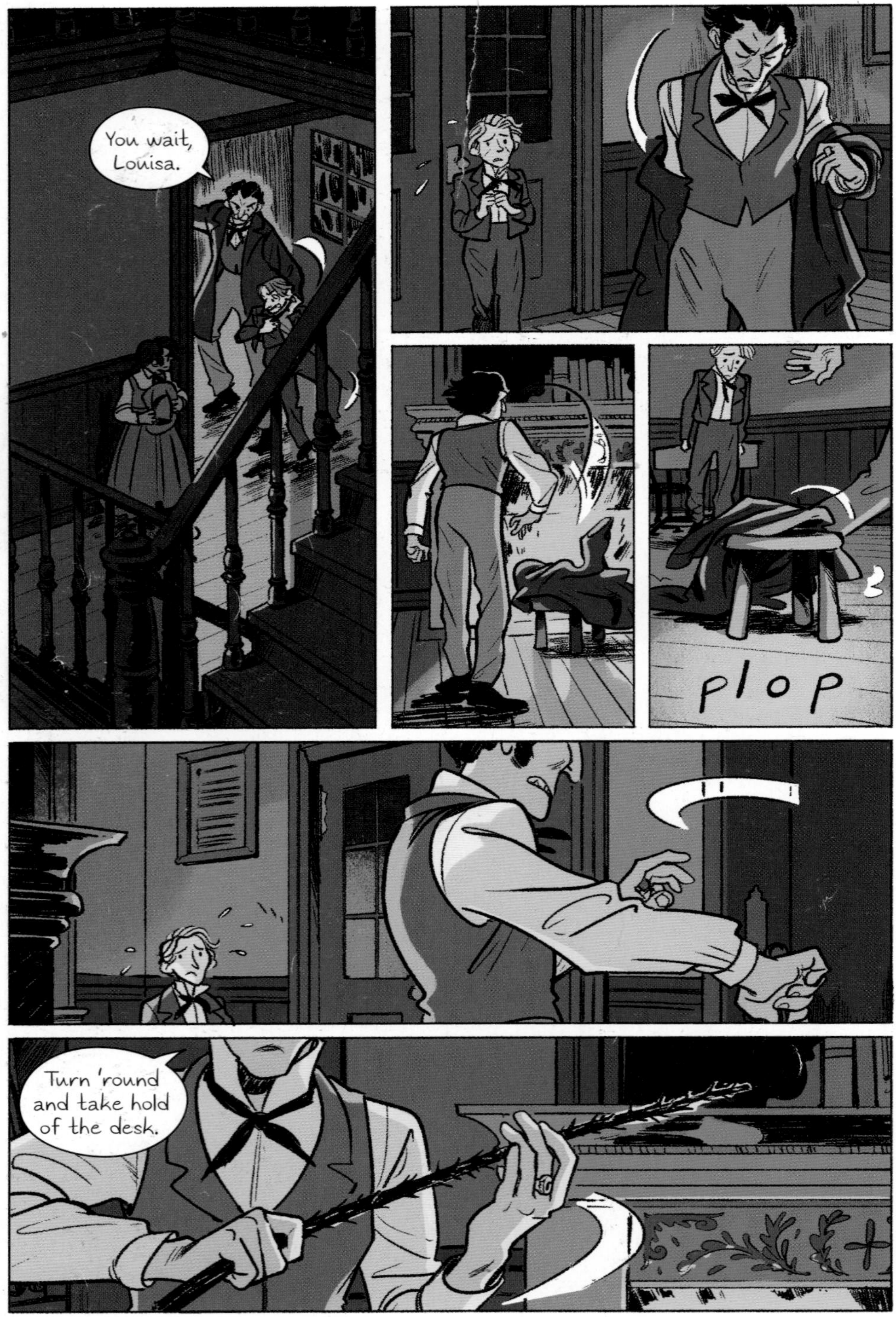
You wait, Louisa.
plop
Turn 'round and take hold of the desk.

No.

What?!

Turn around or I'll strike you 'cross the face.

I won't do it.

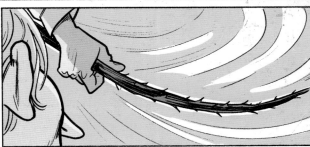

173

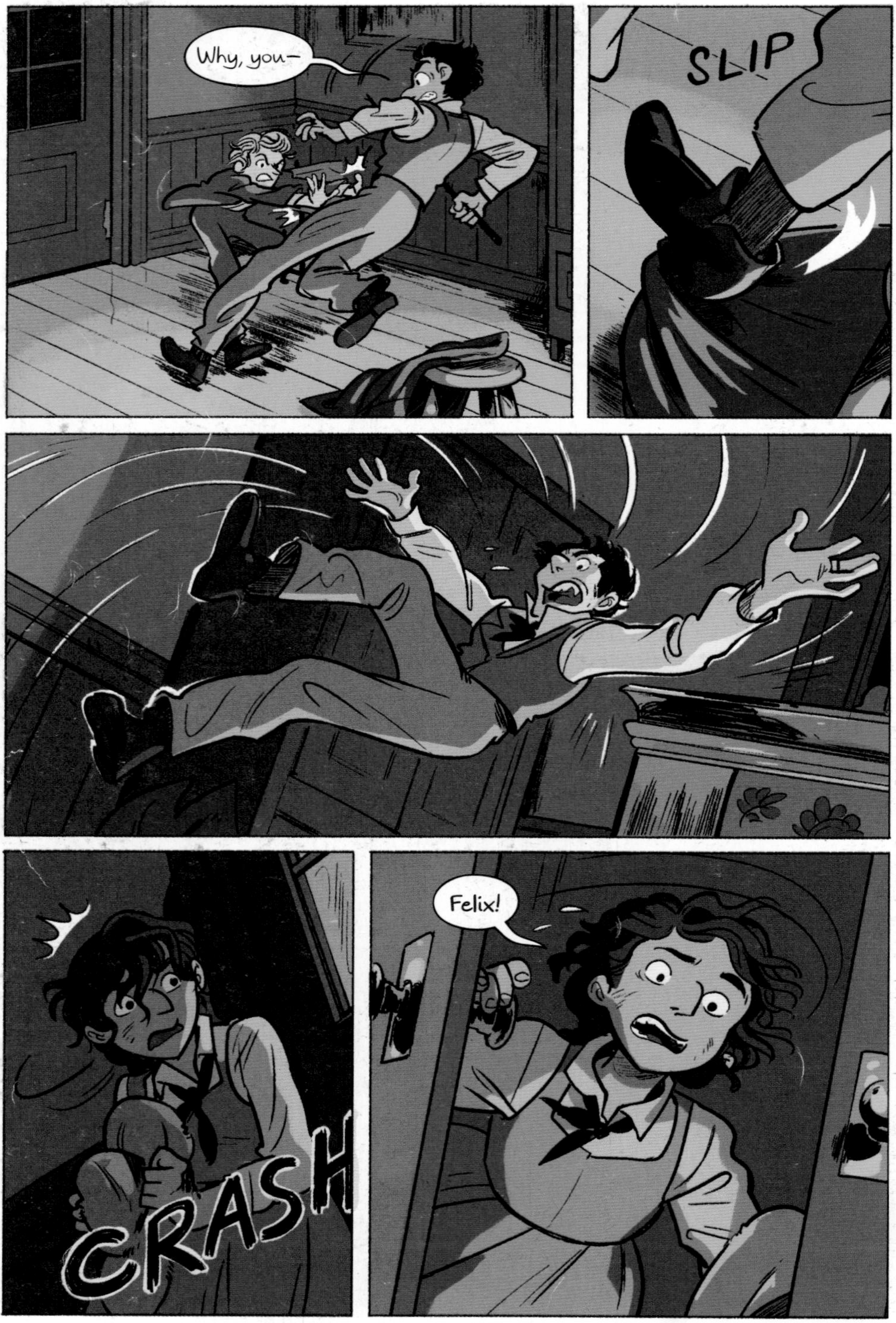

Why, you–
SLIP
Felix!
CRASH

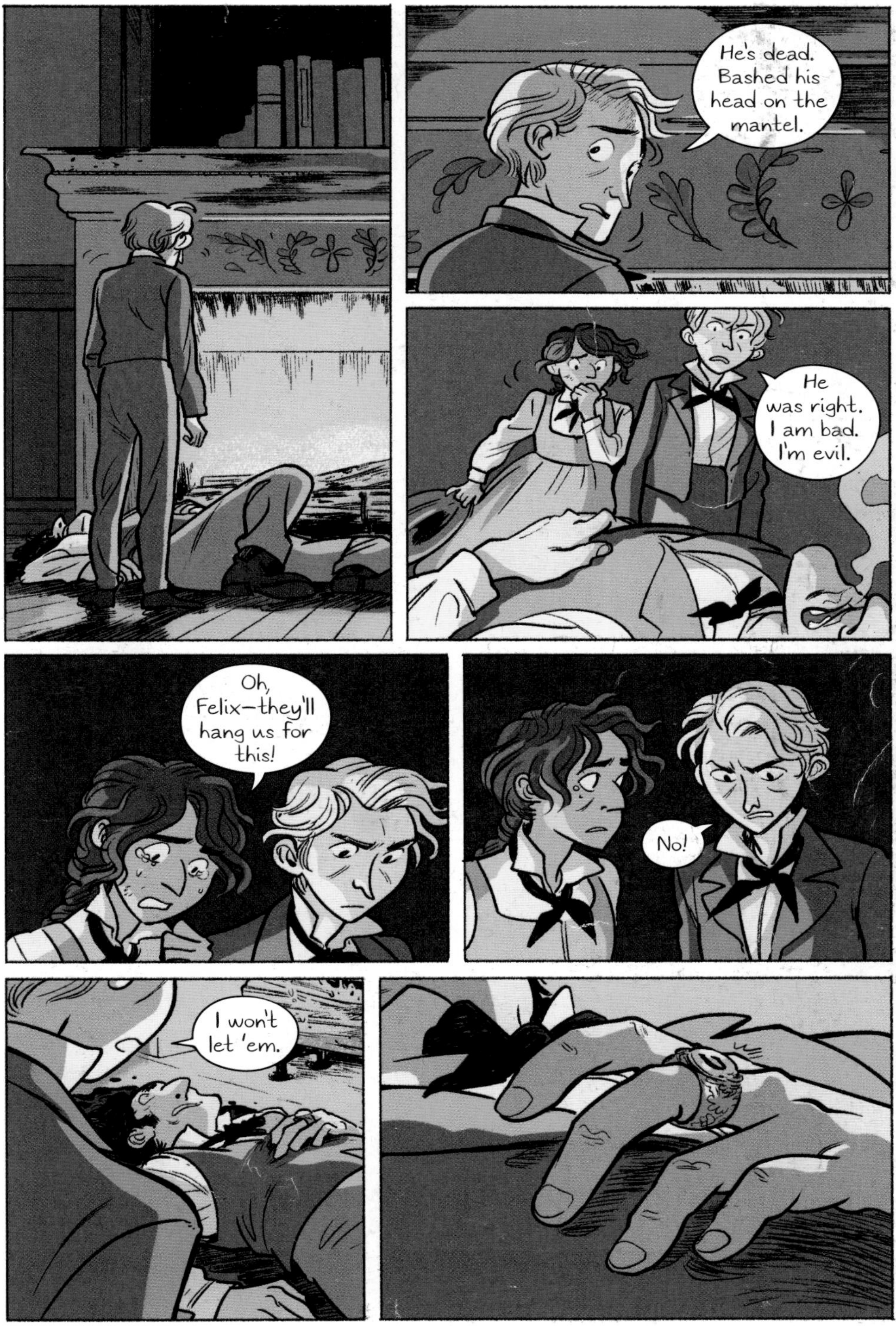
He's dead. Bashed his head on the mantel.
He was right. I am bad. I'm evil.
Oh, Felix—they'll hang us for this!
No!
I won't let 'em.

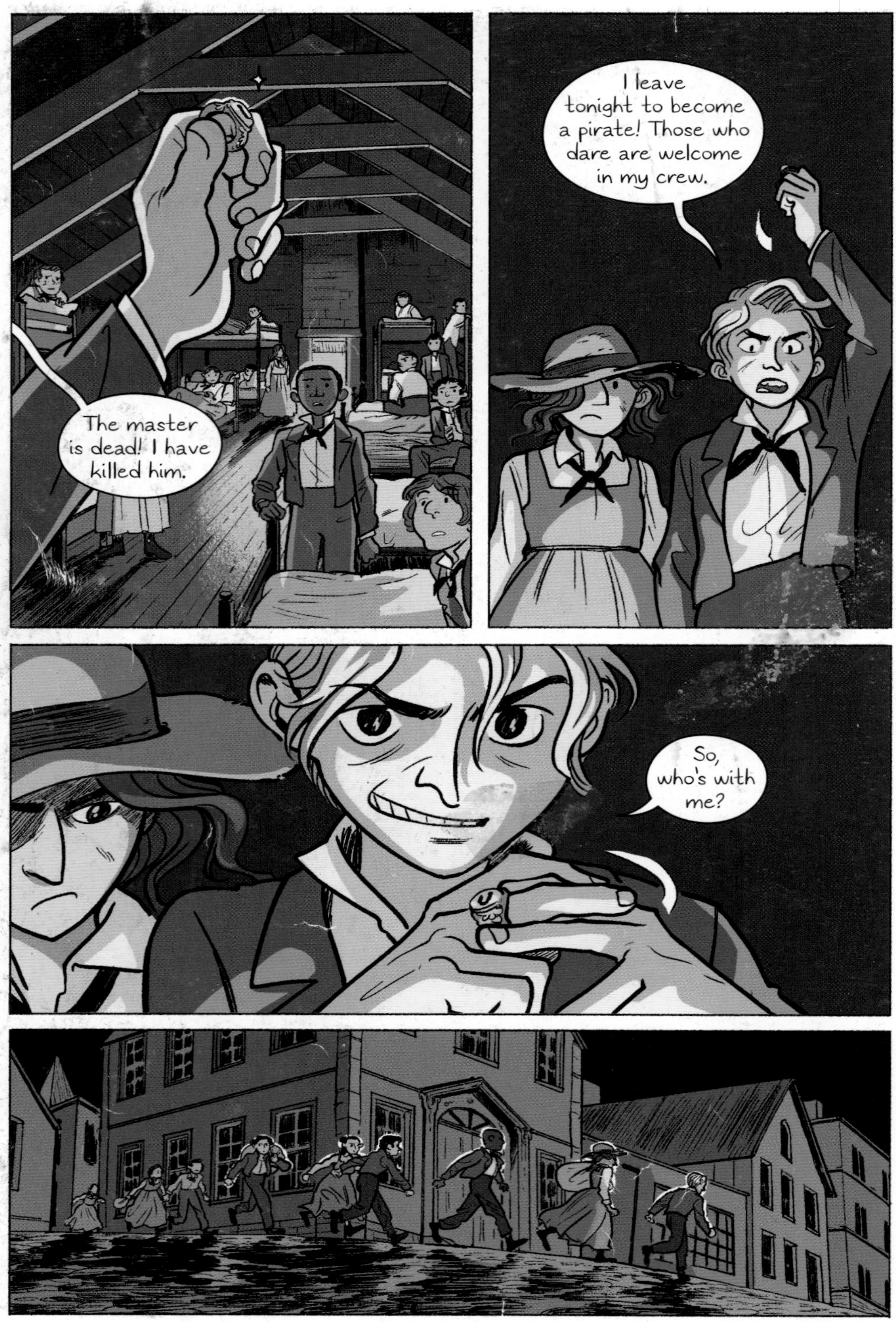
The master is dead! I have killed him.
I leave tonight to become a pirate! Those who dare are welcome in my crew.
So, who's with me?

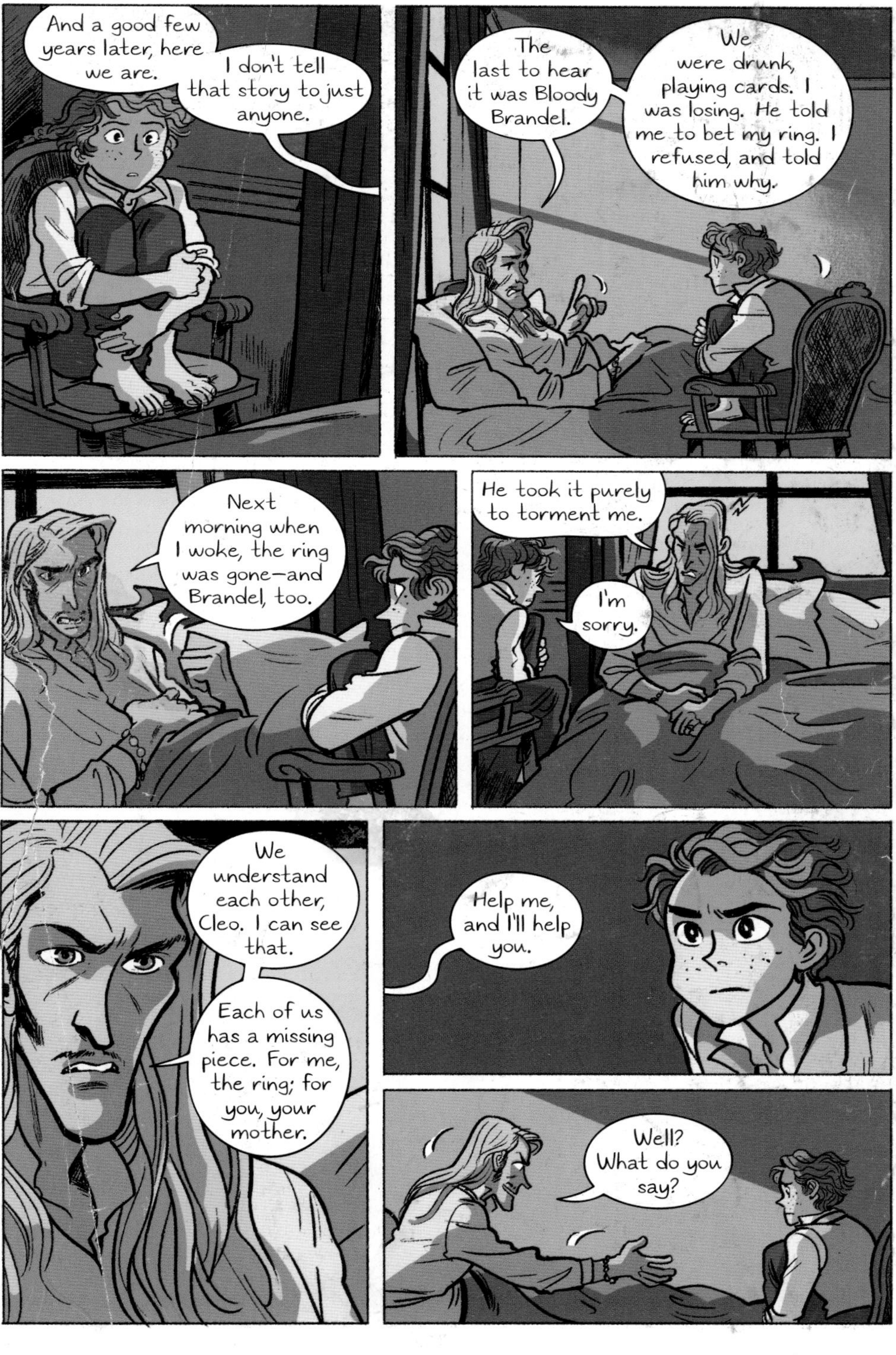
And a good few years later, here we are.
I don't tell that story to just anyone.
The last to hear it was Bloody Brandel.
We were drunk, playing cards. I was losing. He told me to bet my ring. I refused, and told him why.
Next morning when I woke, the ring was gone—and Brandel, too.
He took it purely to torment me.
I'm sorry.
We understand each other, Cleo. I can see that.
Each of us has a missing piece. For me, the ring; for you, your mother.
Help me, and I'll help you.
Well? What do you say?

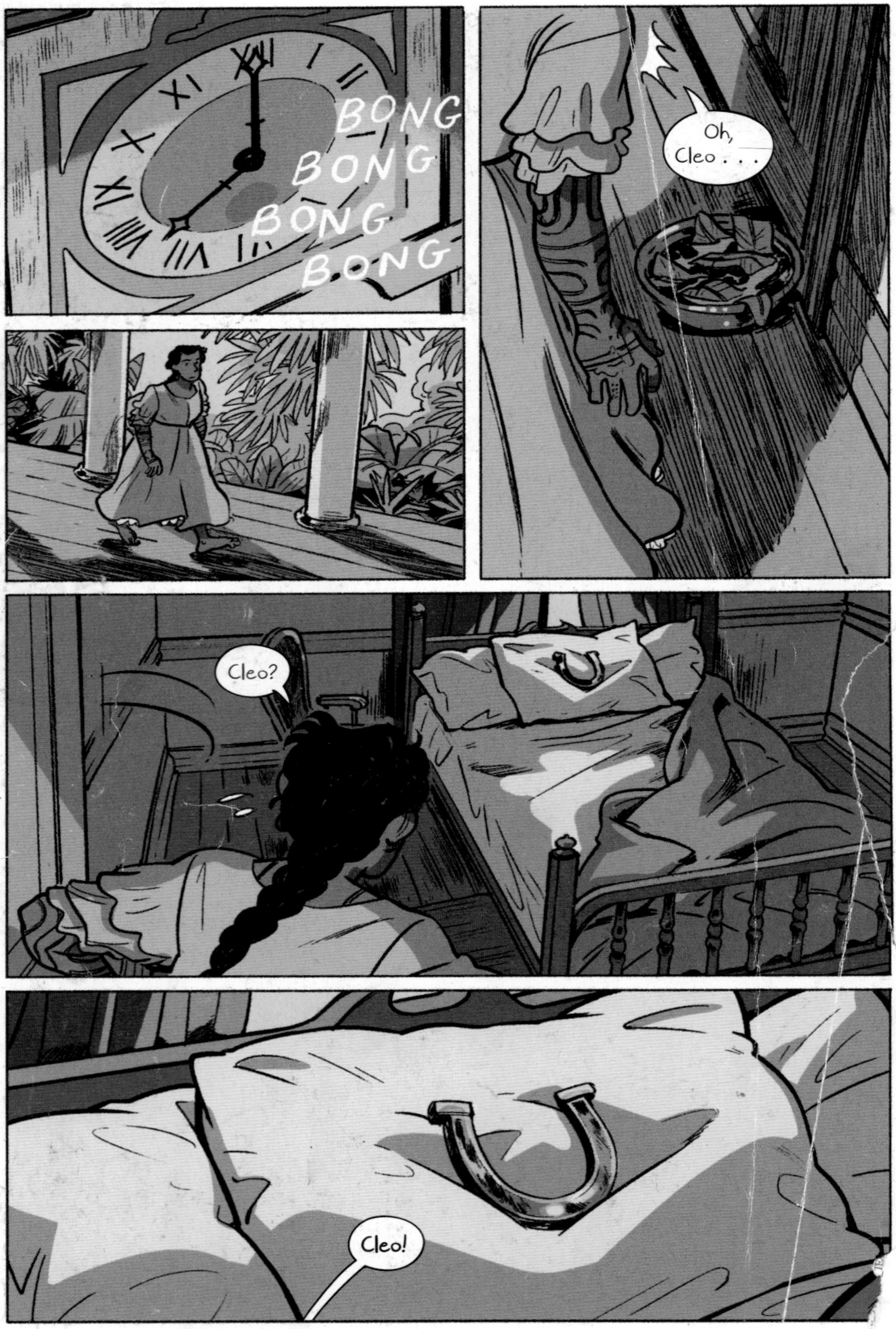
BONG
BONG
BONG
BONG
Oh, Cleo . . .
Cleo?
Cleo!

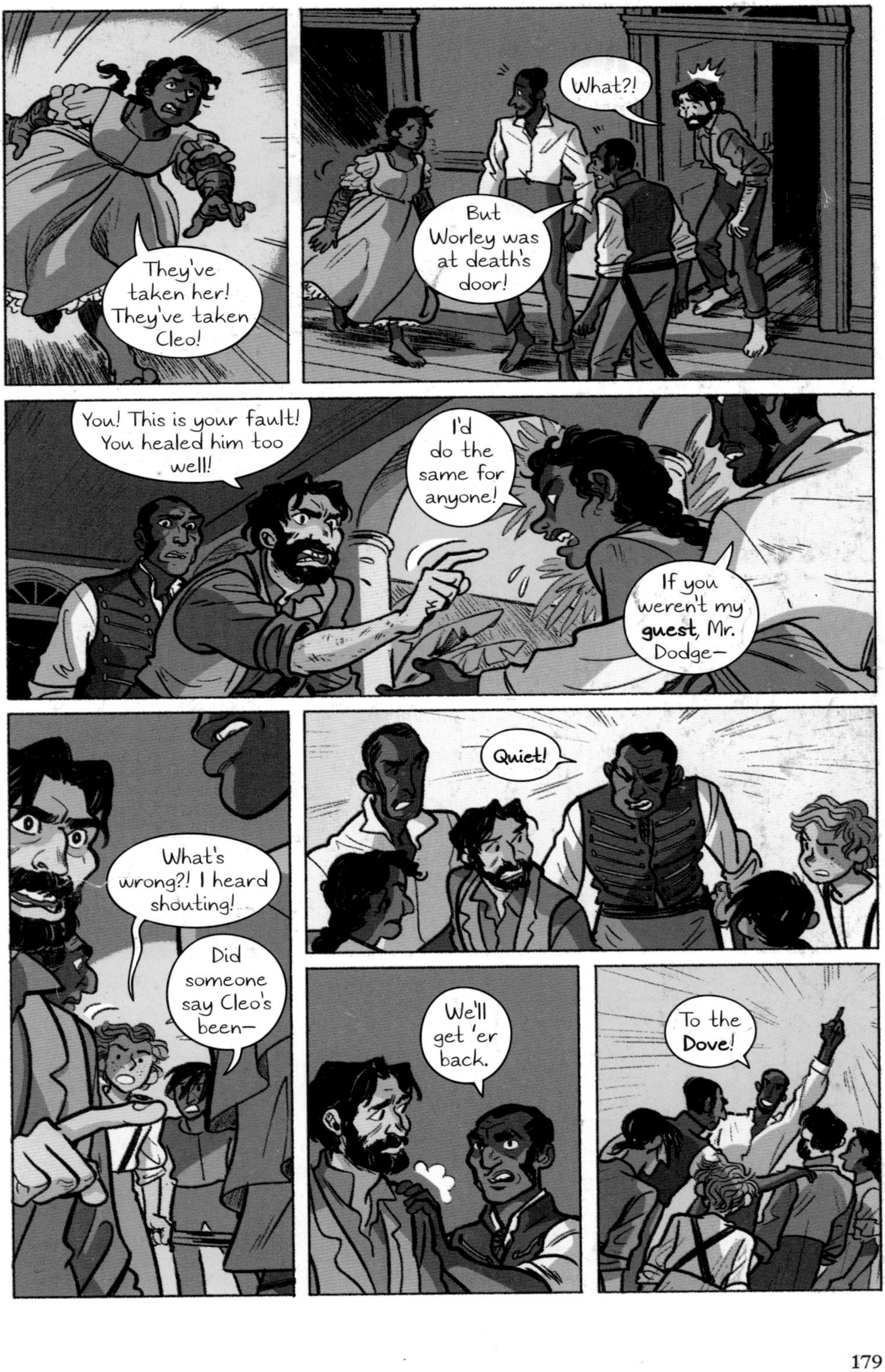

They've taken her! They've taken Cleo!
What?!
But Worley was at death's door!
You! This is your fault! You healed him too well!
I'd do the same for anyone!
If you weren't my **guest**, Mr. Dodge—
What's wrong?! I heard shouting!
Did someone say Cleo's been—
Quiet!
We'll get 'er back.
To the **Dove**!

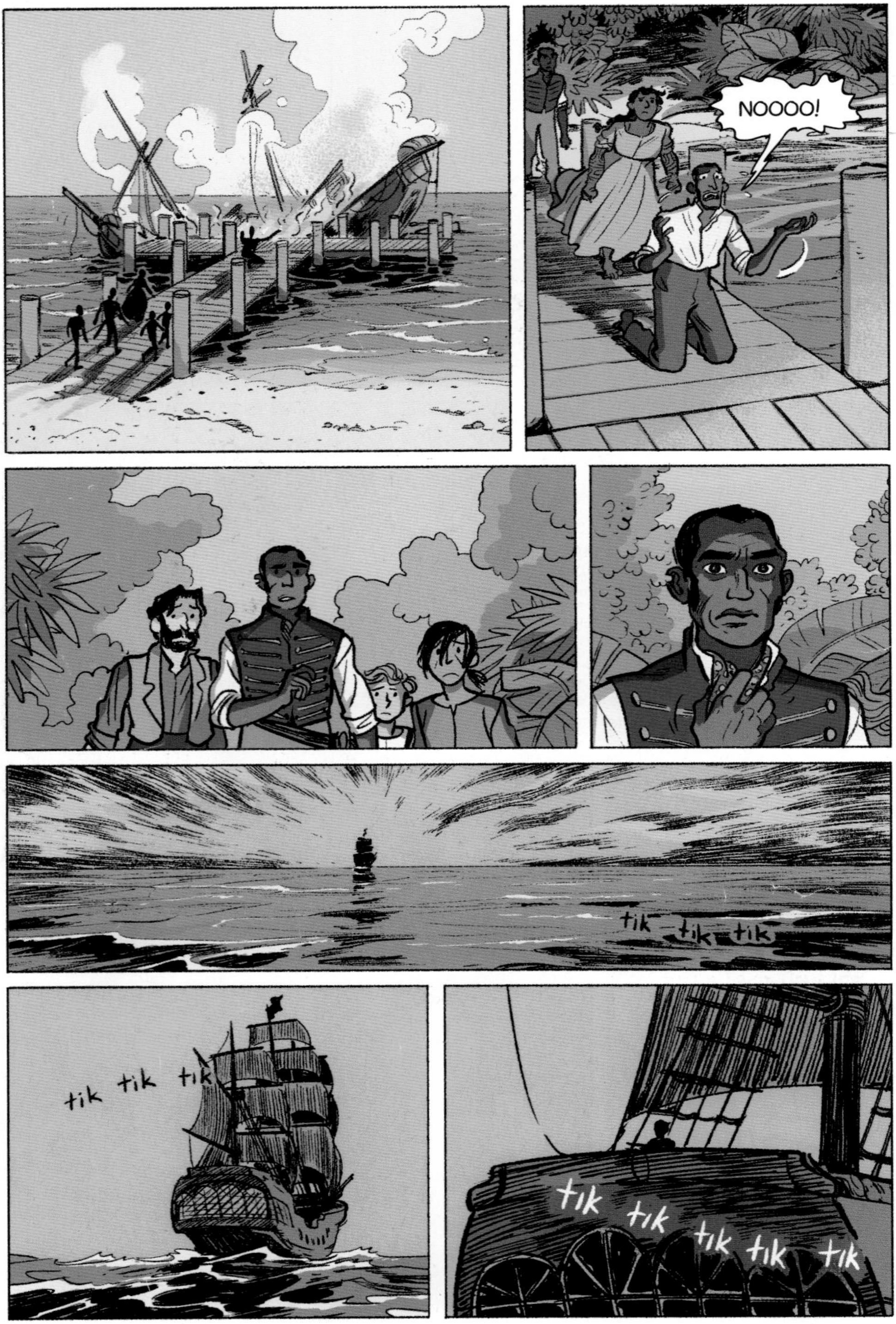
NOOOO!
tik tik tik
tik tik tik
tik
tik
tik
tik
tik

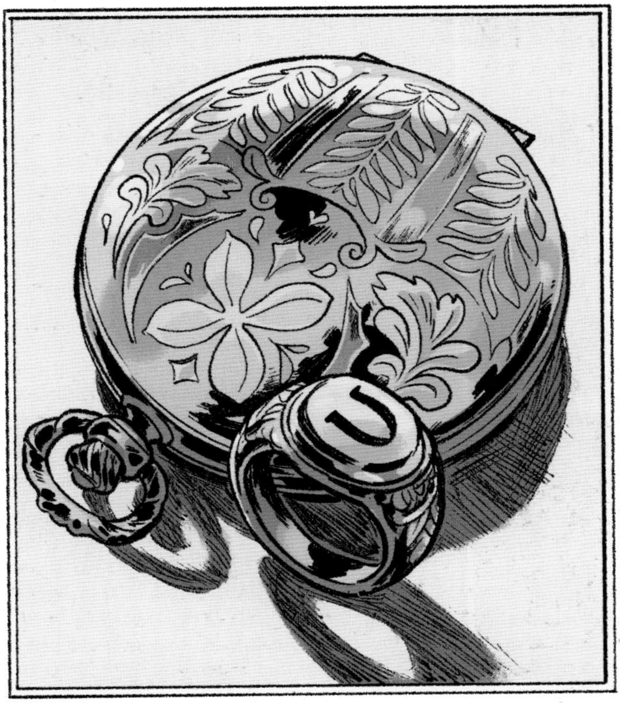
U

CHAPTER TEN

ETERNITY

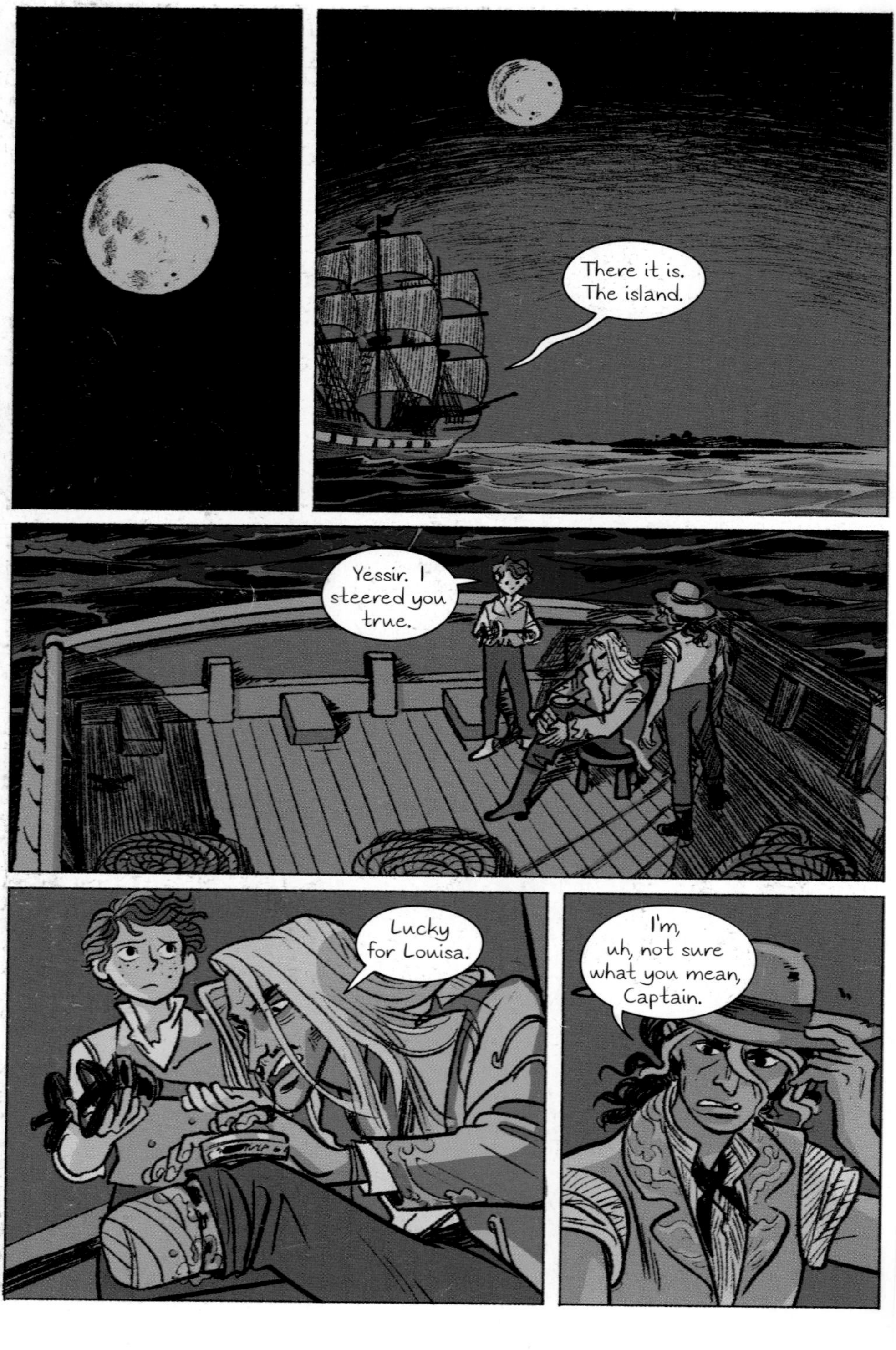

There it is. The island.
Yessir. I steered you true.
Lucky for Louisa.
I'm, uh, not sure what you mean, Captain.

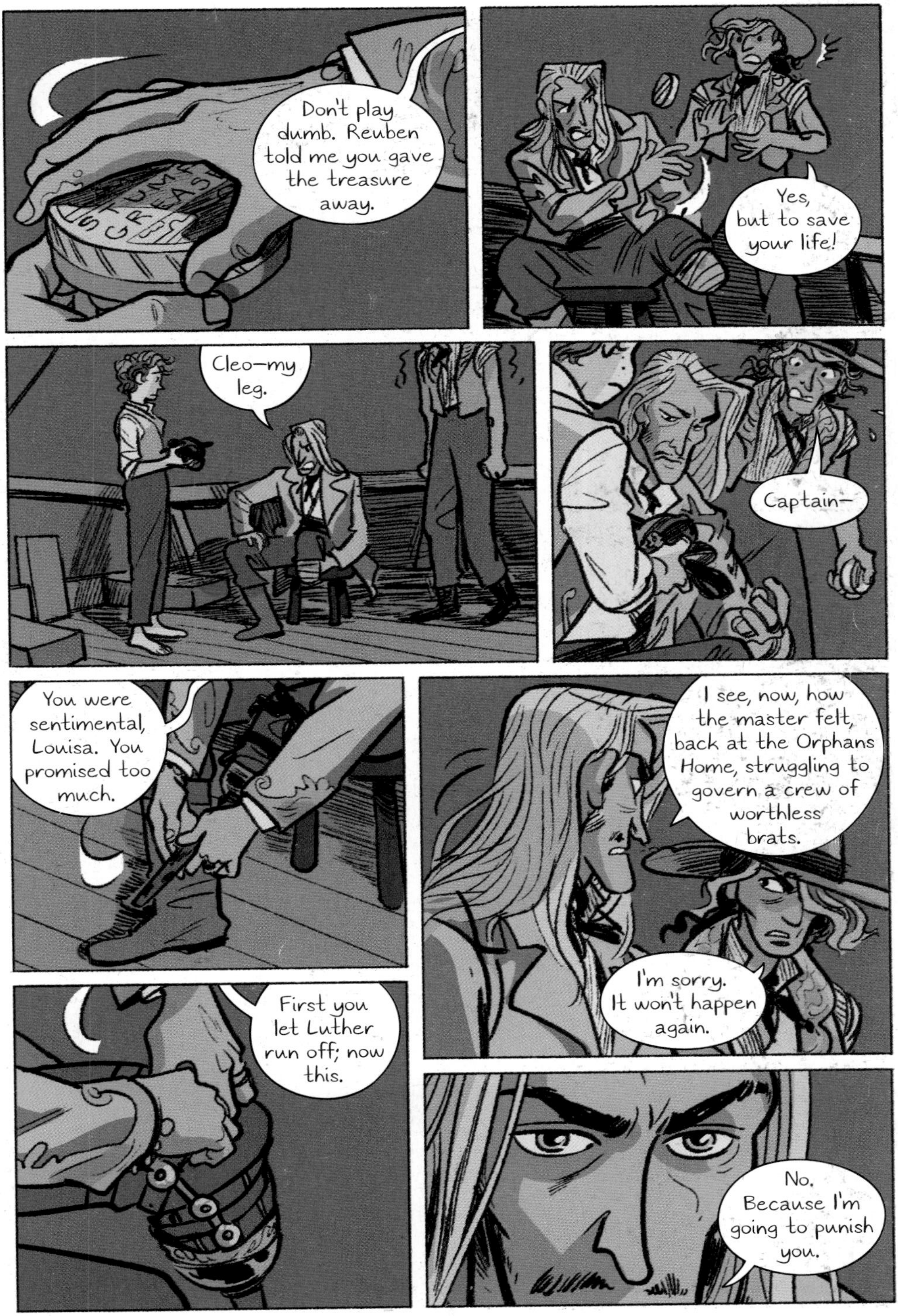
Don't play dumb. Reuben told me you gave the treasure away.
Yes, but to save your life!
Cleo—my leg.
Captain—
You were sentimental, Louisa. You promised too much.
I see, now, how the master felt, back at the Orphans Home, struggling to govern a crew of worthless brats.
I'm sorry. It won't happen again.
First you let Luther run off; now this.
No. Because I'm going to punish you.

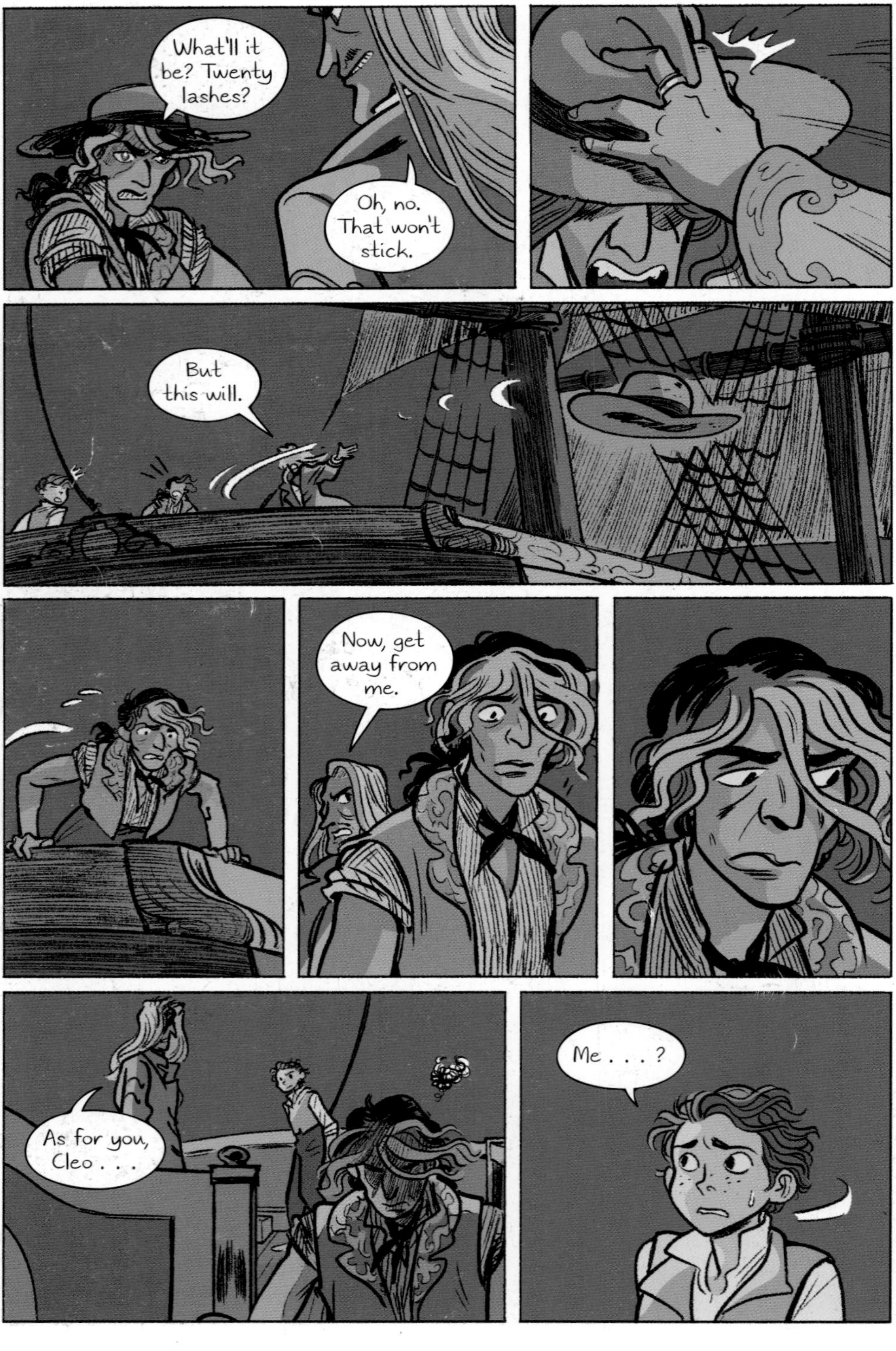
What'll it be? Twenty lashes?
Oh, no. That won't stick.
But this will.
Now, get away from me.
As for you, Cleo . . .
Me . . . ?

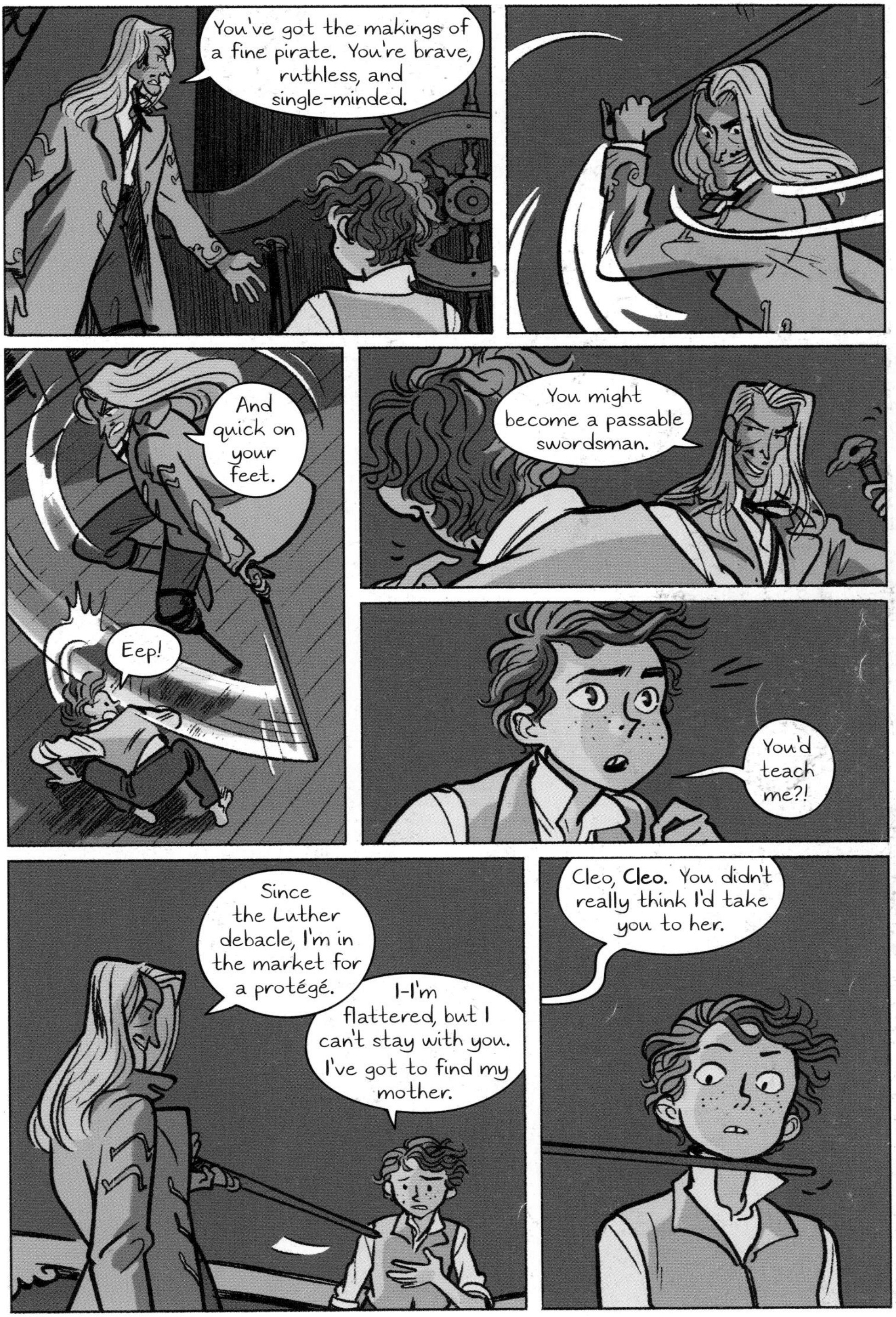

You've got the makings of a fine pirate. You're brave, ruthless, and single-minded.
And quick on your feet.
Eep!
You might become a passable swordsman.
You'd teach me?!
Since the Luther debacle, I'm in the market for a protégé.
I-I'm flattered, but I can't stay with you. I've got to find my mother.
Cleo, **Cleo.** You didn't really think I'd take you to her.

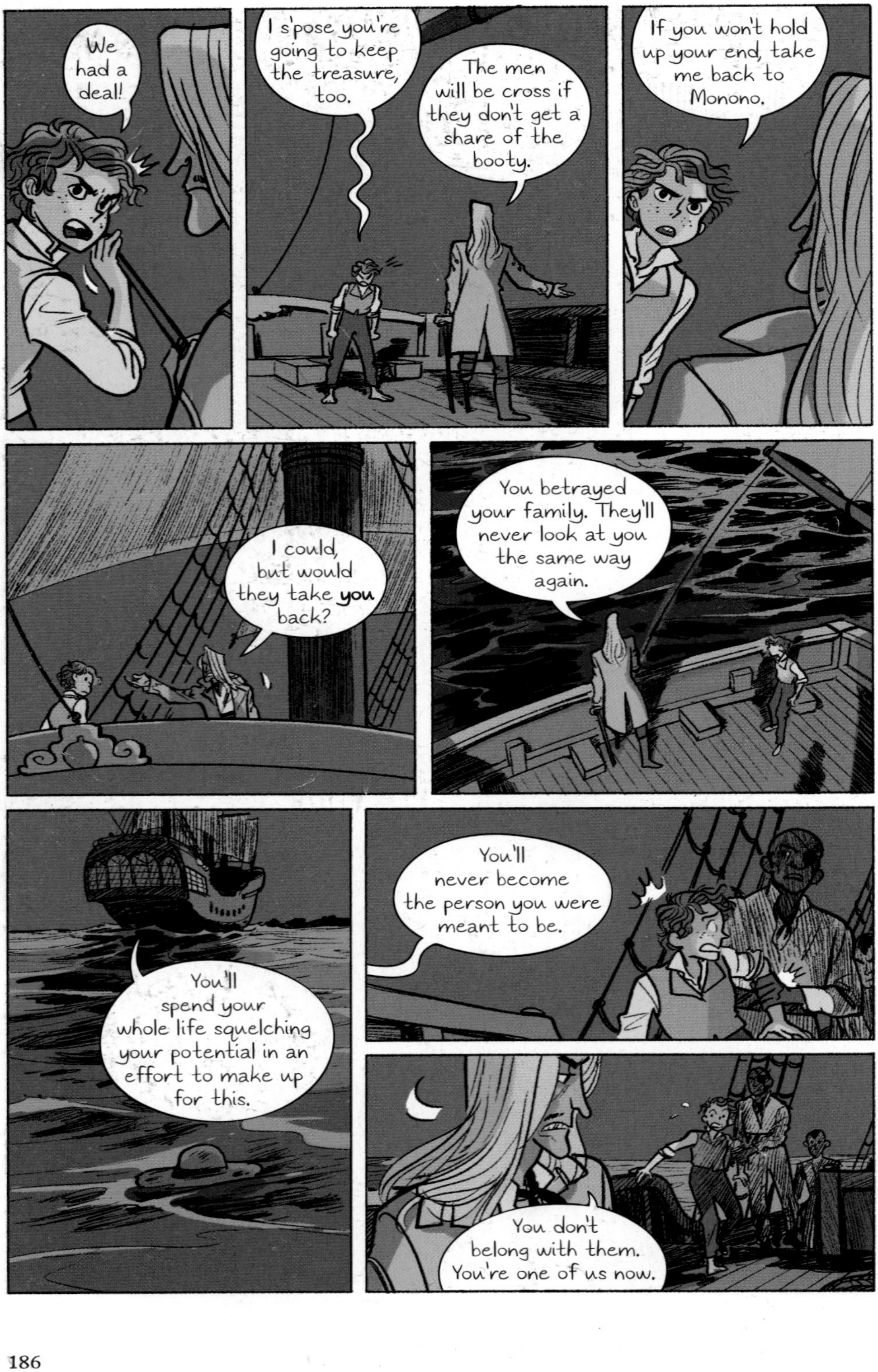
We had a deal!
I s'pose you're going to keep the treasure, too.
The men will be cross if they don't get a share of the booty.
If you won't hold up your end, take me back to Monono.
I could, but would they take **you** back?
You betrayed your family. They'll never look at you the same way again.
You'll spend your whole life squelching your potential in an effort to make up for this.
You'll never become the person you were meant to be.
You don't belong with them. You're one of us now.

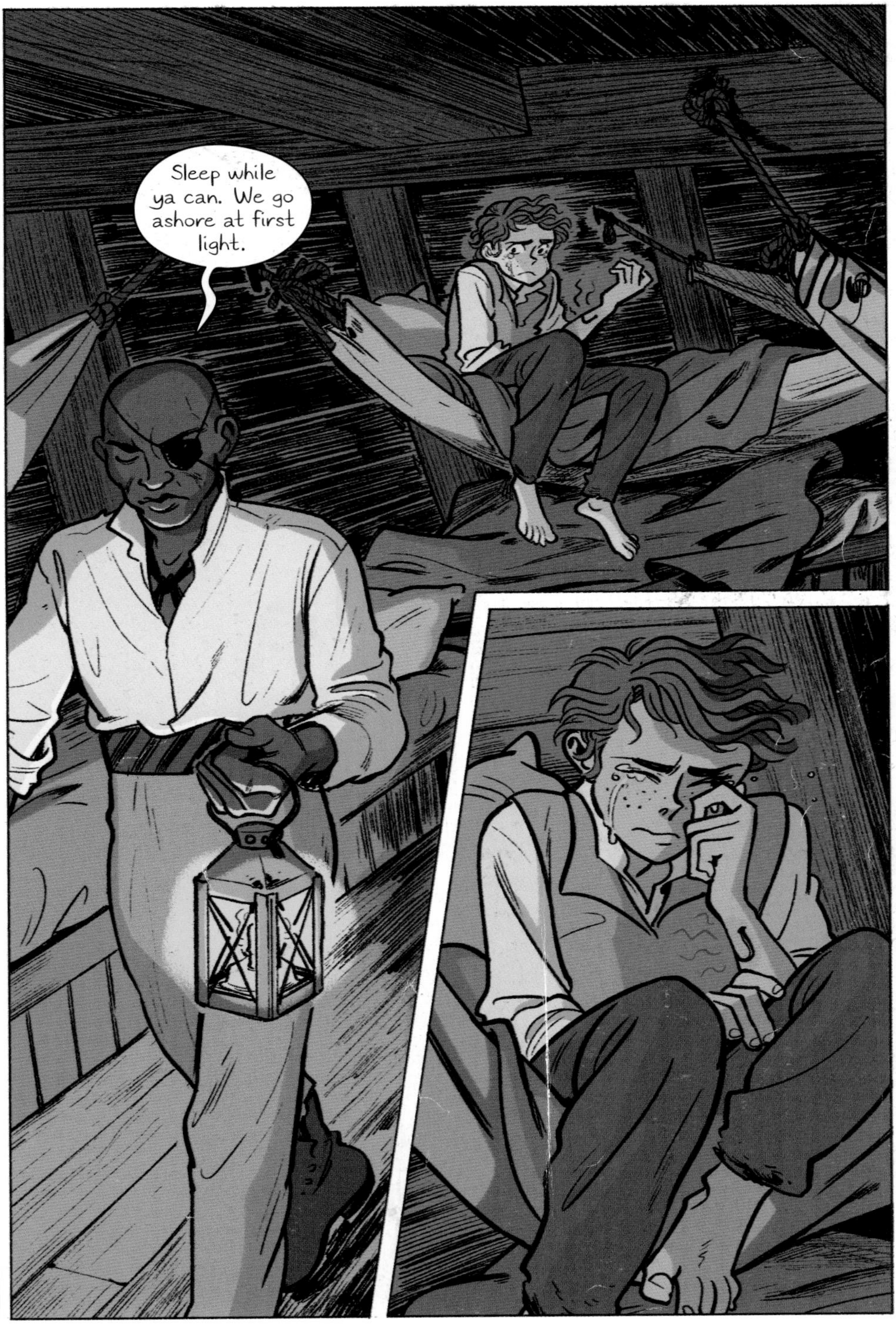
Sleep while ya can. We go ashore at first light.

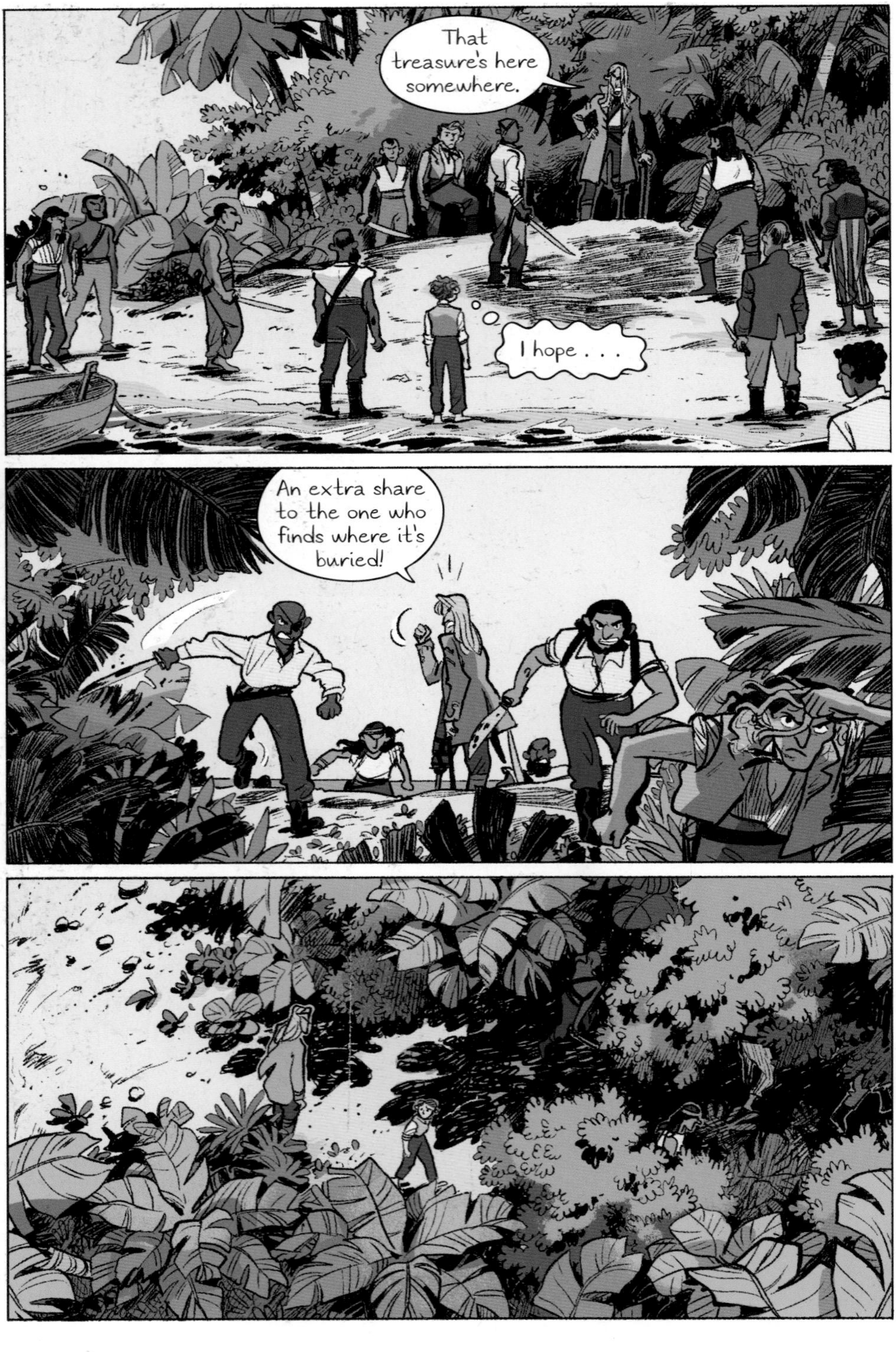
That treasure's here somewhere.
I hope . . .
An extra share to the one who finds where it's buried!

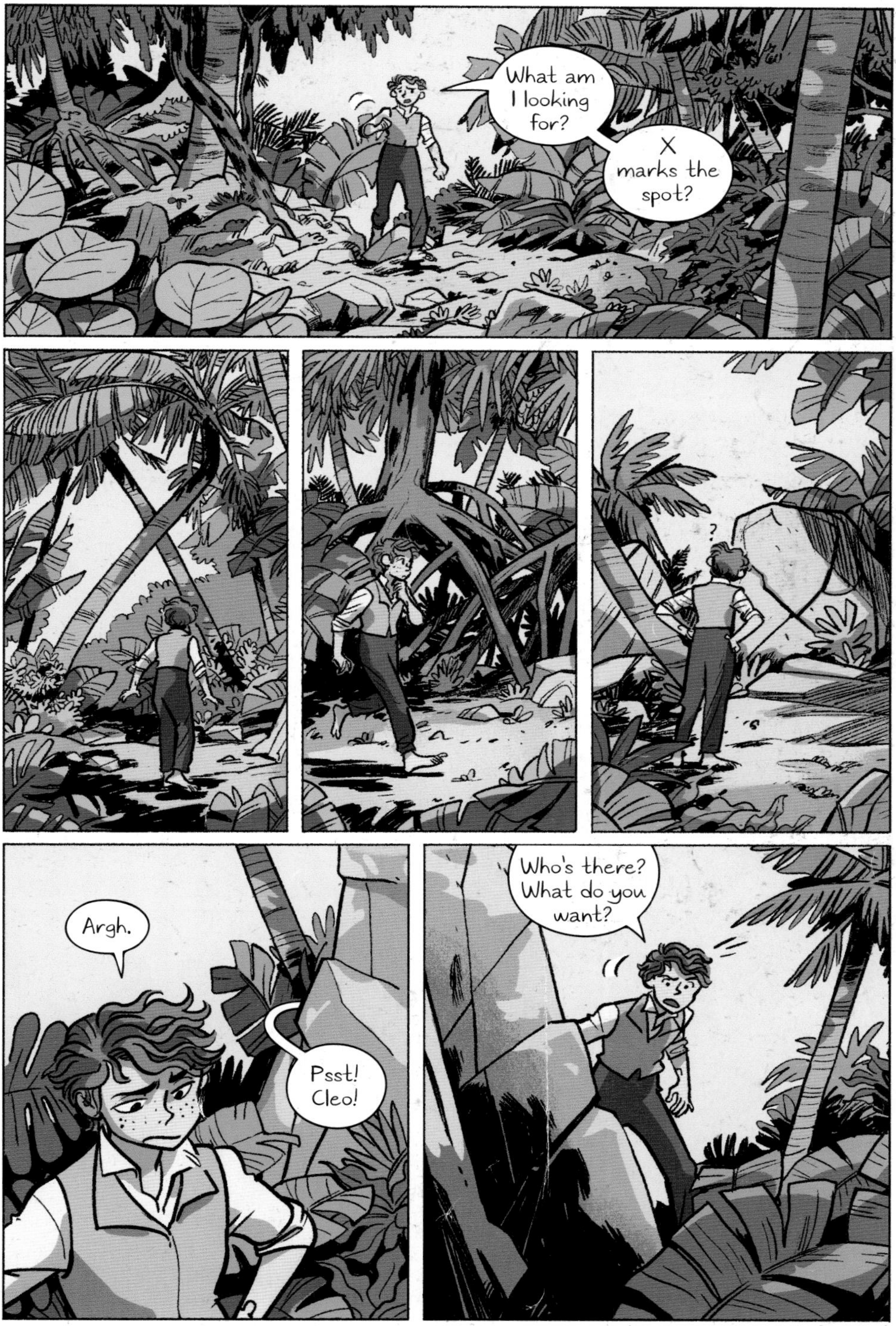
What am I looking for?
X marks the spot?
Argh.
Psst! Cleo!
Who's there? What do you want?

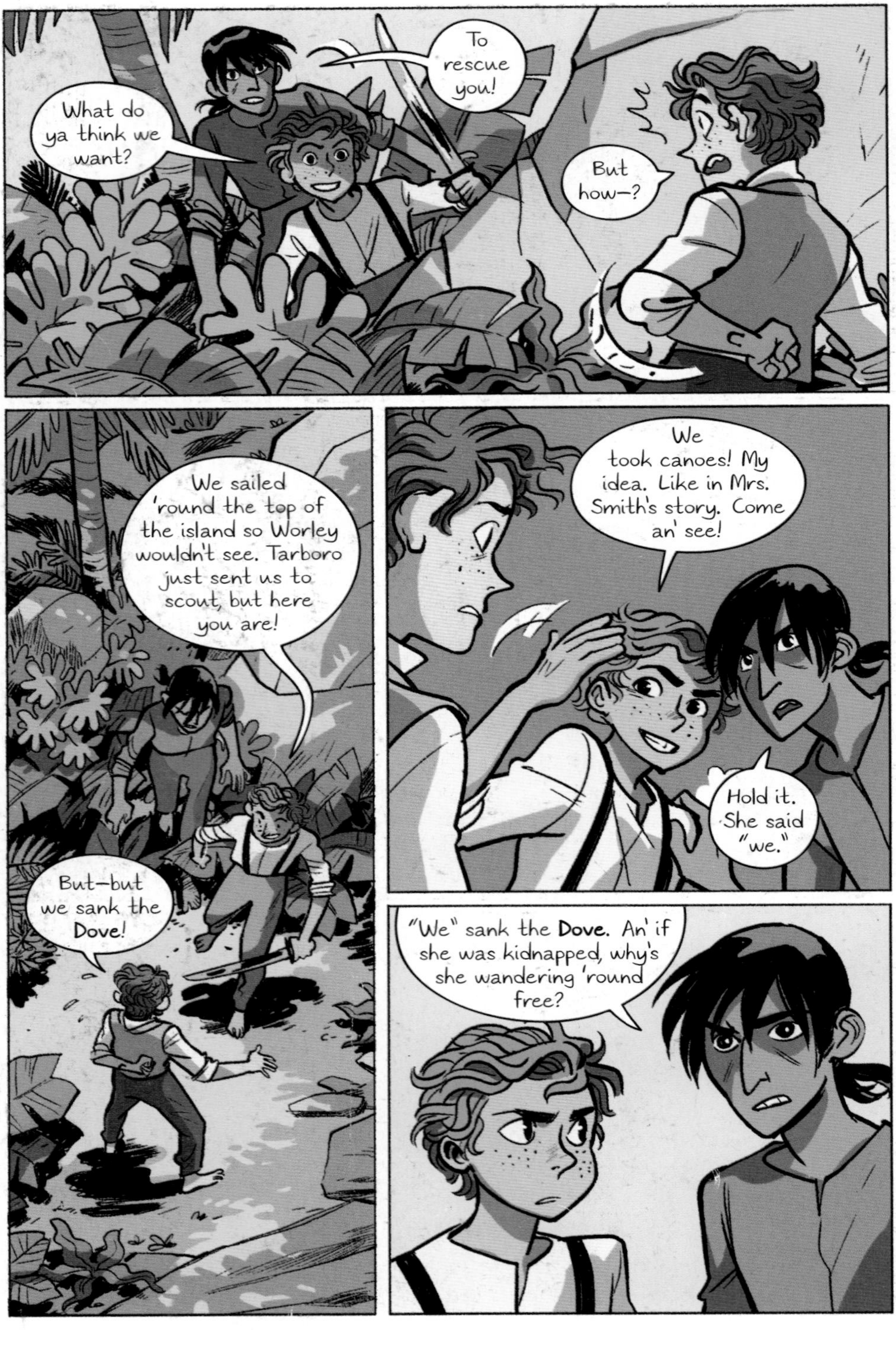
What do ya think we want?
To rescue you!
But how—?
We sailed 'round the top of the island so Worley wouldn't see. Tarboro just sent us to scout, but here you are!
But—but we sank the Dove!
We took canoes! My idea. Like in Mrs. Smith's story. Come an' see!
Hold it. She said "we."
"We" sank the Dove. An' if she was kidnapped, why's she wandering 'round free?

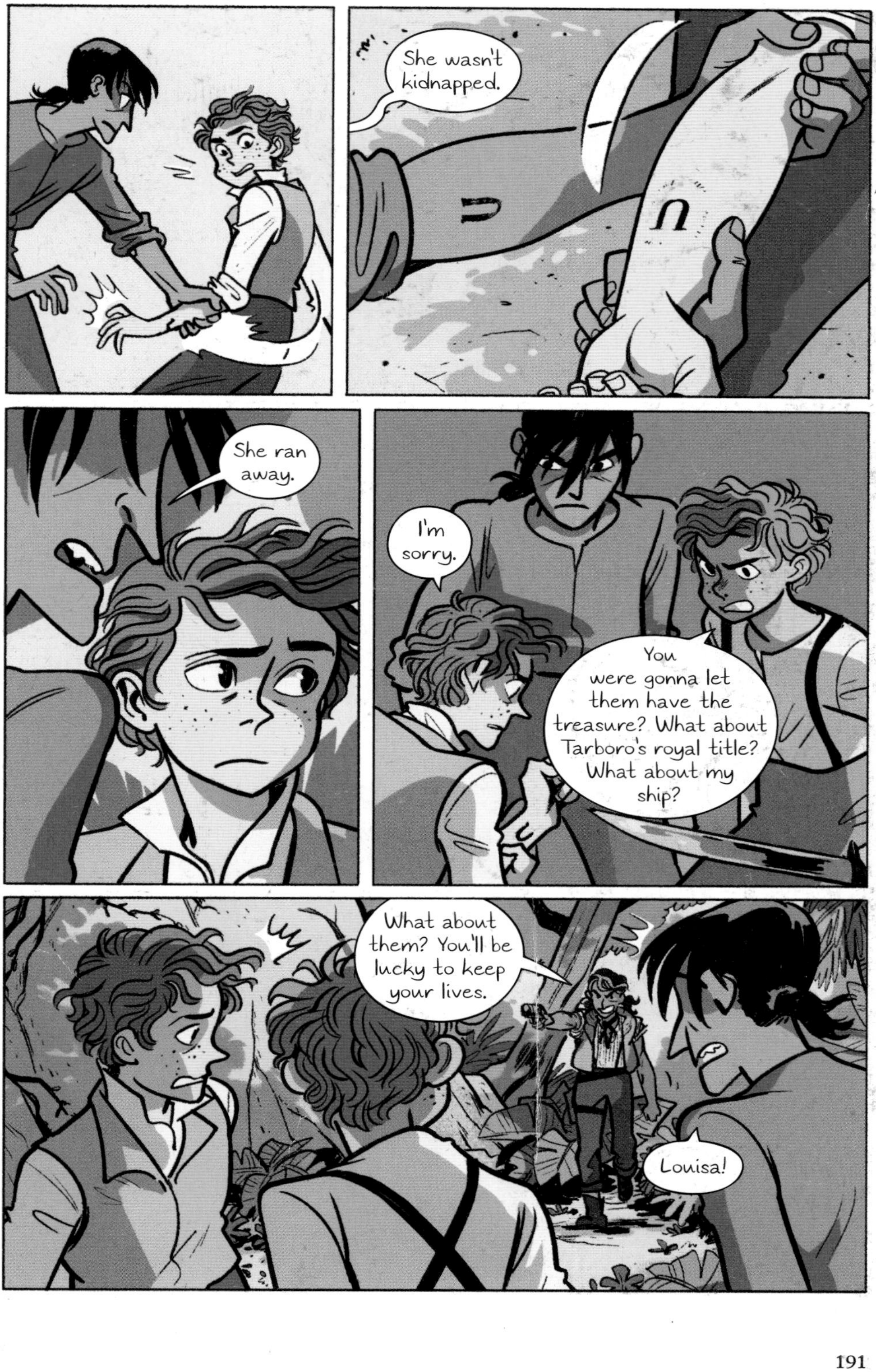
She wasn't kidnapped.
She ran away.
I'm sorry.
You were gonna let them have the treasure? What about Tarboro's royal title? What about my ship?
What about them? You'll be lucky to keep your lives.
Louisa!

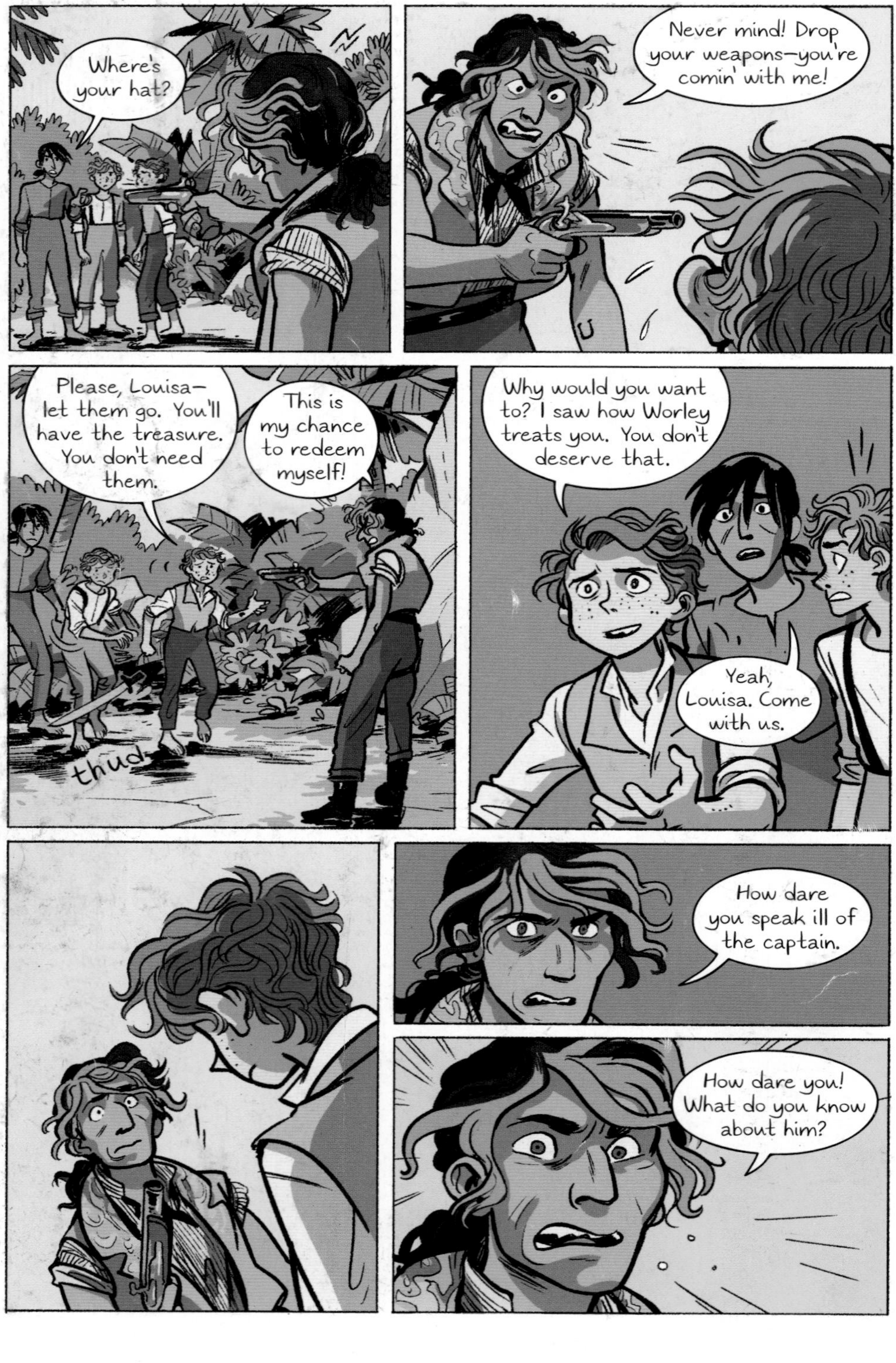
Where's your hat?
Never mind! Drop your weapons—you're comin' with me!
Please, Louisa—let them go. You'll have the treasure. You don't need them.
This is my chance to redeem myself!
thud
Why would you want to? I saw how Worley treats you. You don't deserve that.
Yeah, Louisa. Come with us.
How dare you speak ill of the captain.
How dare you! What do you know about him?

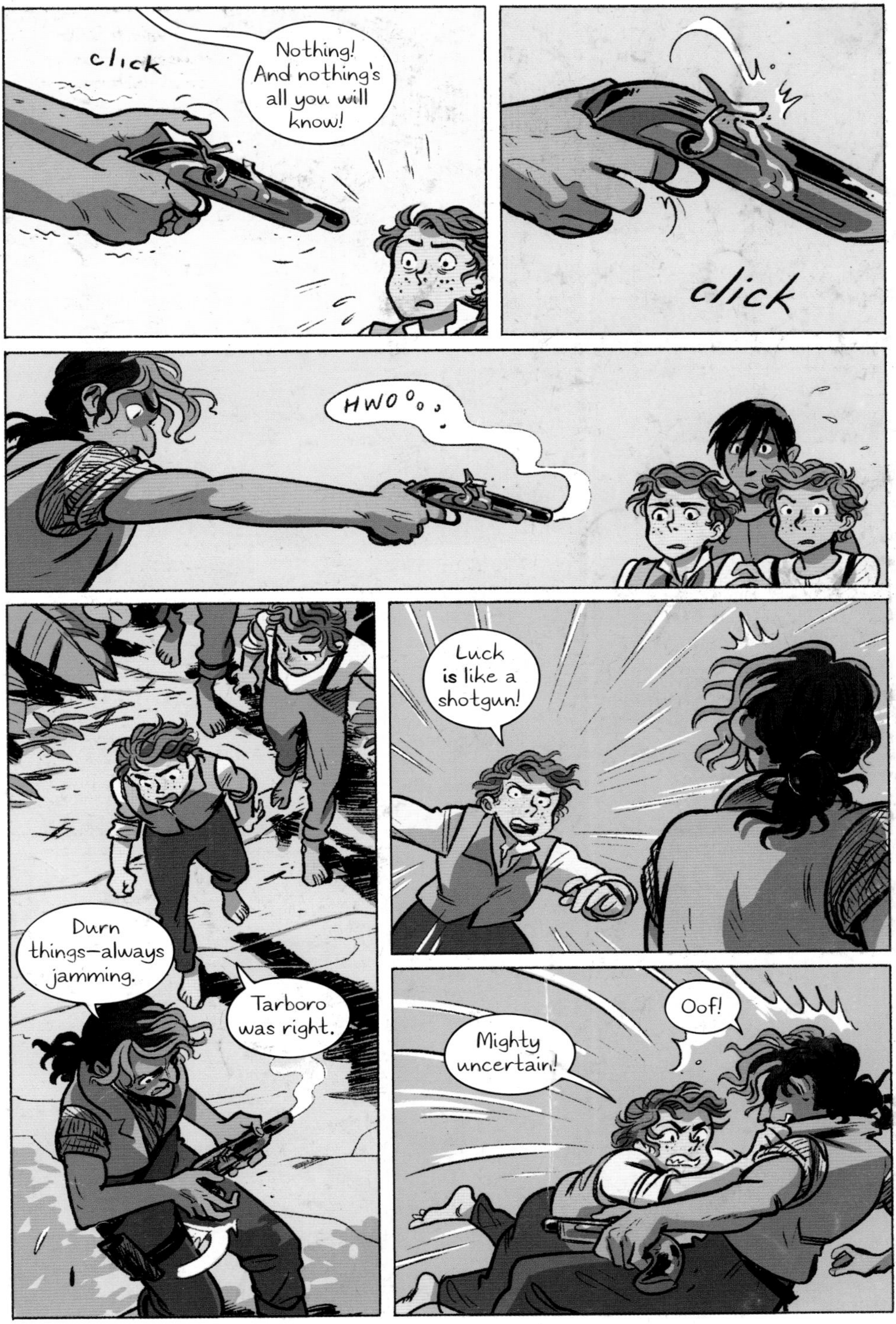
click
Nothing! And nothing's all you will know!
click
HWOo o o
Luck is like a shotgun!
Durn things—always jamming.
Tarboro was right.
Oof!
Mighty uncertain!

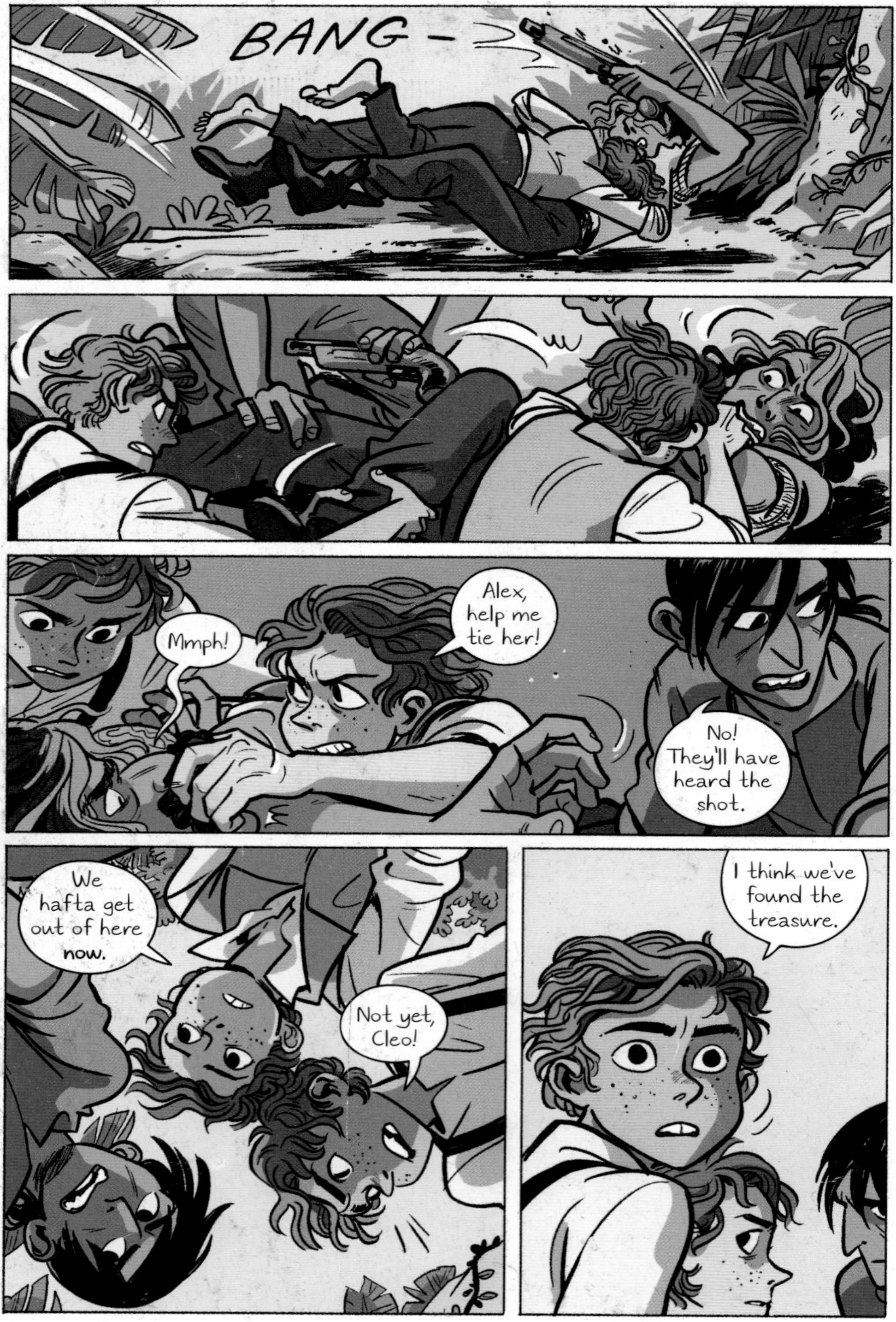
BANG—
Mmph!
Alex, help me tie her!
No! They'll have heard the shot.
We hafta get out of here now.
Not yet, Cleo!
I think we've found the treasure.

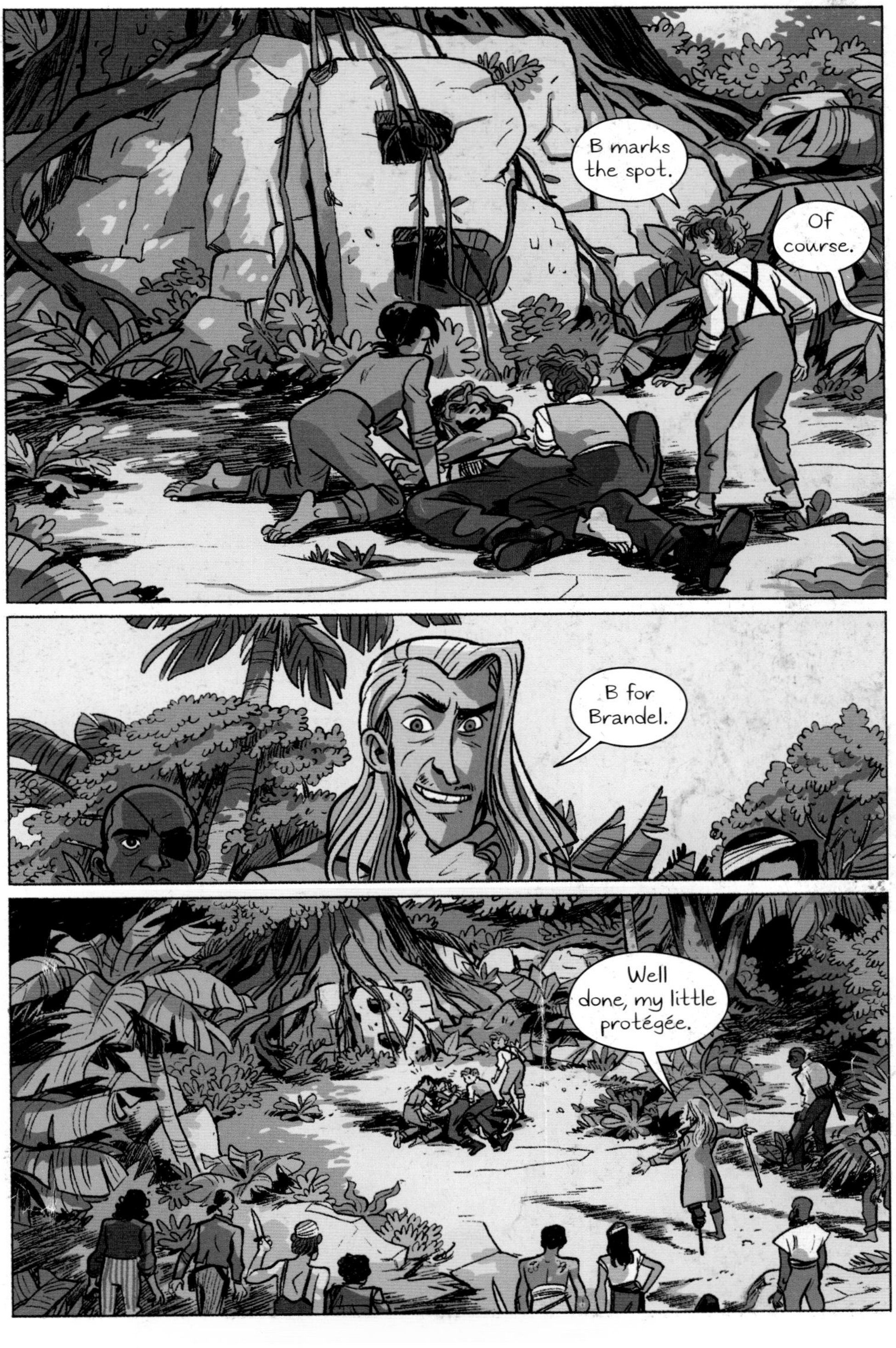

B marks the spot.
Of course.
B for Brandel.
Well done, my little protégée.

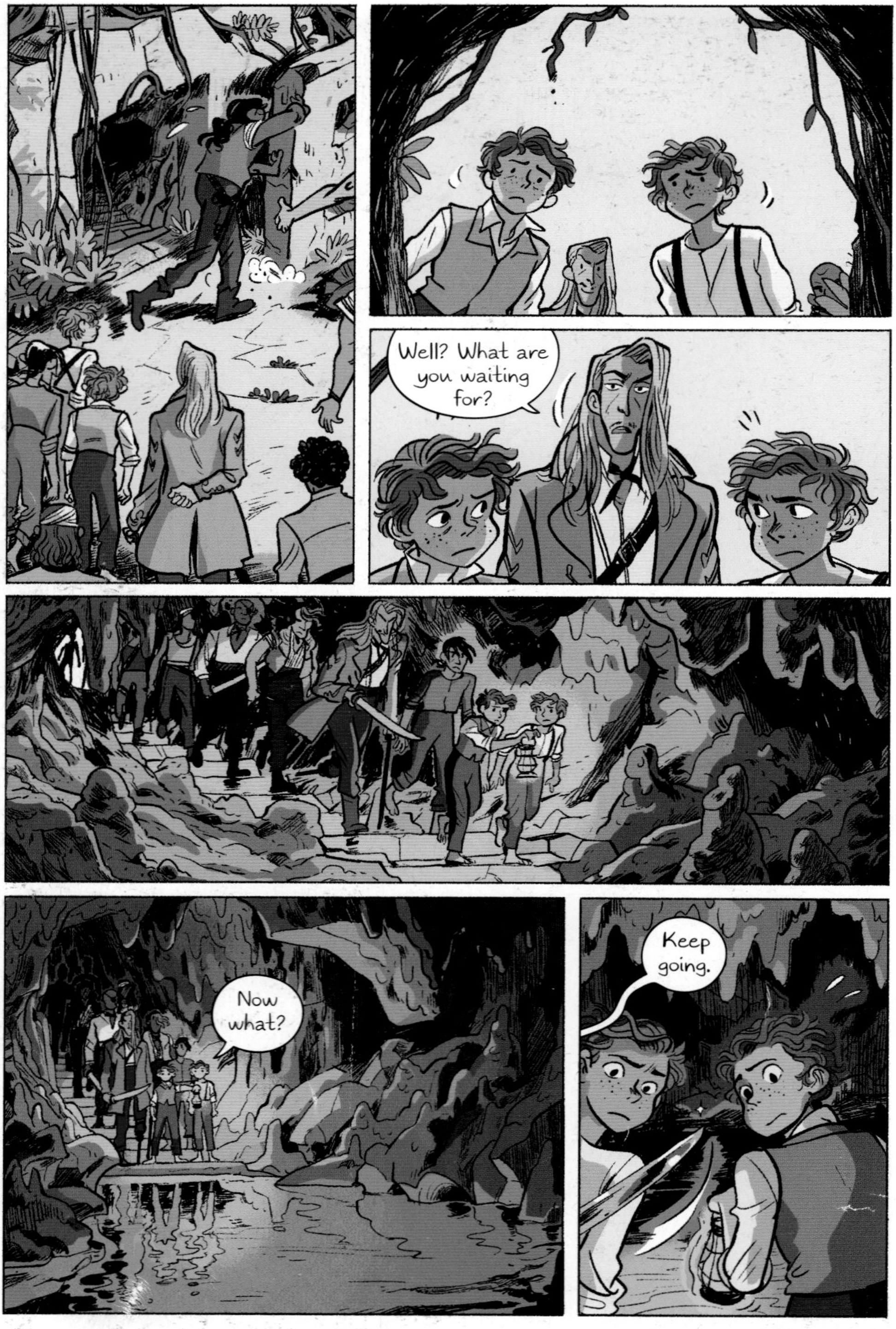
Well? What are you waiting for?
Now what?
Keep going.

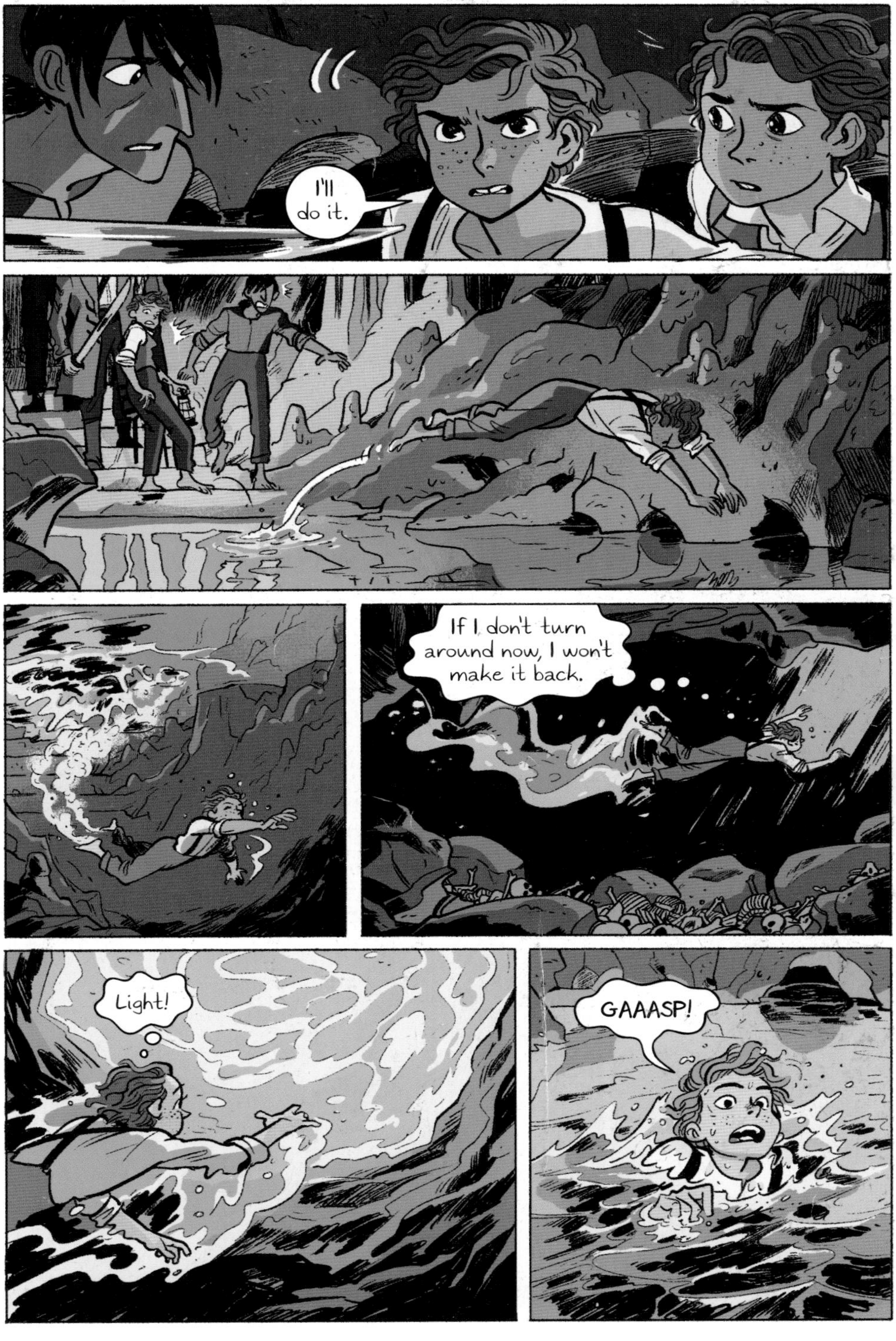
I'll do it.
If I don't turn around now, I won't make it back.
Light!
GAAASP!

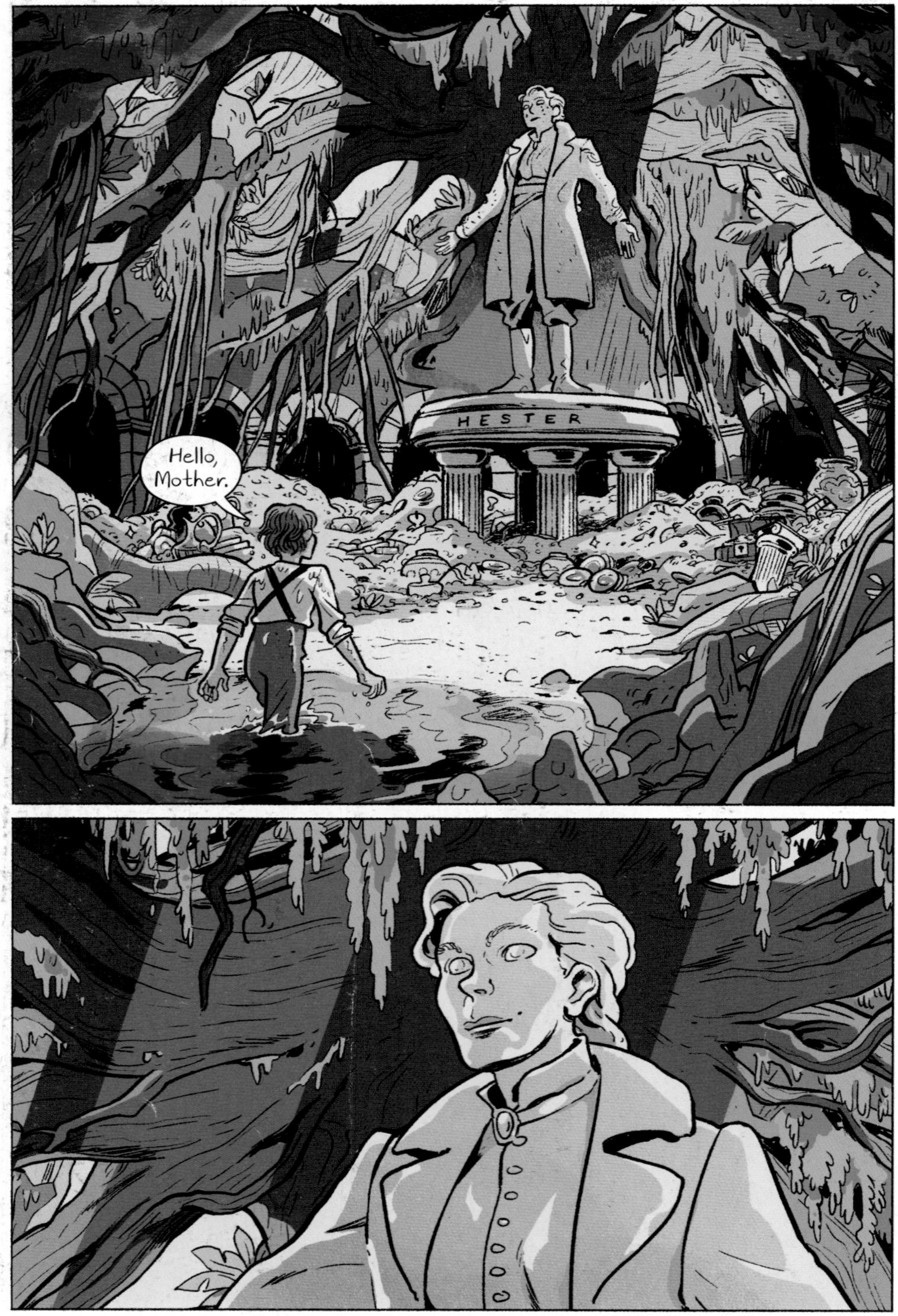
HESTER
Hello, Mother.

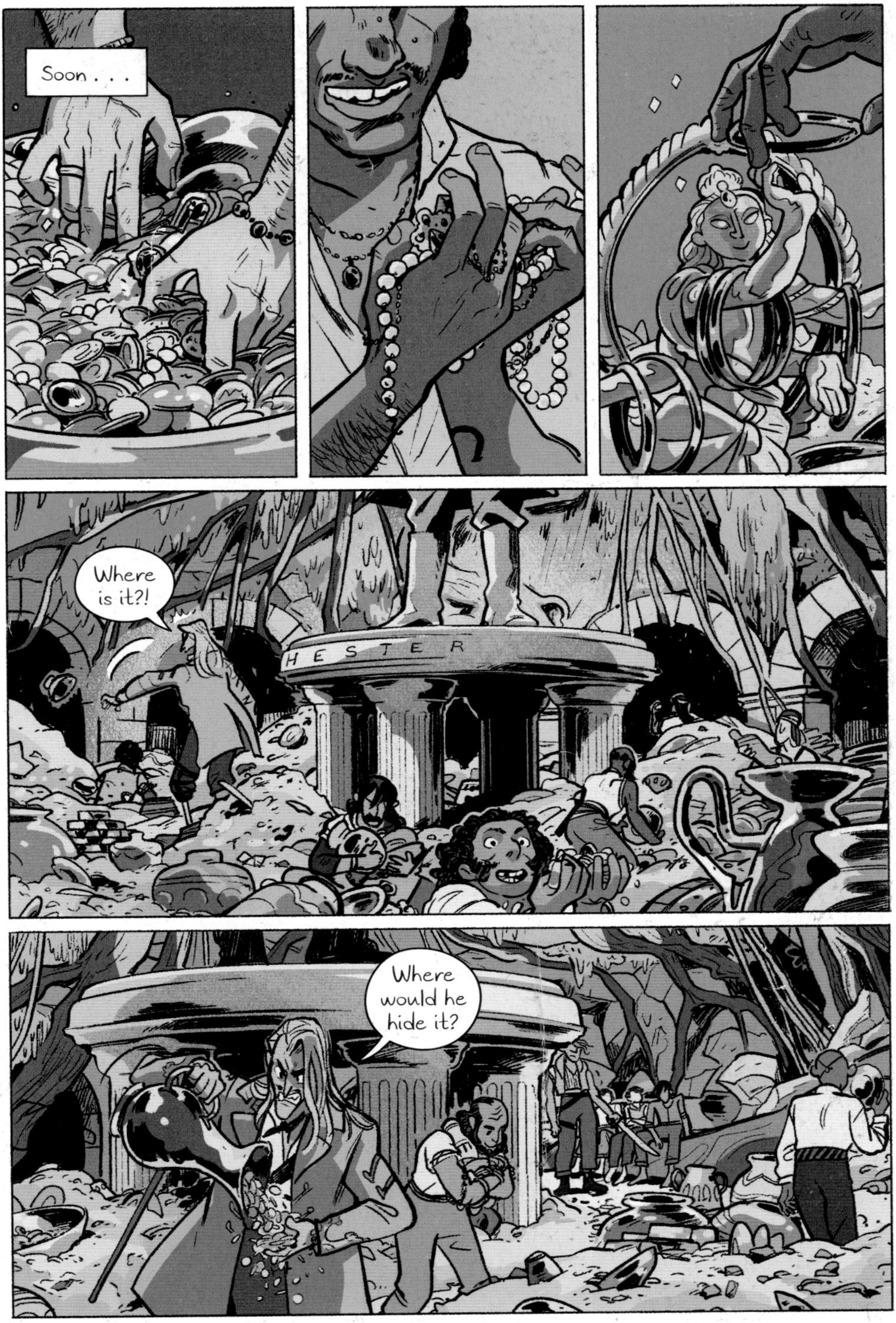
Soon . . .
Where is it?!
HESTER
Where would he hide it?

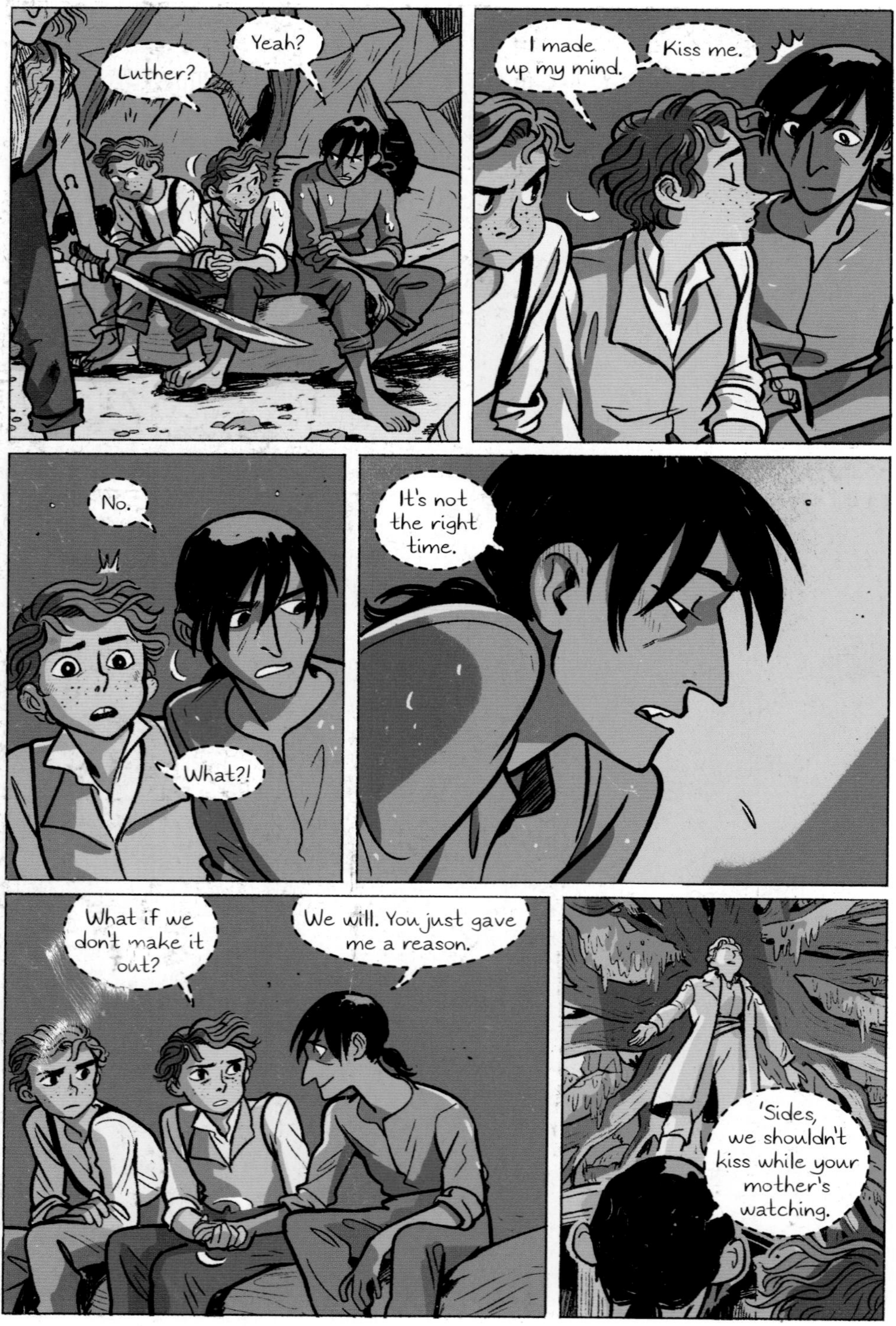
Luther?
Yeah?
I made up my mind.
Kiss me.
No.
What?!
It's not the right time.
What if we don't make it out?
We will. You just gave me a reason.
'Sides, we shouldn't kiss while your mother's watching.

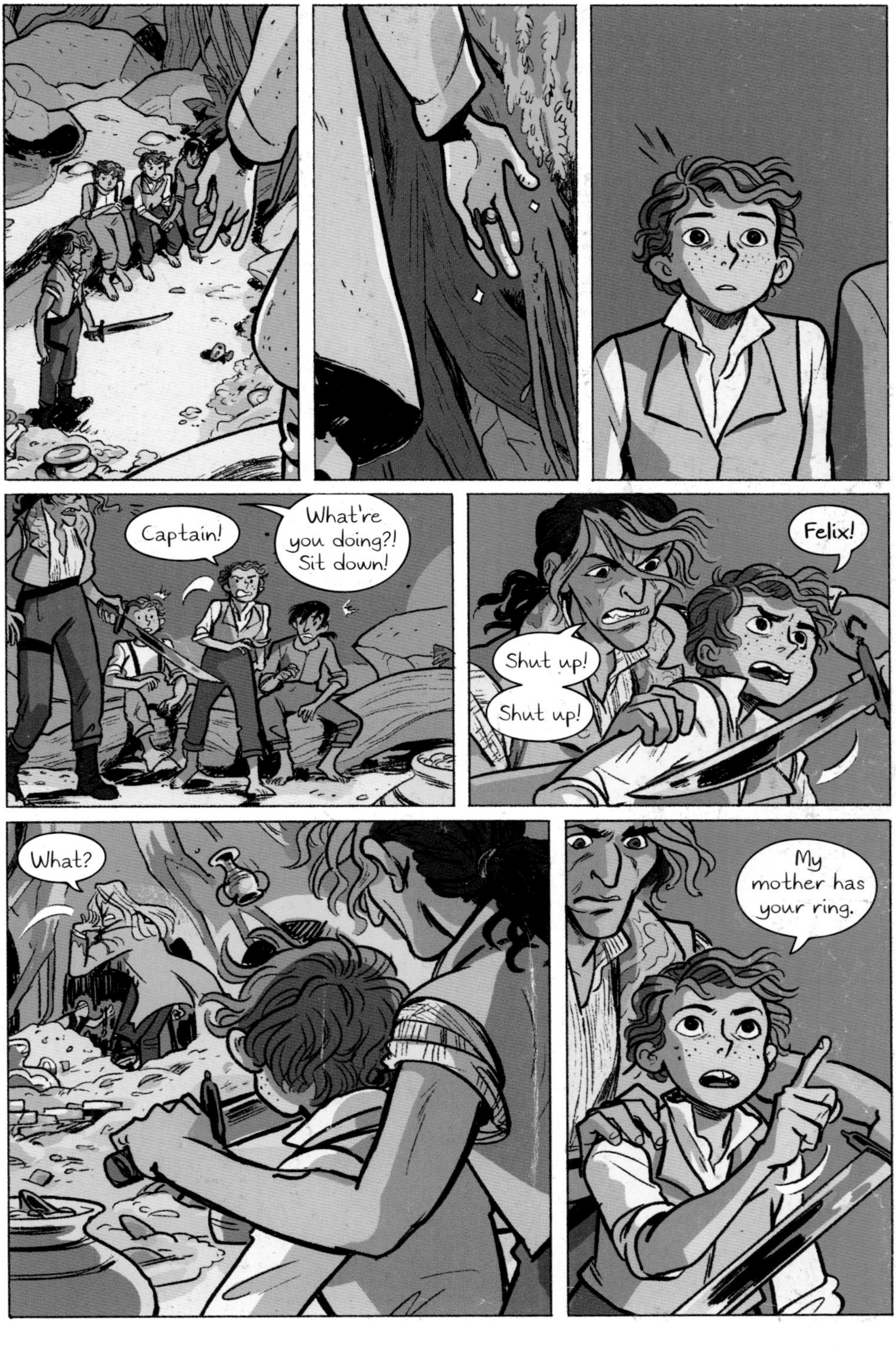
Captain!
What're you doing?! Sit down!
Felix!
Shut up!
Shut up!
What?
My mother has your ring.

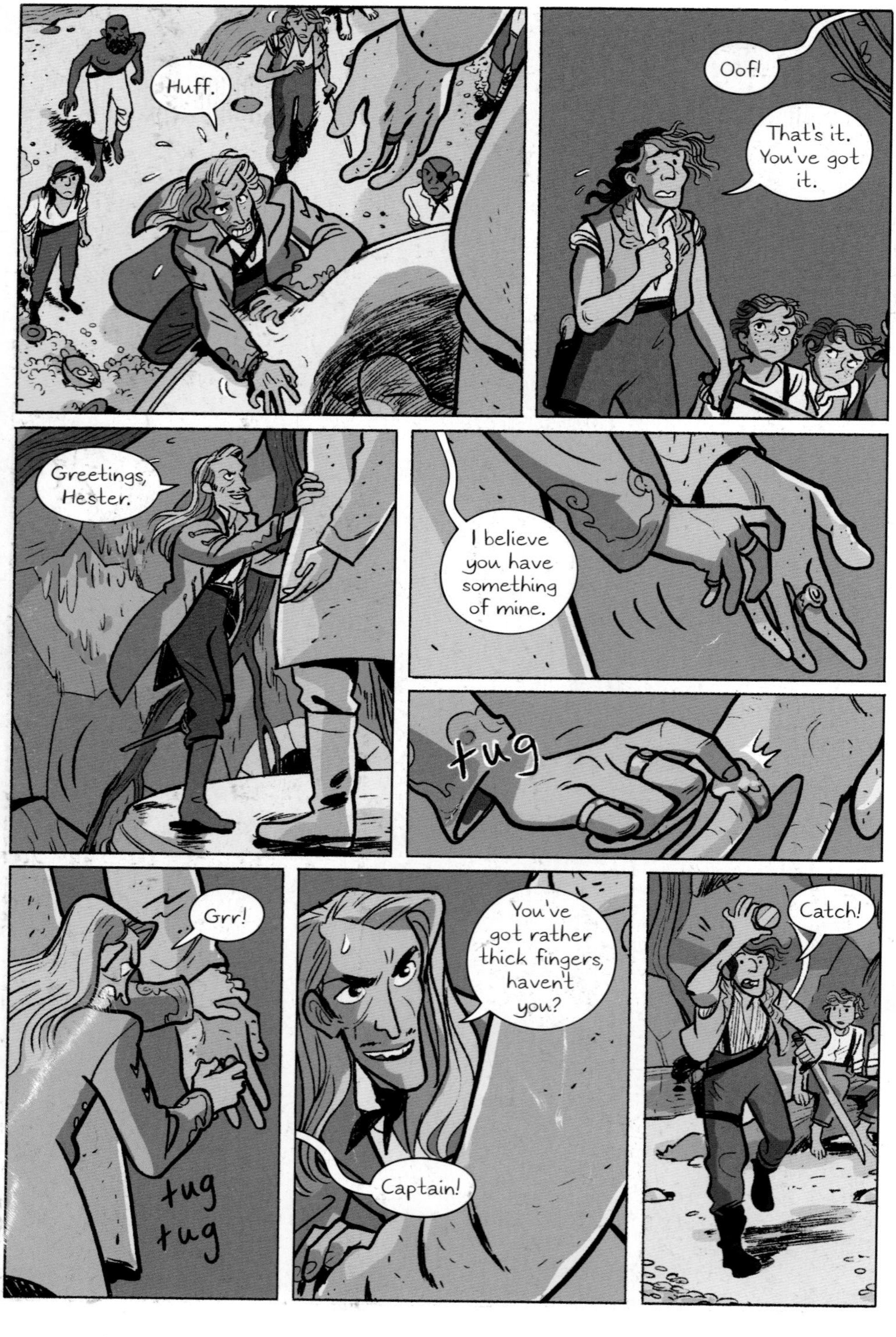
Huff.
Oof!
That's it. You've got it.
Greetings, Hester.
I believe you have something of mine.
tug
Grr!
tug tug
You've got rather thick fingers, haven't you?
Captain!
Catch!

Well done, Louisa.

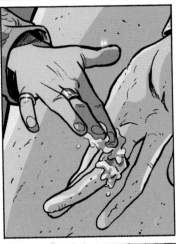

click

Aha!

tik tik tik

What do you say to that, Hester?

tik tik tik tik

"Tick tick tick..."?

tik tik t—

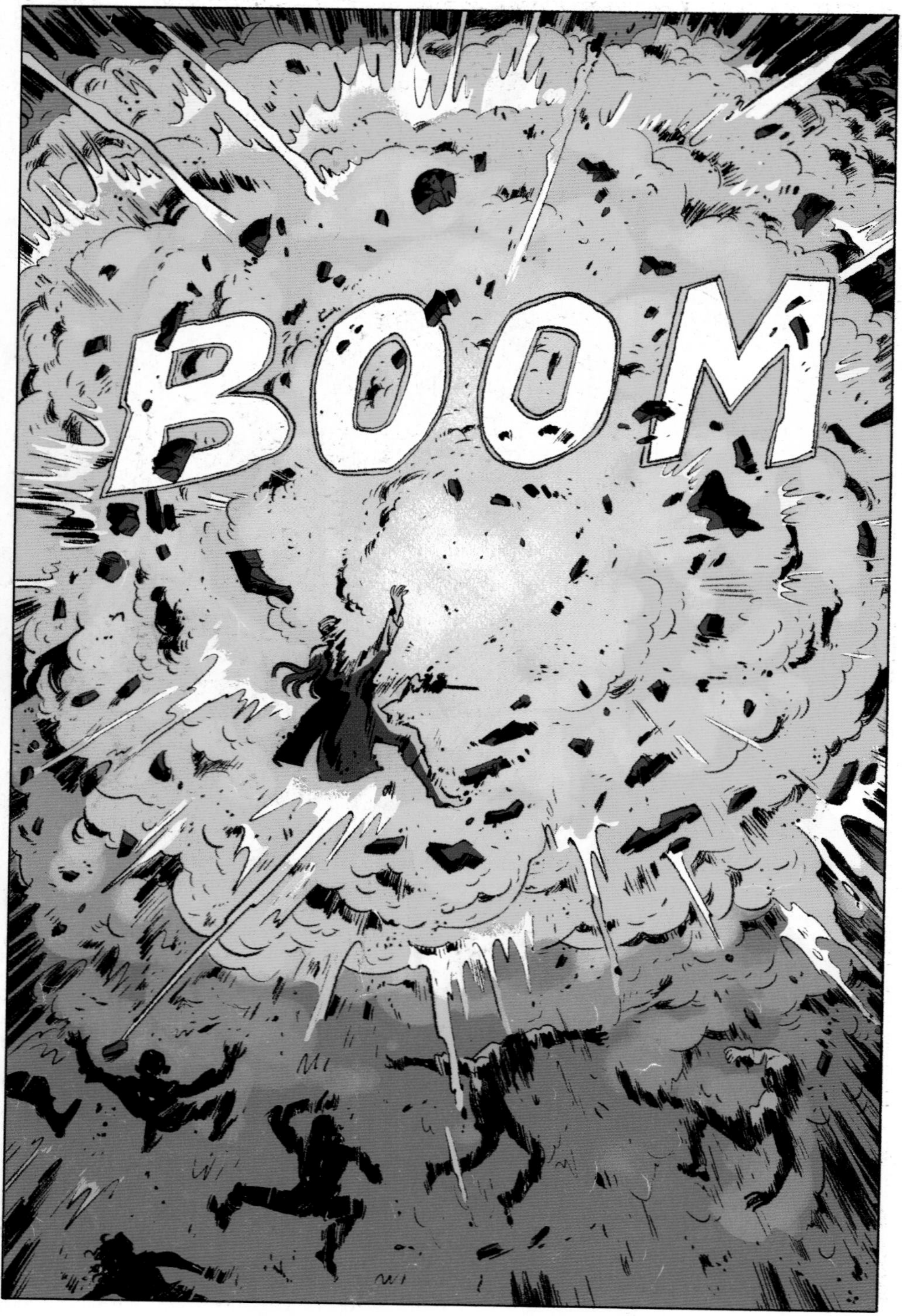
BOOM

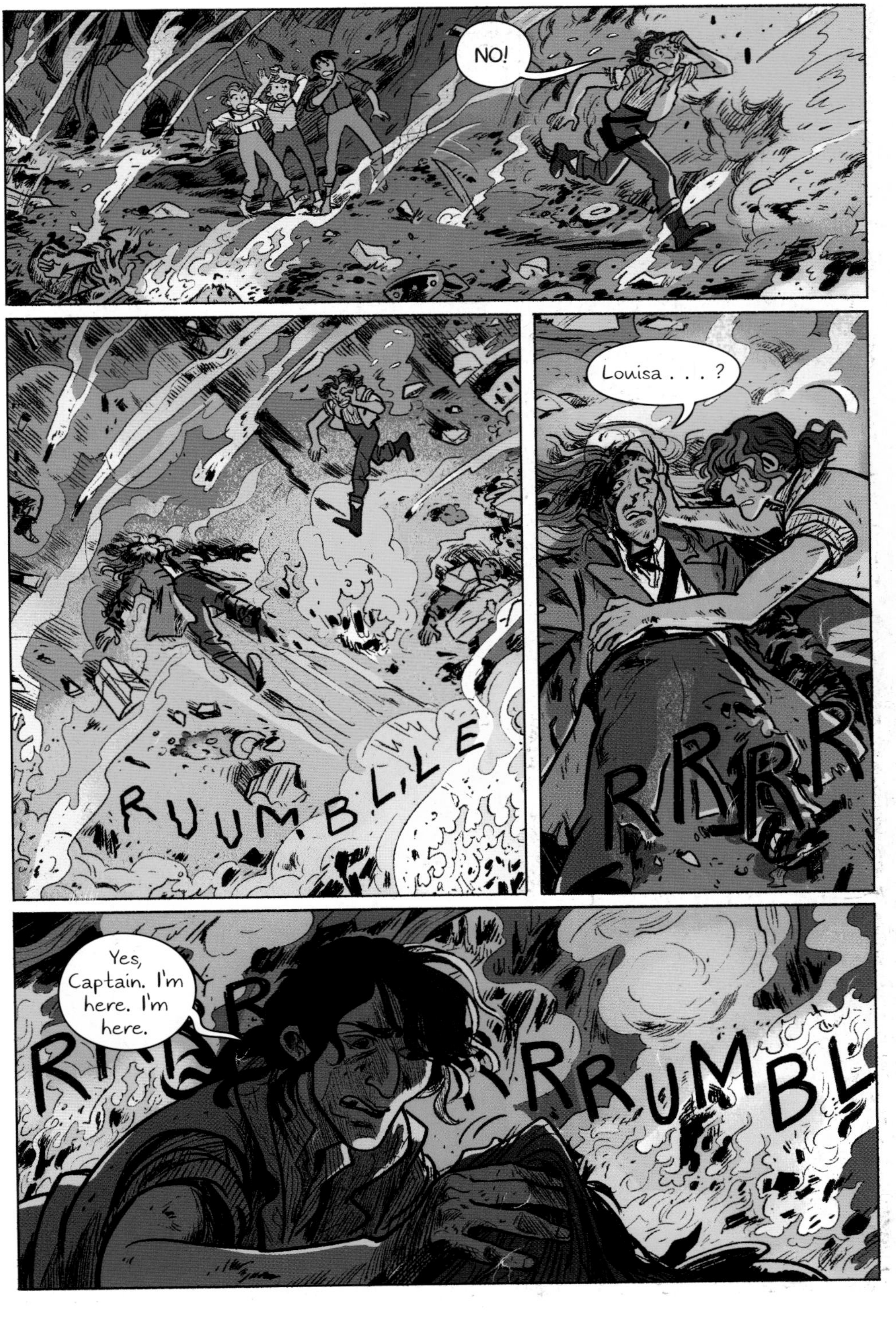
NO!
RUUMBLLE
Louisa . . . ?
RRRR
Yes, Captain. I'm here. I'm here.
RRRRRRUMBL

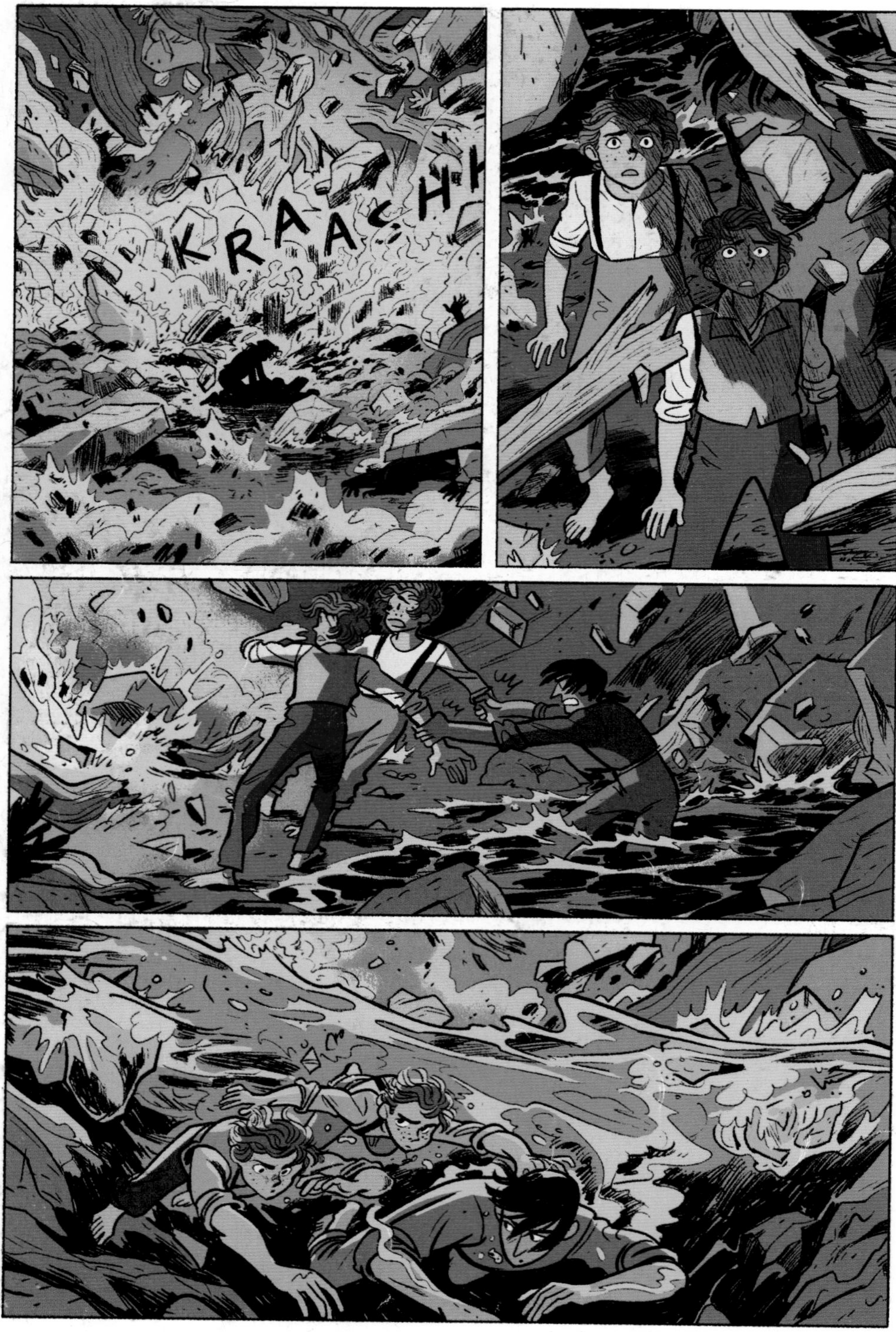
KRAACHH

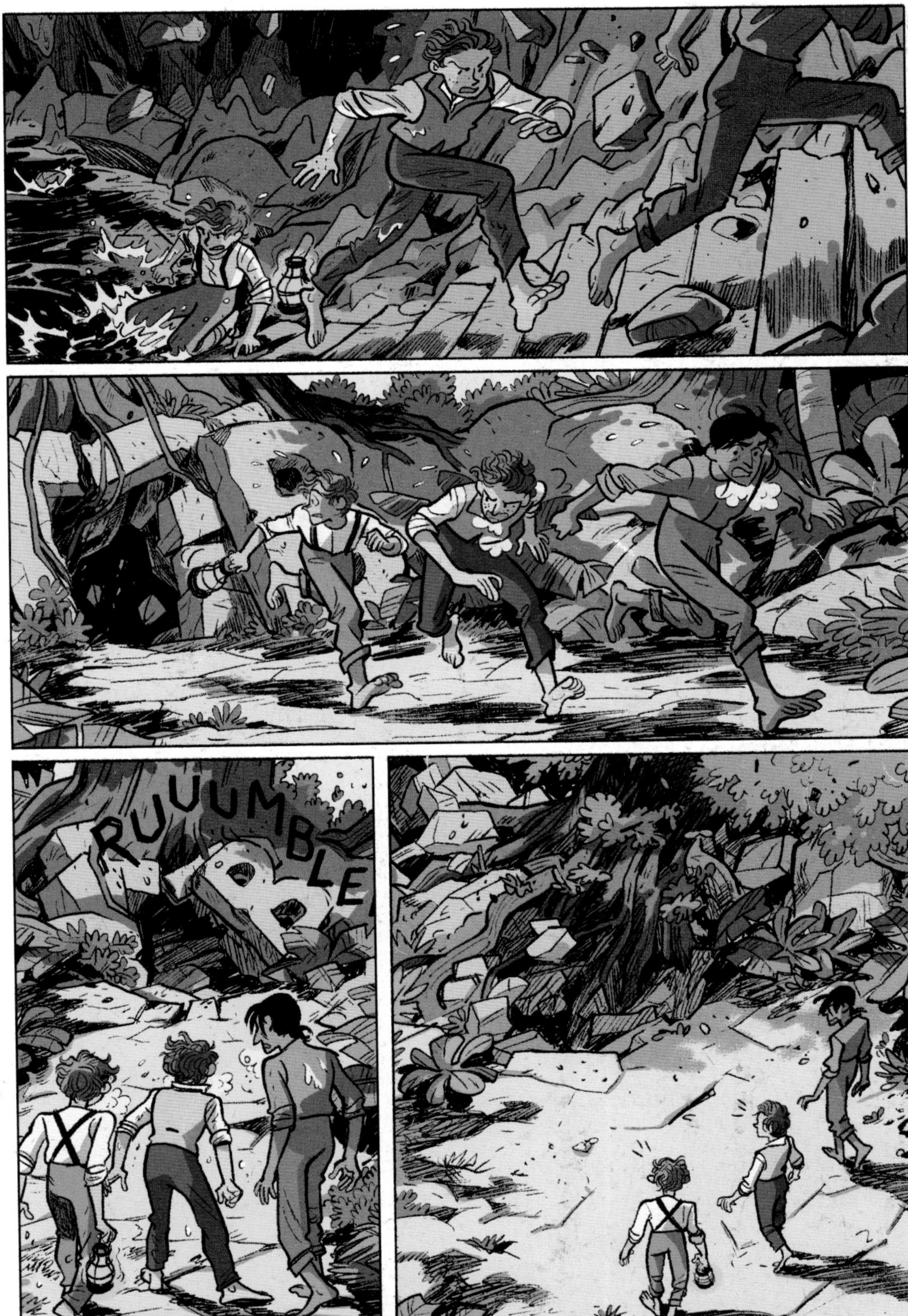
RUUUMBLE

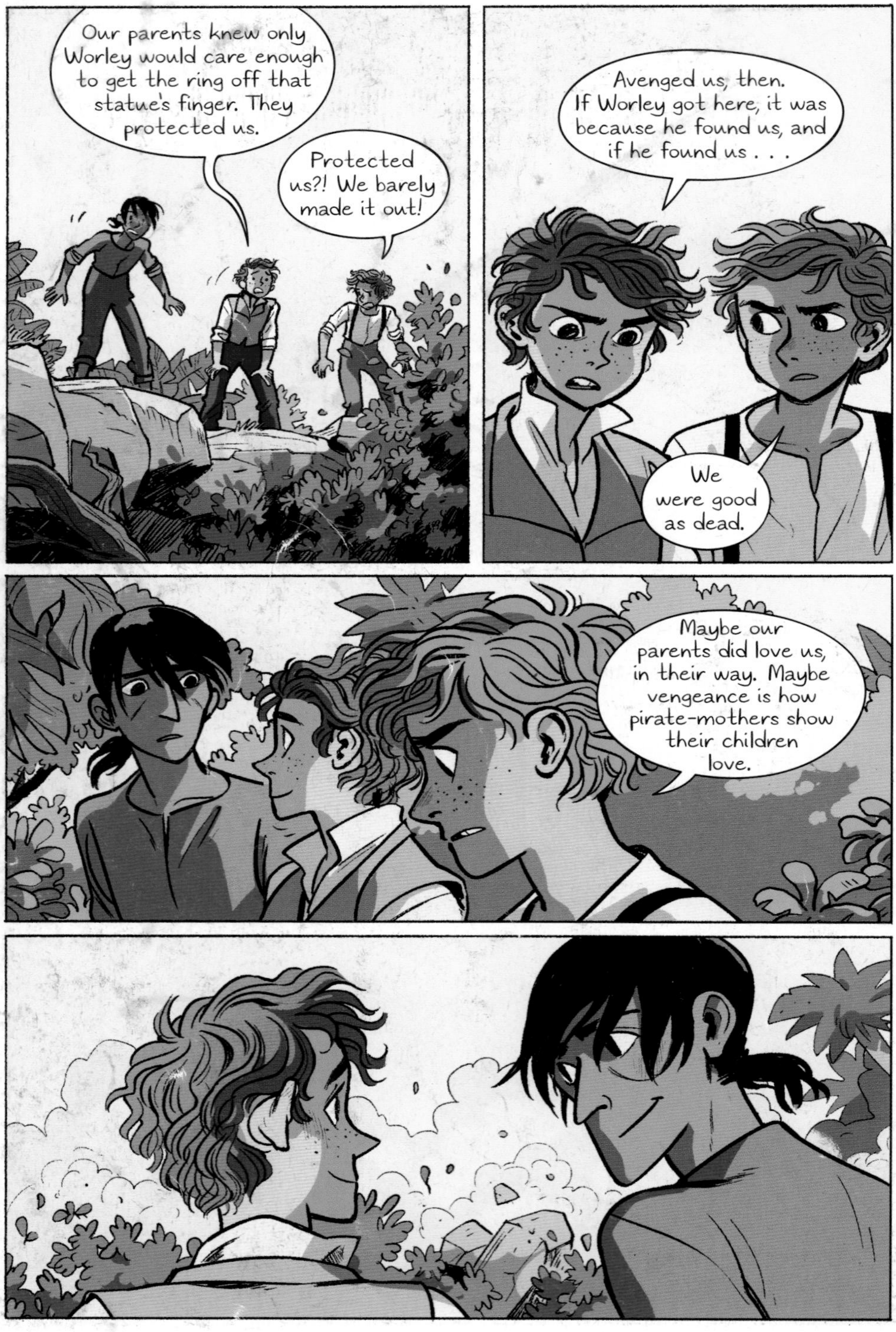
Our parents knew only Worley would care enough to get the ring off that statue's finger. They protected us.
Protected us?! We barely made it out!
Avenged us, then. If Worley got here, it was because he found us, and if he found us . . .
We were good as dead.
Maybe our parents did love us, in their way. Maybe vengeance is how pirate-mothers show their children love.

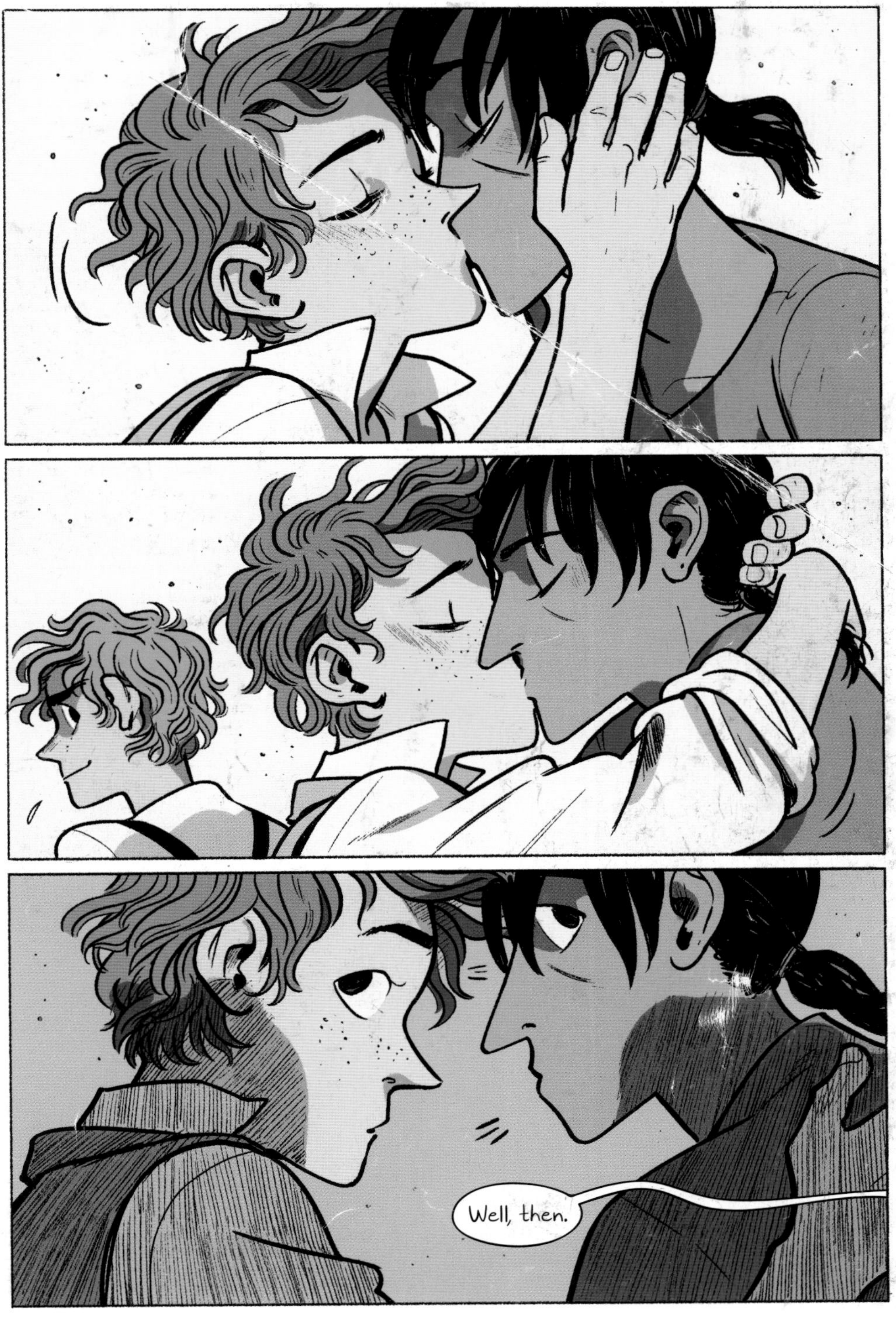
Well, then.

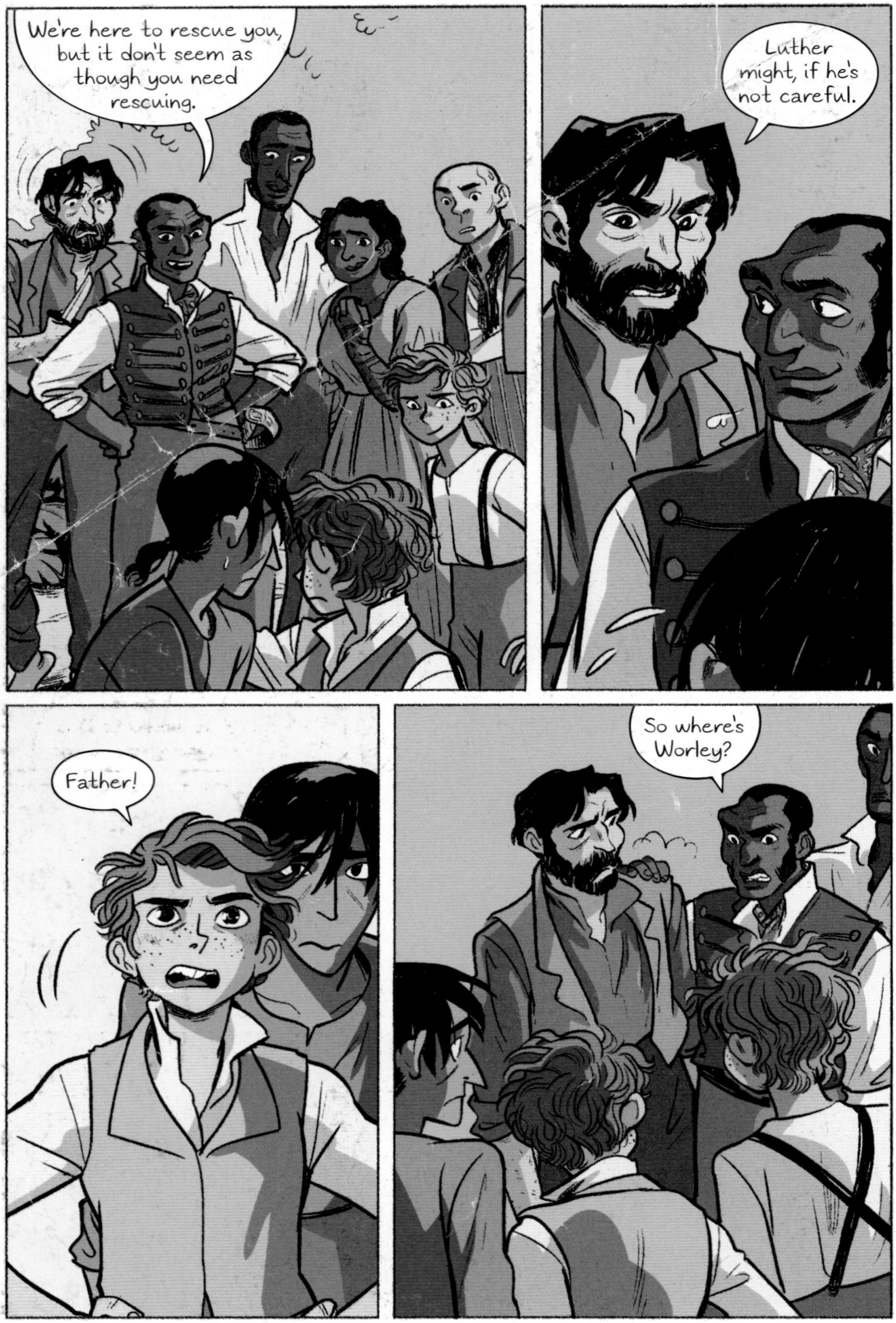
We're here to rescue you, but it don't seem as though you need rescuing.
Luther might, if he's not careful.
Father!
So where's Worley?

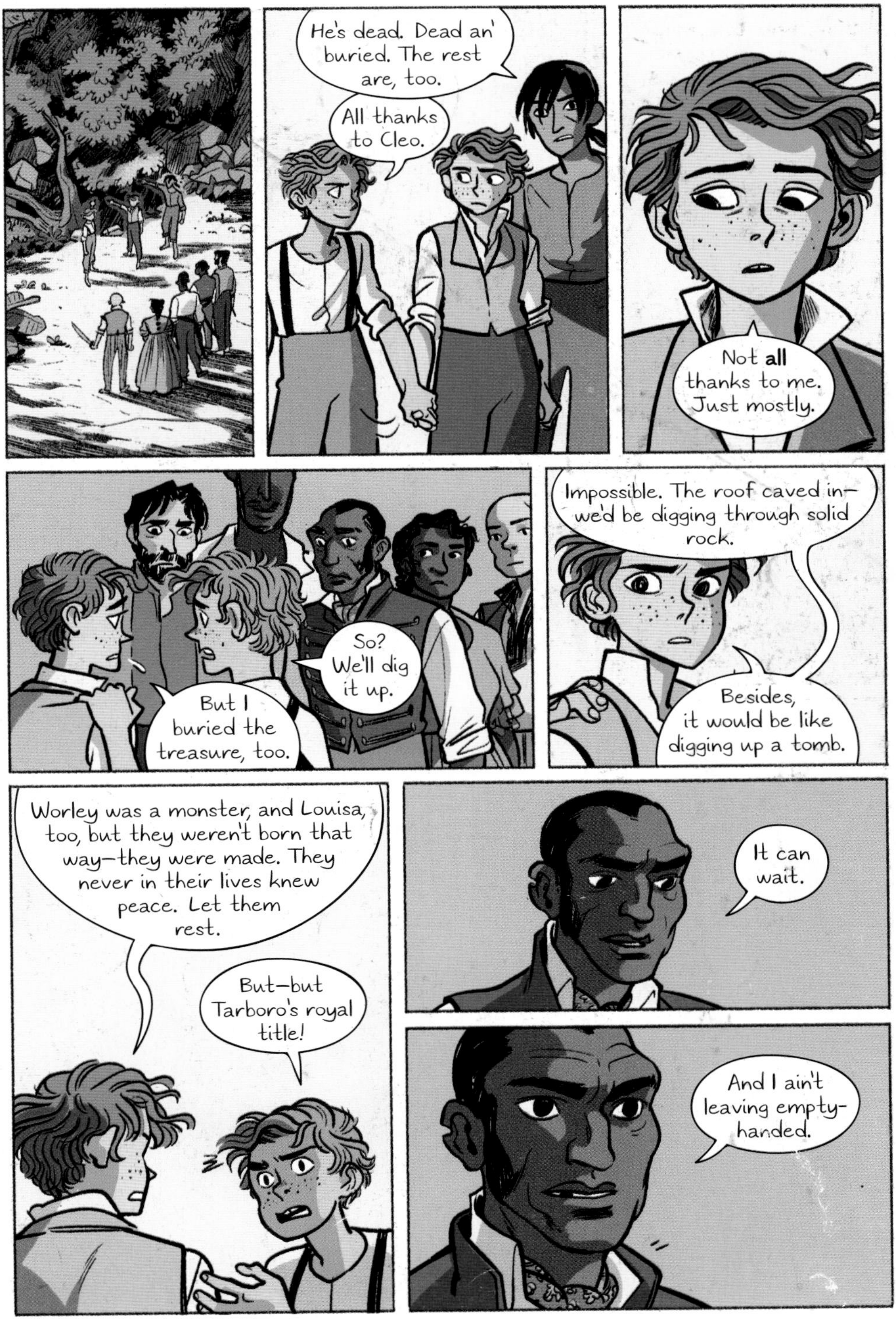
He's dead. Dead an' buried. The rest are, too.
All thanks to Cleo.
Not **all** thanks to me. Just mostly.
But I buried the treasure, too.
So? We'll dig it up.
Impossible. The roof caved in—we'd be digging through solid rock.
Besides, it would be like digging up a tomb.
Worley was a monster, and Louisa, too, but they weren't born that way—they were made. They never in their lives knew peace. Let them rest.
But—but Tarboro's royal title!
It can wait.
And I ain't leaving empty-handed.

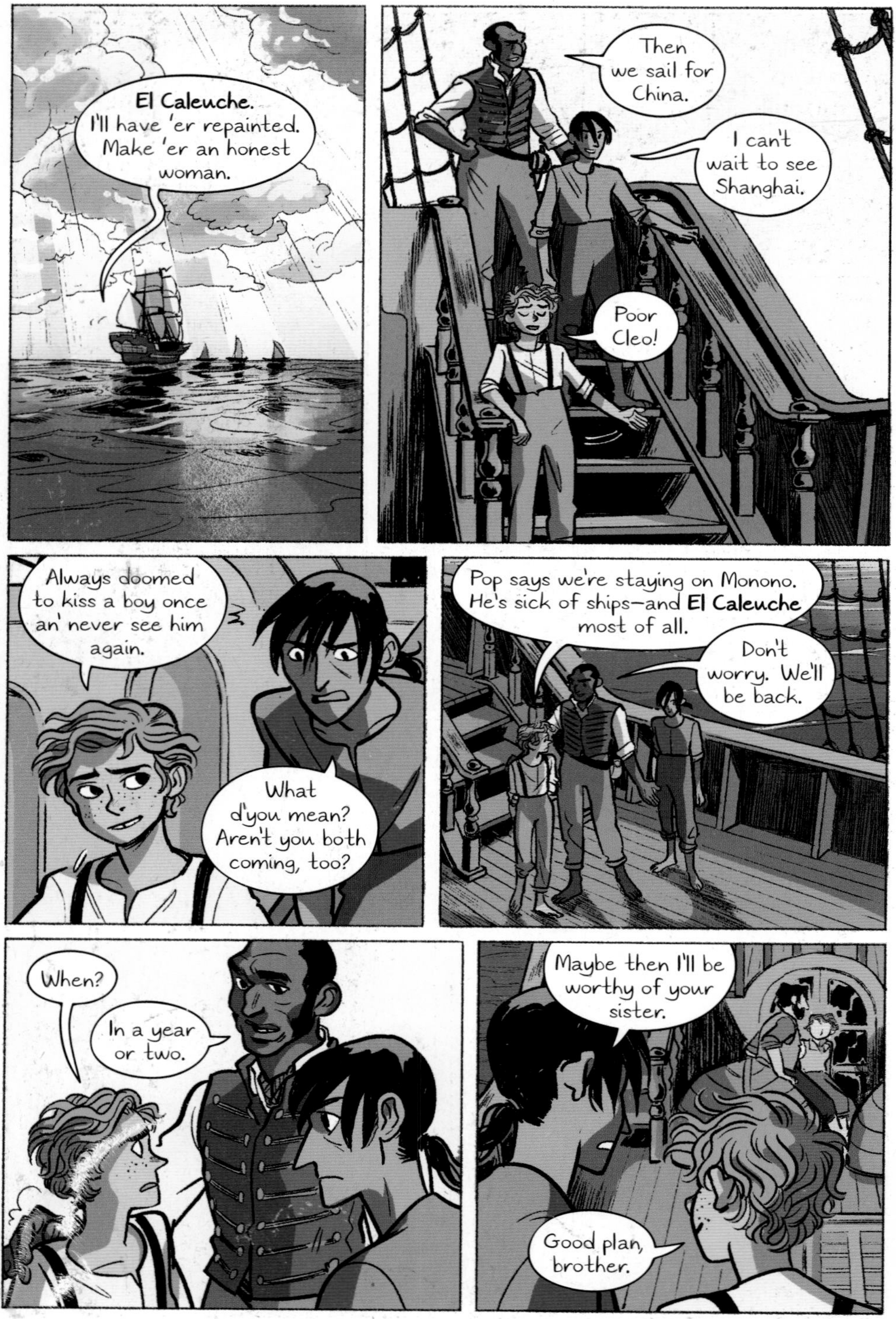
El Caleuche. I'll have 'er repainted. Make 'er an honest woman.
Then we sail for China.
I can't wait to see Shanghai.
Poor Cleo!
Always doomed to kiss a boy once an' never see him again.
What d'you mean? Aren't you both coming, too?
Pop says we're staying on Monono. He's sick of ships—and El Caleuche most of all.
Don't worry. We'll be back.
When?
In a year or two.
Maybe then I'll be worthy of your sister.
Good plan, brother.

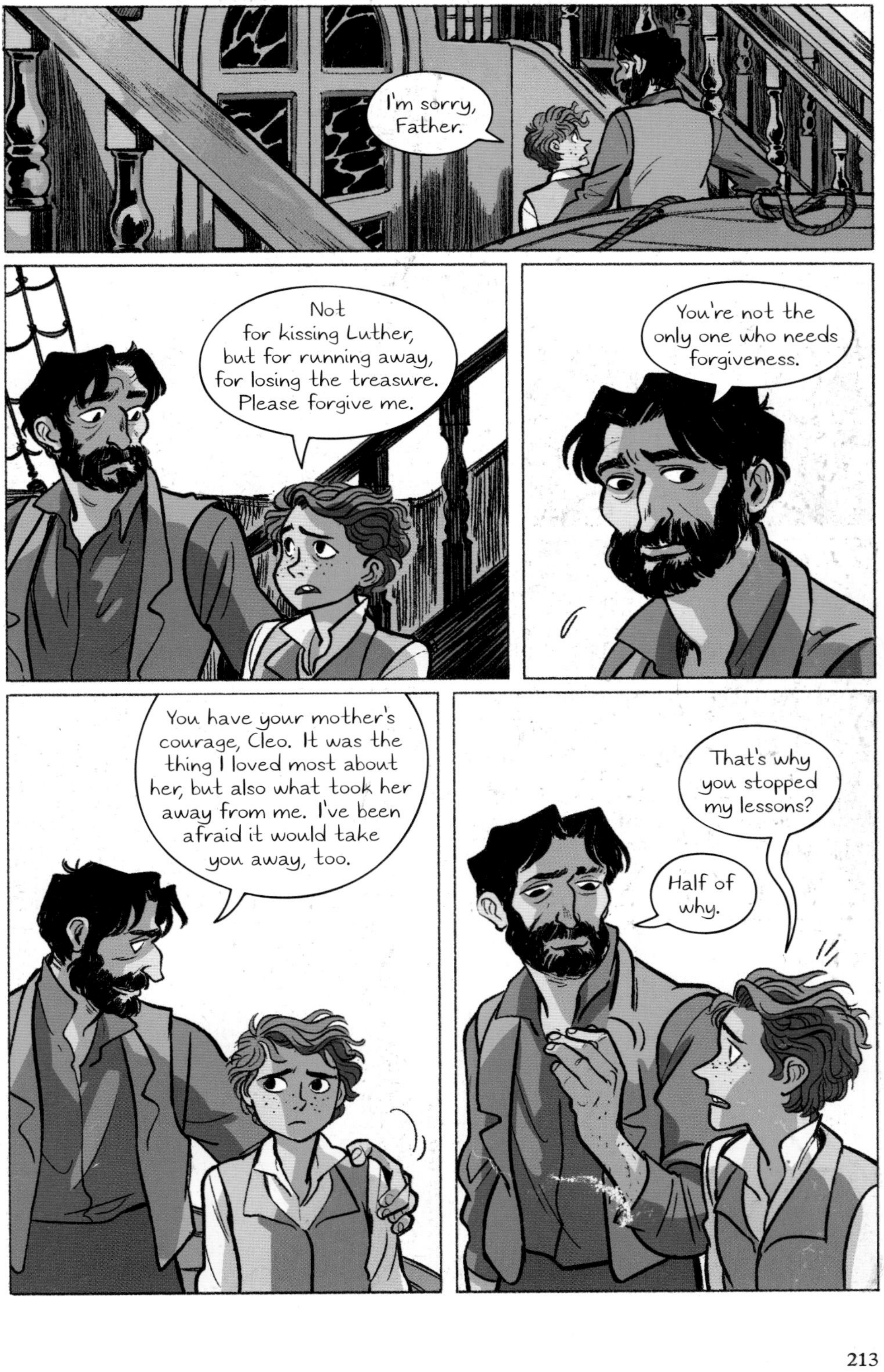

I'm sorry, Father.
Not for kissing Luther, but for running away, for losing the treasure. Please forgive me.
You're not the only one who needs forgiveness.
You have your mother's courage, Cleo. It was the thing I loved most about her, but also what took her away from me. I've been afraid it would take you away, too.
That's why you stopped my lessons?
Half of why.

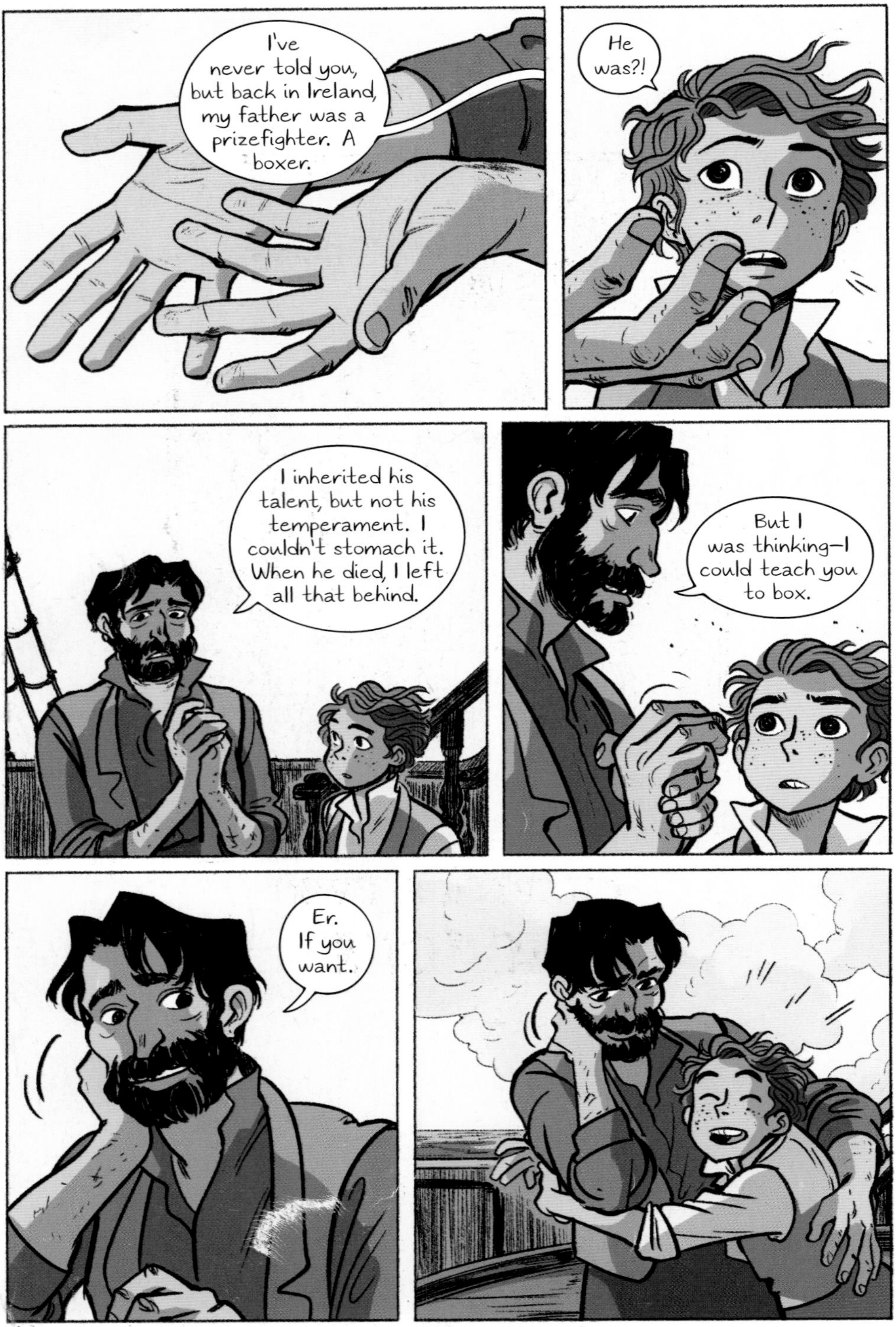
I've never told you, but back in Ireland, my father was a prizefighter. A boxer.
He was?!
I inherited his talent, but not his temperament. I couldn't stomach it. When he died, I left all that behind.
But I was thinking—I could teach you to box.
Er. If you want.

CHAPTER ELEVEN
ECHOES

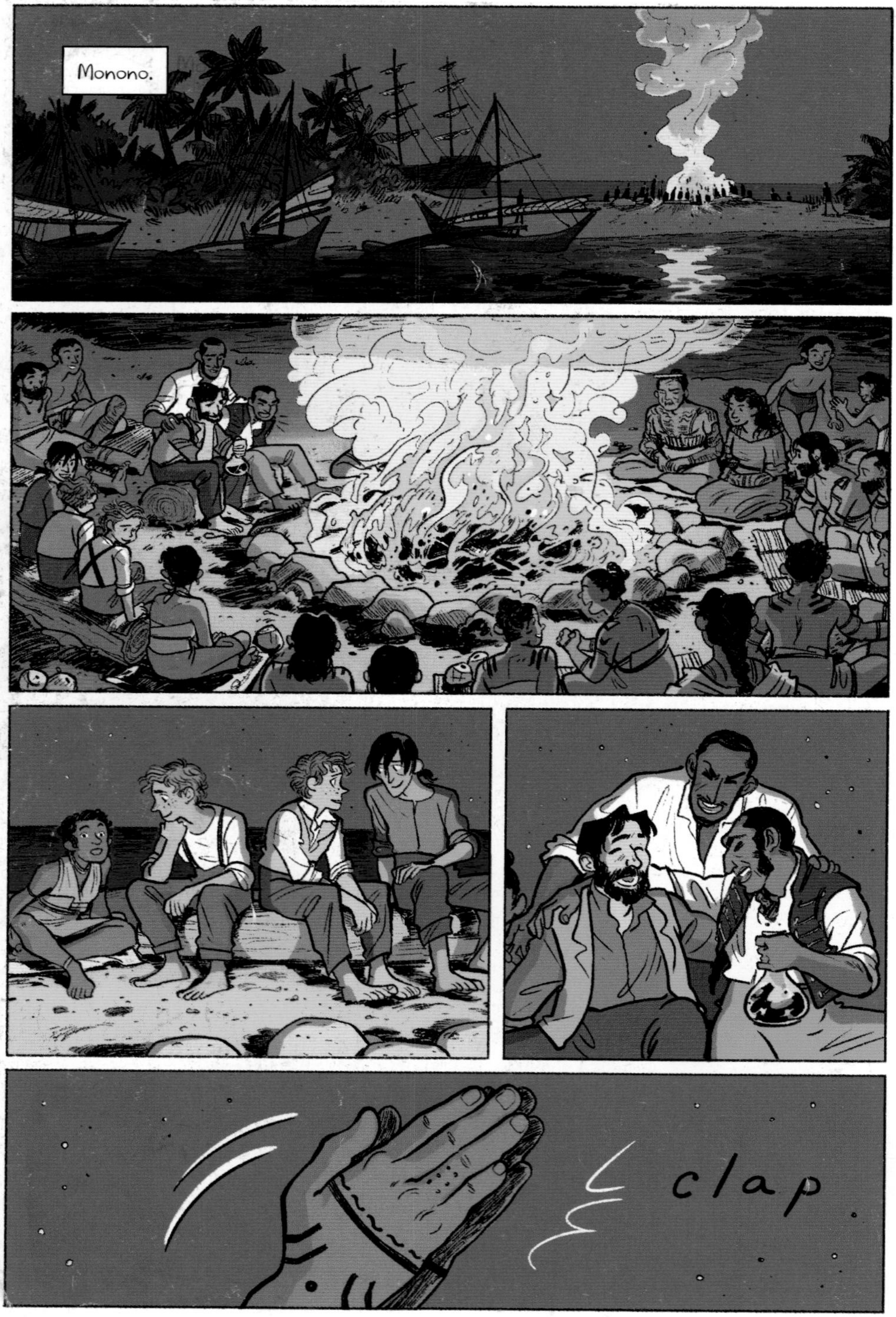
Monono.
clap

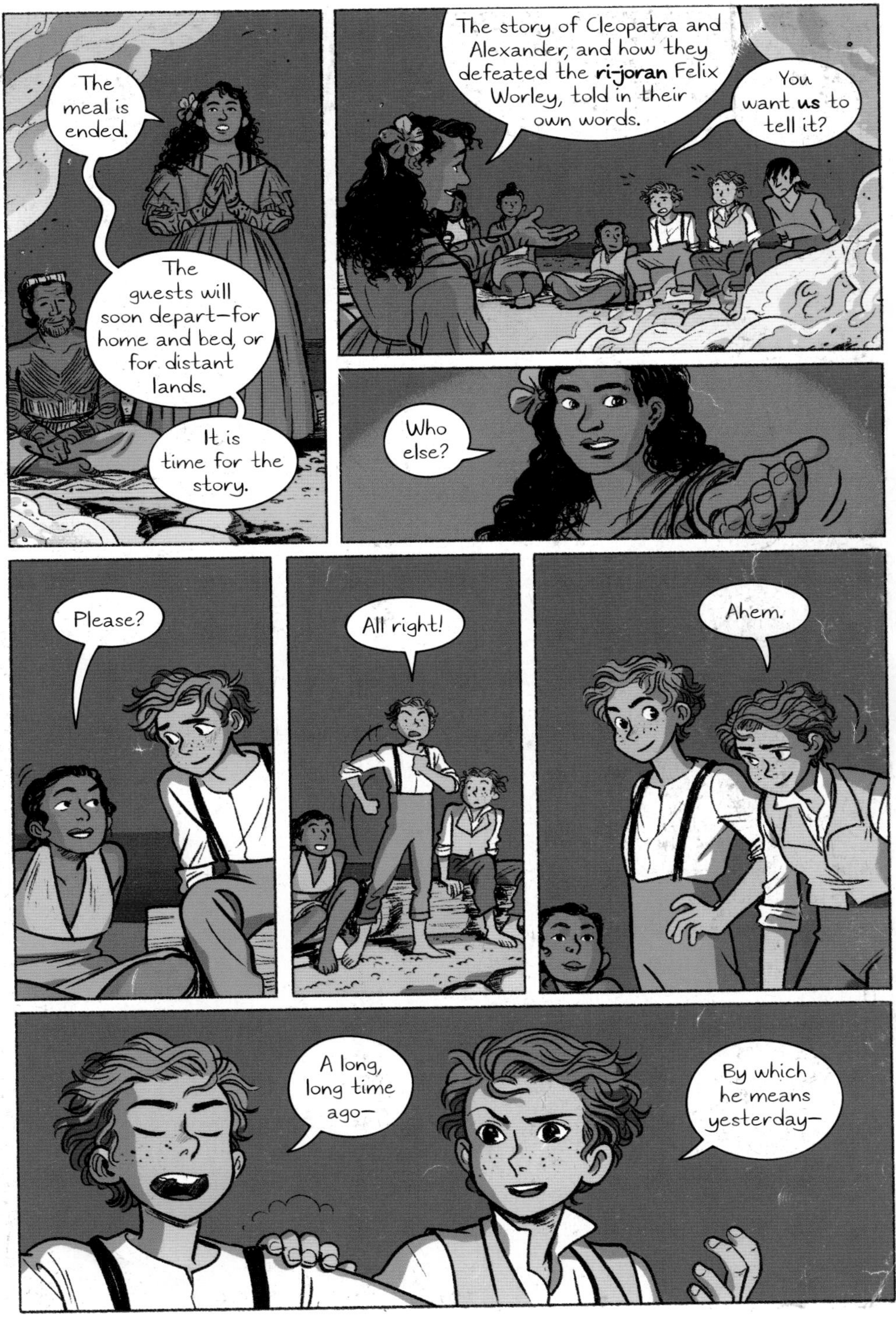
The meal is ended.
The guests will soon depart—for home and bed, or for distant lands.
It is time for the story.
The story of Cleopatra and Alexander, and how they defeated the **ri-joran** Felix Worley, told in their own words.
You want **us** to tell it?
Who else?
Please?
All right!
Ahem.
A long, long time ago—
By which he means yesterday—

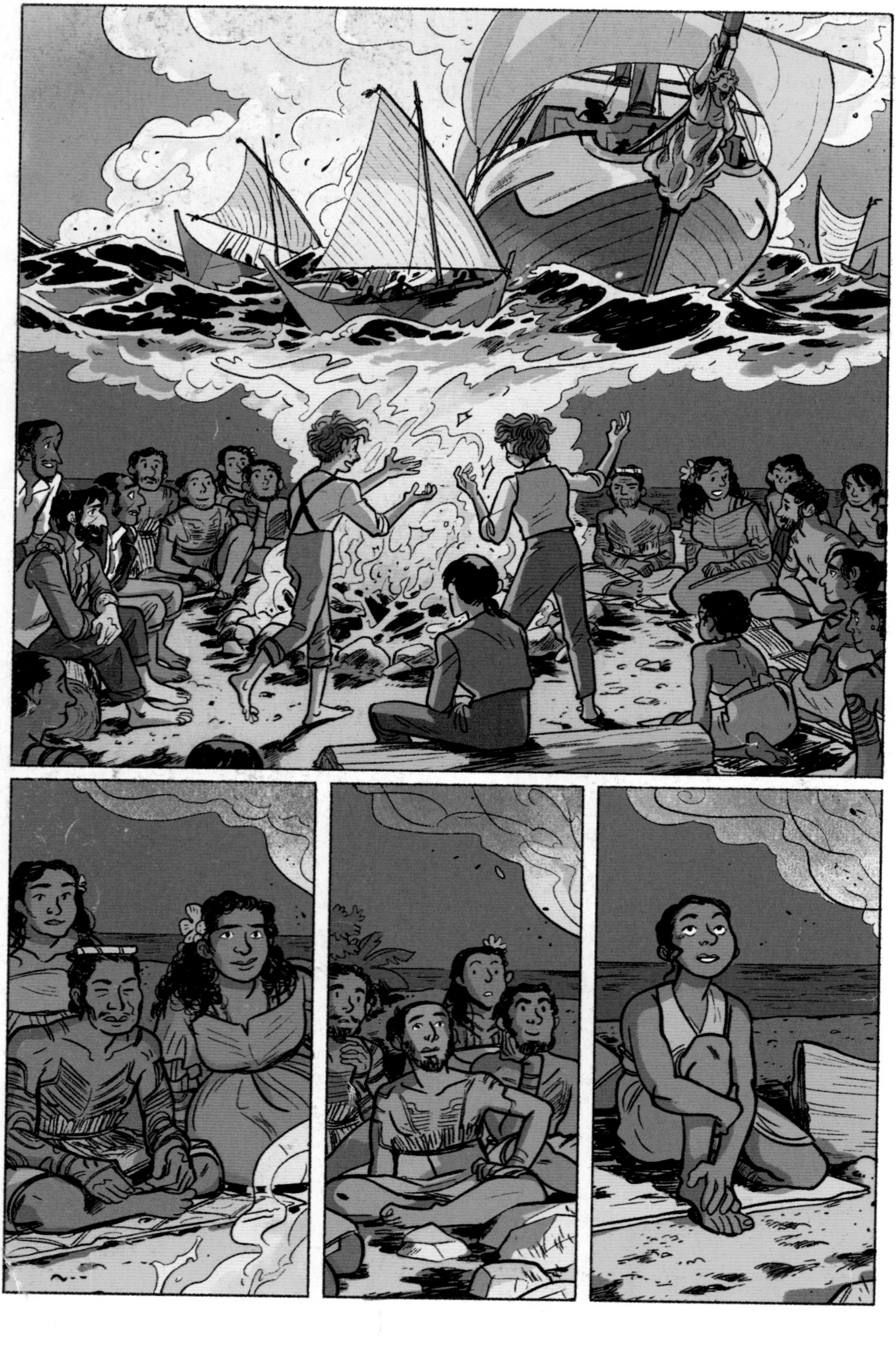

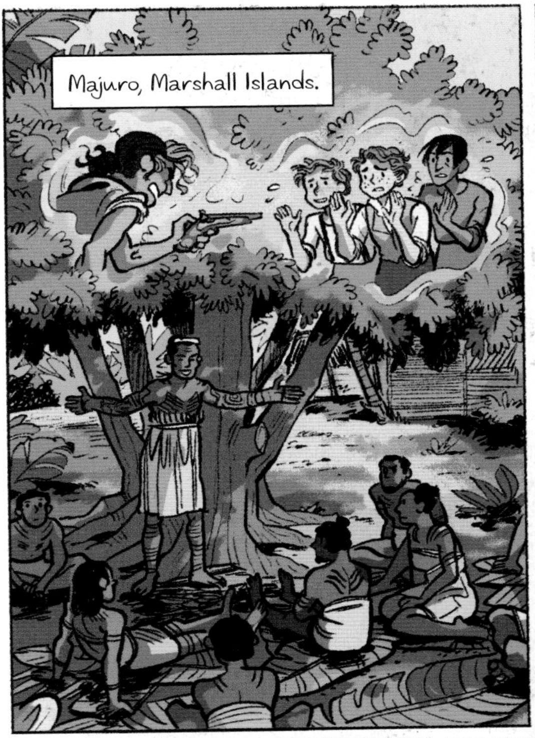
Majuro, Marshall Islands.

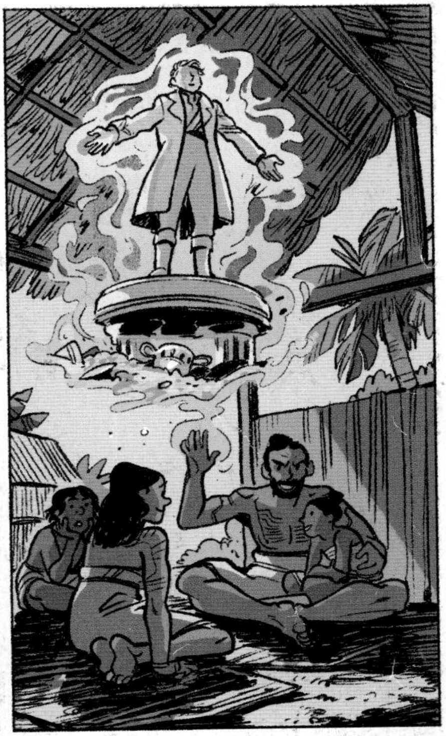

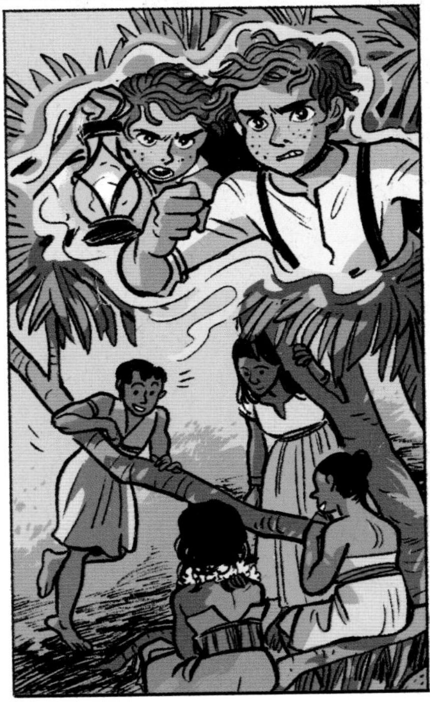

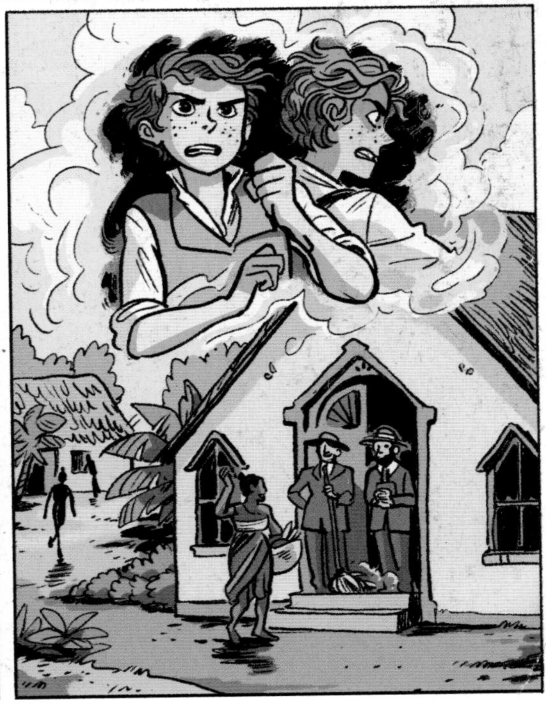

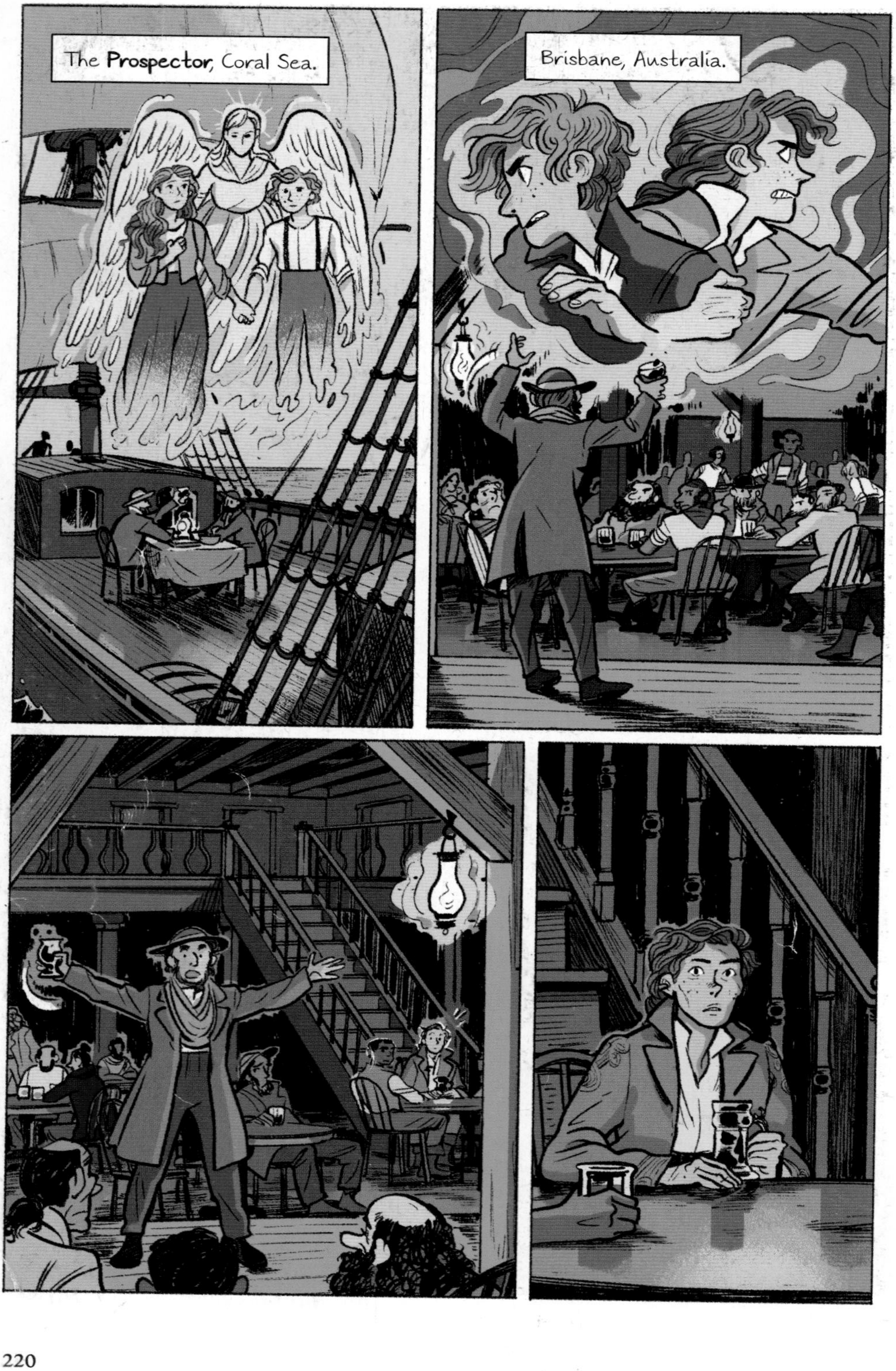
The Prospector, Coral Sea.
Brisbane, Australia.

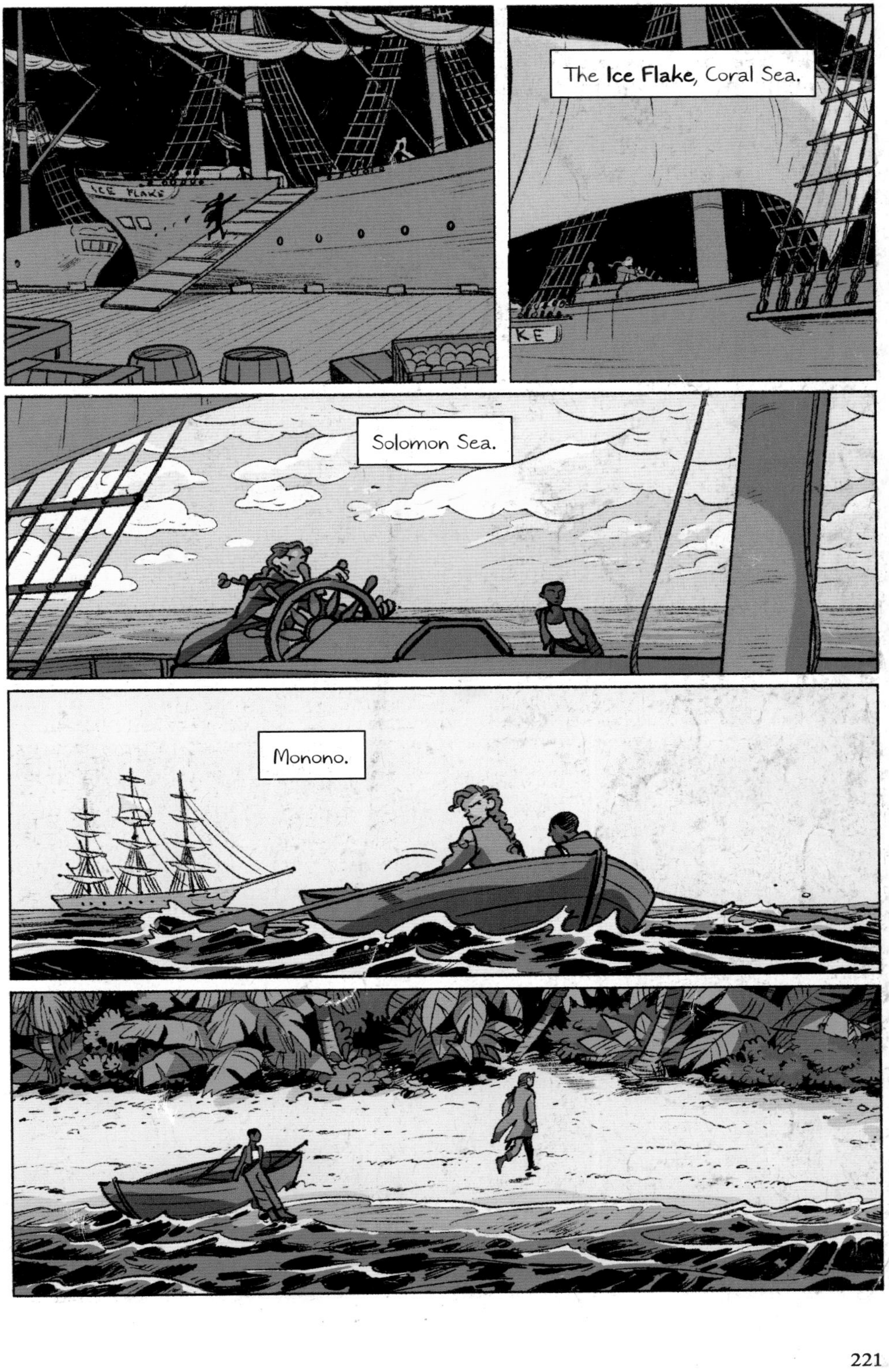
ICE FLAKE
The **Ice Flake**, Coral Sea.
KE
Solomon Sea.
Monono.

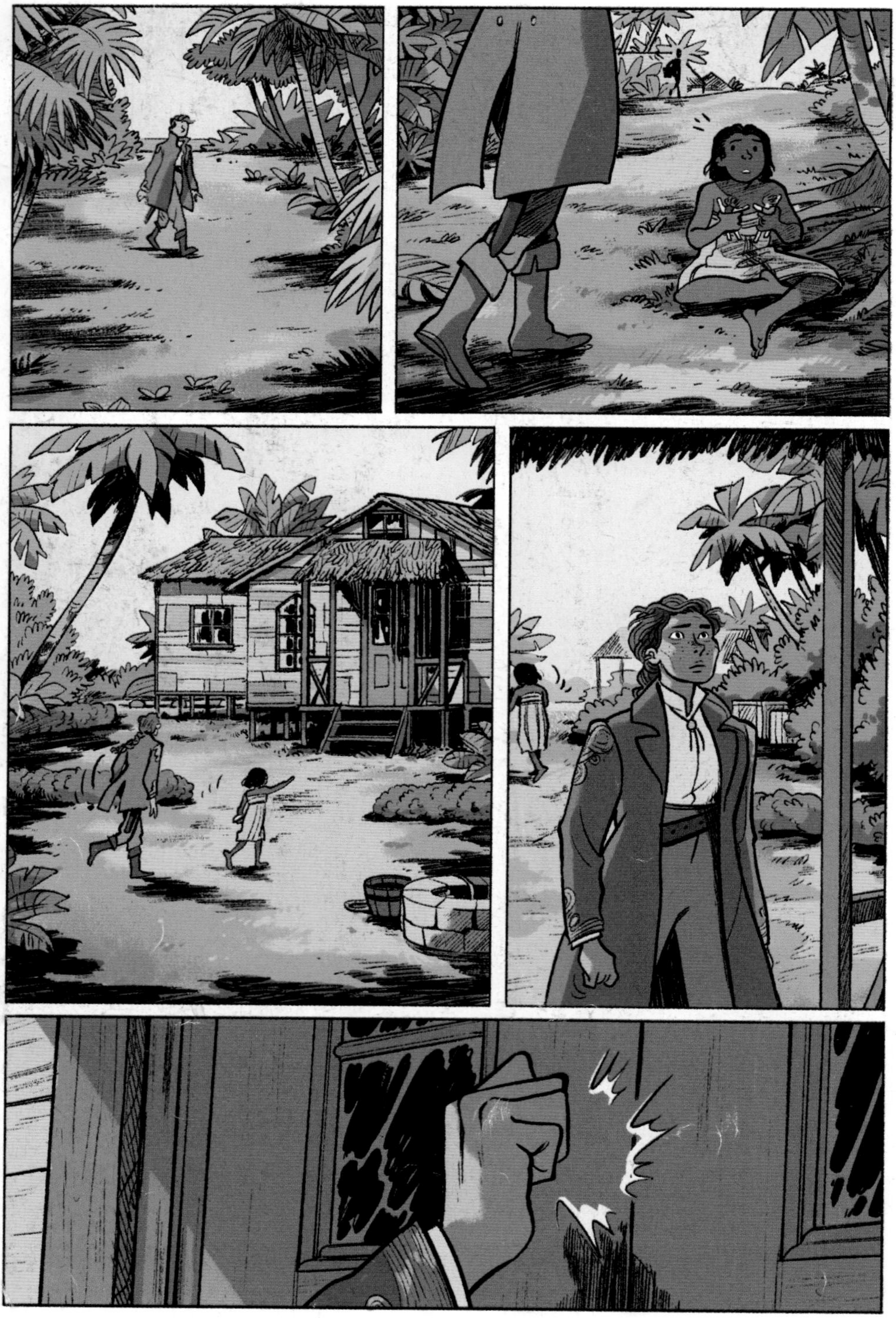

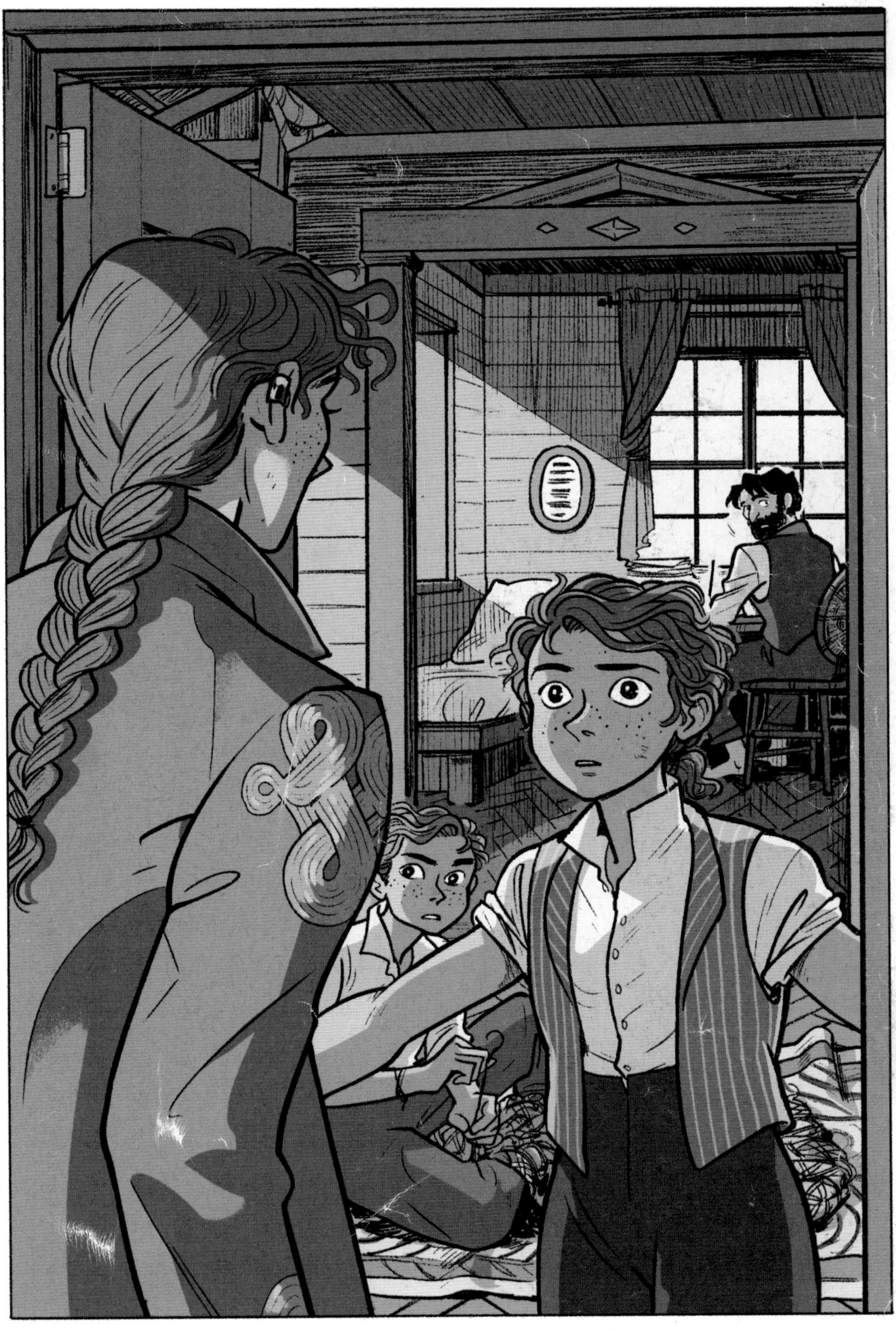

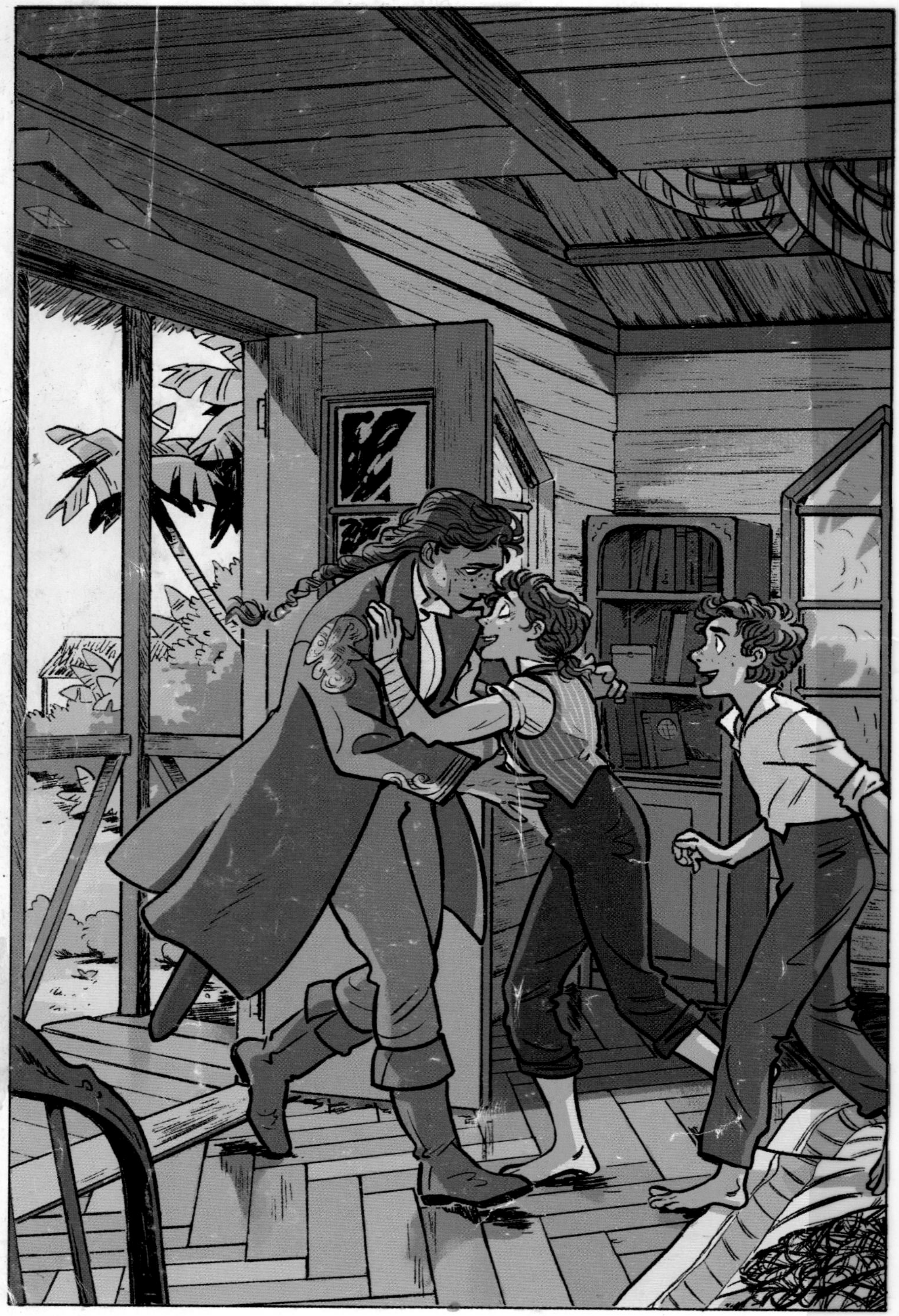